# EXCHANGER

*Happy Reading!*
*Karen Bumgardt*

# EXCHANGER

**K.E. BRUNGARDT**

Copyright © 2019 by Karen Brungardt. All rights reserved.

No part of this publication may be reproduced or transmitted in any manner whatsoever without the author's written permission, except in the case of brief quotations contained in critical articles or reviews.

Copy edits by Karen A. Thomas (www.KATediting.com)

Cover designed by Kat Domet / Domet Design
Book interior designed by Richard Fenwick

ISBN: 978-0-578-51117-7

*For my husband, Larry Brungardt,
who bravely said he would read my book
even though he is somewhat baffled
by science fiction / fantasy*

# EXCHANGER

## CHAPTER ONE

The cold metal door was hard against my back where I pressed against it, scared down to my toenails of being caught while my hair adjusted its coloring to match the drab paint of the gently curving corridor. Fear and reluctance dragged me down with a million tiny weights. The lighting was dim since it was technically nighttime on the ship and we students were supposed to be asleep in our beds in our quarters. Obviously, I wasn't following the rules.

*Hurry up!*

A strand flicked me on the cheek; that's what I get for being cross. *Ouch.*

D̄o̅n̅e̅. Smugness came through loud and clear.

I heard the shush-shush of air blowing through vents, my soft breathing and my heart thumping in my chest and thankfully nothing else. I slunk slowly toward the elevator, staying alert and close to the wall while moving. The elevator doors seemed a mile away, although, in reality, maybe 50 feet, closer to one end of the locked-off portion of the ship in which we were quartered. Doors at both ends of our section were firmly locked, as were all the doors along the way. The elevator was the only way out and it was secured by a palm reader and a number pad for back-up use, just not for Human use.

When I reached the elevator, a thin section of my hair—my hair has abilities I don't understand nor have I puzzled out why it has abilities—tapped the code on the numerical pad so I could press the numbers. It discreetly watched an Imurian officer input the information earlier when my classmates and I were going to the Viewing Deck. When the elevator doors opened, I stepped into the empty space, moving out of sight to the side, pushing the deck button, hoping night officers weren't watching for activity from this elevator. I didn't know why they would, since everything should indicate we students were safely asleep in our rooms, but I fretted, anyway. My hair had done something to the motion sensor in the door to my quarters; I just hoped it had done it right. We were only allowed to be in the Human section or else be accompanied by an Imurian and if I were found, well, honestly, I didn't know what they'd do but I doubted it would be kind.

I clenched my fingers into fists, heart skittering as I slowed my breath for a second, trying to calm down. I fervently hoped the viewing deck was empty and wasn't sure what I'd do if anyone were in there. Some of my hair stroked my arm in support and I breathed out. If it was busy, I'd push the down button, go back to my room and claim to be sleep-walking. How I could explain being able to access the elevator didn't bear thinking about so I ignored it.

The doors opened with a shiver of noise and I looked across the hall. The lights were off in the viewing area room and I took a calming breath in and out. *Okay, Jessi, before the doors close, you gotta move.* I stepped into the hallway after peeking right and left, making sure it was clear, then hurried across to the open door and the dark space beyond, the light from the dim hallway barely enough to see my way across to what I was interested in.

I stepped close to the thick transparent area and I looked out the viewing window at the stars outside. With the room dark, it felt as if I were one with space and I took an involuntary step back as I caught my breath at the overwhelming exquisite beauty. I didn't know constellations so I didn't have any idea where we were but the stars outside swirled in a pattern reminding me of the painting by that ancient Earth guy, Van Gogh, called Starry Nights. Painted in the year 1889 on Old Earth, with presumably no knowledge of space or other galaxies, it was uncanny how much the current view from that window looked like his rendition and how that painting had endured for all these centuries. The many millions of pinpricks of light against the absolute darkness mesmerized me.

Shaking my head, I pulled myself back to the task at hand, looking at the information tablet chest level to me. I checked the sides carefully for a place to put my forbidden memory chip, the one Mom had gifted me at the last second, breathing into my ear, "Info on Devon. Guard it closely."

It was too big for the slot on my own personal device, brand new Imurian technology given to each student for this venture, so I had to find something on the ship that could play it and this was my best bet, mainly because I'd seen it here when we were here earlier. It's doubtful the Cats would've upgraded their internal attached devices recently since they all still function. It was only Personal Devices that were the latest and greatest. *Will this pad play the chip?*

MAYBE.

My hair doesn't talk, exactly, but gives impressions that come across as words. It's complicated and I definitely don't understand why or how it does what it does but it has a mind of its own—literally. When I entered the Transition Years and my body started to change, so did my hair. It had been normal before that but then it developed its own personality, ability to act on its own and to communicate—somehow—with me. I was old enough to realize how bizarre this was and made a solemn vow to myself to keep this completely secret from the world, even my parents and, so far, I'd kept my vow.

*That's not very reassuring.* My waist-length of auburn ringlets shrugged, then fanned out around me to shield the light glowing from the screen, also still camouflaging me now to match the darkness. I wore charcoal gray pants and top with dark shoes to help the illusion of invisibility.

A length of hair tapped the top of the screen. I peered at it; yeah, it was a slot. I offered it the small square and it sucked in. *Please let it work and please don't let anyone be monitoring this room or pad.*

I scrolled through the menu; many of the words from my school years of Imurian language were familiar but many weren't; I only hoped I'd recognize the words for opening the information on the chip. I was puzzling out the menu when a small, impatient hank of hair tapped on one line.

*How do you know this stuff?*

REMEMBER.

I hit the Play icon, holding my breath for the split second it took for the screen to change to my mother's voice and face. Tears welled up in my eyes as soon as she spoke and homesickness hit me with a sledge hammer. A soft sob escaped my throat and I wiped my eyes, hastily turning down the volume to where I could barely hear the words. My mom had been uber-protective of me until I passed the same age Devon had been when he died and would've continued being so if my Dad hadn't finally intervened at that time, saying I needed to learn some independence.

"Jessi," she began. "Always remember we love you with all our heart and soul and if trying to find out about Devon's death puts you in danger, we want you to stop. Please. We're hoping," a pause for her to breathe, "you can find something out but if not, we've lived with the mystery of why he died all these years and we'll still be okay if we never know. Okay, what follows are my memories of that day on the StarFinder, your current ship. Understand getting the brain delve done was highly illegal and giving it to you is even more so. Be very, very careful. You need to know," her voice broke a little, "Dad and I have been under threats of death ever since Devon died, or worse, your removal from us." *That explains why she watched me with hawk eyes when I was little.* She whispered the words and I thought she was sitting in the bathroom to record this, from what little I could make out. The vid camera was tightly focused on her face. The bathroom made sense because it's the only place in all the civilizations to be guaranteed 100% private.

She smiled, more a pressing of her lips together than anything, sorrow etched into every line of her face. "Just—be careful. There's no way Devon should've died." She wiped a wet mark off her cheek, and gave me a one-finger wave after blowing me a kiss.

My heart wrenched in my chest. I never knew my older brother; Mom was pregnant with me during that ill-fated trip on the

StarFinder Imurian transport ship. Now I was an Early Prime Adult on the same ship, traveling to Amorpha to be a first-ever Foreign Exchange Student for my final year of Advanced University schooling before I started medical school. The pain of Devon's death never left my parents and I'd felt the weight of it all my life. Everyone who emigrated to a new planet was allowed to have three children, but my parents only had me. Devon died before I was born and they couldn't conceive again despite the best medical care and advances and there were no children for adoption on a newly settled world. Right now, I felt resentment welling up as she spoke; finding answers covertly about Devon for Mom was not something I envisioned myself being able to do. I saw the world through fear-filled eyes thanks to Mom's overprotectiveness.

Voices in the corridor shocked me, and my heart started hammering from the adrenaline rush as I whipped my head around to scan the room as I snatched the chip out of the reader. *Crap on a crutch! I need to hide!* The floor-length drapery next to the viewing window was only a few steps away so I scurried over and stepped behind it. *For once in my life, I'm very, very glad to be so little.* The folds settled in front of me, releasing dust, tickling my nose when I breathed in mustiness with a very quiet, shallow breath as the lights in the room flicked on and I fervently hoped my feet were hidden. *They need better cleaning people.*

I quit breathing, hoping they couldn't hear how hard my heart was thumping in my chest. I willed my nannies to suppress the adrenaline so I could calm down and stop shaking, but of course, they didn't listen to my silent plea. My hair clenched around me in a protective way, like it could prevent me from getting harmed.

"Smells like Human in here." An Imurian male voice murmured, my internal translator kicking in.

"They were here a bit earlier; must have left their stink on the upholstery."

An audible sniff. "Yes, they certainly did." Another sniff. "It is really strong, like they were just in here." A second of silence. "Why is the info pad on?"

*Fairy farts! It didn't turn itself off.* I groaned silently to myself.

"I do not know. Perhaps Fla're'te used it with the Humans and he did not to key it off again."

"Was that not an hour ago? Or more?"

"I think so but he said the elevator palm pad had a glitch and he had to use the numerical pin-pad so I to suppose this screen might to have a glitch in it, too; they are connected on the same circuit, I to believe. Why else would it to be on?" A couple of muffled footsteps toward the viewing window and my hiding spot. "Huh. It is on a list for the Human classrooms. Perhaps he looked up the location for one of the Humans earlier." *I wonder how it got on that screen.* My hair felt smug. *Of course. Thanks.*

"Maybe."

"Well, whatever. I will to shut it off and we can to continue our rounds. I will to make note of it for the record."

I strained my ears to hear what they were doing; they were very quiet and I couldn't be sure if they were in the room or not. *Can you…..?* One strand of hair slithered around the edge of the curtain and snapped back to the mass of curls.

wAIT.

Well, that answered that question. I wondered what the two officers were doing and I really, really wanted to scratch my nose,

I hoped I wouldn't sneeze and now I needed to pee. I wiggled my nose to dispel the feeling, taking shallow, cautious silent breaths and very carefully avoided thinking about water.

I fervently wished I had my gun but passengers weren't allowed weapons of any sort, no matter how well trained and licensed. I wondered what they'd think of my proficiency with a gun or my training in Cat-Fighting. No pun on the cat-like Imurians, actually; it was a specific form of fighting to train girls to fight like, well, girls. Plenty of hair pulling, slapping, biting and fingernails were a large part of the technique.

"All right; I have made the report. Let us to finish our rounds. I need to clear my nostrils of that Human stench. We will have to make sure room cleaning occurs here."

"Speaking of the Humans, did you notice the females?"

"Yes, yes, I did. That little one is no bigger than a kitling and I wonder at their wisdom in allowing her to participate as an Exchanger. And what is with those long, tightly coiled red-brown hairies? Does she not know having her hairies that long makes her look shorter?"

*Well, how rude!*

"My thought, too, but we do not to make the decisions. That tall one with the yellow strings? I would to mount her in a moment, but only as an experiment, you know. I will to bet she would mewl and squirm under me." He laughed.

A chuckle from the other one. "Yes, I to know what you mean. Perhaps there will be a chance in the next two weeks; she will be on board for that long, after all. She exudes willingness in her hormones. The others will to depart in the morning so no reason to think about them, although there were a few I could to like."

My hands clenched into fists; I hadn't liked Zoe from the day I met her in Early Childhood, and that hadn't changed, but I couldn't wish this on her. Interspecies sex; I really hoped Zoe wouldn't go for that and I really hoped they didn't mean rape. No matter how oversexed I thought Zoe was, she didn't deserve that. The other students would depart for their worlds early in the morning before we would be awake so they had nothing to worry about.

"Yes, I would to take the tall one. That little one, no, that would be like mounting a kitling and I could not to do that. Although she does have padding." *At least they have a few principles. Wait! Did he just call me chubby?*

"No, I could not, either, and she is too short and round to be sexy, anyway."

*Hmph! I'll show them what short can do.* My eyes narrowed as I imagined delivering a kick or two where it would hurt the most.

Growling laughter again. "Everything is in place here; do we need to check behind the curtains? Maybe one is hiding there." He snickered. *Oh, my shattered nerves! What do I do if they come over here?* My heart sped up again in preparation for fight-or-flight and I curled my fingers into claws so my fingernails could be used as a weapon.

"If it is the blonde one, I would to take the time but she is too big to hide there. The little one? Pffft. Besides, the drapes are undisturbed."

More chuckling. "I was making a joke." A tapping sound. "No, they are all in their rooms with the doors locked." It sounded like they were moving away from where I stood.

Okay, now I was *really* fuming. I was little, yes, but not sexy? And was round? I can't help it if I like my meals! It's hard to keep the weight off when you're as short as I am, especially in such a tall society. How dare he say that! Even if it was completely true, he didn't need to have noticed.

"What do you to say we to take our break next? I could to use some stimulant drink to stay awake for the rest of our shift."

"It is a little early for it but who cares? It is not like anything ever happens on night shift, anyway. I am hungry, too, so, yes, break room next."

One strand of hair snuck around the drape again, watching, then what seemed like hours later, pulled back in, and relaxed into place.

Go Now.

I rubbed my nose hard to get rid of the tickle and cautiously slid out of my hiding place, ignoring my bladder. I silently thanked the outside stars for not being found, grateful for once to be small enough to fit behind the material, but I was indecisive for a second about what to do next; I was afraid they'd return here again. I had no idea at all where their break room was but hoped it was far away.

Then I squared my shoulders and decided I had to see what was on the rest of the memory chip. I tiptoed over to the pad, which was now dark, and tapped the screen to wake it up. I slipped the square into the slot again; a little pop-up rectangle offered the choice of 'Resume', 'Start Over', 'Save as' or 'Erase.' I poked the Resume button and a couple of seconds later, Mom's voice sounded again and I frantically looked for the volume button to turn it down; the Imurians had turned up the volume for some reason. Too bad I couldn't use captions only but I didn't want to take the time to figure that out.

"We were expressly forbidden to discuss Devon's death with anyone, especially you, and we were paid a great deal of money to keep our mouths shut, along with threats of taking you someplace no one would find you if we broke our silence. We couldn't take that risk, you understand that; we couldn't risk leaving you an orphan or, worse, losing you.

Who gave us the money? We don't know. It arrived over several months into a special account that couldn't be traced. The threats were credible. We believed them and we had surveillance chips placed into our upper arms as part of the deal." She drew in a breath.

"Why the secrecy? Devon should not have died. Something happened to him after I took him to that class where the air quality was altered. Dad and I believe it was on purpose but we have no proof. Devon was fine for a few days after and then he got sick. Changes happened to his body, distortion is the only way I can describe it, and apparently his nano—you know, his nannies—system couldn't heal him. He lived for a couple of days in great pain and then he....died. Yes, of course I had the physicians on board treat him and I tried, also, but didn't have access to their medical equipment. They all said he died of a viral contamination he picked up while still on New Horizon but I know that's not true. However, we've been forced to tell that story.

We went through an extremely secret, illegal and expensive brain delve to get these memories of that time for you; we will continue playing our part at home. You must destroy this when you're done to keep all of us safe. We love you and good luck. Please remember this could be very dangerous and we don't want you getting hurt or killed so do what you can, if you can, and if you can't, we love you anyway. We've managed this long without knowing the truth and we can continue to do so."

The narrative ended. There was an attachment of her actual memories but I didn't dare take time to review those; it indicated an hour's worth of memories. Now I knew the floors were patrolled plus I didn't know how often they came around. I wiped tears off my cheeks, drawing shaky breaths to compose myself.

I took in a big breath, held it and let my muscles go loose as I breathed out. *They think he was murdered! Maybe accidentally or maybe on purpose, I don't know which but Mom seems certain it's related to that low-air-quality problem. I wonder what she meant by 'he was distorted' thing? I suppose that'll be in the rest of the vid.* I gave a quick shake of my head to clear my mind, then making sure the screen went dark, I made my sneaky way back to my quarters. Homesickness still dogged my steps so as soon I was safely back in my rooms, I turned on the hologram setting for New Eden for comfort.

## CHAPTER TWO

I woke up feeling surprisingly refreshed in the morning as I lazed in bed for a while, reluctant to move or get up because I was so very comfortable. "What time is it?"

The female voice assigned to this room answered, "It is 0530 in the morning. You are required to be at the safety drill at 0600."

"Thanks."

"If you return to sleep, I will to awaken you."

"Okay." I yawned. I rolled over to my side and sat up, swinging my legs out of bed. As I stood, I asked, "Coffee?"

"Madame. It is ready."

I sniffed, smiling. I liked how it seemed like caffeine reached into my brain from the aroma. Going to the kitchen, I rummaged in the cooler for cream, then settled on the living room chair to take my first sip, while closing my eyes to savor the flavor. Incredibly rich flavor exploded on my tongue as I slowly swallowed. I wondered where they got their coffee from. This wasn't from the allotment I'd brought; this was so much richer and more flavorful than mine. *I wonder if I could buy some? And where did they get cream from? Oh. They probably stocked it before leaving New Eden. Duh.*

"Room?"

"Yes, Madame," the mechanical voice answered.

"Can I buy some of this coffee for myself? Also, please notify me of the time in five minutes."

"I am now programmed to notify you in five minutes." A pause. "The coffee is not available for purchase."

"Thank you." Disappointment made me twist my mouth but I wasn't surprised at the answer.

"Yes, Madame."

I finished my coffee just as the room announced, "Five minutes have elapsed."

"Oh, okay. Um, thanks". I stood up and made my way to the bathroom to brush my teeth, take a speedy cleanse in the refresher and dress in jeans and a casual, long-sleeved purple top. I slipped on soft-soled shoes.

"Madame, the map for the drill is on your Personal Device for your use."

I picked it up and headed for the door, opening and stepping through as my fellow students were emerging from their rooms.

"Can you believe we have to do this? Why didn't we do it yesterday before we took off? Don't you think that would've been more logical?" Zoe complained, looking perfect as usual in a butter yellow tailored blouse tucked into black form-fitting pants with a turquoise studded belt circling her slim waist, charms swinging from her collar, breast pocket and along the bottom of the belt in the latest fashion, her blonde hair swinging around her shoulders. "I could've slept in some more."

Mitchler shrugged as he joined our little group trooping down the corridor, his dark hair tousled but looking freshly shaved.

"Yeah, I guess it would've made more sense...but then, maybe not. After all, if something happens during landing and take-off, there's usually nothing left to save. On the other hand, during space travel is usually when emergencies happen, so since we survived the departure, I guess they figured they could wait until today?"

"Right," Keaton added. My heart rate sped up a little looking at him with his chocolate brown hair and eyes, arched eyebrows and his smile. I wanted to tousle his hair but kept my hands to myself. "Besides, when's the last time you actually heard of a Cat—I mean Imurian—ship having an in-flight emergency? Have you ever heard of one?"

Soli nodded. "I've heard of one, myself."

We looked at him, surprised he actually volunteered a comment. He's a very quiet guy but in a drop-dead gorgeous kind of way, with gray eyes, black lashes fringing them and black hair with a slight wave, all of which set off his fair skin. His mouth was perfectly formed with a small, straight nose. He added in an off-hand way, "I think it was this ship, actually. I believe there was something about one of the reactors...?" He shook his head, then said, spreading his hands apart, "I only remember my mom saying something once about something that malfunctioned and affected the air circulation while all the pregnant women were taking a class but that's all I remember."

I mused out loud, "There was more than one ship used for emigration but was this the only one transporting pregnant women?" I shrugged. "Now that you mention it, I remember Mom telling me about that incidence. Something about the air quality became bad, everyone fainted, and they had to treat everyone for it." I kept Devon's death to myself; if they didn't already know about it, I wasn't telling. A shard of pain pierced my chest, remembering my parents' sadness.

Zoe clapped her hands together. "Well, whatever! Our moms were part of the pregnant women that emigrated on this ship and as far as I know, the only group ever allowed to emigrate with midway pregnancies. If that's why we were chosen for this program, I'm glad of it! And speaking of adventure, let's have a safety drill." She flipped her head to toss her blonde hair.

I said in a mild tone, "Well, good morning to you, too, Zoe. I guess you answered the question about our moms being the only group of pregnant moms."

She sniffed, dropped her pose and gave me a cutting look. "Yes, I have always known that; didn't all of you?" Without waiting for answer from any of us, she went on. "It is an adventure, wouldn't you agree, little Jessi?" Then she smiled, an insincere look. "You know, I think your full name is taller than you are, Jessalya."

I gritted my teeth. "Yes, Big Zoe, this is an adventure." I saw her hand twitch as if to slap me but just then, an Imurian stepped out of the door at the end of the Human section opposite the elevator, gesturing for us to get to his position, the door marked on our maps as the safety rendezvous. The other twenty students had left the ship at 0500 so it was only the five of us. Five makes a very small crowd.

The officer in the doorway said, "Please, to have your attention. This door, please to memorize its location, is marked with this red sign." He pointed at the sign, displayed both in our language of Standard and Imurian, and it proclaimed "Safety/Emergency Exit". "If an emergency exists in which you must to leave the Human section, you will to make your way here."

He waited for nods of acknowledgement as he looked at each one of us, then continued. "All doors remain locked at all times unless the Captain has declared an exit emergency, then they will automatically open. An Officer of the Ship, such as myself, will be here to direct you to the life preservation shuttles. We will not to go there now but I now to show you the location and their design look." He held up an electronic device showing the life boat location. "All have a place on the shuttle and there is stored food and water to preserve life. Please to remember, we will always be there to help you in this event." He tapped on his device. "I now take names to make sure all are here."

He went through his short list as I yawned, waiting for my name to be called. *Have to agree with Zoe; I could've used some more sleep.* After saying, "Yo" to my name, getting me a grin from Keaton and a dark look from the officer, we were dismissed to get ready for breakfast and the day.

We had about 25 minutes before being ushered to breakfast. Keaton asked, as we walked toward our quarters, "Hey, anyone want to come to my room for a cup of coffee or tea? I have plenty and nothing else to do until breakfast."

Zoe purred, "That would be delightful, Keaton. Count me in."

Soli said, "Sure, that would be good. Do you have cream, dude? I don't like black coffee."

Mitchler flashed a thumbs-up motion. Keaton said, "Nope. No cream."

I said, "I don't like it black, either. But I have to, uh, use the facilities, you know? Then I can bring my cream over, if you want."

Keaton said, "Sure, Jessi, bring the cream."

Zoe said, "Going to leave me all alone with the guys, Jessi?" She tilted her head, looking very pleased with herself. "I think I'm equal to the task."

I rolled my eyes. "Yes, Zoe, I think you can handle it all by your little ol' lonesome. At least for the two minutes it'll take for me to get there with my stash of cream."

I made a face as I entered my room, used my facilities, then, taking the cream from the cooler, went across the hall to Keaton's room, ringing the Access bell. After a short pause, the door opened and I entered, holding the cream up in a triumphant way, and Keaton said, "Jessi, let me get you a cup of coffee." He poured me a mug, handing it to me with a spoon, and I thanked him, sitting down on the couch next to Soli, taking a sip.

"I asked if I could buy some of this coffee and I was told no. Too bad; it's delicious." I took another sip.

Keaton smiled and nodded. "I tried, too," he confessed. "Heh, probably they don't want us knowing their supply source." He chuckled. "For all we know, it's made from some unknown planet's petrified bones."

"Yeah," Mitchler chimed in, "Probably some planet they won't put up for their Rent-to-Own program so they can keep their source secret!" We raised our mugs in salute to that.

"Anyone else nervous about our immersion classes?"

I said, "Yes and no", my hand tilting back and forth. "Mostly I'm nervous about how little sleep we're going to get!" I said. "You do realize, once we get to Amorpha, we'll all be in different cities, the only Human for hundreds of miles around? That's what I'm most nervous about, quite frankly."

They nodded, suddenly sobered. Zoe crossed her arms. "That's true but it'll be like moving to a new city at home and not knowing anyone. I'll make friends." Then a sly smile slid across her mouth. "For you, Jessi, though, if you make friends, they'll be from the Middle Childhood school."

My hand tightened on the mug handle. I wanted to dash the remains of my coffee in her face but words from my Cat-Fighting instructor entered my head. *'Let it go, Jessalya; it's always better to not fight than to fight. Decisions made in anger are bad decisions.'*

I smiled sweetly at her instead, putting as much sugar into the look as I could. "Oh, I'll make friends at the University, more than you, Zoe. With adult Amorphans. After all, I'm officially in my Early Prime Adult years, same as you." I bit off the words at the end. *Just once, I wish I could come up with a Zoe Zinger but I always think of them too late.*

Keaton's room voice, a male tenor, interrupted, "Time for class. All must depart now." Saved by the Voice. Yeah, it always took me an hour to come up with a perfect rejoinder and then, of course, it was never right for the next time.

## CHAPTER THREE

Our escort Imurian Officer, looking bored with his job, waited for us in the corridor with his hands linked behind his back, tail carefully held out of reach, many of the pockets on his tan jumpsuit empty but the utility belt full of objects. He led us to the dining room and as I plopped into a chair at our designated table, Zoe slithered gracefully into hers across from me and between Keaton and Mitchler. *Okay, I'm a klutz especially when she's around. I admit it. But not out loud.* We tapped in our orders on the screen; drinks were delivered first, with my cup of coffee taking all my attention until the food came.

"I wonder who our teachers are." I remarked as I buttered my muffin. "Since I guess the Imurians know as much as anyone does about other societies, I'm thinking they'll be the ones teaching us."

"Yeah," Keaton said, "The Cats find the peoples to populate their Rent-to-Own worlds, after all, so I'd think they'd know the intricacies of all societies. I hope they're not as boring as our University profs were!"

"Sure hope they're not listening in on us!" Zoe said, grimacing prettily. "That could be embarrassing especially since I don't know if they like being nicknamed Cats." She flicked her eyes to the officer standing guard at the door. "Of course, if they didn't look so much like cats…" She flipped a hand in a dismissive way. "Since they're all taller than most of us Humans, at least we know they're not pets."

Keaton said, "I've always been happy they let us Humans keep dogs and cats for our pets and horses and cows, too."

I chuckled. "You have a pet cow?"

He rolled his eyes upward. "You know what I mean."

"Yeah, I do. Just teasing." I watched the officer's ear swiveled toward us, his whiskers twitching. I dropped my voice softer. "I think he can hear us."

"Probably." Soli agreed. "They do have very large ears, after all, the better for hearing. If the Imurians are our teachers, we'd better listen to what they say and not what they twitch or whatever."

I snorted in agreement. "They do twitch things a lot, like those tails, whiskers and ears." The bell chimed, letting us know breakfast was over so we walked out into the corridor as we joined the officer at the door.

Mitchler said, "Sure hope it's a fun-filled day for us."

"Yeah, right." I said.

A few minutes later, we were in front of our classroom on the Human deck several doors down the curve from our quarters. I opened the door to enter and I stopped so suddenly Keaton ran into my back, crowding the doorway. Keaton poked his finger into my back and growled, "Jess, you HAVE to quit stopping like—"

My mouth gaped open in surprise and from the sudden silence behind me, the others were as surprised as me. I snapped my mouth closed. An Amorphan, a *real* Amorphan, was standing in the room watching us with what appeared to be a smile on his—her—its face. He or she was taller than any of us, taller than the screening vid suggested when we first met our Amorphan families.

His-its-her translucent skin flashed different colors as the light danced across it from his gesture toward us. Wide-set, large almond-shaped eyes were more to the outside of the face than ours were and were multi-faceted in appearance, while slanting upward at the outside corners. No one color could be defined but the effect was arresting. The breathing area was a swelling down the center of the face with two openings at the bottom, similar to our own nostrils. The mouth was wide and thin without discernible lips, and all on a very round head. Feathery, soft brown and gray growths were short on top of the head, becoming longer as they went down the back and sides of the head. If there were ears, I couldn't see them or maybe they were covered by their equivalent of hair. Of course, we had all seen our Amorphan host families in videos but seeing one in person was way different, especially how the skin flickered and twinkled with different colors.

Long arms were covered to the wrists in a diaphanous type material which also appeared multi-faceted with reflecting colors. The garment itself flowed to the ankles, pleated from a neck band and left to fall free without constriction to mid-ankle. The two feet were encased in a covering of an unknown material with an open toe box. There looked to be seven toes to each wedge-shaped foot. I couldn't see nails on either the hands or the feet but other than that, they appeared to be very similar to our own design, except they were, well, different. Then I realized there were no knuckles; in fact, I'm not sure there were bones in the fingers or the toes. My stomach lurched.

My translator kicked in as the Amorphan spoke in a lower register, suggesting a male. "Welcome to my classroom! We will have much sport and information together. Please untangle yourselves and find a seat." He swept his arms up and around and made a motion inviting us to come forward. I'm positive he enjoyed our profound surprise.

I gathered up what dignity I had left and entered the room after a shove to my back propelled me forward, releasing the other four from the bottleneck. "Hello." I nodded to it, "I'm happy to be here. I'm Jessalya but I prefer to be called Jessi or Jess." I hoped his translator was as good as mine. The other four introduced themselves, also, and the being gestured to us to take a seat.

The Amorphan bowed to us, multicolored robes swirling. "I am named Datro Aelotro of family Swi:lerano. I am volunteered to teach you of our society during this journey so you may arrive at my home rock prepared to live as an Amorphan. As your teacher, you call me Tatro while in the classroom. When I'm not teaching you, you name me Datro Aelotro."

He continued, "And questions you may have? I am answering what I may of them before we proceed with class information. As example, perhaps you tell me what you interested in learning? I am to teach you mainly things of our family units, society and language, but I will tell you what I may of other things."

While he spoke, I looked around the room. A vent low on the wall to my right blew cool air our way, recessed lighting in the ceiling brightened the room, small vents were dotted around the ceiling and one landscape painting hung on each wall. A sudden inexplicable urge to go stand by the wall vent lapped over me. It was a soft feeling, not compelling, but puzzling. I resisted the pull toward it and dragged my attention elsewhere. I didn't see a comm device anywhere in the room; couldn't use this secluded place, then, for the memory chip.

Since this was an interior room, there were no windows. I didn't see a second entry into or out of this room but perhaps it was so snug a fitting I couldn't see it. The floor was soft underfoot and I didn't know what it was made from. Our chairs were lined up in front of a metal desk with a viewing screen on it and a chair. Tatro stood between us and the front of the desk. I blew out a soft sigh; I guess I thought there would be something extraordinary about an Imurian classroom. In fact, if they'd put the same furniture in here as in my room, they'd be identical, except for no sleeping room. My attention was caught as Mitchler said, "I want to know about sports on Amorpha and if I'll be able to play on a team."

I'm more of a spectator than a participant in sports, but thought their competitive games interesting and so, apparently, did Mitchler. The Amorphans appeared to be about as aggressive as Humans on a sport field, so no wonder Mitchler was interested in a new game. He'd said he liked playing in competitive team sports and was on a regionally known soccer team.

Tatro looked at him and shrugged. Who knew Amorphans shrugged like us? "That depends on how good you are. You would be allowed to try out, I think, if you want."

Zoe asked about forms of entertainment, particularly dancing, and I said, "I'm interested in dancing, too." I ignored the narrow-eyed look Zoe gave me. "But what I really want to know about is your medical system and really, all types of life on Amorpha. Especially which insects to avoid." I grimaced. "I hate bugs."

Tatro tilted his head a little. "I will arrange such information be sent to each of you."

Soli raised his hand, "Museums and engineering," surprising me as I'd figured him for an interior design person, suspecting he was male-oriented by the looks he gave Mitchler and Keaton when he thought no one was looking. Keaton grinned and said he wanted to learn it all.

Tatro Aelotro bowed to us, saying, "I will teach what I can of all things." He looked us over. "We are peaceable beings on Amorpha. However, you will each have bodyguards on our planet, as you already know. Not everyone agrees with bringing aliens to our world. That being said, you are to be taught self-defense specific to Amorpha, even though some of you are already trained for your world. There are differences in anatomy between our peoples that must be addressed. Of course, it is only to be used in the most extreme of times."

He smiled and his eyes crinkled at the corners. I liked him. His lipless mouth had the same motions as ours: upward for smiles and downward for frowns or puzzlement. His eyes twinkled when he spoke to us. I mean, literally, they twinkled and he seemed very kindly and friendly. However, when he opened his mouth, I saw razor-sharp teeth set in two rows, small in length but reminding me of a serrated knife edge, suggesting they were predators at least at some point in their history.

All in all, I liked this Amorphan with his warm personality, the very first one we'd met in person, more than the regimented Imurians. He reminded me of the intro video from the family who chose me to live with them. I was quite amused when the younger of the two children approached the filming device and poked at it with a finger, saying, "Is this thing working? Is it on? Do we start to talk now? Hello, hello?" His face loomed into the screen until I had a close-up view of his eye. I laughed at his actions and most of all at the look of contrition on the parents' faces.

Tatro moved around to sit in the chair at the desk in the front of the room. "Now," he said, "Today we speak phrases in my language. Tomorrow we talk about dinner manners and other politenesses of our society. But today, you need to know how to use common helpful phrases. From now on, you will only speak Amorphan as part of your training whether with me or not, except at meal time when you are with only yourselves until you become more proficient. Then you will speak it all the time. You were all provided language lessons while still on New Eden so I must hope you used them to further your knowledge of our speaking."

We'd been required to meet three times a week as a group for review of the language materials to make sure we squeezed them into our already over-busy schedules of interviews, ongoing University classes, TV appearances and, in my case, hiding from the press although Zoe ate up the attention with a large spoon. Trying to fit in family and friend time and going-away parties, while fun, had been difficult. It had been a very hectic time getting ready for this journey. In our group Amorphan lessons, Keaton had asked why we were instilled with one-way translators instead of two-ways; the latter would've allowed us to speak in Standard but it would be translated audibly into the other language.

Mr. Chul, director of the program, intertwined his fingers. "That would be the easy way out. It was decided, for this first-ever program, you students are to be fully immersed in the culture," and he held up one finger, "*and* language as a fully-speaking participant." He paused for effect. "Your internal translators will do the job until you become fluent at speaking and comprehension and then they will become dormant."

Tatro made a ratcheting sound and I looked at him, pulled from the memory. "First, our alphabet. We repeat it together while looking at the symbols for each sound." He drilled us until he was satisfied we could each identify by sound and sight all the components of their language. Their alphabet had 53 characters but it was hard learning the liquidity needed for each sound. Their language sounded musical when spoken with a blend of speech and tones. It wasn't like singing a song, exactly, nor was it like our speech with distinct words and inflections. It took a lot of concentration. Tatro then said, "You all have done very well but you will continue to practice it again tonight and of course in class tomorrow. But time for something different, so now we will move on to common phrases."

"Now, this is to ask: Where is the toilet?" He broke it down into individual words and we repeated the words one by one until we got the hang of the tones and pronunciation. Then Tatro improved our pronunciation. I did the best of the five of us causing Tatro to exclaim in delight and with a splat of his boneless hands, "How well you are doing!"

Zoe gave me a pissy look so I smirked at her, giving me a burn of satisfaction. Take that, Miss Perfect Blonde Tall and Slender. *If you only knew what the Cats thought about you*—okay, so only the two I'd overheard the night before but still, I knew something she didn't.

Tatro promised it would get easier as we went along. "I will not make you fluent in two weeks. At least you are able to read our language and also ask for the toilet and a restaurant with a reasonable accent. Tomorrow we review everything from today and I will also teach you pictures of flora and fauna on our world and their words."

When the bell chimed for lunchtime, I was surprised how tired I'd become. Concentrating this hard took a lot of energy. I was more than ready to eat before the next class on local politics and manners started, which quite frankly sounded boring.

Classes were scheduled for 12 hours every day, all day, because of the total immersion process. We were allowed one free hour a day before our scheduled bedtimes, either in the viewing deck or we could stay in our room and use the entertainment system.

Yesterday, we'd been on New Eden time and now we were on Amorphan time. The time-lag effect hadn't hit us yet but then, the time and day had just changed this morning. They didn't take a subtle approach to it; one day we were on New Eden time and now we're not. The Imurians did, however, believe in schedules and regimentation.

Tatro Aelotro announced, as we were ready to go to lunch, "Very soon you will be fitted with traditional clothing of the Amorphans so you get used to wearing them."

Lunch would introduce us to various Amorphan dishes on the menu at our meals until by the end of our journey, that's all we'd be eating and drinking, at least the ones safe for Human consumption. The only exception was the one Human food or drink we could retain for ourselves for the year. Guess what I chose. Yup. Coffee.

After lunch, Tatro Aelotro settled himself on a chair saying, "We will begin by telling each other of ourselves. Even though we each have a translator, they are not universal in our society. Are they in yours?"

"No, because we all speak the same language so there is not much need."

He slanted his head to the right in assent. "Yes, the same on Amorpha. You understand what others say because of your translator but they will not understand your language when you talk, therefore you must learn to speak it well. Your bodyguards can also translate but that is not their purpose and they will not all be fluent in your Standard."

Keaton raised a hand. "I'm still not totally sure why we need bodyguards."

Tatro looked at him, his mouth tightening. "Is everyone on your world happy about this Exchanging program?"

"No, not everyone."

"The same on my world, as I mentioned this morning. There are those who believe we should always stay separate and not cross-contaminate our societies. While we have learned to be a peaceful people, this experiment has never been performed before so we cannot presume that all will be well. Therefore, in all cautiousness, we assign bodyguards to each of you. As parents ourselves, we want our offspring returned whole and healthy and your parents do, too. All students on all worlds are given guards. Now we move on." He gestured for us to open our reading app. As pages appeared, I saw the swirly, loopy writing of Amorphan.

"We have learned the alphabet and now your translation device will help, yes?"

"Yes," we agreed. Our translator nanny could take what we scanned with our eyes and tell it to us in Standard. It's weird, actually. Somehow the translator nanny knew when we were speaking our own language and didn't translate but when Tatro spoke, it chimed in and we heard it in our heads as Standard words. I'll never understand the molecular world of electronics or how things get programmed and how the translator could work that way. I knew it was in my brain at the language center somehow and that it integrated with the brain circuitry, but I didn't understand any more of it than that.

Oh, my aching head; I rubbed my forehead to relieve the tension and when that didn't work, moved my hand to my neck. A lot of my hair had been hanging over my shoulders in front to watch but the section over my neck started doing a massaging type of squeeze. Good thing no one was behind me to see.

"We will now take a small relief time from all this study." Tatro announced. "Officer Sir'et'eh is coming to answer general questions while I take a small break from this room."

I asked in Amorphan where to find the toilet and Tatro nodded in approval. He pointed to the inset door at the opposite side of the room from the chairs and desk as he moved toward the door. After relieving my bladder, I grabbed a snack and a drink from a cart just outside the door in the hallway, as did the others. I took the opportunity to wander around the room, passing close by the vent set low into the wall. Something made me pause there without my knowing why I needed to stop. Without knowing how or why, I suddenly felt complete as if a tiny part of me had been missing.

My hair breathed an extended OHHHHHH, like sudden comprehension of a problem solved. I shook my head in a small motion; I didn't have a clue why or what had just happened.

I looked at my classmates to see if they noticed anything. Keaton looked very interested in his PD, Soli was frowning at his fingernails and Mitchler was openly yawning, arms crossed loosely, leaning back in his chair in a casual manner.

Officer Sir'et'eh walked into the room, nodding hello to us before taking his position at the front of the room. He said in the clipped tone of Imurian, "What do you want to talk about?"

Zoe fiddled with her hair and then, raising her eyes from her device, asked in a plaintive voice, "Can't we talk about something interesting like, oh, you know, what kind of entertainments they have or dance clubs or whatever?"

Sir'et'eh gave her a withering look, slightly flattening his ears, mouth tightening and forehead wrinkling in disapproval.

I raised my hand, "Sir? How long would this journey be in FTL?"

He tilted one shoulder up and the other down in their version of a shrug. "Two days. It is necessary for you to have this training, however, so we are not using FTL for two weeks and then we will for the last day of the journey."

Mitchler asked, "How does FTL work?" A hopeful look flitted across his face although we all knew the Cats closely guarded this secret.

Sir'et'eh looked at him for a long second. "This we do not discuss. Just to know if we did not have this capability, there would be no new worlds for populations to buy."

I was no physicist or rocket scientist so the sheer immensity of space in between galaxies was overwhelming, I forget how many gazillion light years away Amorpha was from New Eden; we were truly and scarily far away from anything familiar. We five Humans would be so alone on Amorpha and once there, we would live in different cities around the world with no contact between each other as we were to be 100% immersed into Amorphan society. It was enough to make me gulp air.

I raised my finger to get the officer's attention. "I know many years ago there was a circulation problem during the emigration of our families. What are the chances that will happen again?"

His eyes narrowed as he glared at me, whiskers back tight against his cheeks and his ears flattening to his head. His tail twitched in irritation. "Madame, that was a one-time incidence of many, many years ago. We do not to allow things like that to happen again. The Captain makes sure of that and you are advised to not worry about such things." There was more than a touch of threat in his tone.

I nodded while holding his gaze to let him know I wasn't intimidated, although, in reality, I wanted to run back to my room and lock my door. "I just, ah, wanted reassurance since it happened to our parents, after all."

His sharpened gaze flicked away for a split second, breaking eye contact as I blinked slowly at him and his whiskers relaxed. "Of course. Please feel safe in our presence. Such a thing cannot happen again."

I noted astonished looks on my classmates' faces. Well, fairy farts, even I didn't know I was going to ask that until I did. If I'd thought about it first, I probably wouldn't have but I couldn't take it back. I wished I could; I really didn't want to call attention to myself.

The officer stood and said, "It is now time to go to physical moves class for instruction and practice moves for defense of your own body."

## CHAPTER FOUR

Language, social customs and behaviors were in the mornings and afternoons were self-defense classes with Imurian officers and dance classes with Tatra Meleandrea, Tatra Hilodria and Tatro Aelotro.

The two female Amorphans' skin sparkled and changed colors, also. Their robes were similar with a loose and flowing style but with a feminine flair, more pleats, embroidery and sparkles added to the neckband and Meleandrea wore a belt around her waist area, apparently a fashion statement. The belt matched the color of the robe with inset bling flashing and twinkling. She was hard to look at without getting dizzy from all the changing colors.

The feathers on their heads were longer and curled around their faces along the cheek line in a very becoming way. All the Amorphans had multi-faceted, multi-colored eyes and their pupils, while round like ours, were hard to discern among all the twinkling.

They had an hour to start our dance instructions to their native music and with their own dancing styles. Even Zoe was rapt with attention as they flowed through the movements to music sounding as if it, too, twinkled. When it was our turn to try, we all fumbled with the steps, even Zoe, and we all broke a sweat.

We switched to self-defense lessons in the same room, two rooms down the hall from our classroom and the door opened to allow the two Tatrans to leave, framing an Imurian with stiff posture and severe looking eyes. He pointed to chairs so we made our way to them and sat. He took up a pose before us, head held high, hands behind his back and feet spread, uniform crisp with creases on the legs and everything arranged with precision. He looked at us in silence down his flattened, wide nose; I felt like squirming in my chair under the intensity of his gaze and my classmates started to fidget.

He snarled out some words and I realized I could understand them even before my translator kicked in. "What a bunch of weak kitlings I have to teach." My translator kicked in with "weak kittens, I will teach." So the translators did have some limitations but I wondered how I could've understood his words without my translator.

He continued speaking. "My name is Rank Officer Mer'lout'e and I am here to teach basics in self-defense against potential threats by any Amorphan. This teaching is directed toward saving yourself in case of aggression against you, although you will each be assigned your own set of bodyguards while on their planet." His tail twitched around his left ankle. "You perhaps to wonder why this is necessary. It is because we work to fully realize all aspects of this new adventure which has never been tried before. Reports from your world and from theirs show most peoples to be accepting and curious about the Program but there are also threats received against the Program. Because we promised that all involved would stay safe and alive, we must teach you basics of self-defense, although your chances of using this information will, most likely, be non-existent. Any questions?"

I raised my hand. "Um, sir?"

"Rank Officer, if you please, Madame."

"Um, Rank Officer, how will we practice these techniques if they are to be used against an Amorphan in case of dire need? Wouldn't it be better if we were to have Amorphans to teach us?"

He bared his teeth, whiskers twitching. "We have recordings for you to watch on actual such fights between Amorphans. We will provide commentary for those viewings to provide further details you might need to know. However, it is much to be preferred that you avoid all such possibilities. Your assigned bodyguards are highly trained to protect each of you and have been fully investigated before being assigned. We wish not to worry you but must let you know the microscopic chance might exist because among any people, there will always be those who oppose such change."

I didn't think he had really answered my question but nodded anyway.

"Other questions? Then we move on to the fundamentals."

The fundamentals consisted of first learning about Amorphan anatomy and soft points on their bodies, nervous system vulnerabilities and similar things. At the end of the first didactic class, we viewed a five-minute clip of an actual fight. How the Imurians got video of an Amorphan back alley fight was curious but good for teaching. Rank Officer Mer'lout'e promised us, or perhaps threatened us, that by the next day, we would start actual physical training. The Amorphans and Imurians were a lot taller than me; truth be told, any adult was way taller than me—I barely nudged five feet tall in Human terms and that was if I stood up very, very straight. However, I did have a few fighting elements on my side, especially my fingernails.

During my Cat-Fight training years, the owner developed a nail polish, luckily with many pretty color choices, to harden our fingernails so I keep them polished and sharpened on the rounded ends as secret weapons. Although my hair can camouflage by matching surrounding colors, it takes a couple of minutes to change to match my environment. This ability would be a lot more useful if it was instant but it isn't. It had also tried to grow as long as the floor but, a lot of pain and scissors later, it turned into very tight ringlets instead to disguise how long it really was and never hung longer than my waist after that.

Outrage washed through me from my hair. *Hey, I'm proud you can change colors; don't get me wrong. But instantaneously doing it would be even better but hey. No one else can do what you do so don't take it personally.*

HMPH. My hair relaxed just a bit, feeling sulky.

After much drilling and testing, we were dismissed to dinner. After dinner, which involved new Amorphan menu choices, we were escorted back to the classroom to study and practice until, finally, we were done for the day and could take our one hour of free time. I was very tired and judging by the yawns around me, so were the other four.

I felt a huge desire for my bed and sleep but I hadn't finished the forbidden knowledge on the memory card. I needed to stay awake so I could sneak out later; if I laid down now, I'd miss my chance. I wondered about the classroom we were in today, if it was the same room Mom and Devon had been in that day so long ago. Could be; I didn't know how many classrooms they had for Humans but it couldn't be that many, I didn't think.

"Hey, Jess, wait up." Mitchler stepped up to my side. "Are you going up to the space view?"

"Yeah, for a while before going to bed. You?"

"Yup, me and Keaton are going. Since we're out of FTL drive for now, wanted to see if I can figure out where we are in the universe by the stars."

I nodded. "I don't know that stuff very well so maybe you can teach me something about it?"

Zoe sauntered over and placed a hand on Mitchler's arm. "I'm sure you can teach *me* a thing or two, Mitchler." She almost purred while snuggling in close to his side. I rolled my eyes. *Obvious much, Zoe?* "Oh! Keaton's coming, too!" She actually wiggled in seeming delight and Mitchler flushed pink. Parts of her, after all, snugged up against his arm.

Keaton glanced over from where he was speaking with Soli and grinned. He raised a finger, saying, "Be right there!" and then clapped his hand on Soli's shoulder, while Soli smiled at him and then turned to wave at us.

"Soli said he's really sleepy so he's going to his room; it's just us going up."

Sir'et'eh stepped into the room, "How many are going to the viewer area?"

"Four." Mitchler said. Soli left for his room with an escort after saying good night.

The elevator was quite roomy with only five of us on it and the journey took a couple of seconds. The palm pad had been fixed, I noted, and hoped they hadn't changed the numerical code.

Apparently using the code pad without inputting a palm print didn't trigger anything; it seemed the palm pad was more for convenience than security.

The lights were on in the viewing room and we walked over to the window while Sir'et'eh stayed by the door. The outside scenery was magnificent with the sweep of infinite dark space before us with pinpricks of light twinkling in the velvety black. There were patterns among the lights, with discernable swirls of milky-white displays and some of the stars glowed reddish or yellowish. There were areas with swirls of color and amorphous shapes and they were beautiful. I felt as if there was nothing between me and the distant stars, that I would fall forward at any second, causing my stomach to flip in panic. Sudden fear washed over me as a part of me inexplicably yearned to be returned to the stars beyond the window while the rest of me wanted to step away. I blinked rapidly and turned my head away from the vista outside and washed a hand over my face.

"Jess? You okay?" Keaton said, putting a hand on my shoulder in support. I pressed my lips together, shaking my head. I held up a hand, closing my eyes and took a large breath in and out, then looked at him and twitched a small smile.

"Got dizzy for a second; sorry about that. I felt like I was almost outside or something was going to suck me out the window. It was rather….unsettling."

Keaton nodded, Mitchler and Zoe both watching me with concern on their faces. "You're pale, and that's saying something with your light skin." He grinned. "I think you'd better step away from the window, though. I'm not sure the Cats would take kindly to your barfing on their floor."

Zoe said, "Ewww, neither would I."

I turned my back on the viewing area, gulping back nausea, and was relieved to see a snack cart arriving. "I need some water."

Sir'et'eh frowned as he walked over to me. "You are very white. Sit and I will bring you a bottle. I think perhaps the viewing deck is not for you."

I swigged down half the bottle as Sir'et'eh asked me, "Are you afraid of darkness?"

"No, it's not that. I—I think I'm just tired. I think maybe it was all too much and it looks like there's no window there…I think it all combined to make me dizzy and nauseous." I drank some more water. "I'm feeling a lot better." I shook my head. "I don't think I want to look out the window anymore, though, at least not tonight."

"That is understandable." He remarked. "Sometimes people of any species to react that way; this I have seen for myself."

"At least I'm not alone in the universe, then."

Mitchler snorted a small chuckle. "No, you're not alone in the universe, Jessi. I'll admit the first time we stood here, my stomach wanted to flip upside down but the more I looked out, the more I became used to it and that feeling went away. Maybe that would help you?"

"Maybe. I think I'll try another night, though." I stood, wiping my hand over my eyes. "I think I'd better go back to my room."

Sir'et'eh looked torn; he needed to stay with the students in the room as an escort but he also needed to take me back to my room. "I can get back to my room all right if you call the elevator. I mean, where else could I go, right?"

His ears twitched back and forth as he thought this over, the end of his tail keeping time to his ears. "All right." He said finally.

"I will to get the lift for you and program it to your deck. That should be all right. As you to say, where else could you to go?"

Leaving the room to a chorus of "Hope you feel better in the morning" from the rest of them, we walked to the elevator. I was thinking hard about how to go to a different floor than mine but in the few seconds I had, I didn't know what I could do. The door opened and he stepped in, tapping the square for my deck, nodded to me and I entered the lift.

I couldn't pass up this opportunity, as unplanned as it was. That view really hit me hard for some reason but I decided I couldn't let it stop me. When else would I get an opportunity to explore unknown areas? The doors closed and I impulsively put my finger on the square for the maintenance deck. To my surprise, the elevator moved past the Human deck and went down further. My hands started shaking a little; what would I do if the doors opened and there were people there? That thought sped up my heart rate to match my trembling hands.

I didn't have much time to be scared, though, because within a couple of breaths, the doors swooshed open again. I peered out into the corridor and saw no one there and heard nothing. *Must be too late at night for maintenance workers. I hope.* I stepped out into the hallway and looked both ways again. *Huh. Now which way do I go?*

My hair undulated in uncertainty as I looked both ways again. In the stillness, I felt a slight desire to go to my right and my hair concurred, so I turned that way. I mused as I walked on silent feet that turning right was a default way to go for Humans, most of us being right-handed. I walked quickly for fear of discovery but it was about as silent as I imagined a grave would be. I came to a

*Exchanger*

large dark opening on my left and the industrial smell to the air hinted I'd found the area I wanted.

I sidled into the large room, keeping my back flat against the wall to minimize my profile while glancing around the room. The light only spilled into the space so far leaving the ends of the room shrouded in black. I felt an affinity to—something—in this room but why that would be was far beyond my comprehension.

My hair slithered over my body and uncoiled enough to reach my feet. I watched as the color changed to match the inkiness around me and my fair skin disappeared from sight. I was mesmerized by the sight, quite impressed and wondered how by the seven gates of hell this even happened. My hair radiated smugness.

I carefully felt my way down the wall; matching the darkness didn't mean I could see in it. As I silently stepped forward away from the light but following the wall to my right, my eyes adjusted so I could see the shapes of machinery and other objects scattered around the area. Something kept tugging at me to the right diagonal from where I was so I inched my way toward it, following the feeling to stay on track.

I stumbled over something on the floor and irritation flashed through me. That better not be my hair tangling my feet! A zing of indignation from my hair—*NOT!*—and I realized it was something like a cord stretched across the floor.

*Sorry.*

If my hair could've sniffed, it would've. I didn't dare use a light and could only hope my eyes continued to adjust to the gloom. The inner feeling became stronger and I used my outstretched hands to make sure I wasn't going to run into anything while

I now slid my feet forward to make sure I didn't trip over anything else. I was far enough into the room the light from the door couldn't reach this area and it was very dark indeed.

There. The feeling inside coalesced around me. This was it. Whatever this was.

# CHAPTER FIVE

Risking a dim light from my device, I stared as I swept the light over the small, square object before me. It was like a small mobile cart, painted dark gray, perhaps three feet high and two feet wide, completely enclosed with a grating over the upper third of the front. An inset panel on top had AKRION printed on it in Imurian. There was a small control panel next to the printed word, blank and dark. It was set on a base of caster wheels and was shoved against a much larger metal box. It felt abandoned and I had no clue as to why I felt an affinity for it. And what was Akrion?

Baffled, I ran my hands over the exterior; it was smooth and cool to the touch, except where the word was printed, inert as it sat there unused and unwanted. No doors were seen or felt on the front or sides. I couldn't get to the back of it without moving it and I didn't want to risk any noise.

I peered at the panel but couldn't read anything on it. I shone a very dim light from my PD on the control panel and touched the ON indicator but nothing happened. If it was battery run, it was out of juice and if it had to be plugged in, I didn't know where outlets were in this cavernous space.

The more I stared at it, I realized it was the right height for the vents in the classroom. Surely there was a maintenance corridor between main hallways for plumbing, electricity and whatnot. Ok, so now what did I do with this information? I was certain this box had everything to do with what happened to the women and my brother, but what was it? What did the Imurians actually do with this cart? More importantly, why? It was definitely a mobile unit since it had wheels, it was small, and then I saw small stickers written in Imurian proclaiming CAUTION and HANDLE WITH CARE and ONLY FOR USE BY AUTHORIZED PERSONNEL as I ran my light over the sides of the unit.

It was welded together along all seams so the only access to the interior had to be on the back of it. Whatever they placed in this, they did *not* want it to leak out. I tried to push it away from the other thing but it was much heavier than it looked or the wheels were locked and since I was afraid of it scraping along the floor and making noise, I stopped those efforts.

I tapped my fingers on the top of the metal box, thinking. It seemed to me they used this to blow something through the vents into the classroom where all the pregnant women were gathered for a class. My brother was there to play the role of "unruly child" and must've received a dose of whatever it was the Imurians introduced into the air. But why did they do it, who did it and why did it kill my brother and no one else?

My hair clenched around me to get my attention; I heard footsteps walking rapidly down the uncarpeted hall toward this area. I couldn't be caught here; I felt very exposed in spite of my hair's disguising ability so I felt the urgent need to hide. I scuttled around behind the large metal thing that the smaller one was butted up against and pressed my back to it, now facing the opposite way of the door and deep in the darkness. I held my breath, hoping my hair would change to match whatever I was standing against and closed my eyes. The whites of my eyes could give me away even through the veil of strands in front of my face, I feared.

I heard male voices speaking in Imurian, two of them as best I could tell. "...and the quicker we check this out, the quicker back to our dinner." *He sounds different from the two from the viewing deck.*

"That is true. Who would want to come to this area, anyway, unless it is one of the workers for the maintenance?"

"I do not know. Perhaps something important broke and needed fixing." A deep sniffing sound. "Do you smell Human?"

"Human? Seriously?"

Light suddenly glared into the room. I'd opened my eyes a crack but I squeezed them shut again, breathing as shallow and light as I could, my hands flat against the metal back behind me. I'd no idea what I stood against or if it had a pattern, which made for easier camouflage, or plain metal, more of a risk. I wished it had a door so I could slip inside of whatever it was but it didn't matter, I couldn't move for an instant. The Imurians had very keen eyesight, along with hearing abilities beyond us and a nose like a bloodhound.

*I'm so glad I don't wear perfume; they'd smell that a mile away.* My hair didn't like any shampoo with fragrance, either, so that helped. I wished fervently they'd just go away; this was the second time I was trapped and it was getting a little old.

"Do you not think it smells like Human in here?"

A coughing laugh. "I think you need time off, Rah'get'eh! I do not smell anything other than oils and dust." A sound like one slapping the other's shoulder. "I think you have Human on the mind, that is all! Which of them has caught your eye? Hmmm?"

"None of them, of course. You know I am courting Xla're'tah."

"Just because you are does not mean other females cannot attract the male eye."

"That is true…" His voice trailed off and I heard their footsteps recede a little. "I think you are right; I think one of the Scitterers made those tracks. Those little pests; I do not to know why we to tolerate them on our ships." *Ye gods and little fishes, I left tracks? I didn't think the floor was that dirty. Must not have been footprints or they'd know it was a Human.*

"Because they to keep the corridors and small spaces clean, of course. But yes, I agree, they can be quite a nuisance."

"The small ones are cute, like that little Human female. The young of any species are cute, though."

*Do they mean me? What?*

"The only thing attractive on her are those sky-blue eyes." A pause. "Well, and maybe that long mass of reddish strings. I have never seen such coils on any Human."

"I like the tall female better. That yellow hair looks delicious!"

*At least they like my blue eyes but since when does hair look yummy? Yuck.*

I heard their footsteps as they stepped around the room. "We will have to speak to the head maintenance Officer about those Scitterers leaving their tracks everywhere."

*What the heck is a Scitterer?* I didn't spare much thought for this as I was concentrating on tracking the sound of their walking.

One strand loosened enough to creep around the corner to check out the space just as the lights snapped off. I stayed frozen in place, not only to adjust again to the darkness but to allow them to leave the area before I tried to sneak back to my room.

My hair gave me a sign it was okay to leave. I slid out from behind the metal box I'd been plastered against and then decided to risk a photo of the Akrion box. I didn't know if Akrion was a company name or an item but it didn't hurt to have a photo. I took a few, wincing at the flash of light, and then I turned and headed for the door as rapidly as I could go without making noise. My hair hung over my shoulders in front as if poised to attack if needed but thankfully, we reached the elevator without any incidence after making sure the hallway was clear. Thank the stars the Imurians had skeleton crews on at night.

I stepped into the elevator and plastered my back against the corner back from the control panel after touching the button for the Human floor. My hair suddenly fell in front of my face, stretched to the floor and pinned me in place. *What the---!*

SHHH!

I forgot to breathe as two night officers stepped into view, the one saying to the other, "Hey, the elevator is already here. It must have known we needed to change floors."

They stepped into the elevator side by side and turned to face the door as the one reached out to punch a floor number. "Huh, it is already pushed for the Human floor. That is different."

The other one twitched his ears, one half-pointing at his companion. "You tapped the wrong number, that is all. It is not the first time you have done such a thing."

"I had not even touched them yet!"

"I think you did when we entered, you put your oversized paw over the edge of the door and you must have hit the number then." He shrugged. "So what? We need to check that corridor anyway."

The other one growled, reaching out to punch his companion on the shoulder, who swatted him back. "Stop that! Your too-huge hands hurt, you piece of slime."

The first one barked a laugh. "Slime? That is the best you can do?"

Frozen in place behind them, I watched this through my veil of hair. Well, guess my camouflage job worked. They didn't see me when they stepped in—*thank you, hair!*—and then like everyone, they immediately turned to face the doors. They weren't expecting anything out of the ordinary which only helped me. *I have to stop being trapped by night officers! This is getting old.*

My hair tapped me. SHHH.

Thankfully, the elevator doors opened then and they stepped out to survey the hall, holding the doors open with a hand. I saw their heads swivel back and forth and then they crowded each other getting back on, shoving and pushing each other with their shoulders. I hastily closed my eyes lest they see the whites of my eyes through the hair veil and held my breath, wishing my heart would slow down from galloping. Luckily, they were making enough noise to cover anything they might've heard.

"I do not to know why we have to check the Humans. They are locked in at all times and our indicators show them in bed."

"I do not to know, either, but if we skipped it, sure as a planet has a moon, that would be the time something was wrong. So, we to take a minute to check. Big deal. Get the knot out of your tail, you big kitling."

The elevator doors opened again and they stepped out, still rough housing as they jeered at each other, laughing and trading slaps and punches. When the doors whispered shut again, I slumped against the wall, knees weak. That was too close for comfort but at least I knew the camouflage job worked perfectly. I tapped the button again for the Human deck.

I gratefully entered my room. My hair was trying to dust itself free of debris from being on the floor so I took my brush and helped it out. *This is why I don't want you on the floor all the time.*

A flashing light caught my eye as I was yawning. "Room? What is the flashing light?"

"You have one message, Madame. Shall I speak it for you?"

"Yes."

"Message from Si'neada." The room's voice changed. "This is Si'neada, the tailor, and I will be making your Amorphan clothes. It is important we meet for measurements so you may be garbed correctly. Please affirm you will be ready for my attendance at 0500 in the morning, ship time. I to understand you returned to your room early due to discomfort and I am sure you are in bed so I will to return in the morning as stated. Please to be dressed and ready."

I made a face. 0500? What a horrible time, the butt-crack of dawn, but I figured I might as well suck it up and confirm. It sounded like he was going to show up whether or not I agreed.

"Room, please confirm for me."

"Message sent."

I shucked off my shoes and padded into my bedroom, got ready for bed and crawled under the covers. As I lay there waiting for the curtain of sleep, I wondered again what a Scitterer was and if it was important to my quest or not, and then thought about that Akrion machine thingy. I felt an affinity for that machine which I couldn't define or explain as it was nothing but a small portable metal box and maybe it could've released something into the classroom. But what? Who would do that and why? With those questions swirling through my thoughts, I fell asleep.

I was jarred awake early next morning by my room, who insisted I get out of bed to prepare for Si'neada's visit. I grumbled and turned over but the lights kept flashing and the room's voice was insistent so after a minute of this, I said, "Oh, all *right*." I swung my feet out of bed and went directly to the kitchen for coffee first and then I brushed my teeth and my hair. I dressed in jeans and a red T-shirt that proclaimed, "Exchangers Switch Places", sliding my feet into my sneakers. I attached a few charms to the bottom of my T-shirt showcasing aliens and Human figurines to go with the printed theme. My room chimed with an alert of someone being at the door, so I asked who it was as I peered at the vid of the person outside.

"Madame Jessalya, my name is Tr. Si'neada and I am your tailor assigned to help you with your wardrobe."

I wiped my face with one hand, rubbing my eyes, as I hadn't bothered with make-up yet. "Okay, enter," I yawned.

A dazzling figure minced into my space. His jumpsuit, a lovely shade of lavender, showcased embroidered flowers at the edge of each pocket and there are a lot of pockets on their jumpsuits. Added bling shone from the cuffs and collar area and it was impeccably ironed. He smiled at me, showing perfect white fangs and teeth as he bowed low, sweeping one arm across his body, and I swear all he was missing was a hat with a feather. His fur sported a pinkish tinge and his stripes were blonde, something I'd never seen on any other Imurian.

His whiskers looked like crystals, winking colors in the light, and I was pretty sure he had something like mascara on his lashes. His gold eyes with their slit pupils regarded me with a softness missing from any other Imurian officer and as his tail curled around his legs, I noticed it was tipped with a ribbon. Earrings in the edge of his upright ears winked purple at me, matching the three rings he wore on different fingers.

I said, "Welcome to my space, Tr. Si'neada." I gestured to welcome him into my room. Unless I missed my guess, he was completely male-oriented. He seemed very feminine even though his outfit had the required pouch for his male parts. I realized I hadn't seen any female Imurians yet and wondered for a second if Tr. Si'neada was actually female but the male sac spoke otherwise. I knew these were family ships so they had to be somewhere but being confined to the Human quarters limited how much crew we saw and it appeared they only assigned males to this sector of the ship.

The Imurian tailor fascinated me; he was the first I'd seen with feminine traits. How could those claws handle something delicate like needle and thread? Or maybe they didn't use those mundane types of things; after all, they had technology beyond what I could understand.

He frowned in a delicate manner and sighed, then his expression lightened as he put one jeweled claw-tipped finger over his mouth and his eyes looked me over, long lashes sweeping over his eyes. "Ah, Madame Jessalya."

"Please, call me Jessi."

"Jessi, then, thank you. You are so, shall we say, delightfully petite? Although, as I to understand it, that big ham of a trainer will be forcing you into a more streamlined muscled shape." *Did he just say I'm chubby?*

"Of course, muscle is good and allows you to dress with grace but, tsk, tsk, you will to save me from using much fabric." He nodded. "Yes, to save much fabric. Now please to turn around for me." He twirled his finger.

I turned in a slow circle. "Ah, yes," he remarked, "You will be a delight to dress. You will look like a miniature Amorphan and they will to think you are a doll. And my darling, your hairies are a delight! So wonderfully coiled like that! And what are these that all you Humans wear? It seems to be a required part of your outfit." He pointed at my jeans.

Amused, I said, "Hair, not hairies. It's called hair. And yes, I suppose jeans are almost a requirement for us Humans."

"I will perhaps try one of these jeans things soon but no room for the tail so I will have to modify. But you call it only hair?"

"Hair, yes."

"But there is so much of it and it is made of individual strings, yes?"

"Strands, and yeah, there's a lot of it. But it is called collectively 'hair.'"

He rolled his eyes, which startled me into grinning. I thought only Transitional Year girls did that. "Very well, then, your 'hairs'. They are still a delight to see. How did you get that wonderful reddish color?"

"That's my natural color; it grows that way."

"And the length? I have never seen such a thing!"

"Yeah, it's rather long, I know, and it's unusual even for us Humans." I shrugged and my hair rippled in a wave at his obvious delight. "I've always loved having long hair so I don't cut it." I didn't mention that my hair rebelled if I tried. Waist length was too long, in my opinion, but that's how we compromised; as long as it stayed at my waist and didn't give me headaches with the curls, we were fine. Since it took care of itself and stayed out of my way, I could live with it.

Tr. Si'neada clasped his hands in front of his resplendent outfit. "Well, I love it, I just love your hairies!"

Amused, I smiled. "Well, I just love your furries!"

"Now, Madame Jessi—"

I corrected him. "No Madame, please, it's just Jess or Jessi."

"Ah, yes, of course, my little Jessi, I will finish the body measurements and then we to discuss materials and colors. I have swatches!" He actually clapped his hands together in delight much as a child would.

I had to grin; he was very entertaining. He fussed around me, pushing my arms out to the side so he could take measurements with some type of instrument, and when he was done, he stepped back, again tapping his finger against his mouth, a purple ring sparkling in the light. "All right." He said after a few seconds of scrutinizing me. "I think you will look best in reds, blues and dark greens. Especially the blues with those sky eyes. No yellow or orange, hmmm?"

"That's right," I said. "I look terrible in yellows or oranges and I definitely prefer the jewel colors."

He opened the small suitcase type thing he'd pulled into the room and opened the top. "Here, hold these." He handed me a bundle of material swatches he pulled off the top of the contents as he continued rummaging around in the case. "Yes, this and this, too, I think."

He faced me and said, "Now hold that up to your face." He pointed an elegant finger at the bundle I was clutching. I did as he requested and as he motioned, I flipped through the squares and held them next to my skin. He then took that bundle from my hand and gave me three other pieces to do the same.

"Hmmm." He murmured. "Yes, I think so." He nodded briskly and smiled at me. "Well, my little delight, I have what I to need from you and tonight you will to have your Amorphan fitting for all the new robes with one to start wearing tomorrow." He packed everything up while I stood there.

"Um, thank you?" I instinctively liked Si'neada; he was amusing and seemed very efficient.

"Of course, my little kitling. I will return tonight at 1000 this evening, ship time."

"I'll be here."

He laughed, more of a chortle than anything. "Of course, my little star. Where else would you be?"

*Probably trapped in another room on the ship with the night watch.* "True; where else would I be?" I smiled at him brightly but he gave me a sharp glance with a bit of a startled look. "Sorry I missed you last night; I must've been sound asleep to have missed the door alert. The viewing deck unsettled me a lot and I wasn't feeling good at all."

"Oh, my!" He exclaimed, blinking at me. "I trust you are recovered now? Did I make you rise out of bed too soon?"

"It's definitely a bit early for me," I admitted, stifling a yawn.

"Not feeling well had to do with the viewing window and when I got away from it and into bed, I felt so much better. I think it's just the adjustment to space travel and time lag and all the excitement." He gazed at me in concern but there was a hint of sharpness to that look.

"How unsettling for you. I am glad to know you are feeling better this morning, my little friend. Well, I shall to return later for your fittings and of course, you will continue to feel better."

I smiled. "I shall indeed."

After he left, I drank another cup of coffee. Who knew? Perhaps the Amorphans would like it as much as I did and I could start an export business for it. Or be their first Human doctor, perhaps with a coffee place on the side. I thought about dispensing medical advice along with lattes and I grinned.

I left my room on time as our Officer of the Day escorted us to breakfast. One after another, we each yawned although I was irritated to see Zoe being delicate about hers and wished I'd thought to cover my mouth with my hand, too. Since I was never going to be as elegant as Zoe, I might as well get over it but I could take maybe a note here and there. The thought that I might need any instruction from Zoe grated on me even more.

"So how did everyone's fitting go?" Zoe asked. "I'm very curious to know what I'll end up with; the tailor wouldn't let me know exactly which of the materials he was going to use for my robes. How about all of you?"

Keaton winced. "That was a very interesting experience, I must say. He measured me every which way and I thought he was going to try to feel my.." he flushed a little..."um, guy parts, but he didn't. Maybe I just worried that he would." He turned redder. "At least they're robes or gowns or whatever and not those jumpsuits with the male," he gestured, "pouchy thing up front."

Mitchler and Soli chuckled, although both looked embarrassed. "Grateful for that, too." Mitchler said.

Soli said, "I hope it doesn't feel like wearing a dress but I guess we can get used to anything, right?"

I glanced at Soli. *I'm sure he's male oriented but I guess he's not the girly side of that. And maybe he's not comfortable talking about it; he's sure never confirmed it or said anything. Huh. Maybe his hormones haven't let him make a full determination yet.*

Brain wave study results and hormone manipulation weren't discussed among us Humans. When we reached a milestone, the doctor discussed it with the person and their parents, if they were still young enough for that, and then tweaking would be done to our nano systems to allow the appropriate hormone to be secreted.

Doctors, of course, were sworn to confidentiality; the person could choose to share the information but most of us kept it private and in-family or told only to best friends. So maybe Soli was adult by brain waves but not quite ready for sex hormone tweaking, or perhaps he was a slow starter…or maybe he was still deciding. I didn't know; I had enough trouble figuring out my own level of interest in guys. I knew I was definitely male-oriented but also knew I wasn't quite ready to explore any physical relationships with them, especially since it would be over in less than two weeks if I did have one on this ship.

I also remembered the excruciatingly embarrassing conversation with Dad and Mom about sex. Two evenings before I left for the stars, I stayed overnight just because I could. We finished dinner and lingered over dessert, enjoying a cup of coffee with our berry pie.

Clearing his throat, Dad said, "Jess, we realize you have reached Early Prime Adult brain wave maturity levels. And you don't have to answer this but have they tweaked your nannies to start allowing for sexual hormones to increase yet?" I nodded, not knowing where to look.

He continued, "Of course, that means sexual desire and probably sexual relationships." He sighed, looking away from me with a blush. He sucked in a breath. "Now, we want you to know that whatever orientation you become, male or female, that's all right with us. We hope you're male oriented but if not, we love you no matter what. We really want you to know and understand that." He paused for a second. "And now you're officially an Early Prime Adult, doctors can no longer talk to us about you about anything."

My face flooded with heat, probably as scarlet as my favorite blouse. We had always been open in our family of three but now this subject seemed so personal and, well, quite embarrassing.

I darted a look at Mom and then Dad and then didn't know where to let my eyes land. She was colored pink, also, and Dad looked like he was braving a lion. I realized they were waiting for an answer from me. "Uh, yeah, that's what the doc said. For what it's worth, I'm pretty sure I'm only interested in guys." I mumbled.

Dad nodded. "Good, then let me fill you in on a few things. I don't think I've told you, because frankly it wasn't your business, but when I was a young man—certainly before I'd met your mother—and my hormones started increasing, I thought, 'Oh, wow! This is great! No worries about pregnancy or disease and I can get all the experience I want!' Because men of the Early Adult Prime years, yeah, it's just about all we think about once the hormones hit." He blew out a breath.

"So I did. Played around, that is. There were some women who wanted more from a relationship but I only wanted to have fun so I made sure they knew I didn't want an ongoing relationship with anyone, just wanted to have fun and, uh, sex. Then I met your mom. "

He covered Mom's hand with his own and smiled. "She wasn't having any of that nonsense about fooling around. She made sure we had a real relationship first and then when we both knew we were going to be committed to each other for life, then we moved into the sexual part. "

He shook his head. "I had no idea how huge a difference a real, committed partner made to the act of making love. It's the difference between night and day, ice and heat…well, you get the idea."

Mom chimed in, "Yeah, before I met your Dad, I, too, played around a little bit. I went with one guy for a while but when I realized he was only in it for the sex, I dumped him. I tried a one-night stand once out of curiosity after that ended…."

She rolled her eyes. "Well, all I can say is that I felt like a wad of toilet paper, used up and then thrown away. I decided casual sex wasn't for me, I needed a commitment and then…I met your Dad. I really, really wish I had waited for any type of sexual relationship for your Dad but of course, I didn't know he was out there yet."

Dad nodded. "Actually, I wish the same thing. We could've learned together and without the baggage. I didn't know how lonely I was, even with all the girls I dated, until I settled down with your Mom."

The guys laughing about being in dresses and Zoe joking with them jolted me back to the present and I joined in as we ate our food. I was looking forward to our Amorphan robes and I hoped they'd be as pretty as Si'neada promised.

We were trying to talk in Amorphan but weren't fluent enough yet to be very understandable, about as well as young children learning their language, making us laugh even more as we stumbled through our conversation. I felt sure my nannies and translator were working overtime somehow to teach me while I slept but I was still bumbling along with the others with pronunciation. Knowing the words and saying them correctly were two different things.

I reminded myself it had only been a few days of immersion and I'd get better with time. I felt a little smug, though, when I noticed Zoe really struggling with speaking Amorphan as compared to me. For myself, it almost felt like my vocal cords adapted to form the words—nonsense, I knew, but it's what it felt like—but I was glad to know how to do one thing better than Zoe, even as bad as I still was at pronunciation. Zoe snapped in frustration, "This is so hard! I thought we'd be better at the language by now."

"We've only been immersed for a little while, Zoe. We'll all improve, every day, because we'll have to. Don't be so tough on yourself." Mitchler said in a calm voice, placing his hand on her arm. She glared at him for a second, then nodded.

"Yeah, you're right." She rubbed her forehead. "I just thought I'd be further along."

"We all did," Keaton chimed in. "I had no idea how tiring it is to try to think and speak in a foreign language at the same time and also to listen and understand while doing it. And it's weird how the translator echoes the words, so that's part of it, too." He stood from his chair. "Let's get to class."

After language all morning, dance class was a good relief from all the sitting. Then we learned more about doing enough to an Amorphan body to keep ourselves safe. Rank Officer Mer'lout'e put up images of Amorphans after the didactic part and said, "You will each to come up and show me on these where the hurt points are and how you can access them."

He pointed at me. "You will be first, Madame Jessalya."

I walked over to the mock-up and as I neared it, my classmates laughed. Standing next to the image showed how short I was. "Rank Officer, can you lower the image so I can reach the head of the Amorphan?"

Silence for an instant, then he said, "They are full sized and standing on the floor."

"Huh. Well, there's no way I can reach up there without a step-stool."

"Yes, I to see this is true. Please to demonstrate for me other points on the body you can access. It is clear that you will not access their head unless they stoop over or sit down."

"I could always ask them to sit down first before I self-defend. Do you think that would work?" I grinned.

Rank Officer Mer'lout'e' s whiskers twitched in what I recognized as amusement, even though it didn't reach his voice. "Yes, that would to be the best solution. However, for now, please demonstrate what you can reach and you can tell me about what you cannot reach."

The rest of class went well, each student showing their knowledge to the approval of our teacher. "Tomorrow," he announced,

"You will to learn on a real person and then there will be practice sessions." Unexpectedly, his voice filled with mirth. "Madame Jessalya, you will practice on asking an attacker to please sit down first." Then he laughed and walked out of the room.

We all looked at each other. "Did he just laugh?"

"Did we really hear that?"

"Did he just tell a joke? I didn't think he had a sense of humor!"

## CHAPTER SIX

Self-defense classes moved into the physical contact portion after we all passed the didactics. Rank Officer Mer'lout'e figured out a way for me to defend myself using other points on the body. Today we were to be introduced to our live sparring partners, Imurian officers in training, probably at the cadet level.

*Stay in a braid, no matter what. This is all pretend fighting.* My long hair caused a lot of head shaking and whisker twitching from Mer'lout'e, who informed me in a stiff voice, "Your hair can be used as a weapon against you, as someone could to grab it and to yank you off balance or to pull you into his attack or any number of other nasty things."

I nodded like I was paying attention, then shrugged, saying, "I'm not cutting it. And I can't believe it'll ever be an issue, anyway, since we'll have bodyguards. Besides, I have trained for years in personal defense with long hair, so I'm not worried." He narrowed his eyes at me but didn't say anything. I flipped a hand over. "If you'd let me have my gun with which I've trained for years and have the license, I could really defend myself." He narrowed his eyes even more at me, still not saying anything. I sighed.

"Of course, I wasn't allowed to bring it along." I made a face. "So, okay, no gun. Got it."

We filed onto the mats provided and bowed to our sparring partner.

"I am Jess Lilienthal, your partner." I announced.

"I am Junior Officer in Training, My'xty'l. I will to teach you moves, defense and offense until I and my ranking officer are satisfied with your ability."

My'xty'l was dressed in a typical Amorphan robe. He was tall (wasn't everyone next to me?) and his fur looked ruffled like he'd fought his way into the gown. I had to bite back a grin at the notion. His feet were encased in Amorphan style shoes, which allowed his toes to seen and I verified they did, indeed, have claws on them, seemingly not quite as retractable as their hands. On the other hand, his ears were tilted back at an angle that bespoke uncertainty, probably at being dressed like this and having to spar with us puny Humans, and his whiskers were tight against his face, expressing irritation. I wondered if his toe claws were out because of that.

When Officer Mer'lout'e came over to me, I pointed out on My'xty'l the parts I would be able to reach on a warm furry body. Satisfied I knew where to poke or prod in case of emergency, he moved on.

Rank Officer Mer'lout'e barked out the order to advance into each other's zone. As My'xty'l moved forward a step, I moved back a step. It felt like a dance with choreography programmed for us. He reached out, I slapped his hand away and we circled around each other. He snapped a hand forward and tapped me on the shoulder while staring into my eyes, a snarl on his lips.

"I have to admit, you look quite rumpled. When's the last time you brushed those fangs?"

My'xty'l blinked and as his attention shifted for an instant, I dove to my left side and danced out of reach. Rank Officer Mer'loute stalked over and bowed to me. "Very good, Madame Jessalya. Avoidance is the best way to go with your diminutive size." He then turned to J.O. My'xty'l. "We are teaching her to avoid but you are training to not be distracted. Next time, to keep your eyes open and on hers." He wheeled away abruptly while ordering us to resume. The rest of the class was like that: I tried to distract My'xty'l and he worked hard at keeping his attention on me at all times. He swatted me far more often than I was able to score a hit on him, however. I felt like one of those little rodent things at home getting batted around like a toy.

I rubbed my shoulder. "Jumping Jingo fish, My'xty'l, that one hurt!" He had swatted me extra hard on the last pass while I was dodging his other arm. I knew I would find bruises later.

He had the grace to look abashed and muttered, "I apologize, you are difficult to pin down and I was perhaps overzealous."

"Yeah, perhaps." I shook out my arm, panting for breath. "I'm not blaming you….exactly. It's just you're so much taller than me that if I stay within your arm range, I'm going to get hit. And I can't run away every time you move." I wiped my forehead, then crossed my arms.

He grinned, unsettling me with the amount of sharp teeth that appeared. His whiskers trembled in mirth and he stroked his chin with one hand. "No, you cannot all the time, because if you were surrounded, for instance, it would not to help you to run. And with their longer legs, they could outrun you, anyway. I will to speak to the

Master Officer of Defense about you and to see what solution we can to devise. Now let us to finish our training steps as designed."

We had been given specific maneuvers to memorize and use in class and we had to demo to the instructor we knew how to do each one. Mine was modified for my shortness and finally I was able to show the Rank Officer I could do the moves as designed.

I was sweating at the end of class, both from concentration on the steps and physically performing them over and over. By the end, I wanted to go back to my room and fall into bed. And here I'd thought I was in good shape but I wasn't used to being constantly on the run. Apparently, none of us had worked on the right set of muscles as I looked around at the sweaty, tired faces of my classmates. I also had the extra burden of keeping my hair under control mentally, as I'd had to convince it over and over again this was training time and I needed to learn these things, even if I received a bruise or two. It finally relaxed back into a braid that didn't give me a headache from the tension.

"Man, that used muscles I didn't know existed!" Zoe moaned as we left the gym as a group, all of us still a little short of breath and the guys still mopping sweat off their faces.

"Yeah, I know what you mean. I spent more time running than I have in my entire life, and, boy, are my legs tired. In fact, I'm going to order my dinner in and just relax with the entertainment vids tonight. I don't think I can face the walk to the dining room."

The others shook their heads in sympathy. "Jess, you were doing a great imitation of a flash-rabbit. But really, you need to come to dinner; you know it's always fun to be with us. And besides, once we get separated on Amorpha, you'll wish you had spent the time with us." Keaton patted me on the back.

I flashed Keaton a grin. "Well, if you put it like that…."

He put an arm around my shoulders and gave me a friendly squeeze. "Pleeeease?" He wheedled. "Right, everyone? We need to hang together while we can."

I rolled my eyes. "All right, you win! I'll come to dinner but first, a little time to relax in my room."

As I entered my room, I ordered it to set the bathroom to sauna mode. Once settled into the delicious heat, I told Room to make sure I was awake in time for the group dinner.

My hair coiled on top of my head and relaxed after it gave me the impression of "yeah, boss, this is goooood". I was too tired to do anything that night other than eat dinner and go to bed. I knew I was wasting time but what else could I do? Besides, Si'neada was coming tonight with my robes and I had to be in the room. He'd made it clear I was his last stop and he wouldn't be here until 1000 ship time, just before my bedtime.

I had dinner with my classmates, as promised, and we were a rather quiet group tonight as we rubbed our sore muscles and grumbled about hurting. These 12-hour days were beginning to take a toll on us but the time was already getting shorter to our destination so we had to do this. We could, however, complain to each other which helped and we moaned and groaned a lot tonight at the table.

"I thought we were supposed to let our muscles rest in between work-outs." Mitchler complained.

"Ha. Try telling that to the Imurians." Keaton retorted. "They said we would be immersed every day for 12 hours and that's what we're doing."

"Look on the bright side," I said, "it's only for two weeks and we're half through the first week."

Zoe threw me a dirty look while wrinkling her nose. "That means 10 more days of this daily torture."

Soli laughed. "That's true, Zoe, but at least the mornings are in the classroom sitting down. It's only the afternoons we get pushed around so much. At least at dinner, we get to speak Standard with each other. That helps relax *my* brain, anyway."

We nodded agreement to that. I finished scraping up the last of my dessert and looking up, said, "Okay, I'm ready for study time. I'm not facing the viewing deck tonight, sorry, everyone."

Keaton said, "That's okay, Jess, we understand. We'll see you in the morning for breakfast."

Our escort arrived and everyone but me decided to go to the viewing deck. I asked to be taken to my room and the officer gestured over another Imurian to go with me. Back in my room, I sat on the comfortable couch and considered whether to try and sneak out. However, it was too early and too many people would be around, so I decided I'd have to wait until another night to view the rest of the chip memories.

That reminded me, though. I pulled up the search engine on my PD and typed in Akrion to see what popped up. Nothing came up other than the usual, "do you mean…." which meant there wasn't anything. The suggestions given weren't even close to the word I was searching for and after trying several other ways of researching it, I closed the screen in frustration. Maybe it was just the name of an Imurian company, after all, and of course it wouldn't be in my data base. I could query Room but didn't want to take the risk.

I shook my head and opened my Amorphan language teacher. I immersed myself in vocabulary, past and future tense, and worked at improving my pronunciation. Funny how it felt like my vocal cords again adapted themselves to the new sounds but thought nothing more about it. As I repeated the words again and again, I was startled when the door chime sounded. I glanced at the time piece on my screen; 1000 ship time so who would be at my door this late?

I almost smacked myself on the forehead but stopped myself in time. There was a habit I needed to get rid of, I thought, while realizing Si'neada should be outside my door.

## CHAPTER SEVEN

My door chimed again, announcing, "Tr. Si'neada has arrived and requests admission."

"Yup, let him in."

The door whisked open and Si'neada stood there, swathed in a multi-color display of fabric. All I could see of him were feet, hands, ears and eyes.

"Did a fabric store just explode and land at my doorstep?" I inquired as I stepped aside to let him enter. "Here, let me take some of that." I scooped an armful off the top, tossing it on my couch and he minced over, dropping the rest.

"It started out as a neat pile, I will to have you to know." He sniffed. "Somewhere along the line, it went 'poof' and got messy."

"I'll say it did. I didn't know there were that many choices on the ship!"

"Those Amorphans each brought different fabrics with them, and I was running late, so I grabbed your everything and came here."

He ran his hand over his head, smoothing the disturbed fur. He looked with distaste at the couch and blew out a breath. "Now we must to sort it."

I laughed. "That's an easy job, no problem."

The problem was the fabric was diaphanous, hard to gather into a neatly folded bundle. As I picked up the first robe, it billowed into the air until I finally wrestled it into some semblance of order and discovered Si'neada had folded five to my one.

I made a face. "Not as easy as I thought it was going to be. I will say, though, the material is beautiful with all those colors and the lightness of it. I love how soft the fabric is."

"It is beautiful and luckily for me, it does not take too many seams to make it into an Amorphan outfit. They to like their clothing open and airy to allow for their changeling habits."

"So it's true? They can morph into other things?" We'd been told about their ability to change their fingers and toes into other usable appendages but our Amorphan teacher didn't discuss it and none of us had had the nerve to ask about it yet.

He pursed his lips. "Yes, well, they can only to change certain things, like their fingers and toes. They don't truly shape-shift but can to change appendages as the need arises. Were not you taught this?"

"Yes, we were. But we've not seen it happen and the Amorphans haven't told us about it yet."

"Do you tell Tatro whenever you brush your hairies or your fangs?"

Taken aback, I said, "Well, no."

He shrugged, a fluid motion. "Then he does not talk about his changeling manner because for them, it is as natural as your hairies getting brushed or your fangs cleaned."

I nodded slowly, considering this. It's true, we all have traits that are so common to our own kind that we wouldn't think to mention or demonstrate them to an alien. Like my toenails growing and needing clipping when they became too long. Part of life and not something needing to be discussed. I'd never thought of that before.

"Now, Jessi, let us put these robes against you to see how they will to look."

He made me stand in the middle of the floor and picked one out. The colors were in the purple group, with edges blurring together in a harmonious blend of colors. I loved it at first sight.

He held the folded material against my skin. I exclaimed, "I love these colors!" He nodded; his mouth was full of straight pins, a bristling border around his mouth. He snapped open the material which wafted through the air and he held it up to me, indicating I should pull it on over my clothes. After I did, he plucked a pin from his mouth and started gathering the materials together in folds, pinning as he went.

"Ouch!" I yelped. "That was *me* you stuck that in!"

Si'neada removed the pins from his mouth and said, "My little wiggly one, if you would please to hold still, you would not to get poked." His glistening whiskers twitched in an annoyed manner. "I need to get your measurements in an accurate manner, and I cannot to do that if you to move. And please to move these long stringy spirals out of my way."

"Hair. It's called hair." I muttered as I gathered it into one hand and held it away. "And please don't stick me again." I paused. "I must say, I do like the colors you painted your, um, nails? Can you do mine like that or is there someone else who can?"

He smirked and I swear his whiskers also smirked. "We call them narrrdila which probably translates to—" and he cocked his head to one side as if listening—"claws, I think the word is. Of course I can paint your fingers that way."

I chuckled. "Not my fingers, Si'neada. My fingernails. The things on the ends of my fingers."

He rolled his eyes. "It would be prettier if I could do the whole finger. Those things on the ends are so, well, little and blunt. Not very much room for a talent like mine to work." He continued fussing around me as I stood on the riser. "I could to paint your—hairy, too."

"Hair, the word is hair. You are hairy but I have hair."

He wrinkled his nose. "I do not to see the difference. But never mind, do you want it painted, also?"

"I'll think that over and let you know after I see what you do for my nails."

His ears deflated just a bit and his whiskers drooped a little. "Well," he said with a sigh, "All right, my little hairy one, I will to prove myself to you first. But oh! The fun I could to have with your hairies!" He ran his hand over the strands that dangled from my hand. "Ooo, and it is so soft. Too bad it's not prettily striped like mine…but I could to fix that shortcoming, you to know."

I couldn't help but laugh. He was so cute the way he pranced and danced around, whiskers glistening with whatever he used on them to make them shine and his colored claws flashing with colors from rings that matched his earrings.

On sudden impulse, I reached my hand out and said, "Fair's fair. You petted my hair, um, hairies, now I get to pet yours."

He winked at me. "Well, if you must, my cute little Human."

He bent his head down to me. "Please do not to muss my style and only to go with the direction it grows, or it hurts."

I put my hand on top of his head, surprised how warm he was. I stroked along the pattern, enjoying how soft it was and how vibrant it felt.

He pulled away. "Yes, that is enough, my little pin cushion, and we are now, what do you to say? Even?"

"Yes, even."

He nodded. "Touching our fur in such a way is considered intimate among us but of course, you would not to know this. But because you are young and we need to be this 'even', then I to permit it this once." He winked again at me. "But, please to know that you do not to do this with anyone else without their invitation." He raised his eyebrows. "Especially our tails."

I angled my head downward. "Of course, Si'neada."

If he'd had dimples, I swear he would've used them right then. "We are now friends."

I smiled and nodded. "We are now friends."

He laughed, a guttural low sound in his throat that sounded like a purr. "I need to finish your numbers so I can to make the Amorphan clothes to fit you better."

"I would much appreciate it. Thank you, my friend Si'neada."

Si'neada minced around me, flipping out a measuring device again as I continued trying on gowns. "I am glad to have the pleasure of dressing a Human female and Amorphan clothes are so floating and graceful." He plucked one from the pile and handed it to me. "To wear tomorrow in compliance with the Amorphan requirement."

"They look so, mmm, airy and comfy. I like that but I might miss my jeans."

He smiled, which involved showing a bit more fang than I was maybe comfortable with seeing. "I think in the privacy of your room in your new home you can to wear your jeans." His ears flattened slightly as he said, "You *are* a little Human, I must to say again. No bigger than a Transition kitling. "

Seizing the opportunity, I tried a casual tone as I asked, "Are there kitlings on board? Will we be able to meet any?"

Si'neada's whiskers twitched in surprise. "Oh, no. Our living areas are strictly off limits to all but Imurians. This is our home, after all, although our livelihood is moving people and goods and finding new worlds for settlement. Are you not friends with the other Humans in your section?"

"Yeah, we're friends and all but I'm curious about meeting others my age, and not Human, that's all." *Yeah, okay, I lied. Zoe and I are not friends but not the time to share.*

"Ah, you will to be meeting plenty of others your age on Amorpha, I think."

I smiled. "Well, that's true enough. Can't argue with that logic."

"Now to hold your arms out to the sides so I may to get the drape of these folds correct."

When he was done, I picked up a white robe and said, "This one is different." I squinted at it. "It's like I can almost see color in it but yet, it's white. It's not transparent, either, and seems to sparkle and I can't call it plain white. There's something different about this one."

Si'neada looked at me with surprise. "Amorphans can to see in a different color spectrum than Humans. That is interesting you can even to see some of that, like the sparkles. Most Humans would only to see it as a white fabric."

"So there's color in there that I can't perceive? That's what you're saying?"

He nodded. I brought the fabric closer to my eyes. "I don't see any color, that's true, but it's like I almost see color, if that makes any sense." I smoothed my hand over it. "It's so soft, that's what I really like about their material."

Si'neada said, "Well, if you had Amorphan eyes, you would to see the colors. I can to see a few of them but our eyes are tuned more to the spectrum of Human eyes than Amorphan. I wish I knew how they made their fabrics, but that is their secret, and will be a good trading item."

He started gathering his tools into his bag. "I will to see you tomorrow, Jessi, when I have the rest of your robes ready for fitting. And to remember, to fasten the holders that are under the robes to hold them into place. They may to look all floaty but they are anchored to your body with the internal strappings. Ah," and here he fluttered his eyelashes at me with a wicked grin, "Be sure to do the strapping first, then your undergarments."

"Thank you, Si'neada." I gave him a half-grin. "I'll figure it out, I'm sure. But thanks for the hint."

He smiled at me. "Ah, my little flower, you will to look good in any of these I am to provide."

I yawned and stretched my back. "Ok, I look forward to that. Good thing they've given us enough time to get used to wearing these clothes, although I'm going to miss my jeans. And please make sure there's no prickly parts on the straps to irritate my skin."

His whiskers twitched in amusement. "Perhaps you will to start a new style trend on Amorpha with these jeans."

I laughed. "Maybe!"

He promised to have the gowns at my room at 0530, and after making a face at the early hour, I asked him, "Don't you plan to sleep tonight?"

He smiled and said, "Oh, yes, I will to sleep. These are minor adjustments for all of you and will only take a few minutes for my staff. So I will be to bed at a good time, my little delight."

He left the room, taking the swirls of colorful material with him and I already regretted their loss. However, it was late by now and I felt like I would drop where I stood if I didn't go to bed, like *right now*.

I yawned and scrubbed my hands over my face, no longer caring about mascara and heard a soft sound, almost a squeaking, and I looked around, frowning while trying to identify it. Maybe it was a vent fan; it was faint and I wasn't sure I heard it in the first place until I heard it again and I cocked my head to hear better. I couldn't really tell where it was coming from and rooms make all sorts of noise so what was one more?

Then I noticed my hair on high alert and I tuned into it. *Do you hear that, too?*

Uncertainty.

A scritching sound came next, along with faint squeaking. I frowned harder; I was going to have to call maintenance if this kept up. "What in the six heavens *is* that noise?" I started walking around so I could pinpoint where it was coming from. "Maybe I'd better have Room call maintenance."

A much louder squeak, off to my left, near the vent inset into the wall. I walked over and looked at the vent. A mesh front covered the 2x2 foot square and I peered into the mesh, trying to see into the dark interior. "Huh. Maybe a gear needs oiling?" The noise stopped. I straightened from my stooped position and stood there for a couple of minutes, listening, my hair relaxing down my back and I shrugged, making a face. "Okay, I guess it's fixed. I'm going to bed."

# CHAPTER EIGHT

That night, I dreamed I was looking at a color wheel and kept poking someone next to me with my elbow. "Look at that color! We don't have that in our spectrum. If I could only change my eyes enough, I'd see them all!" The person next to me, some girl I didn't know, pushed my elbow back and said, "Stop that. I don't have changeling eyes like yours." Her face morphed into Zoe's and I stepped back from her as the dream changed into a classroom where I joined a line of students muttering the same words, "We're Exchangers" over and over as their faces changed into other people.

I woke the next morning with the memory of the dream echoing in my mind and I wondered what it meant, if anything. Some people put a lot of meanings into dreams, others said they were only the mind cleansing itself of the day's nonsense. I knew, for myself, sometimes a dream had a lot of meaning and I could feel the intent of it and other times, they felt like the brain throwing out the trash. I figured this was one of the trash dreams but I couldn't shake the feeling there was more to it than that.

I was reluctant to push back the blankets but I needed to get out of bed and get ready. My muscles protested the movement as I swung my feet out and sat on the edge of the bed. Everything hurt and I wasn't sure it would ever get better. Then I remembered the first several weeks of classes at Cat-Fighting when I'd felt the same way but it had gotten better with time. Well, my muscles needed to hurry up and feel better, is all I could think.

I slowly eased out of bed and into the refresher room, cleansing first to wake up. Coffee aroma wafted into my nose, encouraging me to finish my ablutions and grab a cup. I suddenly wondered what animal the cream in my cooler came from or if they had a barn on a different deck with cows or if it was manufactured. I smiled to think of a deck with cows mooing but since it was delicious, I didn't particularly care as long as it was available to take to my room for when I wanted a cup or two.

I revived even more with the first sip of that heavenly drink and headed out to breakfast, meeting everyone in the corridor. Keaton walked over and draped his right arm over my shoulders and his left arm over Zoe's. "And how are you ladies this morning? Are you two ready for your next piece of adventure? Jess, you look more rested this morning."

"I am, thanks, Keaton." I grimaced. "I'm too sore to think about adventures." I complained.

Keaton chuckled. "Yeah, me, too. The Imurians aren't into rest and relaxation, are they? I guess they're doing what they have to do, though, to get us ready for Amorpha."

"That's true enough, I guess." Zoe rubbed a hand over her shoulder and winced. "I think I pulled a muscle yesterday. Maybe you could massage it for me, Keaton?" She looked at him demurely through her eyelashes as she pointed to a spot on her neck. *Were guys really that susceptible and gullible?* Apparently so as Keaton grinned wider, taking his arm from around my shoulders and started rubbing the indicated area on her neck. Well, easy come, easy go, I guess.

I glanced over at the group, saying, "Forgot my device; I'll be right back." I turned around, saying, "Go on without me. Be right there."

The escort said, "We will to wait for you at the elevator, Madame."

"Okay." I nodded.

Arriving at my room door, I became aware of my hair moving in a slight but agitated way. *What in the world is bothering you?*

There was a slight quiver throughout my hair. OUR ROOM.

I didn't know what that meant so I mentally shrugged it off and palmed my door open. As I stepped into my room, the air felt different and my hair became highly alert. My entire body alarmed but I didn't know why. All I had done was step into the front room and nothing was out of place that I could see. Besides, how was anyone else to get into my room? It was keyed to me and only to me, by touch or voice. We grew up knowing Imurians to have very secure systems; after all, it's Imurian technology. Break-ins were rare in our society because of it; if it happened, it's because someone was attacked and forced to open their space or they were robbed at gunpoint. I was always cautious approaching my own space at home after hearing about this on the news one time but on the ship, I didn't worry about it at all. Although, come to think of it, there had been that funny noise last night but after it stopped and didn't reoccur, I dismissed the thought. After all, there was no place to hide in my room.

I took a cautious step forward, my hair questing around me as if sniffing the air. *What are you sensing?* All I felt in return for the question was uncertainty.

I looked around, not seeing anything changed from when I left a few minutes ago. I went to my bedroom area and looked in. It all looked the same to me although I wasn't sure if my pillow and covers were the same as this morning. I hadn't made my bed because I'd just be getting it again tonight. Was my pillow that skewed when I got up this morning? I didn't know.

I absently rubbed the skin on my upper arm near my armpit. After checking out my entire living space for a secure hiding place for Mom's memory chip , I couldn't find anywhere I thought no one else would think of, either. Finally, I felt an itching sensation on my upper arm where the arm joins my torso and as I started to scratch the area, it seemed to part open, which startled the heck out of me, I'll admit, and my hair plucked the memory chip from my fingers and placed it in there. The skin closed over, there was no pain and no blood and it was like nothing had happened.

The incident was so weird I decided thinking about it would give me headaches so I made the tough decision to not be freaked about it. It was the most secure place to hide it, I thought, no matter how it happened. And in a small, tiny part of me, I wondered just how my body had done that? With no clear answer, and the heavens knew there was no one I could ask, I put the question aside.

My hair was tugging at me to go over to the tree in the corner and when I got there, I saw the soil had been disturbed and clumsily patted back into place. Was it actually possible, in the few minutes I'd been out of my quarters, someone had somehow gotten into my room and had searched for my memory chip or something else? How would they have gotten in, since we had all been in the hallway? Any of us would've seen someone entering my room and none of us had. I then saw small prints in the dirt, circles with rays around the circle like little tiny sausage imprints, too small to be Human or Imurian.

I stared at the dirt, finding it difficult to accept someone or something had invaded my space, then thought to take a photo of it. As soon as the picture was taken, my hair pushed me toward the air vent on the wall. Vents were part of any building, but on this one, I could see fresh marks on the metal around the attachment screws and those hadn't been there last night. That explained how they or it or whatever might've gotten in and out.

On impulse, I grabbed one of the chairs and dragged it in front of the vent. Didn't look too aesthetic but at least I felt a little safer knowing I would have warning if the, uh, cat burglar tried to come back. I snorted a little at my pun. However, no full-grown Imurian would've fit through that opening. *I'd* have trouble fitting through the opening. Maybe they'd placed something *into* the vent? But what? And why? I picked at the edge of it with a fingernail; it was tight to the wall and a little wet paint smeared onto my finger. I peered through the mesh again, this time using my flashlight feature, but still I didn't see anything on the other side.

I didn't know what to do about it, nothing was missing or broken, so I picked up my personal device, and left my room, taking extra care to secure the door behind me. I strode to the elevator where the group was waiting for me with impatience. I waved my

PD and lied, "Forgot where I put it, sorry about that." The elevator doors opened, we got to the breakfast table, and tapped in our orders.

"Funny how we can't feel any movement at all on the ship." Soli said out of nowhere, shaking his head. I raised my eyebrows in surprise and the others looked at Soli with startled looks. Soli seldom started a conversation.

"That's exactly what I was thinking!" Zoe exclaimed. "That must be some kind of technology to never feel the ship move or dock or whatever." She touched her hand to his arm and he shifted it ever so slightly away from her.

Soli said, "They've got technology far beyond what we Humans have dreamed up." He frowned. "Although our technology has stagnated since meeting the Imurians. After all, could you do math without your computer? I couldn't, I don't think, or at least it would be tough. I think that happened with technology. Once the Imurians started selling us Humans their technology, we seemed to have lost the drive to keep inventing our own. Like I said, if you use a calculator to do math, you lose the ability to do it in your head, so to speak."

I made a face. "My dad says the same thing."

"He's right. And I'll admit the Imurians have it far beyond what we could've come up with on our own, at least in this period of time. Maybe I'll change that someday."

"Maybe…" I raised an eyebrow at him. "So you want to design, eh?"

"Yeah, I'm interested in designing technology." He smiled. "In the meantime, think of all the cool things we'll get to experience and learn about on a whole new world with new types of people. Maybe I can learn their tech stuff to bring home."

"It's awesome, right?" I grinned back.

He nodded. "It is at that."

Zoe cut her eyes at me. "Sure, Shorty Pants, it's awesome." She smiled to show she didn't mean the nickname in a mean way but the smile was only on her lips and I knew in my gut she meant it in the nastiest way possible.

"I don't have pants on, Zoe, I'm wearing my robe or hadn't you noticed?"

Her eyes narrowed a fraction before she smoothed out her face. "Yes, it's purple; trust me, we noticed." Then she glanced at the guys and smiled again. "We talked about coming up with some things to do in our free hour, like I offered to teach these guys some dancing." She tilted her head. "What in the world could *you* teach, Jessa Little?"

"More to the point, what can they teach me?" I said in an even tone. Soli raised his eyebrows at that, Keaton chuckled and waggled his eyebrows up and down while Mitchler barked out a laugh. I felt my face become red star hot. "That's not what I meant!"

Zoe rubbed Keaton's arm and practically purred as she said, "Oh, Keaton here has already taught *me* a thing or two."

I felt a sudden rush of physical feelings pulsing in areas I hadn't thought much about before. Face flaming, I said, "I'm going to go study now until time for class. You guys are impossible!"

Embarrassed and angry, I crossed my arms as I stalked over to ask the escort to return me to my room. I stomped off the elevator when the door opened, turning toward my room, stopping short when I saw two Imurians in front of my door. *Were they trying to get into my room?* They turned at my approach and bowed. "Madame Jess."

That's when I realized it was Officer Mer'lout'e and someone new, B'le'ru, as I saw from his name tag, standing at my door. "Why are you at my room?"

Mer'lout'e eyes flitted to B'le'ru and back to me and then he said, "We are to make sure you are all right."

"Why wouldn't I be?"

"We have a report your personal space was entered without your knowledge or permission."

I stared at them. "How do you know that? I didn't report anything."

Their whiskers quivered with agitation. "The room reported the intrusion. You are all right?"

"Yes. I'm okay."

"Why did you not to make a report, Madame Jess?" B'le'ru' s ears moved back in disapproval and his mouth tightened. I think I saw his stripes even squeeze together a little.

"Because I wasn't sure of anything." *How much do they know? Did they really just get here or have they been inside already?*

He said in a curt tone, "It is not your job to be sure. You should have reported even if it is only a feeling." He stared at me, eyes narrowed. "Was anything taken, broken or disturbed?"

"Not that I could tell. I came back to my room this morning to get my PD and thought I noticed something, but like I said, I couldn't see anything missing. It was a couple of small things that made me think someone had been in there without me."

"What small things?"

I frowned. "Oh, the dirt around the tree in the pot seemed to have been disturbed but I wasn't sure, since I don't have a habit of looking at it. And there looked to be marks around the fasteners on the vent in the living area."

My hair was vibrating a little bit against my back, urging me to be cautious. I had no way to know if these were the ones actually responsible or if there really had been a report made. I wished some of my co-students would show up then or the escort had come off the elevator with me. I was nervous about being all alone, the only Human, with these two and not knowing who to trust.

I felt more than heard a door open down the corridor and I heard Si'neada's voice humming along to some tune I didn't know. I turned my head to see him moving toward us with his arms full of robes. He saw me and quickened his pace until he was next to me and said, "Well, now, what is happening here?" I felt a huge relief wash over me at his presence at my side.

"B'le'ru, Mer'lout'e, what are you two doing here?" He nodded his head at them, his eyes narrowing, his whiskers trembling, and his ears springing forward, on alert.

They stiffened, staring at Si'neada. "We are here to investigate an intrusion into Madame Jessalya's room." Their ears flattened as their nostrils flared in apparent dislike.

*I wonder who's intruding on who's territory here? Whose toes are being stepped on?* Si'neada looked distressed. "Intrusion? Into her room? Why would anyone to do that? Who did that?" He turned to me. "Are you all right?" He reached out and touched my shoulder as if to reassure himself I was intact.

"That is what we are to here to find out. We were about to ask her to open her door so we could to investigate."

I looked back and forth between them. They were glaring at

each other, two against one. *Like angry dogs circling each other. Cats would be spitting and hissing and striking with claws by now. Huh. Just goes to show cats can be dogs.* I almost snorted in amusement but caught myself in time.

Si'neada sniffed haughtily, raising his nose in the air. "Well, I am sure if you to ask her politely, she will to let us all in." He looked at me and raised his brows.

I felt an instant rush of relief at having a friend with me and I glanced at the two bigger Imurians. I was still uncertain what I should or shouldn't do next, when I felt Si'neada's tail barely tap my leg and whisk away, as if not to be seen. :*I am your friend and will to watch out for you*:

My eyes widened but before I could figure out if that just happened or how to respond to it, B'le'ru turned to me. "Madame Jessalya, please to open your door."

I nodded. I moved to the door, palming it open, then gestured for everyone to enter. My hair quivered for an instance and then relaxed as Si'neada joined us. I was the last one to enter my space, leaving the door open behind me.

B'le'ru, Si'neada and Mer'loute all looked at the chair in front of the vent, their brows crinkling into questions, whiskers twitching. "I did that," I volunteered, "because I thought whoever it was came in through the vent. It's not much protection, I know, but it made me feel like I'd done something."

Their brows cleared at the same time after a short pause of silence. "I see." B'le'ru said at last, his tail twitching.

The three Imurians moved apart and started sniffing the air, a little like my hair had done earlier, except I could hear them. "The scent is obscured." Mer'loute remarked. He walked over to the tree pot and ran a claw through the dirt. "The dirt was loosened and replaced into place."

"That's what I thought." I murmured. "But I didn't think anyone would believe me—I mean, after all, it could've been whoever comes in to water it."

They all turned to survey me with disapproval.

I crossed my arms and stared back. "Well, I didn't. Think anyone would believe me, that is." I stopped short of saying, "so there" and sticking out my tongue at them.

B'le'ru walked to the chair and moved it back to its original place, then returned to examine the frame of the vent. "It is a small opening so a full grown Imurian would not to fit through this. But it has been tampered with and I can to smell the fresh paint used to disguise the removal."

"So it could've been a young Imurian who did this?"

He turned disapproving eyes toward me. "It is forbidden for younglings to leave our home deck and they are under supervision at all times." He shook his head. "The vent cannot be removed from inside, only outside."

I rolled my eyes, thinking to myself, *Yeah, like that ever stopped a youngling from taking on a dare. I don't care what species they are; younglings are younglings. I wonder if I should mention the Scitterers?*

*No!*

"Is there another small species on board that could've done this?" I asked instead.

## CHAPTER NINE

There was complete, utter silence as they stared at me, even their whiskers and ears completely still. I was pinned into the bubble of quiet by their laser-like gazes and I couldn't move.

Then B'le'ru's whiskers twitched: *How could she know? She couldn't possibly know.*

Mer'lout'e's whisker reply was: *She cannot know. She is merely asking a logical question.*

As I stared at them in return, I realized I'd understood it all—and they didn't have a clue I could. I had no idea how I could read this type of language, my translator sure wasn't doing the job, but nonetheless, I just had. Wow. If I'd had whiskers, I could've replied.

Mer'lout'e said in a gruff tone, "Perhaps one of your class students did this as a joke?"

That rocked me back a little. I hadn't considered that scenario. I tried to think of who was small enough to get through the vent and I came up with one person.

Me. And it would be a tight squeeze at that.

Before I dismissed the idea, however, I said, "I need to see the actual size of the duct inside the vent to know if a Human, other than myself, could get through there."

Mer'lout'e's mouth twitched and he gazed at me with a hard stare as he asked, "Did you to remove the screws and go into the vent?"

"No! Why would I do that? I have no idea where those vents even go! And I don't have any tools." And it was an idea I hadn't come up with yet, darn it. "Or paint, for that matter." A sudden scenario occurred to me. I blurted out, "Hey! You don't think I did this, do you? Why would I search my own room? I sure wouldn't come through a vent to do it; I just have to open the door! Plus my classmates and I have always been together since getting on board the StarFinder and why would they want to get *into* my vent, anyway?"

Si'neada said, with a soothing hand on my arm, "No, no, Jessi, my little squash, we know it was not you nor your classmates to do this."

Mer'lout'e glanced at him and then sighed. "Of course, we do not think it was any of you. After all, you have no purpose in doing so. You are sure nothing is missing?"

I nodded. "I'm sure."

"All right, we will to make our report. We will to send the repair officer to tamper proof the vent screen and we will to include the repair in all the rooms."

"Do you think I'm safe to stay here now?"

"You will be safe after we to secure the vent openings. There are no other ways into your room."

"What about letting me see the size of the duct? I want to know for sure that no one could've gotten through there."

B'le'ru said, "We will to open the vent for you to look. I will to call the officer to do so." He touched a button on his collar and requested the custodian officer on duty to arrive as soon as possible and to bring tools for repairs.

He then said, "We should to sit down while we to wait." He made a courteous gesture toward one of the chairs and I moved over to it and plopped into its cushions. It felt good to be off my feet, but then, feeling the need to be a hostess, "Drinks, anyone?"

I got myself a cup of coffee with cream, the two officers declined and Si'neada requested an Imurian hot drink. As we two were sipping our drinks in silence, the room announced the repair officer had arrived. I told Room to let him in, after we all viewed him on the screen, and he entered, pulling a small case on wheels, which I guessed had tools in it. I looked at it as it passed to see if Akrion was written on it but I didn't see anything.

B'le'ru stood up and said, "Over here. All the vents in the Human quarter need to be reinforced for security. But first, you need to remove the cover so the Human can to see into it for herself."

I got up and walked over to the vent. The repairer approached and nodded at me. He then looked over the vent cover. "Yes, it has been tampered with. I to wonder why." He pulled something out of his case and touched it to the fastening screws and they all whirled out of their place into his waiting hand. He pulled the vent cover off, snapping on a flashlight. I peered into the ductwork to see that it stretched out straight for about two feet and then angled up ninety degrees. I didn't see how any of the other students could navigate that, and although I could probably fit in there, no way could I climb the smooth, metal walls and even if I could, I most certainly couldn't do it quietly.

A strand of hair snapped up a tiny scrap of white from the floor of the duct, almost faster than I registered it was even there, then returned to the rest of my hair and hid the item. I didn't know if it was important or not nor how long it had been there; might've been there for years or could be a dust bunny for all I knew. My hair was offended by dirt so it could've been cleaning.

B'le'ru looked over my head into the space and said, "Madame Jess, could another Human come through there?"

"No. I could, I think, but I'd have a hard time with that part going up." I pointed to it. "I don't see any way to climb that. And I don't see any evidence that anything has. No scrapes or marks that I can see."

He nodded in agreement. "Then please to go to the classroom for your daily routine. You will to return tonight to your newly safe room. Mer'lout'e will stay here to secure your quarters."

"What are they going to do?"

"The repair officer will to secure this vent so nothing can to go in or out. It will be noisy and so you do not to need to be here for that. Please to walk to the hall with me." He turned and headed for the door, where he paused and looked at Si'neada. Mer'lout'e tilted his head toward the door, twitching his whiskers to say *Time to leave, pal.* Si'neada sighed and then walked to the couch, where he dropped his pile of cloth, saying, "Jessi, I must to go, also. I will to know when you are safely returned to your space." He winked at me and gestured a good-bye. As he walked by me, his tail tapped on my leg in a swift motion. :*Stay safe; I will to explain this later. It is safe to go with B'le'ru.*:

I was totally baffled how I heard his voice *in my head,* but only when his tail tapped me. I hoped he was talking about explaining this mental talking later.

We stepped into the hallway and B'le'ru turned around to tap an order into my wall plate. "This will to keep the door open while he works in here. It will automatically close behind him when he leaves but Mer'lout'e will remain here to make sure all is secure until the work is done."

"Uh, okay, I guess."

"Please to walk with me." We started down the corridor toward the lift, he nodded as if making a decision and then said, "Madame Jessalya, it has been decided to help you to be more secure. You are to be issued a gun, per your request."

"A gun?" I repeated. "Really?"

B'le'ru responded. "Yes. You are unlikely to need it but this incident plus your small size have led us to believe you to need something the others do not. We will go to the range starting tonight at 1000 ship clock hours, after the others have gone to their rooms. This must to remain a huge secret between you and me." He sighed and glanced at me, ears back in uncertainty. "There are many things you do not to know about, Madame Jessalya, and I wish you do not become part of it. Better to get you safely to your new home." He looked sad and pensive. "I to need your promise."

"I promise to keep this secret. But are you sure? I don't have my own weapon with me, after all, since it was forbidden to bring it, so what will I use?" This was supposed to be a safe trip, a fun future and a learning experience, not to mention being part of something groundbreaking! Unknown danger and possible harm weren't part of the deal.

Then I noticed my hair feeling happy about this event. I also realized it had slipped the whatever it had snatched up into my jeans pocket. I could hardly wait to see what it was—*please don't let it be a dead bug*—but I needed to be alone to do so.

"I'm sure. I have been pondering this since meeting you and I to know it is the right thing to do. Please, to meet me here at door #1500 at 1000 ship clock hours tonight. There will be an appropriate weapon for you."

He then nodded to me, called the elevator and took me to the classroom, where the others had started already. When I walked into the room, they all turned to me, asking, "Jessi? Is everything okay? They said there was an issue with your room? Is that why you're late?"

I smiled and raised a hand. "I'm okay. There was a maintenance issue, that's all, something to do with the vent in my room but they're fixing it now and it'll be okay by the time we get back tonight. So let me catch up with you all; what were you discussing?" I turned to the teacher and said in Amorphan, "My apologies, Tatro. I forgot to use your language."

His glittering eyes looked at me steadily and he nodded his head. "It is forgiven and understandable with the excitement."

I bowed my head to him. "Thank you."

Mitchler said, "A vent thing? Like the air quality thing that happened when our parents emigrated?"

I shook my head. "No, nothing like that. The cover was a little loose in the sitting area and they decided it needed fixing, that's all. I'm fine; the air is fine." *Maybe I should've told them the whole truth but it doesn't feel right to do that. After all, I'm still not sure it means anything.*

The class had been talking about mundane things, like weather and entertainment so I hadn't missed much other than practicing the language. I joined in, looking up words as I went for what I wanted to say, as the others did. Finally, I raised my hand. "Tatro? May I please be excused to use the toilet?" There; I'd said it in near perfect Amorphan.

He beamed, his sharp teeth just peeking out. "Yes, of course."

I said, "Be right back." I went in the bathroom and locked the door. I did have to relieve my bladder but I wanted to look at that scrap of something in my pocket. For all I knew, it was trash that had somehow been poked in through the vent but until I looked at it, I wouldn't know.

I sat on the toilet seat, after moving the voluminous folds of the robe to one side so I could get to my jeans underneath and pulled out the tiny scrap carefully. *Thank the moons above it's not a dead bug. It's paper.* The paper looked fresh, not old and grimy, and there was very small writing on it which I had to squint at to read. Written in Imurian, it said "Trust Si'neada". I blinked at it. Who was telling me this? *Were* they telling me this? Was this really left for me to find?

I felt I could trust Si'neada but had no explanation for the feeling. Could this be an Imurian who made the noises in my room last night and then messed with the vent so I'd look inside? How did this unknown person know I'd ask to look in there? Why was the note so tiny and why was it left in the vent and not in the room itself? And why was the dirt around the tree disturbed? I wasn't sure the two were even related except it had happened in the same time frame. I gritted my teeth together in frustration. That's what I needed, all right, more mysteries.

I stood, flushed the toilet, and pushed the note back into my pocket, then let the robe flow back down around me, making sure to keep the material out of the bowl of water and the under-straps were well positioned for my comfort. I'd gotten dressed that morning in my usual clothes, then remembered the gown and had just tossed it on over my other clothes, securing the straps loosely. I wasn't sure how my hair had gotten the note into my jeans pocket under my gown but maybe it hadn't trusted the pockets in the gown as being too flimsy or something. It didn't matter; I got the note.

I washed my hands and returned to the room, saying, "Well! I feel much better now." They glanced at me but paid no more attention than that I'd returned to my chair even though I felt like I was radiating a sign that said, "I have a secret." Maybe the bulbs were burned out in that sign.

The day went on as the other days had; language skills and society lessons in the morning and defense and physical/dance activities all afternoon. When we were finally taken to dinner, I was wrung out. I wondered if I'd ever feel fit again, with all my muscles screaming at me like this. So much for Cat-Fighting and line dancing to keep me in shape! I begged off from the viewing deck. "I'm very tired and I want to make sure they got my vent thingy fixed before bedtime so if they have to come back, I don't have to stay up later."

## CHAPTER TEN

At five minutes before 1000, I was ready and nervous with sweaty hands. I checked the vid to the hallway to see if the corridor was clear of classmates as I wiped my damp hands on my jeans, smoothed back my hair, and then decided to wait a couple more minutes before moving down to door #1500. That was most certainly the longest two minutes I'd ever endured, especially since I kept checking the time like every two seconds. Finally, as the hall remained empty, I slipped out of my door, making sure to fiddle with the motion sensor, and scurried as quietly as possible to #1500, which opened as I approached it. B'le'ru beckoned in a "hurry up" manner and I slid through the barely open door just before it snicked closed behind me. B'le'ru indicated I should be quiet as he turned and padded down the hall. It looked like the corridor I'd just left; somehow I thought it would be more, I don't know, different.

B'le'ru came to an abrupt halt and I almost ran into him. He shoved me into a shallow door recession, stepping in front of me and coming to stiff attention. I heard the sound of boots coming down the hallway and my heart lurched in fear. Obviously B'le'ru didn't want me seen by whoever was coming. The boots came to a halt right in front of us.

There was a pause as I heard them both breathing while I held my breath and wished I was completely invisible or back in my room. I didn't dare twitch with B'le'ru's back only a whisker width from my nose. I made sure my legs were right behind his legs, which were clamped together. Other than that, there was nothing I could do to prevent getting discovered if the person in front of B'le'ru looked behind him. My hair crept around me in a silent veil, covering me as it reached to the floor. *Thank the stars I took the robe off before coming here.* I took in a silent breath and since I was so close to B'le'ru, I inhaled his scent, which was a mixed bag of odors. Fear. Anger. Spice. Acrid sweat. Laundry detergent. Uncertainty.

"Officer B'le'ru. I to see you are out for a prowl this evening. I did not to see you on the evening shift roster." A cold voice with a hint of a growling sneer in it, speaking in Imurian.

"Yes, Sir. No, Sir."

*Someone higher in rank than B'le'ru, then.*

"I trust all is well?"

"Yes, Sir."

"Coming for extra range time, hmmm?"

"Yes, Sir."

An unexpected chortle. "You think you can practice enough to win the next range competition?"

"That is my plan, Sir."

A tapping sound. "Good luck with that. I think you are always destined to come in second. But if by any mischance you to come in first, I will gladly to challenge you to a match with myself. I am sure you would to like that?"

"Yes, Commander. It would be an honor." Sounded like to me that B'le'ru would rather scratch his eyes out than be in competition with this guy but there was nothing else for him to say. It was a wonder the officer couldn't tell from B'le'ru's tone of voice.

"How goes the training of the puny Humans? Is it all you can do to stop from tearing their furless skin from them?" The male voice sounded full of regret he didn't get to do it and would relish the bloodshed.

"No, Sir. They are like kitlings, Sir, and must be handled like them. I have no desire to hurt kitlings."

A short silence, then a long inhale. "You stink of Human, Officer B'le'ru." Another inhale. "You stink of female Human. Which one is it?" Without waiting for an answer, he said, "No, it cannot be that miniature Human; she is hardly worth the air she breathes."

*Ye Gods, another one worried about my air intake! I take up way less air than any of them!* Here my hair tightened, especially across my mouth, to keep me still and silent as I reacted to his statement with a sudden up swell of fury.

"No, it has to be that yellow-headed one; even for us, she attracts the male eye. Have you been mounting her, hmm? Is it good? Maybe I should to have a sample of her."

"Sir, I met her for extra sparring time, is all. She is a *kitling* to me! I would never consider her for a mating."

A snort of derision. "I am sure *you* would not consider her for a mating. However, discipline is good for kitlings, do you agree? A good cuff on the head or bite to the neck to remind them who are the betters." A sigh. "Well, I suppose we must not yet to mess with the Humans. It would not to look good for us to deliver them to their destinations with scratches and bite marks. A pity, though. Perhaps the next time we have a large enough group, one or two might not be missed. Remember when we transported all those thousands of them to their new planet? It took several trips and what made it worthwhile to me is I sampled some of the female Humans. And a few of them liked it."

"Yes, Sir. If you say so, Commander." Anger radiated from his frame as he stiffened even more but he was containing it well. I was outraged as well but my hair had me cocooned so I couldn't move and could barely breathe. *Sure hope you have me well camouflaged. And remember I need to breathe!* My hair let up a mere fraction around my nose.

A beat of silence. "I am not pleased that you are here on your own time to practice. Maybe I should consider—"

"Oh, B'le'ru, my sweetness! Whatever is taking you so long? I am waiting for you with my weapon out—oh, dear!"

That was Si'neada's voice! What in the seven gates of hell was he doing here?

More footsteps, mincing this time. "K'ur'lon, how are you this fine evening?"

"You are interrupting." The answer snapped out in an irritated tone.

"Oh, am I? Why are you delaying my—friend—B'le'ru? I had my weapon all ready for him and now, well, we will just have to start from scratch, but, oh, that will be fun, too. Will it not, B'le'ru, my darling?" Si'neada tittered. I'd never heard a titter before but that had to be one.

"I am leaving is what I am doing." I heard distaste in the voice. "B'le'ru, I had no idea you were a twofur; I must say you have kept a deep secret well hidden. I will to see you tomorrow at muster; be sure you are in a clean uniform. Dismissed."

The boots moved off a step and then stopped. "This is not forgotten." The steps resumed as the sound placed him moving down the hall and then the whoosh of a door opening and then reclosing.

My hair swept back behind me and I felt it shorten as it coiled to waist length again. B'le'ru visibly relaxed and huffed out a breath. He barely breathed out the words, "Follow me. We are almost there."

We only went a few feet when he stopped and slapped his hand against a wall plate on the left which opened the door. He ushered Si'neada and myself into a large, cavernous room as the door whispered shut behind us. He turned to me, whispering, "I am *not* a twofur! Although I do want to thank you for being so still and hidden."

"Um, you're welcome?" I made a small grimace as I looked around at the featureless walls. Then still in a whisper, "That was scary, I gotta say. Who was that?" Then, with heat in my voice, I snapped, "And what does he mean, I'm not worth the air I breathe?"

"No one you to need to know. He is much higher in rank than me and must be obeyed and I prefer he not to know you, also. Do not to worry about what he said; he thinks size is all that matters and better for you that he does not to notice you in any way."

"Yeah, I can see that. I think he takes up way more than his share of air! How dare he say that about me? I'll have him know I take up the least amount of air of anyone!" Still pissed, arms crossed, I looked around the large room again, seeing through my scowl booths but without seats, just small counters in between walls, one right after another in a long row to my left. As I looked over one of the counters, I saw different aliens and Humans standing and moving around at the far end. I realized I was in a shooting gallery, not so different from the one I used at home on New Eden except the figures at the far end appeared quite real.

I gasped; I wasn't going to shoot at real beings, was I? I was good at target practice but had never shot at anything alive, animal or Human. I pointed a shaky finger down the room at them. "I don't have to shoot them, do I? Because I can't do that."

B'le'ru looked where my finger was pointing. His whiskers twitched in amusement. "Those are holograms; they are not real. You will to be practicing against them but not yet, of course. First I have to train you to use your weapon." Then he looked over at Si'neada and huffed. "Your intervention was certainly timely but I am not sure what you were thinking, putting yourself in the middle of that."

Si'neada smirked. "I had to rescue you both before he could to do something nasty to you, did I not? He sounded like he was about to lay some kind of punishment on you." His eyes narrowed. "Although I have to admit that Jessi certainly was well hidden, almost like she was camouflaged. If I did not to know she was supposed to be there, I would not have known she was there, if you get my meaning. Well done, Jessi, my little hidden treasure!" He smiled a wide smile, showing fang.

I nodded my head. "What is a twofer?"

"Ah, that." He tossed his head. "Well, I am a twofur. It is like I have two furs, one male and one female. My brain thinks I am female but my body says male so we are called twofur."

"Oh, I see! Like two for the price of one, which we call a two-fer!"

B'le'ru actually rolled his eyes and Si'neada smiled again. "Yes, I am like two persons for the price of one!" He clapped his hands softly as he grinned with glee. "I to like that! I will to use that, you know." He tapped me on my nose with a quick light prod.

I grinned back at him. "Sure, you can use that all you want. What are you doing here, anyway?" I asked.

"He offered to be your companion so you would to feel comfortable training with me on the range. We are not supposed to be alone with a student at any time and he was available." B'le'ru said in a gruff voice.

"Well, thank you, then, Si'neada. I'm glad you're here for me."

"I am your friend, my little shooter." He winked at me.

B'le'ru moved down the line of counters until it was difficult to see the door, gesturing for us to follow. He tugged a glove onto his right hand and then picked up a small item from the counter in front of him and said, "This will to be your personal safety item from now on. It is a small size for you to carry and easy to use." He held it up. It had a short, round barrel, a handle with a small battery pack and a trigger, some buttons and was a dull black/gray type of color. On top of the barrel were two very small protrusions that were notched. He named the parts, then said, "It runs from a battery pack which will need to be charged when low. This button will show green for charged, yellow for diminished power and red for dangerously low." He then somehow removed the battery and showed it to me. "You will to charge it in an electrical outlet, see where the prongs are. Best to keep it fully charged as much as possible." He then replaced it into the gun. A button turned green after it clicked into place.

"This button controls how much voltage is discharged through the gun, from stun to kill. The trigger, when pulled, delivers the charge. This button is the safety, which you keep on at all times unless you to need to shoot. It will be keyed only to your DNA so no one else can use it against you or anyone else. This button sets the range for the beam and the notches on top are sights so you can hit your target." He then removed the battery from the handle and set it on the table. "We will to work with a dead weapon."

He placed it on the table. "Now you will to drill on all the parts until they to become second nature. Then I will to teach you the proper care of it. Then and only then will you be allowed to use it for practice."

"This is definitely different from my own gun. Ours uses bullets." I moved forward hesitantly and touched it with one finger as it lay on the small countertop. It was a bit cold to the touch but I couldn't tell if it was metal, plastic or some other material I didn't know. I tentatively picked it up; it nestled into my palm almost like it was made to be there. It warmed almost instantly to my body temperature.

"This feels comfortable in my hand."

"It is what we use to teach a Transitional Year kitling to shoot. It is about the right size for you."

B'le'ru then said, "Touch your tongue to the safety button so it will receive your DNA."

I glanced at him but he was serious. He nodded. I touched the tip of my tongue to it and there was an instant of suction and release. The button glowed a white light for a brief second and then blinked green once.

"It has accepted your DNA. Now only you can to use this weapon."

I nodded to show I'd heard him. "Wow, that's so fantabulous! Our guns at home don't do the DNA thing; wish they did, then we wouldn't have the accidental shootings."

They both furrowed their brows. "Yes, the DNA solves the accidental part. I did not to know you do not yet to have this." B'le'ru said.

I gave a quick shrug. "What I've been told is because the world is still rather wild, anyone needs to be able to use a firearm in case of a wild animal attack. DNA would limit who could use it, and it might make the difference in the wild."

Si'neada said, "Ah. That makes sense." He tapped his finger on his chin.

B'le'ru said, "Now to identify each part of the gun." He drilled me for some moments on the various components of the weapon until I was perfect. There weren't that many differences in the parts from my own gun. The main difference, besides the DNA and battery pack stuff, was what it spat out when the trigger was pulled.

Then he said, "Yes, you to know them. Now, with your eyes closed."

I stared at him. "Are you serious?" I'd never had to do that with mine at home.

He looked at me, one eyebrow raised.

"You are serious."

I sighed; I was tired and wanted to go to bed. How long had we been at this? I didn't know and didn't see a time piece anywhere.

I rolled my eyes, then closed them and picked up the weapon. Holy Jumping Cow! I realized how different it was with my eyes closed and how much I'd relied on my vision. I'd never had to do this during all my years shooting at a range. Maybe there was a method to his madness. I ran my hand over it, feeling the smoothness of the barrel, the bumps on the handle, the curve of the trigger and the raised buttons. I visualized it in my head and then started touching and naming parts. I got the buttons wrong at first but with practice, I got better until finally, I could do it with ease.

B'le'ru then said, "You have done well, very well. Tomorrow you will to do this against a time measure. For now, I will to keep the weapon and we will meet at 1030 ship clock time tomorrow night. I have duties until then so it must be a bit later." He put the weapon into one of the many pockets on his jump suit.

"I will first to make sure the corridor is clear and then we may go back to the Human deck."

I nodded. Si'neada said, "I will to walk you to your door."

I shrugged. "Okay, if you insist."

Si'neada said in a prim manner, "I do insist, my little warrior."

I got back to my room, where I zoomed through getting ready for bed, as I was beyond tired, even forgetting to activate the hologram of New Eden for my bedroom. I fell into bed and was asleep about the same time my head hit the pillow. I had a brief thought of regret for not exploring more but I was so tired nothing made sense.

## CHAPTER ELEVEN

I awoke slowly to the room announcing my wake-up time. The last thing I wanted to do was get up but I had classes. I threw off the covers and groaned, rubbing my eyes. I was still worn-out and my hands were sore from handling the weapon last night. B'le'ru had informed me just because I was to have a personal weapon did not mean I could skip any classes or workouts. While I thought that kind of sucked, I couldn't explain my absence if I didn't show up so I had to go.

I stumbled around getting ready, slurping my coffee to help wake me up. I yawned repeatedly. It had been very late when we were done at the range and I hadn't had that many hours of sleep. I pulled on a robe with swirls of reds and blues, skipping the extra clothes underneath this time, fumbled through fastening the straps to comfort, smoothed my hair with a soft brush, slid comfortable flat shoes on my feet and left the room, finding Soli and Zoe in the hall. Zoe's robe was a mix of pinks, lavenders and light blues and looked divine on her. I immediately felt frumpy. Soli's was a blend of yellows, grays and blacks and accented his gray eyes and his long black lashes. We said our hello's, me noticing how Zoe's face reflected a faint disgust as she took in my red outfit as we started for the elevator to wait for Keaton and Mitchler with our escort.

They walked up to us a couple of minutes later, Mitchler looking at me, then saying, "You sure look beat again, Jessi. You okay?"

I nodded, stifling yet another yawn. "Yeah, I'm fine. I was up late last night, that's all. You know, too much to do and not enough time." I smiled.

He nodded, looking sympathetic. "This immersion stuff is rather intense, right?" The Officer of the Day led us to the dining room as we all murmured our agreement and talked about how much we were learning and how sore our bodies were. Then we sat while poking buttons on the menu, now mostly Amorphan choices. I was developing a fondness for a type of breakfast biscuit, crunchy outer crust and soft inside with chunks of fruit and meats. Also, their idea of an omelet was right up my alley, too, packed with a type of spicy sausage and vegetables.

I managed to stay awake through classes that day, and even put in a few good rounds in dance class and self-defense class and in the gym. However, B'le'ru informed me in a soft voice, "We meet tonight at 11:30 ship time night" while instructing me in self-defense moves. I nodded; I would use the extra time to nap after dinner so I could stay awake for tonight's lesson and not get further behind on my sleep.

That night, at the designated time, I stood by the door and heard the soft click of its opening. I slid through after verifying it was indeed B'le'ru; some of my self-defense lessons were finally sticking to me, I guess. He nodded at me in approval and whisked me down the hall to the range.

Again, Si'neada was there, this time with a reader in his hand. He grinned at me when I entered, waving at me with one finger, then using that finger to let me know to continue being silent. The door snicked shut behind me and I let out a quiet sigh of relief.

B'le'ru said in a soft voice, "It is still better to speak low and to avoid notice, so to be careful of your volume." I nodded. He then pointed at my weapon laying on the counter, saying, "Name the parts."

I got them right the first time. He approved and then said, "Now to disassemble and assemble as before."

I was a little clumsy with that; after all, this was only the second evening of practice with this gun. B'le'ru frowned at me, making me nervous which only increased my clumsiness. Si'neada remarked, "B'le'ru, you big hairy oaf, you are making her nervous."

B'le'ru scowled. "She must to learn to do this under pressure; if she really needs it in an emergency, being nervous and still assembling her weapon correctly is only in her best interests." He narrowed his eyes at me. "I to expect any of my students," and here my translator said student but my ears heard 'kitlings', "to be able to perform under pressure and anxiety." His tail lashed back and forth a couple of times in emphasis.

I took a deep breath to steady myself and blocked out his glare. This time, I was able to put it together in an organized manner. I held it in my right hand, squinting down the barrel where the targets would normally be hung.

"It is not yet time for that." B'le'ru barked, making me jump and I hastily put the weapon back on the counter.

Si'neada said with a wink toward me, "Have a tough day, B'le'ru Sweetie?" He chortled softly.

B'le'ru glared at him. "You—you—you and your 'sweetie' stuff! The Commander let it 'slip' he thinks I am a twofur! And you know that I am not! Thank the Universe he is not a twofur also or I would be fending him off, the oversexed male he is!"

I raised one eyebrow, a trick I was always fond of doing. "Oversexed male?"

Si'neada said with a grin, "Who tried to mount you today, my dear sweet muscular male friend? I might want to know for myself, you know. I do rather like the military type."

An inarticulate growl came from B'le'ru's throat. "No one!" He then snapped at me, while ignoring Si'neada's grin. "Now to assemble the weapon while dark."

I obediently closed my eyes.

B'le'ru chuckled, an abrupt change in his mood. "You can to keep your eyes open." He clicked a remote and the darkness was overwhelming, inky black and no light source at all. I gasped, startled. I'd not considered these rooms didn't have windows nor spaces under doors; therefore, with the lights out, it was a fathomless black. I felt disoriented for a few seconds, almost dizzy. My eyes were frantically trying to adjust and I felt myself rapidly blinking. My hair shuddered around me in a hard hug as if to ward off the black. Then I forced myself to relax. It was, after all, only dark and I could hear the two of them breathing.

Si'neada said in a quiet but huffy way, "Hey, you big hairy ball of fur! You did not have to turn off my device! What if I lose my place?"

"I did not to want any light at all in here, and I wanted to see how our kitling would react. And so far, not well. She has not even tried to get her weapon."

Well, crap on a crutch. He was right. I was so stunned by the abruptness of the pitch dark, I hadn't even thought about the gun. I rolled my eyes; some kind of soldier I would make, right? Yeah, not a very good one. I groped around on the counter until I found the butt of the gun and picked it up.

B'le'ru grumbled, "About time."

I asked, "How are you going to be able to tell if I do it right or not in the dark like this?"

He said, "By sound. I to know weapons like I know my own stripes. And you will, too, by the time I am done with you."

He was right.

With classes for 12 hours every day and my extra training at night, I was exhausted. I had no energy for the observation deck at night with the others for our one free hour and begged off, saying there was so much to do I couldn't afford the time. They all nodded and didn't argue, looking about as tired as I felt. I had no time to go back to the deck on my own time to view the rest of Mom's memories and I'd made no further inroads on finding out what Akrion was, who left the note in the vent and if it was even meant for me or anything more about what might've been used in the classroom. I told myself I'd definitely take the time the next night to see the rest of the chip even if it meant a sleepless night. It would have to wait until after my weapons session, however.

We met for breakfast the next morning, even Zoe being half way nice to me; I think she was just too low on energy to be her usual snarky self. Our menu now was fully Amorphan, except it did allow for coffee and tea. I thought of the suitcase I'd stuffed full of coffee and a self-maker that would hopefully last me a year, or at least until the six-month mark, when my parents could send me more.

Anyway, after we all finished, our escort told us, "Today you will not have language. You will have more dancing lessons instead. Dancing is important in Amorphan society and we must to make sure you are well drilled in the nuances." We all sat straighter and grinned. Dancing would be a lot more fun than drilling on pronunciation. Tatras Meleandrea and Hilodria waited for us in the room.

"Today," Hilodria announced, "We will go through casual dances; that is the first hour. The second and third hours, we will commence on teaching you formal dances. You will be attending High Function affairs, after all, and you must know how to do them correctly or people will get offended. Therefore, we must not shirk in that duty."

Zoe clapped her hands together and exclaimed, "Oh, yeah, that's more like it!"

Meleandrea gave her a look with her glittery eyes and said, "Young ones such as yourself need to learn to restrain yourself around the elders and there will be plenty of elders at these functions. As part of these formal dances, you will learn the manners that go with them."

Zoe had the grace, for once, to look abashed while I smirked. "I apologize, Tatra Meleandrea," she intoned.

Meleandrea nodded her head. "There, that is acceptable behavior." She moved to the center of the floor. "Come now, my younglings, so I may better teach you. I will show you the forms as a group and you will practice, and then you will pair up."

Tatro Aelotro joined us for the class so Zoe and I both could practice with a male Amorphan. One of the three guys had to sit out a dance while the other two went through the forms with the teachers and they rotated as such. That meant, of course, that Zoe and I actually danced way more than they did but since we both loved to dance, that wasn't actually a hardship. Zoe, of course, flowed through the dances with natural grace and picked up the odd steps very quickly while I clunked my way through these dances. Some of the moves were similar to Human dances but many were very different, requiring a lot of concentration. I was always astonished how I felt I moved while dancing—light on my feet and graceful—is not how I appeared in the mirrors. If I saw myself dance, I thought I looked like I had heavy shoes on and no grace at all but that's not how it felt.

At the end of our lessons that day, we were standing around sipping cool drinks, wiping our brows, and feeling satisfied with our performance. Tatra Hilodria said, "Tomorrow, you will wear your Amorphan High Function apparel to practice in. We only have a short while left before arriving at our home and you must be prepared." She paused. "Take a 15-minute break and you will flow into self-defense class when you return."

Self-defense class went better that day for me, too. I guess I was finally in much better physical shape than when we started. I noted the guys were quicker and more efficient while Zoe still seemed a bit lost. Oh, well, she had her beauty to protect her, although maybe the Amorphans wouldn't think she was as striking as male Humans seemed to think.

When classes wrapped up for the day, I went to my room to shower and then laid down for a quick nap. I needed the sleep; this night B'le'ru would start me on target training. I knew that weapon now like it was part of me and it didn't matter if there was light or not. I always knew where it was in the room, even after B'le'ru would kick it across the floor in the dark. I learned to use other senses besides sight, like smell and sound, to track its whereabouts. Tonight was the first night I'd have a live battery in it and I was excited to see how different it was from my old weapon.

I grudgingly got up from my nap when Room chimed me awake and got myself into an Amorphan robe for the evening meal, making my way to the dining hall with my group. We arrived to find our table wasn't in the usual place. With puzzled looks, we stood uncertainly in the doorway, none of us quite sure what to do, until our Imurian escort gestured, looking annoyed, pointing the way. A door stood open to our left into a room we hadn't known was there. We looked at each other, raising our eyebrows, and then en masse, moved off toward the open door, arriving to find an expanded table in a private dining room.

"Okay, what's this all about?" Keaton asked. I shrugged, then noticed something. "Hey! We have name placards at our seats." Since I had found mine, I pulled out the chair, fluffed out my Amorphan garb, and sat. They all did the same thing and just then, the three Tatrans arrived so we all jumped up again to bow. This was standard dinner manners, as had been drilled into us; the youngest must always stand and bow until the elders were seated and gave their permission for sitting. The three of them glided to their spots, ignoring us in our bowed positions, pulled out their chairs, and sat in unison. Tatro Aelotro said, "You may sit."

Then he made a chittering sound, which captured our attention. "We did not tell you of the dinner plans, so we could be sure to see how you would react. Other than you were sitting when we first arrived, you did rectify that and your manners after that were acceptable. Now, please, order your dinner choices." Then he gave us a lecture on table manners, including how we couldn't sit until we were given permission, even if no one was in the room yet.

Zoe said, "Tatro, we only followed Jessi; she sat first when we arrived. And now we all know better, do we not, classmates?" She glanced at the guys, looking for support. They looked amused but noncommittal, certainly not the support she clearly wanted.

I narrowed my eyes as I glared at her. *You little tattle-tail.*

Tatro made a dismissive gesture. "It is okay, Madame Zoe; this was to be a learning experience for all of you and Madame Jessalya will not repeat the mistake nor any of you."

*Ha. Nice try, Madame Zoe. Backfired on you. Nyah Nyah Nyah.*

Dinner was fun after that, actually. We got to see our teachers in a different way, talking and laughing and chattering. They asked us a lot of questions about life as a Human and offered more insight into their own society. I hadn't had this much fun for a while and I noticed my translator didn't have to work as much; I was really starting to understand the language. I also noticed that most of us didn't need to look up words as often on our devices. With reluctance at the end of dinner, we asked permission to leave the table, in Amorphan, of course.

They granted their permission, and with bows of respect, we left the table and headed for our quarters with our escort. We had stayed later than normal and I realized I had no time for a rest period before going to my shooting practice, only enough time to change out of my robe. Having that much fun at dinner was refreshing, however, and I was energized from the camaraderie of the group.

## CHAPTER TWELVE

I slipped through the door as usual when Si'neada opened it. We made our way quietly down the hall to the target range into the safety of the room where B'le'ru was waiting. With a nod of hello, I reached past him, picked up my weapon, checking it over. B'le'ru smiled in approval. I said, "The battery is empty."

He nodded. "I have a freshly charged one for you to use after we to go through the basics of aiming and shooting." He then placed me in front of the counter. I could see the holograms at the other end of the room, moving around in a natural manner and I had to suppress uneasiness at the thought of shooting them. *They're not real; I have to remember that.*

He demonstrated a shooting stance, telling me to grip the weapon in my dominant hand and wrap my other hand over it for stability. This was the same as my training from home so I was immediately comfortable with it. He drilled me on it a few times to make sure I really did know the hold and then said as he held out the charged battery, "Time to switch."

Without thinking, I popped out the dry battery and popped in the live one, automatically checking for a green light and that the safety was on. I made sure to keep the muzzle pointed toward the other end of the room. Si'neada appeared absorbed in whatever he was reading, although when I clicked the live battery into place, he flinched ever so little.

"On my say," B'le'ru said. I raised the gun, spreading my feet slightly apart, one foot forward for balance as taught, and looked through the sights. "Shoot the blue top man!" He snapped.

Visually sorting through the group of holograms, an Imurian in a blue top briefly appeared, and I pulled the trigger. A pfffting sound came from the muzzle and a flash at the other end of the room. I lowered the gun and said, "How'd I do?"

B'le'ru shook his head. "You missed him and hit the woman he moved behind. If you to stop to think, you miss. That is why the training is so important."

"Your holograms are so much more realistic than ours on New Eden. I have to get used to them." I said in self-defense.

Si'neada piped up, "It is your first time in here, Jess; we do not yet expect you to be perfect." He smirked and went back to his reading.

B'le'ru snapped, "My job is to get her to perfect. Perhaps the holograms were not the place to start; we will switch to single targets first." He made the appropriate changes and I was much better at hitting the single targets. Obviously, I'd have to build up to the moving holograms. By now, my hands were hurting and my eyes felt like I was blinking over shards of eggshells.

I yawned. "Can't we call it a night tonight? I really need some sleep and that will help with my training, I'm tellin' ya."

B'le'ru considered me through narrowed eyes, whiskers twitching. *She is right, she is overly tired tonight.* "Yes, that is a good idea.

Tomorrow night, then." Si'neada's whiskers twitched back, *Yes, let her rest for a night.* I still puzzled over how I knew their whisker language but then my hair let me know.

WORKED WITH TRANSLATOR.

Well, good. Something I didn't have to study, my hair and the translator did it for me and that was just fine with me. Bad enough to learn how to make those melodious sounds of Amorphan without throwing in a visual language to learn.

After getting back to my room, I made myself a particularly strong cup of coffee and slugged it down. I was going to view the rest of that chip, come hells or high water. I waited until a few minutes after the Dividing Hour of the night, hoping to avoid any and all night shift workers. My hair did its trick on my door monitor and, after my hair and I made sure the corridor was clear, took the elevator to the viewing deck.

Once there, after making sure all was clear, I slipped the chip into the wall pad, wishing I could take it from its place and hide behind a couch or something. A menu popped up, asking me to "Resume", "Quit" or "Restart". I tapped the resume button and it took me to the place where I'd been that other night. I took a steadying breath in and let it out slowly. *Do I really want to see this? Is this really going to help me on this quest?* I was torn with indecision and high anxiety at being caught here in the viewing deck.

WATCH.

*Ok, ok, no need to be pushy.*

I tapped the "Start" button and my mom's voice slammed me immediately into overwhelming homesickness again. I clenched my teeth against it. I heard her voice, seeing her hand reach out to ruffle the hair on a small boy's head. "Devon, yes, you have to go, you know you do. I need you to be the bratty boy today for the class for training, you know that. Remember I promised you an extra dessert tonight if you do this for Mommy."

Devon's high-pitched boy voice said, "I don't care. I don't want to go." I caught my breath on a sob; I'd never heard Devon's voice before.

A big sigh. "Devon, please, we've been through this. You promised to go and I promised you extra dessert. So, little man, let's go. Now."

"I want to stay with Dad." He whined. "Dad, I want to stay here with you!"

"I'm sorry, son; Mommy needs you today but when you get back, you and I'll go do something fun, just the two of us. Okay?"

"Okay." Said in a sulky voice.

The scene shifted. A small caption read, "Edited for content". The view now was a classroom, *my* current classroom; I could tell from the paintings on the wall. The room was filled with pregnant women sitting in chairs and my mom's voice said, "Okay, now I'll show you how to deal with a tantrum from your child while in public places." As she spoke, air blew forcibly from the vents, causing hair to flutter and women to exclaim about the sudden cold of the air blowing. Then, almost immediately, some women slumped to the floor off their chairs, others clutched their pregnant bellies, and a few others vomited onto the floor, pale and sweaty.

My mother's voice snapped in a sharp tone, "Medics! We need medics here now! Devon, are you all right? Lie down, now, on the floor. It's okay, baby, the medics are almost here." Her hand smoothed his hair away from his pale face as she shouted out, "Is everyone okay?"

The medics arrived in the room and took over. Again the scene cut out and resumed in their quarters, Dad sitting across from Mom, worry etched into his face. "What is wrong with him, Mellie? Why is his body doing that?" He gestured and I saw Devon lying on a bed, Mom's hand reaching out to feel his forehead.

"I don't know, honey. I've never seen anything like it and besides, you know my specialty is Reproductive Sciences."

"It's like his body is trying to change. I know, it's impossible, but that's what it looks like."

Mom's hand raised as if to rub her face. "Yeah, that's impossible. I don't think that was just a lack of oxygen in the room, either. It all happened so fast; a few gusts of air into the room and then everyone, I mean everyone, was affected within seconds. No two were affected the same. I felt light headed and dizzy and for a couple of moments, like I could faint, and then I was fine and most of the women recovered about as fast, too. No one's pregnancy was impacted, as best as I can tell, and the Imurian doctors on board say that, too." Her hand dropped to her swollen belly, rubbing it as if to reassure me in the womb.

Again the editing occurred. The next thing I saw was Devon's body just before they unfolded a sheet to lay over his inert body, deathly pale with no rise and fall of his chest. His body showed malformations of his major joints and his ears appeared to be hairy and pointed, almost like an Imurians. "What happened to you, little man of ours?" The sobbing. "Oh, gods, oh, gods, this hurts. How are we to continue living with him gone?"

Tears falling onto clenched hands. "You shouldn't have died, Devon; there was no reason at all you should've died."

I choked back sobs of my own, wiping tears away, as I watched her memories unfold. Something was definitely very odd about his death, with his misshapen body and the only one affected like that. Who was behind this, this attack, for want of a better term? And why? If they, whoever they were, had wanted to kill the women, they did a poor job of it. *Could the target have been Devon? Or was he an accidental exposure?* He wasn't originally supposed to be there that day; it was a last-minute adjustment to the schedule, or so I'd always been told. The playback stopped abruptly and a caption read, "End."

I plucked the chip out of the device with trembling fingers. *Were Imurians involved in this? Or Humans? Or both?* The big question, among others, remained. *Why?* I was missing a lot of puzzle pieces here.

I had been so absorbed in what I was watching I was startled to find myself still in the viewing deck; I had been reliving Mom's memories as if I were there. Could whatever had affected Devon given my hair its abilities? It was a definite possibility. It was my biggest secret, one I'd taken extraordinary means to protect, as I knew no one else had anything other than ordinary hair. At least as far as I knew. Not a question I could casually ask. "Oh, by the way, does your hair communicate with you like mine does?" Yeah, that wasn't going to happen unless I really wanted to live in a lab as an experimental being. Nope. That wasn't for me, so I kept the secret like the world would blow up if I ever shared it. Come to think of it, *my* personal world *would* blow up so yeah, it's a secret.

I crept back to my room, numb by the emotional upheaval of Devon's death. It had never been real; he was just stories to me, told by Mom or Dad. To see it, to experience the whole thing was a shock to my emotional center. I think if an Imurian had come along while I returned to my room, I wouldn't have noticed or cared.

## CHAPTER THIRTEEN

The next night, after our classes all day, I snuck down to the shooting range, wrung out emotionally and physically exhausted. I looked forward to shooting things for relief of the inner turmoil and that had never happened before. I took pride in target practice at home, but they were only paper and no semblance to living beings.

B'le'ru put up some really ugly looking characters, a mix of forms from spider-like to Humanoid, who moved their arms, blinked, yawned and generally looked pretty real, except they didn't move from their spot down the range. These were more than holograms; these appeared to be solid, real beings. He told me to line up, sight down the barrel, and then shoot. The first time a shot landed, I yelped when there was a spray of bone and blood from the horrible spider-like thing. I hadn't realized how real it was going to be and I stared, horrified. This was so much different from my former shooting range!

"Oh, my shattered nerves! Are they real? Tell me they're not real!"

B'le'ru rolled his eyes. "Of course they are not real; I have told you that. But if you have to really shoot someone, you have to be prepared for reality and that means bone and blood…maybe even guts."

I thought I might faint, his words making my head swim and the blood leave my face. "I can't do that, I just can't. I don't care how ugly they are. I mean—I—I—I." Words failed me. I laid down my gun and stepped back. B'le'ru shoved me forward and hissed, "To pick it up. It is my duty to help you stay alive in all events. Pick. It. Up." Si'neada made a gesture meaning to do what B'le'ru said. I sighed as reflexes kicked in and I did, indeed, pick it up. He raised his brows and looked down the gallery with a very pointed look.

The spidery thing I'd shot before was gone and in its place was a new ugly character, this time looking more like a grass jumper type of thing. Well, I hated those and spidery things, too, so I shot at it as it jumped out of range, and I shot again. It jumped. I had to figure out which way it was going to jump and how to track it with my weapon and finally, after about four or five times, I finally hit it. It fluttered out of a jump, spewing something green, fell to the ground with its legs twitching madly…and then vanished.

I finally started believing they were not real after all and then it became more fun as I vented my emotions on them. There were jumpers, slithery things, big things with slobbery mouths, slimy looking things and spinners who spun in circles while moving and spider things with webs. Someone had quite an imagination! Finally, B'le'ru said "Enough for tonight. You have made good progress." He shut down the projections and I started yawning. "Tomorrow night, same time."

I gave a sloppy salute, saying, "Yeah, boss." I tucked my gun, after engaging the safety, in my bra between my small breasts, where I carried it, since B'le'ru told me it had to now be with me

24/7. It was too heavy for the flimsy pockets in the robe and I was afraid someone would notice it there so the personal bank of Bra seemed the best place.

Si'neada got up to accompany me to my room as usual. He grinned as he glanced at B'le'ru. "I think our little one here is a natural at this. I am very impressed with her progress as I am sure you are." He fluttered his hands in the air. "Not too long now and you will to be able to put her in the test room."

B'le'ru's whiskers twitched in agreement as he inclined his head our way. "Yes, I agree, she is coming along faster than I thought she would."

"I told you I'd been trained to use weapons since I was much younger. Guess it shows." I reminded them as pride rushed through me, then B'le'ru punctured my pride balloon. "We will to see how well she does with the final testing. She is not perfect yet. She has an aptitude, yes, but does she to have the instincts needed and the nerve?" He shrugged. "We shall to see about that."

When I got into my room, I headed to the bathroom, closing and locking the door for privacy. I felt like an idiot for doing so since I was in my own quarters but my hair was very firm I do this. Yeah, I had a full bladder but this was more than that. I used the toilet, washed my hands, brushed my teeth and then placed them on my hips as I stared at my hair in the mirror, which was impatiently tugging at me for attention. *Well? What is it? Why did you make me come in here? I want to go to sleep!*

WATCH.

*Watch what? I don't have the energy for games.* I furrowed my brow, irritated. Now wasn't the time for tricks and fun stuff. I was beyond tired, tomorrow was another long day and I still hadn't found anything definitive about what caused Devon's death, so I was very frustrated, feeling time slip away from me and I didn't know what else to do.

THIS WILL HELP.

*Going to bed is what will help me the most.*

I reached out my hand to unlock the door and then pain hit me like an avalanche of ice picks. I couldn't scream, the pain too intense to even breathe. I couldn't see, my hair was cocooned around me in a pillar of support and I felt tears racing from my eyes down my cheeks as I crumpled to the floor. *OhGodsOhGodsOhGods! HELP!*

WATCH!

*I can't! It hurts too much!* I felt like everything in me was being torn apart, and rearranged with a blender. Then the pain stopped. Just….stopped. Completely. I gasped for breath, curled around myself on the floor. I felt sore and bruised all over and…different. I gulped for air and then I peeped open my eyes.

No. Those weren't my hands. These were Imurian hands with claw-tipped fingers but they were on the ends of *my* arms. My arms which had fur with stripes. I climbed to my feet and swiped my hand over my face to wipe it clear of my confusion and tears. I stopped the motion.

*That's not my face. Is it?*

YES. NO.

*Yeah, that cleared things up. So is it me or not?* Rising panic threatened to brim over into a screaming attack.

LOOK.

My heart went into stampede mode in my chest, a quaking took over my body and I gulped for air. *What am I going to see? I'm not sure I can look.*

My hair prodded me to use the mirror. I faced the glass with my eyes closed, then I opened them for a split second and slammed my lids shut again. That was *not* my face in there. I peeked open one eye. Yeah, just what I thought. An Imurian face looked back at me. I opened the other eye and gaped at my reflection, first checking over my shoulder to see who was behind me—nobody—and saw my mouth hanging open, showing, yes, fangs. And cat ears on my head. With fur and stripes and vertically-slit pupils in green irises which widened as I continued gawking into the mirror.

I clutched the sink for support. This is *not* possible. Not in any universe. My hair could do many things, including camouflage, but shape-shifting? Completely impossible. Everyone knew it was impossible. *You're just somehow creating this illusion, like when you hide me? Right?*

NO. CHANGED.

*Oh, big stinking fairy farts. What has happened to me? How did this happen? How do I make it go away?* I touched my face with a furry finger to verify it was real. I still felt like myself inside, thank the stars, but I was still in shock at my transformation. My hands shook as I raised both of them to stroke over the top of my head, flipping the ears down to watch them spring back up. I experimented with moving them, surprised at how much concentration that took. I smoothed the whiskers back and they twitched forward again.

I took in a long breath, odors, scents, smells exploding into my brain, making me reel and clap my hand over my nose, pinching it shut. I panted small short breaths through my mouth, stunned at the confusion of scents and the change of my body. I found myself cataloging smells: soap, cleaning odors, urine, my body odor, coffee lingering in the air, earthiness of the dirt around the tree in the sitting room and more. I cautiously took my hand from my nose and sniffed. The attack of odorous information was less, much less, as my brain sorted through them and dismissed them as benign. "Wow." I whispered. "That was—unexpected." I rubbed my nose and took a few more cautious breaths, relieved when I wasn't assaulted again by the inrush of too many odors.

I blinked my eyes. My vision was sharper with Imurian eyes, the light a bit too bright, colors a bit more muted but objects having a bit of halo glowing around them, surprising me. My brain now calculated distances in terms of "can pounce now, must move to pounce, not worth pouncing" ways. I flexed my hands, feeling claw tips biting into my palms.

I closed my eyes and then reopened them. I was still an Imurian in the mirror and I was awake so this wasn't a nightmare. This was real. *How….?* A sudden realization hit me. *You've been collecting DNA from others? Could we do this back on New Eden and I didn't know?*

NO. NOW. AMORPHAN DNA.

*Amorphan DNA?* I watched my furry face scrunch up in confusion as this ran through my brain. *Amporphan…why would..? Oh! They can morph their hands and feet into other things. But all of me changed, right, not just my hands and feet?*

I looked down, which I hadn't done before, and I noted with surprise a tail and everything else I could see was Imurian. All of me had changed or had it? I groped between my legs at a heaviness I'd never had before, shocked to feel something, mmm, bulgy. I gripped the hem of the hirtatchi, the name of the robe I was wearing, and lifted it. My eyes widened. I had a penis. And a scrotum. *What the bloody hell…?*

The scrotum was tight against my crotch, two globes encased in a furry sac and in between them, the penis lay curled over the top of the scrotum, and all very much front and forward. Human men's anatomy was way more dangly than this; no wonder the Imurians needed a male pouch on their clothes. *No way to hide this stuff in underwear! It's set much higher on their bodies.* I cautiously touched the male parts, not knowing what to expect. The penis was soft and limp, thank the lords of the stars, and curiously looked naked and pale.

*Am I still a girl?*

STILL GIRL. ONLY SAMPLE MALES.

*Ahhhhh, I see.* I hoped that meant we only had Imurian male DNA samples so far, which, since I'd not been around any female Imurians, made sense. *I'm not anyone I recognize, though.*

COMBINATION.

*And I look really silly in this robe; it's way too short, for one thing.* I looked around the small room. *I'm taller now? Can you make me taller when I go back to my body? Hey, I can go back, right?*

ONLY TALLER NOW. CAN GO BACK BUT NOT STAY TALLER.

Well, poop on a stick, I'd still be short. I clutched the sink, sudden dizziness washing over me as I remembered how incredibly painful it had been to change to this form. I shuddered at the thought but then another idea exploded into my brain. *Exploring the ship will be a lot easier this way! But I need Imurian clothing; I can't go in this little gown.* I frowned, watching my broad nose crinkle and whiskers lie flat against my cheeks, then I tilted my ears backwards. *This could be fun.* I smiled then, showing a lot of fang and I ran my tongue over the ends of the sharp teeth. My sense of hearing was enhanced; I heard the rasping of my tongue over the fangs and the whisper of the vent fan as it blew air into the room. I picked up faint sounds behind the walls, sort of a scampering sound.

*What else could I become? Whatever I have DNA for? Or does it take a lot of samples for me to change?*

ANY DNA.

I had to try walking in this form; my perspective at this new height was definitely different and I wanted out of the bathroom. *I'm going to walk to the living room and try this body out.*

My hair didn't object so I figured it was okay. I unlocked the bathroom door, stepping out on wobbly legs; although working the same as our Human ones, the balance and heel strike were different. My thighs felt very powerful like I could leap off the floor for the ceiling, and having a tail drag behind me was weird.

I walked around the living room in the dark to confound any possible surveillance and realized I could see surprisingly well using only the glow from the various devices like the clock and power buttons shining green in the dark. I trailed a finger along the back of the couch as I walked softly by, marveling at how different things looked from up here and how strange the fabric felt under my Imurian finger. I let out a breath and shook my head. *I'm still not sure this isn't some kind of joke my hair is doing to me.* I reached up to my head but all I felt was short Imurian fur. *Where did you go?*

I looked at my first finger and the claw tip looked very sharp, so before I could think things through, I poked it hard into the side of my arm. Blood welled out as I bit my lip at the needle-like pain. I scraped at the fur on my arms to see if maybe my hair was wound around me somehow, but all I got was a messed-up patch of the short strands. Somehow, I had really become an Imurian. *I have become the impossible.* The thought made me stagger.

Oh. My. Shattered. Nerves. If I thought keeping my hair secret was a necessity, this changling ability was galaxies beyond that.

Fatigue then hit me like a flash flood, spilling over me and I nearly fell onto the carpet as I stumbled under the weight of it. I felt prickles start at my feet, swiftly working up my body and I knew a change-back was imminent. I wobbled into the bathroom and shut the door just as the avalanche of pain crushed me into a whimpering mess on the floor. *We are never, I repeat, NEVER, doing that again!*

## CHAPTER FOURTEEN

I woke up with no memory of how I got in bed, achiness claiming my attention as exhaustion worked at dragging me back into sleep. I squinted at the timepiece; it was 0417 ship time morning. Why was I awake and what had I been dreaming about? Oh, that's right. I'd dreamed I'd changed into an Imurian male. I mean, that's a weird dream to have but I didn't want to dissect its meaning right now and why did I ache all over? The daily training had been hardening my body and muscles to the point where I would get a pleasant feeling of the muscles being used but not this overall level pain. Maybe I was getting sick or something but other than the muscle aches, I felt fine.

I rubbed my eyes and turned over, pulling the covers around my neck, but as I did so, I heard a pattering sound near me from the floor, almost like a light knocking. I froze in place, heart beating wildly in fear and my hands clutching the covers as if they were a shield, my breath stuttering in my throat. What was that sound? I loosened one hand from the sheet and slid it under my pillow to grip my weapon, pulling it out to point into the room as my other hand reached quietly for the light switch on my bedside lamp. *B'le'ru would be so proud of me.* Hopefully, the gun would be pointed the right way because turning on the light would be temporarily blinding so I squeezed my eyelids to slits first to minimize the assault and flicked the switch, the glow from the lamp a sudden disturbance in the room.

I clutched the gun with both hands and swung it side to side but I saw nothing out of the ordinary as I slowly let my eyelids open all the way. I felt a tug on the sheet and I jumped, a panicked breath leaving my mouth. I looked down and my mouth dropped open even as I pointed the gun down.

I blinked my eyes rapidly, trying to make sense of what—or who—I saw. There was a miniature *something* standing by the side of my bed looking up, plastered against the edge of my sheet where it hung over the edge as if ready to dodge for cover. About the size of a medium-sized lap dog, the head had an elongated shape, vaguely horse-like, a long sinuous neck with an extended serpentine body but with six appendages and a long lizard-like tail, looking like it was covered in black velvet, blacker than a black hole.

Two absurdly large round ears with a thick fringe of hair were set on either side of the head, currently swiveled back in uncertainty and two large brown eyes with horizontal pupils were staring at me, long lashes curling up from the upper side. Two front appendages looked like arms with two elbows and hands with many digits ringing around the round shape of it. I figured those were hands, anyway, as the whatever-it-was was standing on two sets of middle and rear legs and the torso was reared up with the upper two limbs held out to the side and up like in an ancient cowboy movie, as if either surrendering or showing no weapons. I realized their hands were identical to the prints I'd seen in the dirt around the tree that other day. I had the foolish impulse to reach down and ruffle its ears because it looked so little and cute and soft and like it needed petting. *Huh, it would probably bite me but now I understand why all those adults want to ruffle* my hair.

I carefully lowered the gun to the bed and held up both my hands, now empty. It smiled, a tooth baring grin showing broad flat teeth except for the sets of very sharp fangs on either side of the mouth. It gave me a one-finger wave and I returned the gesture. It pointed up; then before I could react, it swarmed up my covers and plopped down next to my leg, patting my thigh with one tiny multi-fingered hand.

Then it said in Imurian, as it continued to grin cheerfully, "I thought you would never to wake up." It waved one hand in the air. "No need to introduce yourself, we to know you are Jessi. I am Deester, male."

"Uh, hi, Deester. There's a we?"

"Yes, I will to call them now." He made a soft whistling sound and two heads popped out from under the bed to look up. Their bodies followed and they swarmed up the bed to plop down near Deester, grinning.

"Who are you? I mean, what are you? Where'd you come from and how'd you get into my room?" I furrowed my brow, clutching my sheet to my chest. "Why are you here? What do you want from me?"

He patted my leg again. "So many questions, little one!" I snorted out a soft chuckle at him calling *me* little. "We are Scitterers from the planet Dursaria but we now live on all the Imurian ships as crew." He looked sad for a moment then brightened. "Of course, I have never seen Dursaria; that is only history for my people. We to live on our chosen ship and go planet-side when the Imurians to go to their recreation planet. They to take good care of us!"

"What happened to Dursaria?"

"Ah. That. We were the civilized society on the planet but as you can to see, we are diminished in size. Although the most intelligent, we were in danger of obliteration by the big, hungry species and the Imurians rescued us. Then they developed our planet for sale and we were given a part of the proceeds. We are good at living on ships, cleaning and maintaining and being of service." He then looked unaccountably sad.

"But…?"

He sighed. "But we will never to have a ship of our own and are forbidden, as are other races, to learn about space time and travel."

I nodded. "And you're in my room, why, exactly? And who are these two?"

"Oh, sorry, I to forget! This is Mareesta and Exanno." They nodded their heads, giving me a little wave of the hand. "Mareesta and Exanno, Madame Jessalya." I nodded back.

"We are in your room because we think you to need some help. You are looking for answers about your Devon, am I right?"

I stared at him, mouth slightly open which I quickly shut. "Uh, yes. How do you know about him? Did you know him?"

"We to know many, maybe all, the secrets on board this ship. We are everywhere, you to see, and we to hear and to see everything." He shrugged, an interesting gesture since he didn't have shoulders I could identify. It was more a ripple of the area where his arms attached. "We are always overlooked, because we are small and we are always around and the Imurians forget often we can to hear and to think for ourselves, too." He tilted his head as he looked at me. "We also overheard you viewing memories from your mother. We decided you were worthy of our help and interference."

"Yeah," I said slowly, "that's true. I'm small for my race and I get treated like a child who can't understand adult things. I never thought of it as much of an advantage, though. I'm usually angry about it, instead." I frowned. "Wait a minute, did you say you overheard me?" Fear made me choke on the words.

He whinnied a laugh. "Oh, but it is okay, I to assure you! Use this to your own benefit, little Human! Anger and fear gets in the way of thinking but knowing what will work for yourself and your goals is a mighty thing." He tapped me on the knee. "But to answer your question, no, we did not to know your brother. I was born a few journeys later and these two very young. It is through our archives and stories I to know of this." He patted my leg again. "It was accidental to overhear you. You did not to notice us entering the room and we did not to wish to let you know of our presence yet. It is our secret with you."

I considered this. I raised my eyebrows at them. "I wish you'd been around back then; that would've made my investigation easier." I sighed. I tentatively touched his little hand. "I could use some help, I'll admit. And since I also hate being treated like a child when I'm not, I'll do my best to not inflict that on you."

He sniffed and the other two grimaced. "We hate being treated like—what do you call them?—pests?"

"I think you mean pets."

"Yes, those. But we often are and if it is to our goal, we to allow it so we can continue our knowledge gathering. One never knows when a piece of information will be useful."

*Good thing I didn't pet his ears. I wonder what they do with the knowledge they gather, although there's always a market for information of the right kind, I guess.* I was still sorely tempted to run my hand over his soft-looking body but this wasn't the time, if ever there was a time. My strand of hair had glutted itself on their DNA and I gathered it all into a bundle and pushed it over my shoulder to lay down my back. *Stay there.*

"Okay, so what information is useful for me to know? Since I assume that's why you're here?" Then a thought struck me. "Hey, did you leave me that note in the vent?"

He grinned wider. "Yes."

"How did you know I'd find it? Why did you make it so difficult and make it look like an intrusion?"

"It was a test to see if you are observant and how you would to handle our minor interference. Also to see if you would to follow through to finding the note. You passed."

"Oh."

"The reason we are here is to tell you. Pursue the Akrion. Your answers are there."

Puzzled, I looked at the three of them, all nodding their heads. "What *is* it?"

They all made the same face. "We to know of it, we to know it is highly prized by the Imurians and we to know they guard the secret of it very closely. So closely even we cannot discern it. But we were the ones to push the machine to the vent in that classroom." He pointed one of his many digits at me and I was fascinated how the rest folded away to allow one to be singled out. "Yes, the machine you found. We, my people, that is, were asked to do so and were told it would refresh the air in the room so we did it."

"Who told you to do it? How'd you know I found it?"

"Our boss at the time told us to do it but he has left this ship many years ago and is now on a different path." Then he winked at me. "We are almost everywhere on the ship and we were there in the maintenance room when you entered. We watched to see what you were doing. It was most fascinating what your long coverings did."

I fingered my hair, pushing it back over my shoulder again. "My covering?"

"Yes, you appeared to change color to suit the machine behind you. It was very intriguing but hard to tell in the darkened room how you did it." He cocked his head to one side. "We assumed you had on a camouflage outfit."

"Yeah, that's what it was." *Let them think that; I'm not ready to share about my hair or anything else yet.*

I scrunched up my mouth in annoyance. "I'm not sure how knowing about Akrion helps me, other than knowing the Akrion machine did the job, which I already suspected. I can't find anything about Akrion from any source and I have to be careful what I access. Is Akrion the name of a company or a substance?"

"Substance, as far as we can to tell. We to know nothing more about it."

"Where do they normally keep it?"

"We are fairly sure it is kept in the science part of the ship and we are not allowed in those quarters."

"You're not?"

He shrugged, that liquid movement fascinating me. "It is full of secrets and they do not to allow any stranger or other species in there."

We fell silent for a few seconds until the two other Scitterers started playing a complicated hand-slapping game. Deester flicked an ear at them with a narrowed-eye look. "Stop that." They looked abashed and started fidgeting instead. "They are young and have not yet learned patience."

"How does Si'neada play into this? Your note said to trust him."

"Yes, you can to trust him. Si'neada is allowed anywhere on the ship as he is head tailor and Imurians are quite vain and always want to look their best."

"Even the scientific quarters?"

"Except there. We must return to our duties now so we will leave you now."

"How did you even get in?"

He gave a dismissive wave of his hand. "We have ways, not to worry, little Human."

The three of them slid down the covers, the young ones giggling over their game, and scampered out of the room. I threw the covers back and ran after them but they were already gone so I still didn't know how they got in or out. I blew out a frustrated breath and went back to bed. *Ok, so I need to know more about this Akrion stuff. I'm going to have to recruit Si'neada, I guess.*

I crawled under the sheets again, pulling the covers up to my neck while placing my gun under the pillow again with my head whirling with thoughts and confusion. *The Scitterers are potential allies, it seems, and so is Si'neada. I can't help but feel something bigger is going on, though, and I think it started back with Devon's death. Or maybe long before that.* I started to droop into sleep again and as I quieted my swirling questions, I relaxed enough to fall asleep again.

## CHAPTER FIFTEEN

When the wake-up alert sounded, it dragged me from the depths of sleep. Getting to bed late, being awakened by impossible creatures too early and then a couple more hours of sleep didn't leave me feeling refreshed in any way. I felt like a sand lizard had crawled into my mouth, my eyes were gritty and dry and I desperately wanted coffee, lots and lots of coffee.

My dream had been so real about exchanging my body for another. It's impossible for anything to shape-shift except, obviously, in my dream but the Scitterers? Maybe they'd been real. I was so muzzy headed this morning I didn't know what was real and what wasn't. The circles under my eyes were real, though, as I gazed in the mirror.

*I'll ask Si'neada about them. He'll tell me the truth. I think. The other? Had to be a nightmare.*

NOT NIGHTMARE. REAL.

I shook my head. *No, can't be real. It's only a dream.*

REAL. My hair insisted.

I narrowed my eyes at it in the mirror. *I don't care. If it is, I don't want to ever, EVER do that again.* I broke into a cold sweat remembering the horribleness of the agony. *Remember the scissors?*

*I'll use them again on you if you try it again on me.* My hair froze in place for a second.

I resolutely shoved all thoughts of impossible things out of my head. This was the time to deal with dark circles under my eyes and lack of sleep, not anything else. Breakfast time was soon so I needed to get scooting on getting ready for the day.

As I put the finishing touches on my mascara, the door announced Si'neada was outside my door for a fitting. Puzzled, I gave permission for him to enter while I glanced at my PD, wondering if I'd misheard him last night and maybe he'd said this morning, not tonight for meeting. The door swished open and he stood there with cloth draped over one arm, a basket full of sewing supplies over his other arm. He wrinkled his nose at me, his eyes twinkling, as he said, "Good morning, I would to say, but you to look like you did not to sleep well."

"I didn't. Weird dreams for some reason. Please, come in but I warn you, we only have a minute or two before the call to breakfast when the escort gets here."

Si'neada entered my room, chatting about clothing and fabrics and what colors looked best with my coloring and as he stepped by me, his tail tapped my leg. :*Do you hear this?*:

"Yeah, I hear you." I said as I cast a puzzled look his way. "Why are you asking?"

He cast his eyes upwards in exasperation. He put a manicured finger to his lips to indicate silence, then wrapped his tail around my wrist. :*Do you hear me in your head? Nod your head once if you do.*:

My eyes opened wide in shock. How could I hear him *in my head*? I nodded.

A slight smile appeared on his face. :*Ah, I am so pleased. Now, I want you to think your answer to me this time. NOT out loud with your voice but inside your head. I need to know if I can hear you, too. What is your favorite color?:*

:*Turquoise. Or maybe aqua. Although a rich red is nice, too...:*

He clapped his hands together without making a sound, his tail still around my wrist. :*Yes! I can hear you, too! And I only asked for one color.:* His whiskers trembled with amusement.

Then he said out loud, "Yes, the clothing fits you well. I will to see you tonight with the finished products." His tail dropped back to its normal position. :*Do not tell anyone of our mind whispering:* This time, he didn't touch me and watched me closely to see if I responded to the comment.

I nodded. "Good then." Then I pointed a finger at myself, making a zipping motion along my lips, indicating my willingness to keep silent. He smiled a tooth baring grin, nodding his head.

:*It is a rare talent for Humans, my little whisperer. I thought I heard you mind whisper the other day and I wanted to check it out. This secret is safe between us. Let me caution you, though; do not try this with anyone else. No one, all right?:*

My stomach grumbled loudly at that point. "Uh, yeah, that's fine, but right now I've just gotten up and I'm hungry." Growling, plaintive noises from my tummy punctuated my words.

He minced from the room. "Of course! We cannot to have you be unfed!"

I touched his arm with my ring finger. I hesitated. :*Do I always have to touch you to talk this way?:*

:*Until your gift fully develops in strength and range, it is easier.:*

:*Can all Imurians talk like this?:*

He tapped his lip with a clawed fingertip. Today's claw color du jour was stripes of pink with sparkles and a tiny rhinestone on the tip. *:Not everyone; but it is not rare, either, and I think most of the people in the armed guard can if they to choose to. It is considered a huge strength to be able to communicate this way under duress or a need for silence. However, not everyone among us can mind whisper without touching. That is more rare."*

He clapped his hands loudly. "I think I might to join you for breakfast, myself."

"Sure!" I chirped. "That would be great!" I touched him again. *:Can you tell me about Scitterers?:*

His eyes widened so wide I thought they would pop out of his head in surprise as we stepped through the door. *:Later, tonight, you will to explain to me how you know about them. And shush, now. No more mind-whispering.:*

As we left my room, I dropped my hand from his arm as Zoe stepped into the hallway, looking tall, blonde and perfect as always, even in her Amorphan robes. I swear she'd had them nipped and tucked to accentuate her figure, which made me feel quite shapeless in my own voluminous robes.

She wrinkled her nose at me. "I hope you're feeling okay, Jessi. I mean, with the unbelievable amount of sheer *stuff* they make us do! I don't how your tiny body can possibly have enough energy." In Zoe terms, that meant she hoped I was going to die that day. "You poor thing. It looks like you're not getting enough sleep from those circles under your eyes. Well, small things always seem to need more sleep." She sweetened her tone. "I can lend you some make-up, Jessi Little, if you need some quality cover-up." She then turned her look to Si'neada. "Good morning, Si'neada. I hope *you* rested well last night." She flashed a smile his way. He laid a hand on my arm. *:Ignore her.:*

*:Easy for* you *to say!:*

He pinched my arm tighter. "Yes, I rested well indeed. Thank you for asking. I to hope your question does not to mean I was looking tired before?"

She flicked her hand in a dismissive way. "Oh, no, Si'neada, you always look dazzling. And rested. Unlike our little friend here, who looks rather in need of caffeine."

Irritation zipped through me. "Si'neada said he would join us so we can discuss more robe choices over breakfast. I must say, your robe is looking very, mmmm, fitted today." My own robes billowed out around me as we moved down the corridor and I smoothed them against my torso before I snatched my hands away to let the cloth float like a real Amorphan would. Maybe I could tighten the straps underneath for a more flattering fit. Zoe noticed my smoothing motion; she sneered. My hands itched to be able to swipe it from her face.

*:Peace. She only does it to goad you. She feels insecure by you.:*

I threw a startled glance his way. *:Insecure? As if!:* I'm not sure I was going to get used to this mind whispering. His amused face and slight smile made me narrow my eyes at him.

She smoothed the outfit over her torso. "Why, thank you for noticing. I just had to have them a little more suited to myself than you seem to need. I must say, you should try a little more fitted look; you look positively rotund in all that material." She sniffed while smiling in a way calculated to make me think longingly of my gun. My hair twitched like it wanted to reach out and slap her. If only!

Mitchler and Keaton left their rooms at the same time and we grouped together by the elevator and waited for Soli to come down the hall. "Hey, good morning, ladies." Keaton said with a flash of a smile. "Mitchler and I are ready for the day; hope you two are."

"Oh, yes, I'm ready. Not sure little Jessi here is; she's looking even more tired than usual," Zoe said in a snarky tone.

"Just because I'm tired, Zoe, doesn't mean I'm not ready." I snapped. "I'm getting even more tired of people telling me how exhausted I look."

"Oooh, and she's crabby, too." Zoe tossed her blonde hair over her shoulder. "Beware, boys; the midget is cranky!"

"I'm not a midget!"

"Could've fooled me, you're so short." Then she looked at the males. "The better to make to us feel taller, right?"

They looked a little uncomfortable to be called into this and Mitchler said in a soothing tone, "Yeah, Jessi's short, it's true, but great things come in small packages, right, Jess?"

"Sure." I said, looking around, puzzled. "Where's our escort?

Si'neada said, "Oh, since I am here, I sent him a note saying he could to go on to his other day duties." He called the elevator and as the doors opened, we entered for our short ride to the breakfast room.

I did manage to say as we entered the dining room, "My robes blend in better than yours do, Zoe, and we *are* supposed to be looking like an Amorphan."

She looked over at me. "I feel the need to change their fashion sense."

I had to admit I wanted my robes to fit me like hers, once again feeling small and dowdy next to her. When would I ever feel equal to her? Oh, that's right—never. "Maybe they don't want to change their fashion."

Zoe laughed, reached out and patted me on the head in a condescending manner, saying, "You keep thinking that, little Jessi." *Hmpf. If you only knew how close you came to losing your fingertips, Zoe. Good thing we have good self-control.*

I thought shooting her would be a very easy thing to do. And I had a gun again.

We sat at the table, Si'neada pulling up a chair to join us and I punched in my food order with more force than was really necessary. Eating calmed me down, coffee woke me up and Si'neada directed the conversation onto the subject of Amorphan robes and styles and fabric choices.

Soli said, "I'm getting used to wearing these dresses," plucking at his robe while grinning. "I especially like going commando in these things. Or at least, my tailor hasn't made me any underwear." He winked at Si'neada who smiled at him much differently than he did Keaton and Mitchler, Si'neada's eyes softening when he looked at Soli. Hmmm. Soli was male-oriented and Si'neada was a two-fur. *I wonder if they're attracted to each other! That would be—interesting.*

But going commando? No underwear for the guys? Or for Zoe, probably, knowing her. I flashed upon an image of interesting male bulgy parts and then how things might waggle and wiggle under there and suddenly I was blushing at my thoughts. Zoe was giggling, saying in a coy way, "Well, you'll just have to guess if I'm wearing panties!" while she peeked at Keaton and Mitchler from below her lowered lashes. I noticed Keaton and Mitchler looking very intrigued at that comment as they both looked at her with intense interest. Yeah, I'm sure some doctor tweaked her hormones too much, too soon.

I hadn't given any thought to this at all, myself. I just threw on my own panties and bra every morning like usual and that was it. I don't think I'd gone commando since the day I was born and wasn't sure I wanted to try it out now. I did wonder about Zoe, though; did she or didn't she? And what did it feel like? Did she just skip the panties or the bra, also? Thank goodness our nannies weren't yet programmed to let us have our cycles.

Si'neada's voice intruded on these thoughts. "—and the males do not. What you to do is, of course, your choice as it is unlikely any will to look under your robes." Then he tapped me on the arm. "Now, Madame, let us to talk colors for you. Turquoise, I believe, you like?"

I nodded, bemused. "Yes, it's one of my favorite colors. Do the Amorphans wear that color?"

He clapped his hands. "Of course! They to have colors your eyes cannot even to perceive and all the ones you can, remember? But if you could, oh, the brilliance of hues would to dazzle you. This will be for your other set of formal robes for those auspicious occasions they will be sure to make you participate in to show you off, you to know."

That started a conversation about what colors might be like if we could only see them. It's hard to imagine other colors besides the ones we knew but Si'neada still claimed there were 12 primaries in other spectrums. At that pronouncement, he stood. "If you will to excuse us, Madame Jess and I have to do final fittings."

They nodded with Zoe rolling her eyes, sniping, "Of course you can leave, *Madame* Jess. I'd think as small as you are your clothing would've been done long ago as there's so little to work with." She then picked up her PD, very pointedly looking at it, and said, "You only have 20 minutes; we won't be able to hold class for you."

My hair twitched with the urge to sting her. "I may be small, Zoe, but I'm worth the extra care taken to fit me correctly. I'll be on time to class, you may be assured of that." I turned and strode away to prevent her from answering. Let her think what she would. Once we were on Amorpha, she would be half a world away and I wouldn't have to see her again.

My anger carried me into the hallway before I could release its hold on me, letting my shoulders drop. That woman could definitely irritate me to my flash point in a heartbeat. I didn't know then that I would be killing her tonight.

## CHAPTER SIXTEEN

Si'neada followed me into the corridor and I huffed out a breath. "Yeah, she goads me all right." I said through gritted teeth.

Si'neada laid a sympathetic hand on my arm. "We all to have those who can pull our whiskers."

"Yeah, I guess we do." I shook my head to clear my thoughts of Zoe. "So about this fitting?"

He winked at me and tapped my nose twice. "I have a special surprise for you today." :*There is no fitting, that is my excuse to take you away from the others.*:

:*Ooooo-kay, then, where are we really going? To the shooting range?*:

:*No. Not yet, that is for tonight. You are to meet one of the queens today; she wants to talk with you. But you must not speak of this to anyone out loud, ever.*:

I gawked at him. We were still in the Human area of the ship and a couple of Imurians in uniforms were strolling along the windowless corridor as it curved along. I could now understand every word of Imurian but they were murmuring to each other about some duty thing so I quit listening.

Si'neada said in a bit louder than usual voice, "I found material I had forgotten about to suit your skin to a nicety. Too bad you do not have stripes like us; I would have so much fun playing with patterns!"

The other two Imurians then noticed us and nodded hello. "Si'neada. Human."

Si'neada waved a languorous hand motion at them. "Officers."

I nodded in return to them, amused, as the taller one's whiskers said, 'Poor puny Humans without fur on skin. Must be cold all time! Dressing like Amorphan? So funny!'

Si'neada's whiskers twitched back a reply, 'Yes, very amusing. This one's hairies like fur. Oh! The fun making clothing not dull, dreary uniforms!'

"We must be on our way." The one on the left said. "Si'neada, I will to see you soon for a uniform fitting."

"Yes, yes, to make an appointment, please."

We continued down the hall without passing anyone else. After those two disappeared from sight, Si'neada motioned me through a different door than normal around the curve from my classroom.

:*What or who are the queens?*: I dared to ask with a mind whisper, touching his arm.

:*Fully grown adult female Imurians.*:

:*So why am I going to see one of the queens?*:

:*Remember first that no Human has ever met a queen, to my knowledge, by their choosing. That you have been requested to do so is an enormous honor. And I to ask of you, please, to show all courtesy toward her.*:

Okay, so I wasn't getting an answer to why. Wait and see, I guess.

:Does she have a name? And is there anything special I should know about manners?:

:She will divulge her name if she so chooses. Do not stare her in the eye as you Humans are wont to do, and when she looks at you, blink slowly to break your gaze apart to not appear combative.:

:Is that all?: I wondered if sarcasm came through in a mind whisper.

:Common manners will suffice for the rest. Bow your head when meeting her and let her direct the conversation.:

I nodded my head, thinking his advice over. :I can do that. Why me?:

:She will to explain.:

I shrugged and tilted my head at him. :Ok, I guess.: Goody, another adventure I couldn't discuss with anyone.

"We have arrived, my little star. Please to go in first." The door whispered open after a slight hesitation. I'd been so busy listening to his mind whispers and asking questions of my own that once again I hadn't paid attention to my surrounding. B'le'ru would be so disappointed in me, I realized, as I belatedly swept a glance around, seeing nothing but the same hallway as before, before I took a tentative step into the room onto the plush cushiony flooring. Patterns wove through with a fluidity that mimicked water, interspersed with reds, blues, yellows and other colors I couldn't discern. I felt if I took another step, I would sink and I was hesitant to move.

I looked up to see walls painted in soothing pastel hues with framed paintings spotted around the room. There were discreet lights in the ceiling, two doors in the walls leading elsewhere and a kitchen to my left. The light in the room was soft and inviting, lit enough to see everything but not too harsh to the eyes.

Ahead of me was a sitting area with backless burgundy chairs arranged in a semi-circle in front of a large lounging type of couch in a soft shade of gold. It had a back with a large gap between the upper and lower cushions, I supposed to let the tail go through. A low table, made of glass and metal, separated the couch from the chairs. Pillows with fancy weaving were scattered on the couch and each chair had one. I noted the pillow weavings were of fanciful creatures.

A female Imurian sat on the couch, the first any Human in transport had met, if Si'neada was correct. Dressed in a form-fitting lavender jumpsuit, over-sewn with sparkling stones in random placement, she gazed at me as I looked around. She sat with one foot tucked under her, the other foot bare on the floor with polished claws. Her arms draped out to either side of her onto pillows and her hands sported painted claws tipped with jewels. Her stripes, the ones I could see, anyway, were dyed different colors on her tawny fur, which looked to be groomed until she shone.

Her slit-pupiled bright green eyes watched me in amusement, ears forward out of curiosity, a small smile on her face. Her whiskers twitched at Si'neada as he nudged me in the back to move forward. *'Not much of her, is there?'* The queen said, "Please enter. You are welcome to enter my space."

I bowed and said, "Thank you for inviting me." As I straightened up, she beckoned me forward. Si'neada followed me, one hand on my low back to guide me.

"Your name?"

"Jessalya. But I go by Jess or Jessi."

She quirked an eyebrow. "You to prefer the shortened version?"

"Yes, I do. Jessalya is very formal and I like being informal."

"I think it is because you are small yourself and to need the shortened version of a long name." She chuckled, then she tilted her head and surveyed me again. I blinked slowly as her gaze went to my face and after she apparently had catalogued everything about me, she said, "Someone has taught her manners, I see. Well done, Si'neada."

"Come, Jess, and to sit here." She indicated the chair across from her. "Si'neada, please to get us something to drink. Jess, do you to prefer tea or coffee or something stronger?"

I replied, "Coffee, please, with lots of cream."

"Ah, yes, the cream. That is what makes coffee drinkable, yes?"

I smiled at her, keeping my teeth hidden. "I certainly think so."

"Do you know why you are here?"

"No, ma'am, I don't. Si'neada said you'd explain."

She steepled her fingers together and looked at me for a few minutes. I remained quiet, waiting for her to speak first. I started to squirm under that direct gaze but managed to stay still and not stare directly back. After a minute or so under that direct gaze, I heard a far-off voice but it was indistinct and I was unsure if it was outside my mind or in it. I almost put a finger in my ear to clear it from the noise when Si'neada delivered us each a mug of coffee, mine blonde with cream, hers also light with cream and his somewhere in between.

She took a sip of coffee, all the while gazing at me with an intense look, again making me want to fidget. I looked back, but remembered to blink slowly and look away now and then, like Si'neada had coached me. The far-off buzz was becoming closer and I cocked my head to one side, trying to hear it better. The words were garbled as if I could almost, but not quite, understand them.

Then, with sudden clarity, I heard words inside my head, making me jump and spilling a little coffee on my lap. :*Jessalya, do you hear this? Jessalya…oh, there you are. It's about time, kitling! Si'neada, I have found her frequency.*:

:*How delightful! I believe she has more than one, though.*:

:*Yes, you are correct. She needs training and an inner shield for her thoughts.*:

I raised my hand. "Um…I'm right here, you know." Their eyes swiveled to me and my face flushed. "What do you mean, I have more than one? And shields?"

Si'neada settled next to me on the couch. "Shields, my little mind whisperer, to help to keep your thoughts confined to yourself and not to broadcast to anyone who can to receive. We each to think in a different frequency, like radio waves, you understand?"

I shook my head.

"How many radio stations can you to listen to at a time?"

"One."

"You see? You can only hear or send thoughts on one frequency at a time."

"Oooooh-kay. I guess that makes sense."

"Mind whispering is not universal for us but not uncommon. For Humans, it is very rare indeed and even more rare that a Human can hear or send on more than one frequency. Which you can." He flicked my nose with a soft touch. "You are lucky no one other than me has heard you. I, too, have the rare trait of hearing and sending on many frequencies."

I looked back and forth between them, clutching my coffee cup like a lifeline.

The queen chimed in, "Yes, you would have been found in your night time trips if the guards had heard your thoughts."

My mouth dropped open. "I—that wasn't me. We're forbidden to leave our section without an escort at any time!" *How does she know about those? I was very careful!*

:*Yes, you were very careful and clever. But little happens on this ship I do not to know about.*: She smiled at me, showing the tips of her fangs. I'm certain I turned an ugly shade of red. Sweat popped out on my forehead and on my back and I clenched my hands together in my lap to keep them from trembling.

:*No need for discomfort, little one. We are not telling. We to admire your audacity.*: Si'neada patted me on the back.

"How did you know?" There was no use denying it any more. Then, realization dawned. "Oh. Of course. You just heard me confirm it, didn't you?"

Si'neada and the queen—she hadn't told me her name yet—looked at each other and her whiskers said, 'Set up training time. She must have shields. Today.' I caught my thought before it formed and unraveled it into something else, like worry about being late for class, so they wouldn't know I'd understood their whisker talk. A girl had to have *some* secrets, after all.

"Only we to know and no one else will to find out. You will to have lunch with me today so I can teach you this shielding. There is no danger of anyone in your classroom reading inside your head or receiving your thoughts so it can wait until then." Si'neada again patted me in reassurance.

Nonplused, I nodded. "Okay." I agreed in a faint tone. "Lunch today, then." Then I held up a finger. "How do you know the others aren't receiving or sending?"

He quirked an eyebrow at me. "Have they yet?"

"Uh. Not that I know about."

He spread his hands apart, raising his eyebrows. "So, my little coffee cup, I am right?" He flashed a toothy smile at me.

The queen rose smoothly to her feet and stepped over to me, swatting Si'neada on the shoulder. "Enough of that." She placed her hands on the outside of my shoulders, bending in toward me, concern in her leaf-green eyes, "Continue your protection lessons and to heed them well. There are those who to wish you harm, or at the least, to want your blood. You can trust Si'neada and B'le'ru but be careful of others." She stepped back and bowed to me with a small gesture. "Thank you for your time, Jessalya. Until we meet again."

She pivoted and strode out of the room through one of the doors. I stared after her until Si'neada's hand on my arm startled me. "We must to go, my little confidant; it is time to return to your class."

## CHAPTER SEVENTEEN

We sauntered down the hallway the few doors to my classroom. My head was spinning from the encounter earlier and confused about our conversation. How had the Queen known about my night time excursions? She knew before I inadvertently confirmed them. I had to wonder if any of the other students had been called to the queen's quarters but I couldn't ask. I had, after all, promised not to discuss the visit with anyone. Si'neada voice whispered into my head. :*Remember the gallery at 10:00 ship time tonight. And of course, you will to have lunch with me this noon.*:

I groaned. That's the last thing I wanted to do. I wanted to sleep for the next two years, as wrung out as I felt. Instead, I nodded and yawned. "Looking forward to it, I'm sure." *Do Imurians recognize sarcasm?*

Si'neada rolled his eyes. "Yes, I am sure you are, my little pincushion. Not." I cocked my head at him as I poked his shoulder with my finger, like a pincushion would do. *Apparently you do recognize sarcasm.*

:*Of course we do. Yes, you really do to need those shields.*:

I made a face at him, sticking out my tongue before stepping into the classroom where the other four were, thinking about the queen telling me I was in danger, and if not my life, at least my blood was sought after. What was it about my blood that made it desirable? I mean, my nanny system was provided by the government and developed by the Imurians, so it couldn't be those; there had to be something else about my blood, but I couldn't imagine what it was. I really wished I could ask my classmates if they had any special abilities but if they did, they'd keep it secret, too.

The memory of changing bodies in my dream last night came forward. Wouldn't it be totally cool if I really could change shape to anything I wanted—I mean, really totally change my body, not just my hair camouflaging me? Oh, well, anything can happen in dreams, after all.

NOT DREAM.

*Yeah, right.*

Shifting my shape would be interesting, within reason, of course; I mean I didn't want to become an insect or anything nasty like that. Wouldn't there be size limitations? How small or large could a shape-shifter go, anyway? How would one communicate if in a different form that couldn't form words? My head spun to think of it; it was way too complicated to figure out the nuances, but it didn't matter. No one knew the answers because being a shifter was all fantasy movie stuff. The Amorphans came the closest as they could manipulate their boneless hands and feet to become other shapes on a temporary basis but they still stayed an Amorphan in every other way.

"Talk to yourself much?" Zoe inquired in a sugary tone.

I blinked as I looked up. I'd been concentrating so hard on my thoughts I hadn't realized they were looking at me. I must've been moving my lips as I went to my chair, a habit my mother had forever tried to break me of doing. The irony was she did it, too, and yeah, it looked funny. Not ha-ha funny, weird funny.

"Uh, sorry. I was worrying about being late."

"That's not what it looked like you were saying."

"What, you can read lips now, Zoe? A new talent for you?" I bowed my head to Tatro and switched to Amorphan. "My apologetics, er, apologies," my translator supplying the correct word, "if I'm late."

"Not to worry, Jessi; we were only now ready to start."

Keaton gave me a thumbs up and Zoe sniffed as she looked down her nose at me. Whatever. I made a small face at her. "Told you I wouldn't be late." *Nyah, nyah, nyah. So there.*

I was relieved to get to my room that night after dinner. The concentration and hours involved daily were intense, to say the least, and after 12 hours of continuous companionship with my four classmates, I yearned for time alone so returned to my own quarters after dinner time each night. At first, I'd turn on holograms of New Eden, of the forests and trees, and animals. Sometimes I'd put on a beach scene. After a while I realized it only sharpened my homesickness so I switched around to scenes from other worlds, giving me a chance to experience strange fauna and flora along with Amorphan topography every day to familiarize myself with my upcoming world. It also gave me a chance to rest a bit before going to the shooting gallery. As I entered my quarters, I wondered if I would see or talk with Deester or if he, too, was a figment of my imagination. That made me think of Devon and the unusual twists to his body I'd seen from my mother's memories. Had his body tried to become a shape-shifter? Is that why he died? But if so, since my parents are undisputedly Human, how? Who did this to him? And by inference, perhaps to me. I ground my teeth. My parents hadn't had any luck in finding out answers any more than I was, although at least I had found out about Akrion. Just thinking about it gave me an odd pang in my chest and a fuzzy yearning to return. But return to what or where? Ever since the night I felt like the void outside the viewing window would suck me through, I'd avoided the deck like it was a plague. It had felt like the stars themselves and the spaces between were calling to me to join them. I pushed away the fear it inspired in me and refocused my thoughts on Devon.

I'd obviously never known my brother as he died before I was born. I'd heard stories about him and felt like I knew him to a degree, like a ghost that doesn't know how to disappear. I'd often felt like I was a poor substitute for him, although to give Mom and Dad credit, they never said anything like that, being always supportive of me. His presence, however, always hovered around my parents, in the lines of grief etched into their faces and the way Mom would touch a photo of Devon now and again with softness and love. She often wiped a tear away and then, shaking her head, would turn to me and say in a bright voice, "Ok, Jessi, let's get something done." I hated the look of sorrow in their eyes and yearned for a way to fix it.

*It's only fear, Jessi; they are only memories and no matter what, I know Mom and Dad do love me. Stop dreading and start doing.*

ABOUT TIME.

Hair can be snarky? *Oh, shut up.*

One strand of hair nicked at my arm in disapproval. *Stop that!*

*Exchanger*

Chiming rang out, sounding urgent.

I stepped into my sitting area. "Room? What is that sound?"

"Your requested alarm, Madame. You are overdue for bed."

I rubbed my eyes, mascara be damned. "Oh. Thanks. I'll get to it, then. You can turn off the sound."

I returned to my bedroom after turning out all the lights and put on my soft-soled shoes for my nightly trek to the gallery. My hair did its things to the alarm system and I crept down the hall to the appropriate door when it was time and I whisked through as soon as it opened, Si'neada giving me a two-fingered wave to say hello as we made our way to the range. "Where's B'le'ru?" I whispered.

He waved a hand. "Oh, he is preparing your lesson so I came to let you in tonight."

I nodded. We arrived at the range, stepping through the sound proof door to greet B'le'ru who was squinting down the gallery at some targets. "Need glasses, B'le'ru?" I inquired sweetly.

He glared at me. "No, Jess, I do not."

I grinned at him and then thought I'd better not poke too much fun at him; after all, he made up these lessons and I didn't need them any harder than usual. He bared his teeth at me and then said, "Tonight we to have a surprise for you."

"Really? What kind of surprise?"

Si'neada clapped his hands. "Oh, a lovely surprise, my little warrior-ette!"

I wrinkled my nose in puzzlement and glanced between them, looking for clues. "A good surprise??"

"Yes!" He exclaimed. "We have arranged—well, you will to see when you to go through that door over there! We will be a few minutes more out here so you to go in without us. Have fun!"

"But what about target practice?"

B'le'ru waved a dismissive hand. "Not to worry right now. After you have fun, then you will come here to finish."

Puzzled by this break in routine and not sure why they would send me ahead without them, I frowned at them. What were they going to do out here they didn't want me to know about? My mouth twitched. Ok, B'le'ru was probably setting up his most diabolical set of targets yet and didn't want me peeking.

I thought hard at Si'neada. :*What aren't you telling me?*:

Si'neada only smiled and flapped a hand at me. "Go on, my precious kitling! You will to have fun but you have to go in there to do so!"

I gave him a suspicious look but he grinned wider and shooed me toward the gray door inset into the wall at the far end of the gallery. I'd never noticed a door there before but then, we'd really never been away from this area.

I shrugged. "Ok, ok, I'll go."

B'le'ru held up a hand to stop my movement. "Your weapon, Jess?"

I tapped my chest. "Here."

He held out his hand so I pulled it out, checking to make sure the safety was on before handing it over. He inspected it, then nodded in approval. "Good. You have learned well."

I walked down the long stretch between the nondescript wall to my left and the shooting cubicles to my right. When I reached the door, I pushed it open and stepped through into the gaiety of a party, the door shutting behind me, noise, laughter and chattering swirling around me.

I looked around in amazement. The room was decorated with banners reading, "Congratulations, Students, on being the First Exchangers to Amorpha!" Balloons *(where the heck did they get balloons?)* were clustered around tables with our names printed on them; I tapped one and it swayed away from me. My current favorite song, "Till the Woman Laughs" played at a loud volume. The walls were festooned with yellow cloth falling in folds from ceiling to floor and I wondered how it was attached.

Zoe yelled, "Here she is! Short stuff herself has arrived! We have a short drink for you, Jessi Little!" She bared her teeth in my direction, flipping her hair over her shoulders, placing a proprietary hand on Keaton's arm, who glanced down at it, shrugged and winked at me with a quirk of his eyebrows. Then Keaton, Mitchler and Soli all saluted me with the drink in their hands. I waved at them and a serving tray was thrust in front of me with beverages. I picked one up and took a swallow. I was totally bewildered by all this; I thought my lessons were secret and I had kept them that way. I guess they were in on the secret, too, but why was I the only one who didn't know?

I took another gulp of the drink, feeling a little dizzy from it. Had they actually used alcohol in it? I was pretty sure the Imurians wouldn't allow alcohol, but whatever, it was delicious. I moved toward my classmates and when I got close enough, Keaton shook off Zoe's hand and draped an arm over my shoulders for a hug. The problem, I've found through experience, is that when a tall person does that to a small someone—me—they inadvertently lean, like I'm a crutch designed to hold them up. He squeezed my shoulder, saying, "Ah, little Jess! You are so cute, you know, being so little and with your gorgeous long curly hair and those killer blue eyes. I just want to scoop you up and put you in my pocket!"

Zoe narrowed her eyes at Keaton with displeasure and I wrinkled my nose at her for a change. Nice to be appreciated for my size and making her jealous was a big bonus. Although there was that time I'd caught her leaving Keaton's room with disheveled hair while she was smoothing out her robes. I'd wondered just how much they'd been involved in things that I still didn't know enough about but it was, after all, their business, not mine. Just because Keaton made my heart speed up was beside the point. I wasn't ready for a relationship yet, especially a ship fling that would end as quickly as it started. Mom's comment about toilet paper always flitted through my mind and that worked to dampen any attraction. I didn't know Keaton well enough to know if he could be a future permanent relationship or not but I did know with Zoe around, I probably wasn't going to find out, anyway.

Soli touched my arm. "Welcome to the party, Jess! We hope you're as surprised by it as we were."

I was certainly surprised, all right, especially at all the words Soli had used as he seldom spoke more than a short sentence at a time. I frowned at him with a questioning look. "I didn't know you guys were having lessons, too? I thought I was the only one, so, yeah, I'm pretty much shocked." I lifted my glass to my lips only to find it empty, so I set it on a nearby table.

He grinned. "B'le'ru said there would be one big party when the last of us was ready and trained. I guess you're last."

Zoe said in a nasty tone, "Of course she's last. It's hard to keep up when you have a miniature body."

That did it; I was sick and tired of her harping about my shortness so I rounded on her, clenching my fists at my side. "Zoe, why are you always going on about how small I am? Afraid I'm cuter than you, is that it? Or are you tired of always being eye-to-eye with the guys? I can't help being short! And the Heavens above knows the doctors tried hard enough with all the medical stuff to make me tall, and it wasn't pleasant, let me tell you! Actually, the treatments hurt, and they hurt a *lot*." I took a step toward her, gritting my teeth against the swelling noise of the music.

She gave me a narrow-eyed look and then said, "Huh? What was that you said, Jess? I can't hear you way down there." Then she laughed.

My hair fell over my shoulders like a restraint. I wasn't cooperating, though; I had an itch I was determined to scratch with Zoe's nose on the end of my fist, and if I couldn't reach her nose, then it would be whatever I could find. I was more than ready to put my Cat-Fighting skills to use on her.

"I wanted to be friends, Zoe! You and I are the only two Human females for a trillion light-years and I thought we could overcome our differences but you won't let it go. For whatever reason, my size is stuck in your throat and YOU. WON'T. LET. IT. GO. Well, no more MISS NICE GIRL here! I've had it with you." And I threw a punch at her smirking face, although to my chagrin, she leaned back and I missed.

The boys stepped back with haste, although I caught the words, "Kitten Fight!" as they moved. Zoe bared her teeth at me and crouched in a defensive but aggressive stance.

"Bring it on, little girl, bring it on!" She snarled with her fists up. Her eyes were locked on mine, as we were taught in our self-defense classes, and then she rocked forward, swiping at me. I felt something catch in the sleeve of my robe and, with a start, realized she had a knife hidden in her hand. A sharp one, too, by the easy parting of the material. She flared her nostrils and growled, "I'm going to kill you, Jessalya Lilianthal, as I should've done many years ago."

I was shocked by the words. She couldn't mean that for real; it was just an expression…right? But then she lunged while I was distracted and again the knife in her right hand came at me, this time for my throat. I grabbed her hand with my left one, a part of me wondering why the guys weren't interfering, but I didn't have time to figure that out. She was, after all, taller and stronger than me and if I didn't do something right now, I was going to end up bleeding on the floor. Was there something in the drinks that made us do this? I felt a hank of hair move into the front of my robe and pluck my shooter from my bra, slapping it into my right hand. I shoved it against her left temple while straining to keep the knife in her right hand from cutting me and panted, "Enough, Zoe! No one is going to kill anyone here tonight!"

She froze in place for a second and I thought we were done. As my grip on her wrist eased for a split second, she lunged at me again with the blade fully out and exposed. I didn't realize my hair was wrapped around my fingers as it held the gun and we—my hair and myself—pulled the trigger at point blank range.

## CHAPTER EIGHTEEN

The explosion of blood and brain from her head rocked me back. Horrified, I tried to shake the gun from my hand as I scrambled back but my hair wouldn't allow me to let go. I screamed, "I didn't mean to do that! I didn't want to shoot her, oh, shit, I'm so sorry! We need the Imurians in here; they can fix her—somebody call for help!"

Instead, I felt the barrel of a shooter against my own temple and Keaton snarled, "Murderer! She didn't have a weapon." My hair hardened under the muzzle and I wondered if my hair was bullet proof. I didn't want to find out.

"She had a knife and she was trying to cut my throat!"

"We didn't see a knife and we can't let you out of here. We'll take care of this ourselves."

I felt the tiniest vibration from his weapon as he started to activate it and my gun hand whipped up and around to shoot him in the face. As he fell to the floor, the others yelled and pulled their shooters out and I ended up shooting all of them into a heap. I started sobbing, clutching my free hand over my mouth. How did this come to be? What had gone wrong? Why had this happened?

Then a hidden door opened, and our three Amorphan teachers came in, chattering and laughing. "We're here to join the fun!" Then a dead pause as they took in the carnage as they came to an abrupt stop, pulled weapons and aimed them at me. "Murderer! We knew there was something off about you, Jessalya!" As they leveled their shooters at me, my hair-covered hand rose and I shot them before they could shoot me. I didn't even think about it; I reacted and it was deadly. B'le'ru had trained me too well.

Stunned by my own actions, I fell onto my knees on the floor, tears pouring down my face, then sitting back on my butt while clutching my knees to my chest. Blubbering, I rocked back and forth, "I didn't mean to! I didn't want to! I didn't mean to!" I'd had such a good life but now I would be executed or worse, be in prison for the rest of my long life. How could this have happened to me? I was crying so hard I started to retch although nothing came up.

A torrent of feelings crashed through me: guilt, horror, rage, pity, overwhelming sadness, more rage, a tsunami of guilt. The wheel kept turning and spinning off more and more emotions and I didn't know how to stop it or come to terms with what I had done. I wanted to hack my hair off to the roots and gave a split second's thought to grabbing Zoe's knife to do so. Then out of nowhere I sensed a presence standing over me. I couldn't open my eyes to look, I couldn't kill another person, I couldn't stop crying. Let them shoot me. Please.

"Jessi, my little kitling, to look at me." I heard Si'neada's gentle voice. I shook my head and continued rocking back and forth. "Jessi, my Human friend, to look at me, please."

"I can't, look at what I've done, my hair did it, I—I can't." I whimpered. I knew I wasn't making sense but it was all I could sputter out.

:*Jessalya, look at me now!*:

The sharp words bit into my brain and startled, I glanced up at him through swollen wet eyes, then my mouth dropped open. The room was empty.

"But—but, where are the bodies? I shot them all—I SHOT THEM ALL! Don't you understand, I shot them, I didn't give them a chance, I just SHOT THEM!" I sobbed.

"How did you get all this cleaned up so fast? They need funerals; it was self-defense, I swear!" My hair finally let my hand release my shooter and it was—somehow—tucked back in my bra.

Si'neada laid a soft hand on top of my hair and smoothed it back. He looked at me with compassion. I saw B'le'ru standing behind him looking at me with what seemed to be gruff respect.

"Jess, it was not real. Look around; they are all gone. It was a test and you passed. They were all real-D holograms. It is how we to test our soldiers. If you can to kill people you know and like, then you are ready to defend yourself truly."

"It was real! I felt them! I drank from a real glass! I *saw* them die!" And yet the room was now empty, all decorations gone and clean, oh, so very clean.

"Our technology is far beyond what you Humans know. We can to make it very real indeed."

"Oh, my shattered nerves. It's not real." I whispered. "It's not real." Then a flare of pure rage tore through me. "YOU MADE ME THINK IT WAS REAL! How could you do that to me? How am I to live with knowing I can kill people I know!" I shoved his hand off my head, glaring at him, hands fisted, ready to swing a punch as I stood.

"What kind of friend does this? What kind of teacher?"

B'le'ru strode forward. "Madame Jessalya, this is how we to test those being trained. You will to know what you are capable of doing to protect yourself. And you to need the protection. The truth is you will never need to shoot someone you know." He paused. "Probably."

"I want to go back to my room. Now. Please." I was still shuddering from the aftermath of reaction and adrenaline. "Do my classmates know about this?"

B'le'ru replied, "No, they do not to know about your lessons. They are very capable at other forms of self-defense."

I shook my head. I was furious with them for putting me through this emotional and physical upheaval. Si'neada said, "Let me to give you a squeeze, Jessi, to make you feel better."

"A hug, you mean? I'm not ready to forgive either one of you, much less give you a hug! Do *not* touch me." I said through gritted teeth as I scowled at them both. I looked around the room again; there was no sign of carnage, just a bare, metal walled room.

Weakness then hit me like an avalanche. My knees started trembling and I felt like I didn't have the strength to breath. "I need to go to bed. Now." I started walking on wobbly legs toward the door, suddenly grateful for Si'neada's hand under one elbow and B'le'ru's under the other. "I need sleep and to—to process all this. Maybe tomorrow I'll appreciate passing this test."

Wisely, they said nothing more as they escorted me to my room, making sure I made it safely through my door. I shucked off my clothes, crawled in bed, and clutching a pillow, sobbed myself to sleep.

## CHAPTER NINETEEN

When Room chimed me awake the next morning, I felt like a piece of flotsam washed up on a shore somewhere. I wanted to stay in bed, which was becoming a thing, but today was still a class day and Room was very insistent about me getting up. I wondered how long it had been yammering at me. All of a sudden, I was hungry, I could smell coffee and that galvanized me to action. After getting ready, I walked into the kitchen for my first cup of coffee and memories of last night swept in. I set my cup down untasted.

I still didn't know if last night had been real or not since I'd not seen anyone yet to know if they were really alive. It didn't make sense I could've killed them all or that they were even in that room threatening to kill me. No way I'd have been released so easily from the scene if I'd really murdered all those people. I shuddered. It still felt real and I was angry and upset over the test. I finally picked up my cup and started sipping it, the rich creamy flavor starting to soothe me and I thought I'd be able to face the day after all.

I hesitated as I reached for the door opener. What if it had all been real? I stepped out in the corridor as Keaton was leaving his room. "Hey, Jessi! Good morning! Count down is on; not much time left on this barge until we become Amorphans. Where has the time gone, eh?"

I managed to smile at him. He was so cute; the physical classes had certainly improved his already yummy body and I enjoyed looking at him and I suddenly yearned to be in his arms for comfort. I was so relieved he was alive I couldn't speak for a second as I was having trouble reconciling his cheerful face and voice to the carnage last night.

"Jess? You okay?"

"Uh, yeah, yeah, sorry, still a little sleepy. And I've only had one cup of coffee so far, you know?"

He came beside me and lightly punched me on the upper arm. "This is all becoming so real." He looked down at himself with a wry smile. "And I'm actually getting used to wearing dresses." He rolled his eyes and then winked at me.

"And you look so good in them, too." I chirped. *Ah, jeez, was I flirting with him? Better not let Zoe catch me doing that!* "Nothing like a little something swirly to feel masculine, right?"

He snorted. "Yeah, right. Ah, well, there is freedom under here and that is something." Again he winked at me; I felt heat rising from my face as I turned bright red.

I stammered, "Yeah, us girls, well, uh, you're not a girl, but this girl, anyway, loves being able to wear these swirly robes and all these colors. They are comfortable but the straps aren't all that freeing, I don't think. Anyway, the colors alone…" I was babbling, I realized, so I shut my mouth.

He made a face. "Yeah, the colors. Never thought I'd see the day I'd be wearing a rainbow."

That startled a laugh from me. "Really? A rainbow?"

"Yeah, this morning when I put this on." He grinned. He put a warm hand between my shoulder blades, giving me a shiver. He swept his other arm through the air, saying, "After you, Madame Jess."

He kept his hand on my back as we caught up to the other three and I saw Zoe cataloging everything. When we arrived at our table, he pulled out a chair for me, sitting next to me. Zoe looked across at us and said, "Well, aren't we cozy this morning?"

I blushed again, like I had anything to blush about. Keaton smiled at her and said, "It is a cozy type of morning. We only have a couple of mornings left, and I want to make it the best time left."

"Hmph." Zoe sniffed, putting her nose a little into the air, curling a lip while looking at me with a clear message of "he's mine and hands off, squirt."

I opened my mouth to retort but at the same instance realized there was nothing I could say. If I tried to deny, she would only believe we did something together all the more. If I explained, she still wouldn't believe me, thinking I was trying to cover up something. Better to let her think what she would because when it came to me, she would think the worst anyway. Keaton and I both knew the truth and that had to be enough. The truth was, of course, that Keaton made my heart go pitter-patter a bit more than was comfortable, especially with such a short time remaining. Looking at him definitely brought up new feelings that I wasn't yet sure how to handle.

I made my breakfast choices, the closest thing to a pancake the Amorphans had, some fruit I'd grown quite fond of, and eggs. I ate every bite even though my mind kept dodging back to the massacre last night. I reminded myself—again—they were all alive and sitting right there with me at that moment, eating, chatting and laughing.

I suspected what really upset me the most was the fact I had shot people I knew. I'd believed they were real and yet I pulled the trigger. Granted, my hair had a lot to do with that, as it kept my finger on the trigger, shooting, and it all happened so fast, I couldn't override its decision, but I regretted it, feeling guilty and slimy about it.

Soli said, "Starfinder to Jessi! Come in, Jessi! We've been talking to you like forever."

I blinked, startled. "Uh, sorry. What are you talking about?"

"I'll bet I know what you were thinking about." Raising her eyebrows, Zoe threw a sly glance at Keaton. I gritted my teeth, then lied, "I was *thinking* about our classes today. Are you all as tired as I am? 12 hours every day…I'm exhausted."

"Yeah," Keaton said, "I'm pretty worn out, too. At least there's not much more time and then life can become normal." He barked a laugh. "Well, as normal as it will be to be an alien on Amorpha."

Zoe flipped her hair back. "I'm not tired. With my dance classes and everything else, I was in really good shape to start with and now I'm in even better form."

"And your form *is* good." Mitchler leered at her with a grin and a wink, raising his eyebrows up and down.

She looked smug and pleased, smoothing the robe down her sides and giving him a flirty look. No wonder I felt like a broom next to her, useful in some ways but no shape at all.

She quirked an eyebrow at him, saying, "Aw, thanks. I'm glad you noticed."

Keaton said, "Oh, we've all noticed, Zoe." I wasn't sure if he was admiring her or admonishing her, but I would vote for admonish.

His foot nudged against mine under the table and I pretended I didn't know it was there even as I hoped his foot would stay.

A group of Imurian officers strode through the door and walked near our table. They weren't anyone I'd seen before and judging by everyone else's puzzlement, they hadn't either. The leading male halted, looking around at us, and then abruptly said, "You are the Human Amorphans?"

I felt the blood leave my face. That was the same voice as the officer who had accosted B'le'ru in the corridor while I hid behind him. Well, now I had a face to go with the voice but who was he? From the deference of the other two Imurians with him, he was somebody higher up on the food chain.

We all nodded. I almost said, "Duh." but I felt his razor-like gaze pin me into the chair like a bug on a board. I was afraid to move, to attract more attention. His gaze slid over us and then stopped on Zoe. He inhaled a breath, slowly and carefully as if he were testing our scents.

He stared at Zoe. "Come with me, Madame."

She narrowed her eyes and said, "Where are we going and why?" She looked at him with a steady gaze but I could see by how she clenched her hands together to keep them from shaking that she was scared.

Fury flitted over the officer's face, at least to my eyes, and his whiskers twitched with words I apparently didn't know yet. Were they swear words, I wondered? Did the Imurians have swear words? The two with him startled, but kept their gaze up and away from us. One looked like he wanted to intervene but didn't dare do so.

He tapped a claw-tipped finger against his lips, glaring at her. He said, "She will to come with you," pointing at me. Me?

Why me? I didn't want to stand, wasn't sure I could stand, with my legs feeling like rubber. I wished B'le'ru or Si'neada would appear and explain this.

As if on cue, B'le'ru came from the other side of the dining room. I hadn't realized he was anywhere near so seeing him was both a surprise and a huge relief. He came over with a furrowed brow. "Sir?" He made a very slight bow. "May I inquire what this is about? These students to need to go to class now. Is there an emergency?" His voice was deferential, his ears slightly back in puzzlement, with the tip of his tail twitching ever so little. His whiskers weren't saying anything at all, unlike my hair, which felt a knife edge away from protection or violence or something.

"This is not your concern." The officer snarled at him.

B'le'ru stood his ground. "I beg your pardon, Sir, but these students are my responsibility and I am to be involved in all things in their concern. Those are my orders from Captain Lar'nou'te."

Fury washed across the officer's face as he realized he couldn't demand anything more. "Very well," he said in a stiff voice. "I will to arrange something later with the Captain."

B'le'ru asked, eyes lowered a little from the higher-ranking officer's eyes, "Do you have questions for the student Humans, Sir? Perhaps they can be asked here?"

The officer crossed his arms over his chest, obviously thinking this over. "No. No questions here. I was only curious about their thoughts about their journey on the StarFinder. I thought perhaps to interview them." The look in his eye said otherwise, especially when he looked at Zoe. Then he turned his eyes on me. He tilted his head at me and regarded me with a steady stare. I blinked slowly at him to show I was not a threat and did my best to look innocent while I fought the urge to run and hide someplace far, far away.

B'le'ru gestured. "Perhaps later, Sir? They are all free after their dinner time for an hour."

"Later would be acceptable," he finally said. "B'le'ru, when their classes are over today, you will to notify me." He shrugged, a surprising show of nonchalance in his military stance. "If I have time, I will to interview them then. If not, it can wait."

B'le'ru bowed his head. "Yes, Sir." The two other officers looked immensely relieved.

The officer gave a curt nod, spun on one heel, and strode back out the door, his two companions trailing behind. B'le'ru watched him disappear before he relaxed. Keaton asked, "What the heck was that all about?"

B'le'ru shook his head. "I am not sure but I will use today to find out." He furrowed his brow slightly. "Perhaps it is only an interview."

## CHAPTER TWENTY

I hid my trembling hands in my lap and waited for my heart rate to slow down. I didn't know if the others were as shaken as I was, but I knew that officer was bad news. What could he possibly want to ask us about? My shooting range time? My meeting with the queen? What was his interest in Zoe? Was he really going to interview us, all of us, or just us two women? I remembered what he'd said about mounting Human females, willing or not and thought we'd better come up with a reason not to be alone with him. We'd already stood our ground on that but he could possibly override orders.

I had a day of classes to get through and I didn't want the distraction, to be honest, but there it was. It was going to be the elephant in the room all day. Which made me wonder, again, if elephants were even real? I'd seen photos but those could be faked, of course. Why would they have been in a room? They seemed kind of big to be brought into someone's house. I rolled my eyes at myself; there was no answer to that question and really, it didn't matter. It was only a saying, one I had learned from my Mom who loved those old archaic sayings.

B'le'ru said in a soft voice, "I will to escort you all to your classroom now. Please do not to worry about this; I will to find out more and will to arrange to be with you for any possible interviews. For now, there is nothing to worry about."

"Easy for you to say," I muttered under my breath but Zoe heard me and I'm sure B'le'ru did, too.

His whiskers twitched. *Kitlings.*

Zoe said, "I have *no* idea what that was all about; I'm sure *I've* done nothing wrong." She gave me a squinty-eyed look. "What about you, Jessi? Have you done something wrong?"

"No!" I huffed. "No, I haven't." I glared back at her as we all moved toward the door as a group.

Tatro Aelotra stood at the front of the class room, waiting for us to bow our greetings to him. After we gave him our proper respect, he said, "Good morning, Amorphans in the making!" He waved his hands in a flapping manner, which meant he was pleased about something. It really showcased how boneless their fingers were which was rather disturbing but I was getting used to it. My stomach only lurched a little bit.

"Today I am pleased to tell you all are making exceptional progress toward integrating well into our society. The next hours will be a lot of drilling in language and manners. You will now live as Amorphans all day and night. You are to be robed at all times as is appropriate for your status, you will eat and drink only from our menu and you will, in your leisure time, do only Amorphan games, literature, movies and similar things. You will be prepared to assimilate quickly when we arrive!"

I raised a hand. "Tatro, what about our one Human luxury we're allowed?"

He said, "Oh, yes, that. Yes, of course, you can have that daily but you must otherwise be one of us in all ways possible." He then chuckled; I think it was a chuckle. It was a sound we hadn't heard from him before. "Except we know you cannot transform your hands and feet into other things, so in that, you cannot be like us! That is our special ability, developed over millennia to allow us to survive in all circumstances." He beamed at us. "If I could teach you to do so, I would, but that isn't possible."

I felt my fingers twitch in response and they almost felt like they would dissolve into another shape, even without my hair helping. *No, I cannot change shape! Even if I could change shape—which I can't—now's not the time.* Frantic at the thought, I clasped my fingers together to underline the point. I quickly looked around to see if anyone had noticed my dilemma but no one was looking. I eased the pressure the tiniest bit from my fingers and looked; thank the beasts of the woods they were still mine and still Human.

Tatro said, "Now! Let's commence conversation! Jess, since you are most proficient, I want you to start the discussion of the book "Politeness Dos and Do Nots". You have read this text, yes?"

"Yes, Tatro, I have read it." I replied in Amorphan. "I find it especially interesting in the chapter about eating precedence and preferences in the school dining hall. Perhaps you can take us through the proper protocol for going through the line and how to choose what to eat? The book does not discuss this."

Tatro said, "Yes, we will practice going through the line, how to choose what is good. Oh, how to pay! That would be excellent practice for when you are at classes away from home."

He turned to Zoe. "Please ask a question or make a comment

about the book, "The World Beyond Home"; for instance, please discuss the plot in one or two sentences."

Zoe replied, "Sure." She bowed her head slightly. "Oops, that's not Amorphan, my apologies." She paused, then restarted in our new language. "The book is about a young male who sets out on an adventure because he is bored with learning in classes and wants to experience life itself. He runs into danger, finds friends, makes enemies, and ultimately finds that what he seeks has been what he has had all along. He returns home, safe, happy and ready to assume his adult life."

"Wow, I am impressed, Zoe," Keaton commented. "You really did read that book." A smug smile was his answer.

"I'm not just a dumb dancer, you know. I actually like to read and the book was well written, except for the parts that were beyond my vocabulary. I had to look up a few words—"

Tatro barked, "All conversations to be in Amorphan, please!" Oops. We had lapsed back into Standard without thinking.

Zoe cut me a dirty look like it was my fault she was speaking Standard. I made a face at her—after she'd turned away, of course. She was like a sniper; she had a talent for saying cutting things to me phrased in such a way there was no rebuttal or giving me looks to which there was no defense. Was that a learned behavior, I wondered, or something she did naturally? Whatever it was, I didn't have that knack.

Tatro turned to Soli. "Soli, tell me what you think of the book."

He grunted. "I did not read much past chapter two. I did not care for the book." He clenched his hands together. "I apologize."

"You are a fine young male, Soli Dawson, no need to say sorry if you did not like the book. Honesty is good." I reached over, patting Soli's hand in reassurance; hopefully, he'd know we didn't care he hadn't read the book.

That sudden silence filled the room where all talking ceases at once. Mitchler, Zoe and Keaton stared at us and Soli's face became red as did mine, feeling heat creep up my neck and over my face. My hair twitched restlessly as if to cover me from my embarrassment but it knew better than to do so in public.

Tatro stepped back, looking a little flustered himself. "All right! You now will be able to leave for your middle day meal!" He flapped his hands, which made that odd, whistling sort of sound and then said, "Now go! It is time to eat."

We walked as a group into the hallway where Zoe raised an eyebrow. "Why were the two of you blushing so hard? What's between you and Soli? What was that about being honest?" She poked Soli's arm, causing him to set his lips in a grim line.

He gritted out, "Nothing like you think, Zoe. We were only discussing the book." He took in a breath and then said in Amorphan. "And we speak in Amorphan, yes?"

Zoe tossed her hair back with a quick movement of her head. "Oh, that. They're not here so I think we can speak in Standard."

Keaton said, "Zoe, I think we better use Amorphan; remember, they can monitor us almost anywhere." His command of the language was pretty good, almost as good as mine. He pointed upwards with a discreet motion of his finger and his eyes darted around the room.

I interjected, hoping to get a Zoe zinger out first, "Yeah, Zoe, anywhere, well, except the bathroom which is probably where you spend all your time anyway." I lifted one side of my mouth in a sarcastic smile. She gave me a haughty look which made me want to stick my fingers in her eyes.

I dropped back a little to be behind Zoe to remove the temptation. I still felt small, ugly, and overpowered by the tall, lithe blond with the very feminine figure ahead of me. Then I flashed back to the shooting gallery; I'd shot her in the face and suddenly I wasn't so annoyed with her. I was relieved, instead, that it had only been a test and not real.

Despite all the difficulties between us, I figured I had to find a way to talk to her, maybe to mend things between us, I just didn't know how yet. The only thing we had in common was being female. Well, that and we were both the first Exchanger females going to Amorpha. Okay, the third thing is we both loved dancing. Ack, the fourth thing is we seemed to have a crush on Keaton. I think Zoe had a crush on Mitchler, too, and if Soli hadn't been male oriented, she would've crushed on him, too. Someone definitely tweaked her hormones too much too soon.

Otherwise, we didn't connect on any level at all. But we were soon to be isolated Humans on an alien world and I wanted to at least part ways as friends if I could only figure out how to get past her dislike of me.

Keaton looked over his shoulder. "Come on, Jess! We are going to be late if you do not catch up." Our escort was beckoning to us impatiently from the elevator door.

# CHAPTER TWENTY-ONE

We found the Tatrans at our lunch table and, after a moment of surprise, we bowed, received their permission to sit and settled into chairs. I tapped the menu which was now exclusively Amorphan and placed my order, and Tatra Hilodrian next to me nodded in approval. *Nothing like a pop quiz at lunch time. I think I got an "A" for ordering, though.*

Tatra Meleandrea tapped the table with her eating utensil to gain our attention.

"We Tatrans have decided to have fun for you on the last evening on this trip prior to arriving at our world. We want it to be memorable and something the Imurians can also enjoy."

She paused for dramatic effect. "We will have a talent contest with you Humans! The Imurians who watch will be able to select their favorite part of the evening and prizes will be given but only for you Humans! This is a uniquely Human thing to do, I believe, and we Amorphans will love it, too!"

I could feel the stunned silence around me like a coating of oil. "A what? A talent contest?"

Tatra Meleandrea grinned at us with her mouth full of food, making me avert my eyes. "Yes! We researched activities Humans like to do and we learned that Humans like to show off their skills and talents so we decided this would be the way to end our journey and it sounds very fun to us. You know Amorphans like fun, yes?"

Tatro Hilodria chimed in, "Since we have taught you several of our traditional dances, we want each of you to dance with us in the contest!"

"Uh, do we have a choice about this?" Mitchler asked in a mournful tone.

"Oh, no. We have decided and the Imurians have agreed and it is all set. You are all excited with us, yes?"

We all said "yes" in tentative tones; what other choice did we have? One of my favorite shows on the viewing networks on New Eden was "Talent Seek" and I loved watching it, always amazed at what people could—and couldn't—do. I never thought I had anything stage worthy, though, like those people on the show. Having independent hair didn't count as a public talent in my mind.

Zoe said while shrugging, "Well, Keaton and I could do a ballroom dance."

"Yes!" Tatra Hilodria exclaimed. "That is what we thought for you. Also, for you to sing a song for all to hear, too."

Zoe smiled and preened at the suggestion. "I could do that."

Soli said, "I guess I could do a gymnastics routine for the show. The floor mats are all right for tumbling and I can work with that." Soli's Amorphan was really improving making me wonder if he was practicing on his own or with someone else. For someone so ultra-smart, he sure did struggle with the language.

Tatro said, "As long as you can use the fighting mats, then we are excited to see what you can do."

Mitchler chimed in, "Keaton and I could do a stand-up comedy routine. We like to make people laugh, right?"

Keaton smiled, nodding. "Sure, we'll work up some jokes even the Imurians will understand." Then he elbowed Mitchler. "The two of us together…we'll slay 'em, yeah?!"

I laughed. "Just make the jokes like they are: stiff and formal!"

He laughed along with me. "Yeah, they are, right? At least, the military ones. That Si'neada, though; he's a Cat of a different coloring."

With only five of us, it would be a short show if we all didn't do more than one thing. Of course, Zoe could dance and sing and probably do everything perfectly, down to having a perfectly shaped bowel movement, for that matter. Soli would do a floor routine, the boys a comedy act in addition to the Amorphan dances.

What did I have? Well, I could dance and stay in the pocket of the music; even Zoe couldn't deny that, so inspiration struck me. "I could do a line dance for the show."

Zoe rolled her eyes and said, "Line dancing? Are you crazy? It's not even a true form of the art."

"First of all, Zoe, it's been around for a few hundred years now and it most certainly is a form of dance. What I mean, however," I said, "I can do it by myself, without the line. After all, each person dances solo anyway and while they're designed for group dancing, they don't have to be done as a group." I glared at Zoe. "I do know complicated dances, no matter what you think about line dancing. It may not be ballroom, Zoe, but it has its own beauty."

Soli said, "Wow, Jessi, that would be supernova. I've always thought line dancing looked like fun."

Zoe sniffed. "Let's face it, you can't dance as well as me, Jessi, and never will. After all, dance, song and acting are my future, not yours, and I've been studying it all my life, unlike you. And fun? I don't think so; fun is a beautiful ballroom routine."

Oh, brother. "That's true, Zoe, my future is in medicine but dancing is fun, and line dancing is really fun. You should try it sometime unless, of course, you think you can't manage the steps or stand to have some enjoyment." I loved seeing her face redden and anger heat up her eyes. Then I remembered my plan to make her more than an unfriendly face in my life. Oops.

Tatro Aelotro said, "We will have many dances this way! We like dancing on Amorpha so this is good. We, too, can learn some new things."

"So what will the prizes be?" Mitchler asked.

"Ah, we cannot reveal that until the night of the program. They will be good." Tatro shoveled food into his mouth, smiling broadly. I looked away from his full mouth, too, feeling a little queasy at the sight of those serrated teeth piercing his food.

Si'neada sauntered up from behind us. "Oh, Tatro, I must have Jessi come with me this instant. A sewing emergency, as odd as that may seem."

All eyes went to me as I stood and bowed to Tatro. "I'm sorry, Datro, er, Tatro, I will be to class on time." Ok, so I'm still a little confused on when to address him as Tatro outside the classroom.

The Amorphan nodded his head, continuing to chew his food, now with his mouth closed, with a slightly puzzled look on his face. Zoe narrowed her eyes at me, puckering her finely plucked eyebrows together and the boys smiled at me.

"Come with me, my little teapot, to fix this vexing problem of clothing."

He dragged me down the hallway to yet another anonymous door and whisked me through it. "All right, Jessi. You must to learn to shield and to learn it now. We cannot have others to hear you broadcasting your thoughts."

"It's not like I'm trying to broadcast them!"

He smiled, shaking his head. "I to know, I do to know that. You have had no awareness of your mind-whispering ability until now and no one to receive your thoughts. At first, you were very quiet but you are becoming more and more loud. Now, to pay attention to how I tell you to build a metal wall around your thoughts."

A draining 20 minutes later, he said, "Well. That will to do for now but you must practice at all times in putting your thoughts behind this wall. If you to need to mind-whisper with me, you to open a window in the wall in your mind. If it is an emergency, you must to open a door. To receive, you must to always visualize a vent cover over the tiny opening in a window. Understood?"

I nodded. *Not really.*

He chucked me under the chin, saying, "Let us to get you to your class on time, then. You must be aware of and maintain this shield at all times."

Once back in the classroom, Tatro said, "Now time to learn about sensitive things in our society, such as bathroom behavior and dating and sex."

Oh, boy, finally the good stuff. Or not.

Tatro leaned back on the desk at the front of the small line of five chairs. "So, in a, what do you call it in Standard? A public room?"

Keaton said, "You mean a public restroom? Or public bathroom?"

Datro frowned. "Yes. Why is it not called a toilet room? Is that not where you go to relieve your full bladders and colons? Do you rest in those rooms or take a bath? It is confusing to us learning Standard."

Keaton nodded. "Yeah, it is," he said in Standard, then switched to Amorphan, "Yes, it's a place to relieve ourselves. We Humans like to veil such things with the use of other words." He shrugged. "We Humans don't like to admit to our bodily functions, I guess." He showed a palm. "We don't rest or bathe in public bathrooms. I don't know why they're called bathrooms, either."

Datro nodded. "On Amorpha, a public place of relievement is called a Waste Receiver Room and like your society, we do have male and female rooms. There is no shame among us; all peoples have to empty their waste materials. But in a public Waste Room, there is no talking among the entries. You go in, do what is necessary, wash your hands and leave. Talking is considered impolite and rude."

Mitchler nudged me. "Ha, guess that means you girls can actually go to the bathroom by yourself! No need for a girlfriend to go with you to put on your lipstick or whatever it is you do in there. By the way, what *do* women do in those stalls?"

I stared at him. "How would I know? We're all in our own stall with the door closed! I can only hear things from other stalls and, trust me, I wish I didn't! I only know what I do in a stall and that is taking care of business." I wrinkled my nose at him. "I'll have you know, I can go use a bathroom all by myself because I wear my big girl panties all the time now." I chortled at seeing the look on his face.

Tatro Aelotro waved. "What is stall? Does that not mean to come to an unexpected stop?"

I grinned. "Yes, it means that but it also means a small enclosed cubicle, such as in a bathroom for women. It can also mean where a horse is kept in a stable. It has many meanings, as do many words in Standard."

"Yes, it is what makes learning Standard so very interesting. All the words that sound identical and yet have different meanings." He shook his head. "At least Amorphan is easy to learn."

I rolled my eyes. "Easy, Tatro? Maybe the words but the intonations are difficult for our vocal cords." The others muttered agreement.

"Be that as it may," he waved a hand again as if brushing away gnats, "you are learning it and are understandable, that is what is important. Now, on to this." Tatro pushed a spot on the desk and a naked Amorphan projected into the air before us. None of us, I think, were prepared to confront a nude Amorphan and after a mutual intake of air, we expelled it together.

"We now discuss the anatomy of an Amorphan because it is different from Humans." Tatro pointed. "Our genitalia is hidden when not needed…here." He indicated the pelvic area where a fold of flesh lay. "Not only are our feet and hands changeable, so is our genitalia. So, for instance, if the female Waster Receiver room is full, then she may change to a male and use the other one. Or if there are not enough males in a community for procreation, then females may choose to change to become male."

Our mouths dropped open. This was completely new information. Wow, that would be so handy at the auditorium or stadium in a big crowd—or an all-girls' school.

He folded his hands together. "It is not an easy decision to do so, to become permanently male…or female, of course, and changing is a force of will and not without pain so it is not done without thought and decision or, perhaps, desperation." He made a dismissive motion with his hand. "Of course, you Humans cannot do this but you need to know this for the public rooms, as sometime you may come across someone who is reforming and you need to understand that it is their choice of the moment and should not be interrupted." He tapped two boneless fingers together.

"For us to alter from one sex to another for long-term means altering everything within us and so that decision is not a light one. However, to alter to use a public room is not difficult, only a matter of reforming for a small amount of time. This is told to you because you must understand this in our society. This would not happen on your world, I think."

"No, it would not. We have people who are born 'transgender' and their bodies have to be surgically fixed if they choose to become the sex their brains believe they are." Zoe tapped her fingers on the desk. "This would certainly make it easier for them."

He looked at her. "It is too bad that they do not have our ability. We do not have those issues in our society." Then he shrugged. "I believe the rest of our bodies have enough similarities that we need not discuss those." He flipped off the projection. "What else do you want to know?"

Zoe chirped, "I want to know about dating!" *Of course* she would want to know about that, but to be fair, I was curious, too.

I saw Soli shake his head just the tiniest bit as if in disbelief at what she said.

Tatro looked at her and templed his malleable fingers together. "Dating is only within our species and no one would consider mating outside of our species; you must understand this."

We nodded our understanding. He continued, "That is all there is to discuss about dating. If you are asked to an event, ask if it is a date. If the other says yes, then you must say no. If it is a social event with many others there, then it is permissible to be accompanied to that event but it cannot be considered a date in any way. Our Zatras are very firm on this."

Zoe looked disappointed. Did she really think she would be *dating* an Amorphan? I made a grimace. What could she possibly be thinking? We'd already been told many times that couldn't happen between any species. The officer telling B'le'ru he'd 'mounted' Human females…was that even true? There were strong prohibitions in place with all civilizations; he must've been lying. I hoped.

Tatro Aelotro then said, "And about sex. There will be none for any of you while on Amorpha as you will be separated into different cities, as you know. Procreation is limited to partnered adults and they only become partnered after many times of dating and socializing, so again it is not something necessary for you to know."

Well. That certainly stopped the lecture in its tracks. Even Zoe seemed nonplussed by his declaration. "So there is nothing more to be discussed about this. If ever in doubt, ask your host parents as to the rightness of the issue." He nodded his head. "We will now turn to your chapters on schooling, the subjects that are offered, and which ones you should consider taking. You have, of course, an agenda of classes you must take but there are electives."

## CHAPTER TWENTY-TWO

That night, frustrated by my lack of progress on Devon's death, I paced my sitting room. *I have two nights left. Two! I need to visit that machine again and see what I can find out about it.* I frowned as I moved, staring at the carpet, that odd sensation of being pulled toward something. I'd been very, very lucky so far to not get caught venturing into forbidden areas but my luck had to come to an end at some point. I sensed it would be tonight unless I—unless I what? I thought of the dream where I changed into an Imurian; if only that were real. If only it didn't involve all that bone-crushing pain.

CHANGE. HELP YOU.

*Huh? Help me how?*

QUICKER.

*You mean like what you've done before, camouflage me?*

NO. REAL CHANGE. NOT DREAM. Impatience, as if it was tired of explaining.

*Not a nightmare? Are you sure?* A sneaky part of me knew I'd really morphed into an Imurian but I'd pushed the whole incidence away like a nightmare. Because if I could actually do that, I might not be Human after all. At that thought, my heart stuttered in my chest, anxiety ramping up to a new level. If not Human, what was I? A whole new species? A mishmash of DNA? A mistake? I wrung my hands, clenching my teeth.

But—what if? What if it was real and I could become an Imurian? I could move around the ship with impunity, even into the living quarters—and perhaps even the science lab. I sat down with a thump on my couch. The possibilities suddenly yawned before me. If I really could—CAN—then I'd wasted a lot of time. I could've been exploring every night and going into all areas of the ship. Quick anger at myself reared up and I gritted my teeth together. I hadn't wanted to accept the changing ability; I was afraid of the pain, afraid of the unknown, scared out of my big girl panties that I wouldn't be me somehow if I allowed this.

Reality reared its ugly head and pointed out that I'd been busy at all hours every day with the immersion program and the extra training at night. I had to have some sleep! Didn't I? I was getting by right now on about five hours and I could really feel the lack. The one hour I had at night in my room after dinner before I could venture out to the range or exploring wasn't enough; I found if I sat down, I fell asleep. Unless, of course, Deester dropped by for a visit. He was a fascinating friend, if reticent to talk about the StarFinder scientists and crew, insisting he knew nothing more, but I learned a lot about his society and he promised me when I finally got my medical degree, I could practice on him and other Scitterers.

It also came down to the fact that I liked my status quo, as uncomfortable as it often was. I hated change which is why taking this journey was so monumental for me. I dragged my feet at new things, anxiety dogging my steps until I did the thing I feared and then I'd find out I'd been nervous for no reason at all, or worse, avoiding the fear-causing thing and missing out on a lot of good stuff.

With this trip, I'd finally said to myself, "Enough! I have stepped through fear often enough to find out it is only a veil to prevent me from living life and I've had enough. It's only fear, after all; I'll step through it this time, too, to discover new life as an Exchanger Student." I had stared at my face in the mirror, nodded once and then winked at myself. A peaceful feeling settled over me, my hair dancing around me in glee, and I felt a new surety of who I was as a person and, for once, in control of my own destiny.

What was the phrase Dad used? *Yeah, that's it; I'd been comfortably unhappy in my own little world. Coming on this trip to be the only human in a city of Amorphans has been very scary for me and I haven't been ready to accept anything else.* I'd fought through my fear of the unknown to even enter the StarFinder, walking up that endless ramp into the bowels of the shuttle, which was bigger than my imagination had painted it. I hadn't yet seen the full size of this ship but it was as big as a small moon, at least in my mind.

I uncrossed my clenched arms, squared my shoulders, thinking, *Enough of fear! That son of a bastard snuck in again and prevented me from exploring. Well, no more! Let's exchange this body for another! Let's do it, hair. Let's step out of the fear and into the fun. If I'm going to be an Exchanger, then, by glory, let's be an Exchanger in all ways!*

Happiness wafted from my hair. If it could've clapped hands, it would've. F!NALLY!

I removed all my clothes; I didn't want them shredded to pieces by the size change. I sat on the couch and clenched my teeth against the remembered pain to come. My eyelashes dragged my lids down over my eyes as I felt my hair drape over me and I fisted my hands, dreading what was to happen. I felt that indescribable feeling start at my feet, almost tingles, not quite movement but a ripple, perhaps, that was quickly building into a breaking wave with sharp rocks, but still with the tsunami force of the first time. Everything happened at once: I felt my legs and arms elongate, my bones crunching and changing, my ears moving upward, and my feet growing as my tailbone seemed to extend. *How in the seven gates of the hells does this happen?*

YOUR DNA ALLOWS.

I fought to breathe, to stand, to withstand the wave of pain. It wasn't quite as bad as the first time and I remembered something Mom used to say. *"Anticipation of an event is always, always worse than the event itself, Jessalya. Remember that."* Anticipating the bone-breaking agony and the rasping of muscle moving over bone would never, ever make me look forward to the changing. However, knowing I would live through it helped. A little. *Heavens forbid if I have to do this often or quickly.*

I'd dreaded doing this again so much I'd completely denied the ability. The pain was there, oh, yes, let's not overlook that, but perhaps it wasn't as bad as the first time and then as suddenly as it started, it stopped. The end was so abrupt I staggered to catch my balance. Now my eyelashes allowed my lids to open and I looked down at my body to see these longer, hair-covered striped legs. *Note to self, always wear loose clothing. I might not always have time to strip naked first. Thank goodness for Amorphan robes.* Had I been wearing my jeans, they would've been ripped beyond repair.

So—now what? It took me a few steps to feel how these much longer legs worked, to feel the springiness in the feet and knees and the almost-gliding walk I got after the first several steps. This was pretty astounding, actually. My perspective of the room was quite different, too; I saw things from a different angle than "up" because I was taller. *How am I taller? I don't understand. How is this even possible? Why does my DNA let me do this? Can I be other species, too, or only Imurians?*

Then the really big question. *Am I still me? Am I still human?*
YES, STILL YOU. OTHER SPECIES? YES.
*This is all DNA based, right?*
My hair agreed.
*So we take in other's DNA and then—what? I use their DNA to change? What about my nannies and my own DNA? Where does it all go?* I asked as I walked around the space.
NANNIES HELP. YOUR DNA MALLEABLE.

I made a face. Whaaaaa--? My DNA is malleable? What the stinking hell does that mean? I've never heard of such a thing and I suspected no one else had, either. When did I develop changeable DNA?
BORN THAT WAY.

Oh.

The next question, of course, was why I was born this way. My hair shrugged and I realized if it didn't know or wouldn't tell me, I wasn't going to figure it out right now. I hadn't had enough DNA classes to understand this—yet. Besides, knowing how or why didn't help me with the problem of being a nude Imurian. Nothing I had would fit.

I heaved a sigh. Okay, time to look at all of me. I activated the full-length mirror in the bathroom after closing the door and peeked at myself, blinking rapidly. Yeah, I was an adult male Imurian again. Funny how I felt completely female still. I was fascinated with having a penis, because it was so different to me, but then I thought to myself, *No time for fooling around with these body parts, Jess. Maybe later.*

I then looked at my torso and saw the barest hint of nipples in two vertical lines on the upper chest but since I was covered in hair over the whole body, there wasn't much to see. The stripes were intriguing and my tail twitched into view, startling me for a second.

I concentrated on moving my tail back and forth and up and down. I tried to make a circlular motion but my control wasn't good yet. I peered over my shoulder to see the base of the tail appeared high enough on my backside that sitting wasn't an issue. I stroked the hair on my tummy, loving the softness and then petted my arms and legs. The hair there was coarser than the tail but still fun to feel.

I examined my claws on my hands to find my nail polish survived the transition, causing my mouth to open in surprise. I clamped it shut again and then looked at my ears. Yes, my earrings had transitioned with me. The pressing question was how was I to get clothing to fit this form? I definitely couldn't wander the ship naked in any form, that's for sure.

I tapped my lip with my forefinger, careful of the exposed claw. Si'neada could get me a uniform but I wasn't quite ready to share this changing thing with him or anyone just yet. Deester said I could trust him but how far? Could I trust him with this monumental knowledge? I saw my green eyes widen in the mirror and the vertical pupil closing down to a slit. Deester had a better chance of getting clothing to me on the sly, I thought, as he seemed to have free range throughout the ship more than Si'neada. Uncertainty swelled but I had to trust someone who could help me. Since I was going to invade the science labs as an Imurian, better to involve someone who wasn't one so who better than Deester?

I'd been practicing my frequency listening ever since Si'neada had given me my first lesson along with my shielding lesson. I was better at both, I hoped, and discovered I couldn't hear my classmates' thoughts at all, although a time or two, Zoe had batted at her ear like a gnat was buzzing her. I could sometimes hear far-off murmurs and sometimes could make out words; I could catch a stray word or two from the Imurian Escort of the Day but they seemed to be well trained to not let their thoughts leak out.

I'd been practicing listening for Deester's thoughts, too, and whoever he chose to come with him for our visits; he was as curious about me and humans as I was about him and his society. I couldn't get a peek into his head so he was either so far off my radar on either end or so well-shielded I couldn't catch anything. Calling him with a mind whisper wasn't going to work, or at least I didn't think it would. First, I'd better become human again in case he became agitated over an Imurian in my room and called the guard.

I gritted my teeth as the pain wave worked its way through me, wishing I had something to bite on as my teeth might be in danger of cracking someday. Maybe it was my hopeful nature but it did seem to take a tiny bit less time to go through this. I looked down; now I was standing in my birthday suit in the bathroom. I scampered into the sitting area and snatched up my robe as the vents blew cold air over me, making my nipples wrinkle up and stick out. Did guy parts shrink up like that, too, in the cold? I didn't know yet but suspected the answer was yes.

*:Deester?:*

I opened my mental senses as much as I knew how and listened hard for a returning echo. Nothing.

I tried again on a different level. *:Deester!:* Still nothing. I bit my lip, thinking, then walked over to the vent. "Deester?" I said into the vent. "Deester, please, I need to talk to you."

Again nothing. What else could I do? I tried knocking a knife against the vent in a rhythmic way, hoping to attract a Scitterer's attention. A couple of minutes crawled by and I was ready to chew a nail off by that time. If he didn't show up in the next three minutes, I'd have to figure out something else.

"You rang, Jessalya?"

I jumped straight up in the air, I was so startled. I gasped for breath and placed my hand over my heart as if that would slow down its sudden racing. "How in the slimy hell did you get here?"

He smirked. Yup, it was definitely a smirk. "We have our secrets, too, Jessalya." He stood with his upper front arms crossed, looking at me with a tilt to his head and a questioning look, his sinuous body covered with work clothes. "What do you need that is so urgent? I do have a job, you know."

I sighed. "Yes, I know. But, I hoped you could help me with something." I wondered how much I could or should tell him. I felt I could trust him and my hair was relaxed around him but— could I? "I need an Imurian outfit, um, male, average build, I guess."

His eyes narrowed as he continued contemplating me. "An Imurian uniform or jumpsuit? Or casual?"

"Uhhhhh....jumpsuit, I think. No, uniform." I puffed my cheeks. "I'm not sure."

"Do I dare ask why?"

There it was, the question I dreaded. To be fair, I'd want to know, too, if I were him. I bit a nail, stalling, as he raised a tiny, hairy eyebrow. "I need it to wear?"

His eyes widened and then sharp pointed teeth appeared as he started hooting laughter. His arms squeezed his torso as he wheezed out, "Oh, that is fancy! You in Imurian clothing? How much are you going to roll up the sleeves and the cuffs? Yes, no one will suspect you are not an Officer of the ship if you wear one like that!" He wiped his eyes with one hand, sputtering as he laughed. The only thing he didn't do was slap his leg in mirth. "Not to mention no tail sticking out!" He howled again, doubling over this time.

I scowled at him. "I'm so glad to be a source of amusement for you."

He unbent enough to grin up at me, waving a hand in a dismissive way. "Oh, I have needed a good gut laugh like that for a long time." Then he tapped me on the knee. "Now the truth, Madame."

I sat down to be eye-to-eye with him, an unusual thing for me to have to think about doing. "You must swear to secrecy first." I shook my head. "I don't want to think about what would happen to me if it were told to the wrong people." I looked him straight in the eye. "Can I really, really trust you?" I had to trust someone sooner or later with this and I didn't think Deester was in a position to harm me. We'd had enough conversations I felt he was true to his word.

He made some complicated motions with his forehands. "Yes, you can truly, truly trust me." He patted me on the knee while gazing back into my eyes without blinking. "This is truth." He straightened to his full form, both sets of arms held out before him open-handed, balancing now only on his hind legs and his long, pointed tail. "I solemnly swear to keep your secret, except in case of dire need and/or your survival. I swear this by all the stars in the universes and by the piece of God that dwells here." He tapped his chest, presumably over his heart. "This is truth."

Okay, then. That sounded pretty binding, I guess, not being any expert on swearing-to-secrecy pledges. But how to answer? I finally said, "I accept your pledge." I hoped that was the right way to do this. "I consider you a friend indeed and I hope I can trust you." I nodded. "This is truth." *Well, I'm committed to this now. Hope it doesn't bite me in the butt.*

He touched a forefinger to mine, nodding, as if a solemn ceremony had been completed.

I took a deep breath. "Okay, here it is. I'm just going to say this, and then," I took another breath, "I'll show you." My hair apparently agreed with this agenda as it snugged up against my back in a supportive squeeze. "I can change shapes into an Imurian." There. I'd said it. Now two of us knew this deadly secret.

His jaw fell open and his eyes blinked rapidly as he stared at me with astonishment plainly written over his face. "That's—that's impossible."

"I know. And yet I can."

He pinned me with his eyes, searching my face, then he pointed at me. "Let me see." He said this in a very quiet voice. "Let me see if this is truth."

I nodded slightly. "Okay, watch but don't interfere. I'm not sure how or why I can do this and I definitely don't know what would happen if you touched me in transition." I squeezed my eyes shut, clenched my teeth and gave internal permission. The tsunami built up, crested and I felt everything shifting, elongating, breaking, grinding and moving. I felt myself drop prone to the floor. I heard a small gasp but couldn't fight the agony enough to open my eyes. When the pain receded, I saw Deester standing in a defensive mode, open-mouthed with all teeth bared in a snarl, claws extending from his hands. "I won't hurt you, you know." I felt my face; yes, I was a Cat again and I looked down, running my hands over my now-flat chest. I was fully transformed. My robe was quite tight around my neck and I reached back to loosen the binding; I'd forgotten to remove it before transforming. Apparently, my body also changed it enough to not strangle me.

He sat with a thump on the floor, and then fell forward onto his tummy. "I do not know what to say, I do not believe my eyes and yet, as you said, there you are." He abased himself in front of me. "I never thought to see such a thing. I am privileged."

I reached out and tapped him gently on the back of his head. "I'm still me, Deester, so please, don't do this. Stand up and be my friend. The universe knows I need one right now."

After a few seconds, he scrambled to his feet and bowed to me. "This is unbelievable power, you know. I will for certain keep this secret for you may not survive if it is discovered." Then he looked pensive for a second, then asked, "Does Si'neada know?"

"No. Not yet. Maybe not ever."

"He is trust-worthy."

"Yeah, but the fewer who know about this, the better. Right now I need Imurian clothing so I can walk the ship. You understand I have to, *have* to, find out what happened to my brother all those years ago, for my parent's sake, if not my own. I think what happened to him is what happened to me, also, so I need to know, and I suspect it has something to do with the scientists. You yourself told me the only ones allowed in there are Imurians. So I will be one, find what I need to know and then maybe I can forget about this ability."

"Do you know how it has come around?"

"No. I only discovered this," I indicated my new body, "during this trip. It has to do with my DNA and my nanny, er, nano system, I think." I made a tight line with my mouth. "I mean, why me? Why now?" With sudden hope, I asked, "Do you know?"

"No. With all our collective history before the Imurians and after, we have never heard or seen such a thing and we are on all the ships as they explore. The Imurians believe it impossible and they are the most widely traveled of any known civilization."

"Well, a gal can hope, huh."

He grinned. "Right now you're not a gal." He pointed to the obvious male parts as I sat cross-legged, robe riding high on my thighs and I covered the area in haste.

"Now you know the reason I need that jumpsuit." I raised one buttock and freed myself from sitting on my tail; it was uncomfortable that way.

He nodded. "Yes, I can see that." He pointed a finger at me. "You need a uniform, not a jumpsuit; you need to be a ranking officer for authority in the science area. Wait here. I will return with one for you." He paused as he started toward the kitchen and turned solemn eyes toward me. "I will let you see my secret for entering and leaving in exchange for yours. And please, hide in the bathroom; the ones who will have to help me bring it should not see you as this."

I circled my finger and thumb in a sign of agreement. He hurried into the kitchen, opened the cupboard door below the sink and disappeared. *Of course. There must be a hatch under there for the plumbing and they use it for entering rooms. Huh. These rooms aren't quite as secure as the Imurians want us to believe. Good thing Deester is my friend and not my friendly spy.*

## CHAPTER TWENTY-THREE

I came out of the bathroom after a discreet tap on the door to find a uniform, brand-new or at the least, freshly ironed, laying over the couch back. I held it up, finding it bare of insignia and hoped that didn't matter. Then my foot nudged something and I looked down to find a small bag the suit had hidden before. I opened it to find insignia badges, various items to add to the waist belt and a small e-pad. I flicked it on to see a list of the badges, what rank they indicated and other useful information. After I dressed, I slapped a high-ranking Officer's badge on my chest and put the tools into their places on my utility belt. I also added my gun to the appropriate pouch.

Taking a big breath in for support, I viewed myself in the mirror. Imurian in a uniform, insignia and tools, all checked off. Oh, crap. Boots. None of my shoes would fit these feet but I had seen some of the Cats strolling around barefoot so perhaps it would be okay. I had no idea if this level of Officer had to wear boots or not but I'd have to go with what I had and that didn't include boots. At least I'd walk more silently in bare feet. I checked the time; it was well after midnight ship time so the corridors should be relatively free of personnel. The sparse nighttime crew would be out and about but I was pretty sure my badge outranked them.

Nothing to do but try it out. I shook out my arms, drew in a big breath, letting my shoulders relax when I breathed out. I checked to make sure the corridor was clear before I slipped out my door into the darkened hallway and headed to the elevator, directions to the science lab on the pad given to me by Deester. I practiced standing as a Cat would while on the elevator; just because I looked like one didn't mean I naturally knew all the nuances of their body language.

I drew a shaky breath of relief when I arrived at the lab deck and moved down the darkened, empty corridor to my left toward the big blast doors that were securely closed and intimidating in appearance. Not only did the doors seem menacing, the signs helped the illusion by proclaiming "Danger!" and "Stay Out if You are Not Authorized!" and other signs to that effect. All that snarling made me wonder what they were hiding behind those thick metal doors. I touched my gun to make sure it was accessible; with my hair now integrated into being an Imurian, I couldn't count on it being able to physically participate in protection.

When I'd questioned Deester about what went on in the science area, he looked grim and said, with a shake of his head, "We have never been allowed in there ever, not even when our families first joined company with the ships, but there are always rumors and rumors are not ever pretty. I only know the scientists do their work in there and they are highly protected and sometimes people disappear and do not come back."

*I really, really hope those scientists sleep like babies at night knowing there's no way anyone can break in. Besides me, of course.*

I hoped complacency lulled them into no staff being assigned a night shift. I patted my weapon again. If needed, I had that and I had claws, teeth and training.

I stepped briskly toward the doors as if I had every right to be there in case anyone was watching this darkened area on a device somewhere. "*Always look the part*", my Dad said, "*even if you don't feel it. If you look and act the part, people will believe you belong there.*"

I kept my shoulders squared up and envisioned an "I'm a High-Ranking Officer" look on my face. My ears were upright, whiskers at neutral, and my nose slightly in the air with head held high. As I inhaled, I catalogued metal and fiber scents, some odors belonging to beings I didn't know, and cleaning fluids amongst other scents I couldn't yet identify. My tail twitched at my ankles and I hoped I remembered it was behind me when I closed doors.

I looked over the thick doors before stepping onto the painted circle on the floor in front of them. A pad extruded from a panel in the door and I used the code Deester had provided. He was definitely a wealth of knowledge; him knowing this code made me wonder if he had secretly accessed this area on his own.

Apparently, I passed inspection because I heard a click and the door silently moved inward to open but only giving me about two feet of space to enter, preventing a full-frontal assault, if that were my plan. I sidled around the door's edge, peering around to check for clearance. All was quiet and empty from what I could see in the dimmed area.

I slipped through into a short hallway. Closed doors were on either side of me and another door ended the hallway ahead of me. I tested the doors as I tiptoed down the hallway but the doors were locked. The small mesh-reinforced windows inset in the upper half of the doors let me peek in to see what appeared to be individual offices. I thought about entering each one to see what I could find but didn't know how to unlock them, and I was sure their computers were password protected, anyway. The door at the end beckoned to me and, without knowing why, I felt I had to go through it.

I stopped in front of it, drew in a large breath to steady my rapidly beating heart and gently pushed on the door, expecting it, too, to be locked. To my surprise, it swung open a few inches and I listened before entering, my ears swiveling to catch sounds from all directions. I heard intermittent soft rustling and light breathing noises but no talking, no machines whirring or the clatter of keyboards. I furrowed my brow in puzzlement and pushed the door open a little more to reveal soft, barely-there lighting, like a night light in a kid's room. I looked around in confusion.

Two large rectangular tables were centered in the room with chairs around opposite sides and upstanding rings embedded into the table top at regular intervals. The metal chairs had arms on either side and the legs were bolted into grooves in the floor. There were a few open-topped boxes here and there filled with small items. I looked away from the table to see rows of large cages along the nearest side of the large space and there appeared to be something or someone inside each cage. I marveled at how much I could see in the dim lighting with my Imurian eyes.

I tiptoed over to one of the cages and saw a small animal wrapped in a blanket and sound asleep. It had a long, pointed snout with large fluttery nostrils at the end, feathery whiskers ringing all the way around, askew from the sides of the face. The three eyes were closed, and there were four round upright ears on the top and sides of the head. The body appeared velvety but most of it was covered so I couldn't see the whole thing. I looked in the next cage; there was another one like the first one, only this one was curled up with its snout buried under its front legs, which appeared to have small hand-like appendages.

As I stood there staring at these animals, my tail snuck through the mesh of the cage and ever so gently touched the body and then quickly retracted.

WANT DNA.

Oh, so my hair was still active and curious. Well, I was curious, also. What were these things and why were they in cages? Were they versions of lab rats, like Old Earth used to use in ancient times? They appeared to be in good health, no signs of harm, and they were sleeping peacefully.

I moved to the next cage. A different species was in this one, but all I could see was a scale covered backside which winked a pretty blue in the low light. There was a second one in the next cage. As I moved down the line, I discovered there were pairs of everything and all different. The one common thing, and I couldn't say why I thought this, was they all seemed very young. *I don't think this is Noah's Ark but there are pairs of different animals here. Do they come from different planets? Is this a sick ward of some type? They don't seem ill in any way and there are no attendants or nurses.*

As I stared into one of the cages, the small body turned over in its sleep and one arm came uncovered, a metal bracelet coming into view. The little hand-like appendage stretched out and what appeared to be tentacles unrolled, each tipped with a needle-like end. *Those look dangerous. Is that fluid from the end?* I wrinkled my nose as a smoky, oily odor wafted out after a small noise erupted under the cover. *Oof, whatever they're feeding this thing, I think they need to change its diet! That stinks.*

I stepped away from the smell and looked through more of the cages. I noted more of the bracelets, all identical, all on the upper limbs and some with them also on the lower limbs, especially the ones with long, vicious looking talons. *Maybe this is some type of nursery; maybe they take young from the some of their worlds with special needs and help them here. I suppose a cage is no worse than a baby's crib especially if they wouldn't play nice together. They all appear to be well fed and in good health. I suppose it doesn't matter; I need to move on.* As I stepped back, my heel tapped one of the boxes on the floor and I looked down. I peered into the contents; these looked like toys which confirmed my belief this was some kind of nursery. Okay, then, moving on. I moved through the dimness to the far end of the space opposite where I entered toward the other door. When I got to it, I put my ear to the door to listen first before attempting to open it.

I heard a soft murmuring on the other side, like voices but I could barely hear them. I stretched out my mind to try to :listen: but I didn't or couldn't pick up any mind whispering. However, the voices were getting more distinct and an adrenaline rush filled my body, my tail twitching back and forth, my whiskers flattening against my hairy face, ears slanting back in uncertainty.

I felt the buzzing prelude to a change of form from the overload of fear and anxiety so I stepped away from the door, leaning over and carefully slowing down my breathing. I couldn't afford to have the change happen here and now; I had to stay Imurian. I struggled with the feeling, keeping my eyes closed, concentrating on my Imurian form, fighting the urge to become human again, and the wave receded to a distant horizon but not totally gone. If stress was going to bring on exchanging one body for another, it wasn't going to be a very effective way of getting things done. *How can I prevent changing unless I want to?*

PRACTICE. NOT PERFECT AT KEEPING FORM YET.

*So if we get distracted, that could be a problem? Or if we get scared?*

PERHAPS. WORKING ON CONTROL.

Fatigue dragged on me and I felt desperate for sleep but I had to complete this. I was almost out of time on this ship and I didn't have answers about Devon's death or why I had become a true Exchanger. How was this changing thing even possible and why me? A snarky part of my brain whispered, *Why not you?* I ignored that as best I could. Dagbone it, I planned to be a physician, a scientist, not an impossible shape-shifter everyone would want to experiment on!

*Be who you pretend to be, Jessi. That's the only way forward right now. I have to think Imurian, be Imurian, feel Imurian.* Voices coming closer on the other side of the door startled me as I straightened up and moved back. *I think they're coming in here!* I couldn't hide under the tables; they were low to the ground like they were made for children and I wasn't sure I'd fit. There was always my gun—oh, by the blazing fires of hell, my gun required my Human DNA to activate. There was no time to reset the gun's activation settings to Imurian DNA, either, so if I had to pull it,

I'd have to act as if it could be used and honestly, they wouldn't know the difference; they would expect it to be tuned to this self, anyway. *Unless we can change just my finger to human?* No time for an answer, I heard the doorknob rattle a bit as the door was unlocked from the other side.

I ran on silent feet through the room until I was at the closed door through which I'd originally entered. My only plan was to pretend I'd just entered the space and the rest I'd have to make up as I went. Well, ok, my other plan was to press up against the door and hope somehow my hair could still camouflage my body.

The door at the other end swung open and four Imurians entered, two of them holding someone between them in a rough hold, one leading the way and one at the rear. That someone being dragged was slumped, something covering its face and stumbling as he or she was pulled forward into the room.

"To put her on the table now!" A male voice snapped with authority from the lead figure. "To get her secured, quickly now."

Three of them deftly picked up and placed the person face up on the table, none of them noticing me where I was plastered against the opposite wall watching this scenario. They clipped chains from the wrists and ankles to the upright bolts on the table. *So that's what those are for. Oh. Those aren't bracelets on those beings in the cages; those are manacles.* I felt sick to my stomach but after seeing the claws, talons, tentacles on the youngsters, I supposed it was better to be safe than sorry. The person struggled to sit up but dropped back onto the table as the chains were short and there wasn't room for a struggle against the restraints.

"May we now to mount her, Doctor?" One of the helpers inquired.

*Mount her? Just what was going on here?* I didn't want to call attention to myself just yet, not until I could understand what was going on. All of them were riveted on the figure on the table. They weren't whispering, which suggested they didn't care if they woke any of the sleepers but since those sleepers were in cages it probably didn't matter much if they did awaken. They'd kept the lights down which made it difficult to make out just what they were doing or planning to do.

I didn't like what I'd heard, though; this sounded a lot like rape. I wondered what happened to her tail; I hadn't seen one but this had all happened so fast, I'd probably not noticed it. She wore some kind of gown so it was possibly hidden under that or perhaps she wasn't Imurian.

The leader of this scene spoke in a calm, detached voice. "Not yet. I must to administer the memory drug and the fertility drug so there is no trace of this evening left for her to recall. Then you must to wait 15 minutes for them to be effective and after that, I do not care what you do as long as there are no marks or evidence of your pleasure and she remains alive and in good shape."

"Yes, sir." One male answered. "D'ru'ke, set your timer for 15 minutes after the drug is administered." The male to his left nodded and raised a device to tap on it.

The leader spoke again. "Keep her still so I can insert the tubing."

The figure on the table fought, tugging on the arm chains with grunts of effort. The Cats pinned her to the table while the order-giver pulled out an object. "Put a light on this."

"Yes, Sir, Doctor. Right away."

The third male stepped forward, shining a small flashlight on an IV tube and a syringe held in the doctor's hand. The doctor peered at the contents, flicked a finger against it and pushed the plunger up slightly until a drop of fluid shone in the light. "To hold her arm and to hold it tight. I do not want to have to restart the vein access again."

Two of them continued to pin her arm down as she moaned and struggled. The doctor stepped forward, pushing something with tubing into her arm, then put the syringe to the tubing now snaking from her arm, pushing the plunger. He then repeated the action with a second syringe. He capped them after using, tossing them into a container nearby and then pulled the IV out of her arm and tossed it to one of the helpers. "To dispose of this properly or I will to see you punished."

"Yes, Doctor!" He tucked it away in a pouch on his waist. "I will to see it burned myself."

"Make sure you to do that or I will to know. Now, remember, 15 minutes you must to wait or she will to remember you." He turned on his heel and left through the door he'd entered through, closing it behind him with a snap.

As soon as the door closed, they relaxed a little, looking at each other with grins. "I wonder if this will impregnate her and I wonder who the sire will be if this works."

"I do not to know. All I know is what he told us: it will take all of us to overwhelm her system so it works. He wants this done in the actual body and not in a lab dish to study the full effects. What I to find interesting is if we do succeed in impregnating her, he said he had a way to make her body to hold the pregnancy in abeyance until she is on her return journey and she will never to know until it is far too late." He shook his head. "How is that even possible?"

Shrugs from the other two. "Scientists. Who to knows how they figure these things out? At least we get to have some fun in this plan, unlike those other times."

"Has it been 15 minutes yet?" The third one whined. "While we to wait, maybe we should to pull numbers for who goes first. Maybe for once, I will be the lucky one." His hand dropped to the front of his jumpsuit. "I am ready right now."

## CHAPTER TWENTY-FOUR

Horror locked me into place. Whoever was on that table didn't deserve this, no matter what she'd done! Was it an Imurian female, maybe from a different ship, who'd gotten herself into trouble somehow? Whatever she'd done didn't warrant rape! Was this a punishment? Was she a willing participant for some reason? That didn't feel right, couldn't be right, since she was chained down, but stranger things had happened in the universe. How was I going to save her? There were three of them and only one of me, still unnoticed, my only advantage, well, that and to all appearances, I outranked them. If I could take them down, how would I get the prisoner loose from those chains? What if all the youngsters in here woke up and made so much noise that the leader would return while l was rescuing her?

Indecision gnawed at me. Did I let them know I was here now or wait a few more minutes? *If I let it go a little longer and one of them has his pants down or whatever, that would make my fight with them a little easier,* I thought. I couldn't let it go as far as an actual rape and I wasn't quite sure how much time had already passed from the injection into the IV tubing. First I would try pulling rank on them and see if that did the job. That was my best, most peaceful approach and if that failed, well, I'd have to fight it out and win. Then I'd worry about freeing the chained female and hoped she would be grateful for the intervention.

On the other hand, if I waited too long, the memory drug would take effect and she wouldn't remember any of this. I wasn't sure why that bothered me, but it did. I felt she needed to remember, bad as this might be, if only to protect herself in the future, in case she hadn't agreed to this whole thing, which no sane woman would. What's known can be healed but what is buried could ruin an entire lifetime.

A sudden noise attracted attention as she bucked against the chains again. "Noooo! Let me go! Please, let me go!"

Oh, Gods. That was Zoe's voice. That was no Imurian on that table; I had to get her out right now even as a tiny part of my brain whispered maybe she deserved this. I angrily pushed that thought out of my head; no one, not even Zoe, deserved this. Ever. Under any circumstances. Just…No.

I felt around on the wall for a light switch. This had to end right here, right now and light would be my first defense and snapping orders as an Officer would be my second. I had to keep them off balance so they didn't notice I hadn't opened the door to be in there. I flicked on the lights, brilliance suddenly bursting into the room, striding forward the instant I hit the switch, barking out in my best, deepest Officer voice, "What is the meaning of this? What am I seeing here? This is forbidden! Why is that human restrained? Answers! I want answers now!" I pointed imperiously at one of the Cats standing at the table gaping and blinking in the sudden light, his hold on Zoe's arm relaxing.

"Ah, ah, sir, I, uh, we were ordered here tonight by Dr. Le'nar'te."

One of the other two chimed in, "Yes, we, ah, were detailed here to guard this female from, uh, harm. Yes, from harm."

I came to a halt within striking distance of the nearest soldier. "Why is she shackled to the table?"

Discomfort showed on the soldier's face. "She…fought, sir. Dr. Le'nar'te felt she was a danger and needed to be restrained."

"Why is she here and not in her own quarters in the Human sector?"

"I do not to know, sir." A quick sideways glance to his companions told the lie.

"You do to know and I to demand answers! Now!" I pointed at one of the others. "Your name, now!"

"Qu're'te, sir!"

"Answer my questions right now or there will to be consequences."

"We were told she was part of an old experiment and Dr. Le'nar'te said he needed to follow up on it. He said it was very important."

"Which experiment?"

They all shook their heads. "We do not to know, sir. We really do not."

I tapped a finger against my mouth, glaring at them, my ears pinned flat to my head, whiskers bristling, causing them to shift uneasily and glance around. "Unshackle her this instance; I will to take her to her quarters. This is unforgivable but I will to overlook this once as long as you to comply right now. I will to speak to Dr. Le'nar'te about his unauthorized experiment later."

The three of them looked at me. I snarled, trying to weight my words with authority. "Now, soldiers!"

"But the memory drug is not fully effective yet, sir!"

"I do not to care if she is to remember your behavior. Get this done."

One of the officers gave me a narrow-eyed look with his brow furrowed. "How did you to get in here, Sir? I do not to remember the door being opened."

Poop on a paddle. He'd noticed. "You were too busy thinking about your hormones to notice the door admitting me to this space." I sneered at him, hoping to keep them unsettled. He looked uncomfortable, ears flattening out to the sides of his head in uncertainty, whiskers twitching the same emotion, and he opened his mouth to say something more.

"Officer! Did I not to give you an order!"

"Yes, Sir!" He fumbled at his belt for a key, his suspicions on hold while he inserted it into the locks on the chains to remove them and they helped her to a sitting position.

She swayed as she sat there, holding her head in her hands, knees pulled up and one of them put his hand on her arm, which she promptly swatted away. "Don't touch me."

I stepped closer. "What is your name, Human?"

"Zoe." She said in a soft, flat voice. Her face was very pale with dark areas under her eyes telling the story of her stress. She blinked as if trying to focus and a tear dripped from the corner of her eye which she dashed away with a shaky hand. Angry red marks ringed her wrists.

"Zo-ee, I will to escort you to your quarters. Will you to be able to walk?"

"I—I don't know."

"Help her down." I snapped. Two of them helped her to her feet where she stood with her fists clenched, eyes staring at the floor or her bare feet, I wasn't sure which. Sound suddenly swelled to fill the room as the residents of the cages started yipping, chittering or thumping noises but, surprisingly, a few spoke in Imurian, a mixture of, "Is it morning?" "Why are the lights on?" "Let it go!" "Let me go!" "I am hungry, feed me." "I want toys." Several of them were standing at the front of their cages, faces pressed to the bars to take in our tableau, some hanging from the bars, some shaking the cage in an effort to get out.

Zoe raised her head to stare at the cages and then at me, then back to the cages. I shrugged. There was nothing I could at this moment about the nursery situation; I needed to get her safely back to her room and do it right now before these three figured out I wasn't supposed to be in this room. "I will to take her from here. You three will settle these younglings and get them back to sleep before they disturb the scientists." I supported Zoe with my left arm and she sagged a little against me then pulled herself upright.

We shuffled toward the door, sideways to it so I could keep an eye on the three males as they tried to hush the younglings in the cages. I was about to blow out a breath of relief as we came within a few feet of the door; we were almost out of there and safe. I murmured, "Zo-ee, when we get to the door, turn off the lights. The switch is right there." I indicated it with my chin. My right hand rested on my gun. She nodded understanding as

I saw her eyes mark the spot. *Just a few more steps, that's all, just a few more.*

The door at the other end flew open so hard it bounced off the wall as Dr. Le'nar'te strode into the room. "What is all this noise?" he demanded. "Hey! Why is the human not on the table? It has not even been 10 minutes yet!" Then his gaze swung to me. "Who are you? Why do you to have the human? You to have no authorization to remove her!" He back-handed the closest soldier. "Stop them!"

"But, Sir! He outranks us!"

"He does not outrank me and I gave you an order! To stop them *now!* To shoot him, just do not to harm the female."

The soldier reached for his weapon as I pulled mine. "I am taking this Human to her quarters. You know this is illegal! These men were about to have non-permitted sex with her and you know the punishment for that." I snapped out the words, hoping I was right about the rules, bringing my gun up to point at them. *Any chance my finger can become human so my gun works?*

YES.

*Do it quick.* I felt my finger reshape—*holy crap!*—and the gun activated, judging from the vibration of active status.

"*Shoot him!*" Dr. Le'nar'te screamed over the cacophony of noise from the cages. "She must not leave here until I am done with her! Do not to shoot her, though!"

"But, doctor! I'm not sure I can shoot him without hitting her plus he's an Officer!"

"You to shoot him or you will to live to regret it! And I will to see to the regret part myself." The soldier visibly flinched. "I will to take care of his body and all else. Just to get the human back here now!"

I kept pulling Zoe toward the door but couldn't take the risk of turning my back on the group at the other end. Two of the soldiers were advancing toward me, weapons out and pointed at me, waiting for their opportunity. I had to find a way to turn off the lights and get out the door without us getting hurt.

Without thinking about it, I stepped behind Zoe, holding my arm in a lock across her chest, turning us to face the others. "Shoot me and you to shoot her." I held the gun steady on the group at the other end. I whispered into Zoe's ear, "On my say, to turn off the lights, please. I must to get you out of here safely."

She whimpered in reply and sagged under my arm, her heart beating so hard and fast, I could feel the thump on my arm as I held her.

"I am not here to harm you; they will not to shoot you and if they to shoot me, they to put you back into shackles. Do you understand? I am using you as a shield for both our sakes." She let out a ragged breath, and then breathed out one letter. "K."

We were in a stand-off, the soldiers hesitating to attack a superior Officer, and I was unwilling to shoot them unprovoked. Zoe and I inched toward the door ever so slowly so they wouldn't notice our movement. Dr. Le'nar'te pulled the front male's head down to him by the ear and said something into it I couldn't hear. I had a brief thought of trying to read minds but there was too much happening to concentrate and I couldn't take the time or energy to try. The male's eyes widened, whiskers flat against his face like mine and his ears snapping back against his head as soon as the doctor let go. My ears flattened in rage as my tail lashed back and forth and I gave them my best Mom look. Hey, it always worked on me as a kid; couldn't hurt to try.

It didn't help. Quick as a flash, he discharged his weapon just after I bit out to Zoe, "Now! The lights!" Her arm fumbled behind her to hit the switch and she gasped as the shot found its mark on her. I gasped with her; the shot that hit her also hit my side in a searing, wrenching pain. Hot blood gushed down my side; I felt it drench my uniform as I snapped off a shot back at the males and the lead one fell, making the other two jump in surprise and the doctor scamper back. Because I was prepared for the lights going out, it gave us the extra one or two seconds to rush out the door. "Hairy Balls!" I swore. "I sure hope this door locks itself!" The awful thought hit me that maybe the lock would only be against entering, not exiting. I yanked open the door, pushing Zoe out first and then I followed, ducking as shots rang against the door. I hauled it shut behind me, then smashed the pad extruding from it, hoping that would slow them down from opening it again.

"We need to run, Zo-ee. Can you?" I ignored the knife-like pain in my side.

"I—I don't know." A gasp of pain from her. "I'll try." Her robe was scarlet with blood and she held a hand against her side trying to staunch the flow. Her eyes were huge in her face and her lip trembled as tears ran down her face along with mascara. It gave her a bizarre look.

"You have to run. There is no other choice."

I gave her an arm for support as we ran down the hallway toward the elevator. Well, running wasn't really what we were doing; it was more like lurching along. The elevator was our fastest way but I worried the doctor had a way of blocking it. Luckily, in my nightly adventures, I'd found stairs behind unlocked doors—apparently they only locked the doors in the Human section—so as we neared the elevator, I yanked open a door and pulled Zoe in after me, forcing the door closed. There was a manual locking device, which I flipped into place.

I pointed up. "We to go this way." Side by side, she dragged herself up the stairs with her left hand on the railing and the other tight against her right side, me supporting her weight with an arm. We made it to the next landing, out of sight from the deck below, and she slumped against the wall, blood covering her hand where she had it pressed. Blood soaked the robe in front and scarlet dripped off her hand.

"Zoe, we have to keep going. We will to be found if we to stay here. The sooner back to your quarters, the better to treat you."

She nodded and pushed herself up to stand, hitching in a breath. "Okay. Let's do it."

"Wait. Here. Press this against your side." I ripped off one of my sleeves, wadded it up and handed it to her. It would have to do.

We made it another two decks before Zoe held up a hand. "I…need….to catch…my…breath." She was becoming paler by the minute and the wadded-up sleeve was getting saturated with blood. My own wound had clotted already.

"I may have to call the medics right here."

"No!" She gritted out. "I can make it to my room. We're close, right? Please tell me we're close."

"We are close." I reassured her. *I think.* Going to the lab area had seemed quick but coming back was taking forever. Of course, we were using the stairs, not the elevator, and that's definitely the slow way to do things.

We both heard the clang of a door opening below us and male voices shouting in urgency, "They went this way!"

Zoe bit her lip and struggled to hasten her pace, as I supported her with my free arm, my gun in my other hand as I glanced down the stairs. I whispered, "We need to go quietly but quickly." She nodded, face white and eyes wide.

"We have to check every door to make sure they did not to leave the stair well." The voice was a lot closer than I'd hoped, making it more urgent we move faster. I looked down but they were still a few flights away from us. I could hear them but couldn't yet see them.

Voices floated up. "They went up more; see the blood? And I smell her scent, it is strong with blood and adrenaline!"

"Yes, they must to be on the way to her room. We can always to catch her there if we do not find her in here."

They broke into a run on the stairs as we moved closer, step by step, to the door we needed, Zoe's weight dragging on my arm as she did the best she could through the pain. They rounded a landing and I caught a glimpse of them charging up the stairs. I leveled my weapon and shot at them. They both yelped and ducked, zinging wild shots back at us. I bit off a cry as I shoved Zoe upward, the pain in my own side feeling like a hot poker or maybe they had shot me again. I didn't have time to decide and I could only imagine that what Zoe felt must be six times worse.

They snarled as they regrouped and bounded up the stairs, forcing me to dodge shots while shooting back, then one hit my thigh. I yelped and staggered. "Run, Zoe!" I shoved her and she fumbled with the handrail, pulling herself upward toward the door in a shambling run. I had to stop the soldiers or we'd never make it to our quarters, because I'd be dead and she'd be back in the lab in shackles. I knew she couldn't go back to her room but no time to think right now. My side hurt and my thigh didn't want to hold my weight.

I had the advantage of height on the stairs, though, and I changed my weapon to maximum stun, braced myself on the handrail, waited for the opportunity and shot the front one in the chest, who crumpled into a heap in front of the second one, causing him to leap over the limp body. As he jumped, I pulled the trigger again and he crumpled to the floor alongside his companion. No time to stop and gloat or to wonder if they were alive; they'd already alerted the others to our whereabouts over their comm units. *Thanks, B'le'ru, for the hologram lessons.*

My ears flattened tighter against my head as I limped up the stairs after her and I gripped her arm to hold her up; okay, to be frank, I needed to use her as a crutch, too, as my thigh really objected to being used. I opened the door and we spun through into the blessedly empty Human corridor.

*Thank the stars they keep their hinges oiled.* I closed the door with just a snick of sound. "We need to hurry. I do not know why they are not here yet but be grateful."

*What if they're in her room already? Like an eight-legger in a web? I'd bet they're checking in Medical and in her room. It's what I'd do.*

"Zoe," I said very softly, "They are probably in your room already so we are going to Jessalya's room."

"She doesn't like me." She gasped. "She may not let me in."

"She will to let you in."

"I hope so. I can't go much further."

We supported each other as we stopped in front of my door. I contemplated the door opener pad, then felt a sudden flare of pain in my hand so I looked at it. Yup, it had changed to my own palm so I slapped it on the pad and the door swished open. I more or less dragged Zoe into my quarters, taking her to the couch where she dropped onto it with a moan. "Shhh!" I shushed her.

She nodded, her face pale and drawn, eyelids fluttering over her eyes, lips tight, looking like she was about to faint. Blood continued to seep from her wound, my ex-sleeve saturated with blood. I didn't dare call the medics; we couldn't risk discovery so I gently moved her hand and removed the sodden cloth. I ripped open her robe to expose the wound on the right side of her abdomen, adjacent to her belly button but at the side of her body. There was only a trickle of blood now but as pale as she was, I figured that was because her blood volume was low. I felt her pulse; I wasn't a doctor's daughter for nothing, after all. It was thready and weak, her breathing shallow and I realized she had slipped into unconsciousness. I stood there, frowning, as I thought about what to do. *Any ideas?*

BE YOU.

I shook my head. Of course; first I needed to become Jessi again. I grabbed a kitchen towel to press to her side before stepping out of her view. I heaved a sigh, my fists clenching in preparation for the pain as it started to consume me. A lifetime later, I was human again, the Imurian uniform puddled around my feet. *How DO you do that with the clothing?*

TALENT. REARRANGE MOLECULES. I felt smugness emanating from my hair. I cast my eyes upwards but I had to get back to Zoe.

First I ran into my room, threw on pajamas, grabbed washcloths and towels from the bathroom, then ran back to her and applied pressure. She stifled a groan at the sudden push on her wounded side but she didn't open her eyes. *Think, Jessi! What else can I do?* I'm sure her nannies were fighting frantically to keep her alive but they needed all the tools. What did she need the most?

She needed blood and fluids. I didn't have medical equipment and right now I didn't trust any medic; what if that Dr. Le'Nar'te showed up? Or was monitoring the medical clinic for Zoe? What else could I do?

*I'm open to suggestions. Anything? We need to hurry; we can't lose her and we especially can't do it in my room bur we can't call for help.*

Silence but I felt my whole body thinking hard. Finally, my hair relaxed just the tiniest bit.

GIVE OUR BLOOD.

Aack. It was kidding, right? What if she and I weren't compatible blood types? Oh. Wait. My blood type is O negative; therefore, I am a universal donor—for humans, anyway. Ok so how could I give her blood? A blood transfusion would require medical staff and equipment and I couldn't risk that. Zoe's life hung in the balance, though, and I couldn't let her die, even at the risk of her recapture, no matter how much I disliked her.

GIVE HER TRANSFUSION.

*How in the bloody gates of hell can we do that?*

CREATE TUBING AND TRANSFER BLOOD.

Indecision tore at me. Do a field transfusion in the crudest way possible—*using my hair!*—or risk calling Medical? I knew if I didn't do something for her, she was going to die.

TRY.

Well, if the crude way didn't work, I could always call Medical. I heartily hoped I wouldn't have to do that; I had no way to explain what happened to Zoe, or to me, for that matter.

In my overwhelming concern for Zoe and amongst the pain of changing back to my body, I'd forgotten my own wounds. I looked at my thigh, pulling my pajama waistband out so I could look. The wound on the front of the leg was red and angry but not as bad as it had felt. *Their gun must have been on stun, also. But why didn't I collapse when it hit me?*

ADRENALINE. HEAL FAST.

Bemused, I quirked a small smile. *So I see.*

GET KNIFE.

I ran into the kitchen and grabbed the smallest, sharpest knife I could find. *It's not sterile!*

NO TIME.

*Now what?*

SIT DOWN.

I sat on the floor next to Zoe's unconscious body on the couch.

MAKE OPENING IN VEIN.

I took a breath. *Wait a minute, I need something.* I got up and dashed into my room, grabbing a scarf. I ran back, twisting the scarf into a tight length, then tied it around her upper arm. I felt for the bulge of a vein at the junction of her upper arm to the lower arm. I then used two fingers to stretch the skin over the vein and I knicked it open with the tip of the knife. A few drops of blood welled out. My hair formed itself into a small tube and entered her arm through the opening. *How in all the starry heavens do you do these things?* My hair ignored me.

I felt an odd sensation, like someone was sucking through a straw, only I was the straw. I drew in a shaky breath, moving my hands to pin down Zoe's arm, in case she came to and started to thrash around. Her shallow breathing deepened a bit as I felt

*Exchanger*

the suction continue on my body. After a while, I felt an urgent need to lie down, and let me head drop forward but I didn't want to move while the transfusion was occurring. Finally, after an eternity or perhaps two, my hair withdrew from her arm, startling me from my exhaustion and haze. I grabbed an unused washcloth and slapped it over her arm to stop the blood welling out. *Did you give her one unit?*

YES.

*How do you know?*

NANNIES TALK.

I blinked at that. The nannies could communicate? I guess that made sense; they were, after all, microscopic computers. *Okay, then. What now?*

TIME. REST. FLUIDS.

Yeah, I could second that idea. I laid my head on my arms and yawned. A sudden pressing thirst made me raise my head to look at Zoe, now looking less pale and breathing more naturally. Maybe it had worked. There was no way I gave her more than a unit of blood, if that, from my body but maybe I'd given her enough to get the edge on her healing. I didn't want to ever do something so bizarre and stupid like that again. *What about infection?*

NANNIES FIX.

Ah, yes, of course, that was part of their job, to regulate the immune system. It's a very large part of why my brother's death from a mysterious illness was so odd because it was very rare to get ill in the first place, and even rarer for an illness to bypass our nannies. Speaking of which, I'd rescued Zoe and now saved her life but I hadn't gotten any answers in the lab area. Figures Zoe would screw up my sleuthing.

I couldn't go out again, it was four in the morning by now, and we were both exhausted beyond moving plus there were Cats searching for the both of us. I couldn't go out as a Human and it was too dangerous to take on the same Imurian body right now. After gulping down a big glass of water, then placing one next to Zoe on the table by the couch, I fell asleep hearing Zoe's breathing deepening into the soft sounds of true slumber.

## CHAPTER TWENTY-FIVE

I don't know what woke me, exactly, but my arms were numb along with my butt and feet from my position on the floor. I raised my head to look with bleary eyes at Zoe who was staring at me while blinking sleep from her eyes and struggling to sit. It must've been the sound or feel of her moving.

"What—what happened? Why am I in here? Why does my side hurt so much?" Her eyes widened and she gasped. "Why is there so much blood everywhere?" Fear entered her eyes. "What did you do to me?" She shrank back from me. "Why did you hurt me?"

My jaw dropped open in astonishment. "What did I do to you? *What did I do to you?*" I shook out my arms as if that would speed up circulation and get rid of the pins and needles faster. "I saved your sorry ass, that's what I did. I saved your ungrateful life. I'm *not* the one who hurt you, you ungrateful piece of—" I stopped the flow of words and took a breath, shaking my head; she didn't remember what happened, no need to snap at her. "You were hurt badly, Zoe, and I took you into my room and did what I could for you. That's all." I looked off to the side to avoid the shocked look on her face. Why would she believe me? We weren't friends, not even close.

"I—what did you say? You saved me?" Maybe the memory drug had worked after all. Oh, great, now how was I going to explain this if she didn't remember. I opened my mouth to say something, but then her face changed. She put her hands over her face. "I thought it was all a nightmare. I thought—hoped it wasn't real." She looked up at me. "It was all real, wasn't it?" She said in a very quiet voice. She stared at the floor as her hand probed her side and she winced with pain.

I nodded. "Yes."

"Why am I in your room and not mine?" She frowned. "Why aren't the medics here?"

"The Cat who brought you said it was too dangerous and brought you here instead. He said people were waiting in your room to take you captive again."

"Oh." She bit off the word as she shuddered. "So that part was real. Why me? What did I ever do to them? Those Cats…why? Did they…..you know, did they?" She jerked her head side to side. "I—I don't remember all the details."

"They were about to." I didn't know how else to say it so I went with simplicity. "But they didn't. The Imurian said he stopped them."

She shivered. "I'm a flirt and I know it but it's only for fun and only for us, you know, us Humans." She looked away from me. "I never asked for—I never wanted to—I wasn't there because I wanted to be." A beat of silence. "I didn't agree to anything…did I?"

"No, you didn't." I couldn't believe I was sympathizing with her but there it was. She needed gentleness right now and understanding. "It's okay, Zoe, it didn't happen and you're safe now. I don't know the reason why they had you there in the first place. Do you?"

"No. That doctor guy said something about Acne, akron, Ack-something, but I don't know what he was talking about."

"Did he say Akrion?"

She shrugged. "Maybe that's the word he used. Do you know what it is?"

"Nope. But I think we need to find out." I meant that only for my ears; apparently I said it too loud.

"We? I'm not going back there! I'm not!" She clutched her arms around herself, gasping in panic.

"It's okay, Zoe, no one is asking you to, so please, calm down." I reached up and laid a gentle hand on her arm." It was the 'royal we', as my Mom used to say."

She wrinkled her nose and furrowed her brow but stopped rocking her body. "What does that mean?"

"I'm not sure but it's something like orders from on high, I guess."

She made a gesture that meant 'whatever'. "What now? Why does my side hurt so much?"

"We—er, that is, you were shot, or so the Officer told me. He said it's not life threatening but you lost a lot of blood from it." I watched her eyes widen in shock, mouth dropping open. She yanked the cloth away from her side, staring down at the wound on her side. "Bloody hell." She said in a faint voice. "I'm going to have a scar there."

Ignoring that, I went on, "I've been thinking. Oh, quit rolling your eyes, it does happen occasionally." She must be feeling better if she could act like her old self. "I think for safety's sake, neither of us should be alone at night so I think you should sleep here. It's only two more nights but there's safety in numbers, as they say." I blew out a breath. "I also think we should let Officer B'le'ru know about tonight. Or Si'neada."

She clutched my arm. "No! I don't want anyone to know, no one! Promise me." Her fingernails dug into my arm. "Please!"

"All righty, then. You can take your fingernails out of my skin now. I promise." Just like that, we were back to our old relationship except now we had the heavy weight of this secret between us.

"Good. Why weren't you taken to that lab?"

I shrugged. "I don't know why they took you there or why they left me in my room but more reason to never be alone. Although it's damned lucky for you I was still awake."

"Who was the Cat Officer who brought me here?"

"I don't know, actually." *Because I didn't think I needed a name.* "There was no time for all that; you were bleeding heavily from that gunshot and while I was tending to you, he left, saying he'd make sure no one came to my room."

"Oh. I guess that's good." She frowned. "I wonder why he came to that lab."

"I don't know, Zoe. Maybe he found out what they were doing and went to stop them."

"Maybe."

I started to get up but she put out a hand to stop me.

"I have to ask you something, Jessi." She sighed. "I have to know."

"Know what?"

Staring at her hands, she said in a quiet tone, "I have some odd gaps in my memory and I wonder if that wasn't my first time there. There've been a few mornings, when I woke up, I felt like things weren't right, like, I don't know, just not, you know, right." She blew out her breath.

I gasped in a shocked breath. It hadn't occurred to me there might've been other times she was taken to the lab. "Oh, my gods, Zoe." I sucked in another breath. "How would we know? Especially if they used that memory erasing drug on you."

She stared at her blood encrusted hands and then abruptly swung her legs over to the floor. "I have to pee. And wash this blood off." She looked at me, frowning. "What memory drug?"

"The Officer said they injected you with something to make you forget everything." I didn't mention the fertility drug; since they hadn't gotten to the rape part, I didn't figure she needed to know that yet. She'd had enough shocks already.

She washed a hand over her face, then her hair. "I must look a fright. Memory drugs, eh? That would definitely explain why I don't remember everything that happened tonight." She levered herself to a standing position, swaying, then with a determined look on her face, she wobbled off to the bathroom. "I'll be right back. I have an idea."

A few minutes later, she returned to the couch, dropping heavily onto the cushions with none of her usual grace. I'd dragged a chair over near the couch so I could get off the floor. Her hair was combed and face washed, hands now free of blood. The skin around her eyes looked bruised and blue, lips a pale red set against pasty white skin.

She said, avoiding my eyes. "Are you still, uh, intact, Jessi?"

She picked up the water glass and starting sipping, glancing at me, embarrassment evident on her face.

"What?" I wrinkled my nose. "I guess so. I'm in one piece, anyway."

"I mean…" Her face turned pinker. She mumbled, "I mean, are you still a virgin?" She drained the glass, setting it down with a thump.

I gawped at her. "Why in the name of the Heavens are you asking me *that*?"

She twisted her mouth in discomfort. "Please. I need to know because…..I just need to know."

"Okay. Yes. Okay?" I said in my most sarcastic tone. "You happy now?"

"Okay. Me, too." She said in a small voice, holding a hand up.

My mouth opened and closed a few times like a fish out of water. "Ah, okay then. Thanks for asking and thanks for sharing."

She shook her head. "You don't understand." She raised her head to look at me. "Yeah, I know I make it seem like I've had relations with guys but I haven't been willing to go that far just yet. I'm still exploring, you might say, but not ready to commit to sex." She clenched her fists. "But if I'm *not* a virgin now, then…" She waved a hand in a helpless way.

"Ok. Then….oh!" I furrowed my brow. "How will you know?"

"I tried to look in the mirror while I was in the bathroom, but, you know, looking down under isn't easy, even with a hand mirror. Right? You know that?"

"Uh, right." I mumbled. This was *not* a subject I wanted to discuss with anyone, much less Zoe.

"So…Okay." She sucked in a breath. "I need you to look."

I froze in place. She couldn't possibly mean….what I thought she meant.

She waved a hand over her crotch area. "There. I need you to look there. I have to know." Her teeth clenched and she still couldn't meet my eyes.

I buried my face in my hands. *Oh, Gods, shoot me now. Take me out of this hell pit.* "I'm *not* looking at your velvet, Zoe! I wouldn't do that for my best friend and you're not even close!"

"Velvet?" She stared at me with a baffled look. "What the flaming hells does velvet have to do with anything?

I picked at a hangnail, refusing to look at her. "When I was a little girl and my mother was teaching me names for body parts, when she said that word, vulva, I didn't hear it right so I thought she'd said velvet, because that was the only word that made sense to me. My mom was quite amused and told me that was as good a word as any and since that part of our bodies was soft like velvet, it was more appropriate than vulva." I dragged in a breath as I looked at her with defiance. "I'm not looking."

She drew her knees to her chest. "Please. I have to know. I have to. I have no one else to trust so it has to be you."

"Zoe, you don't even *like* me. And now you want me looking *there*? That can't be undone, you know. It'll be something I can't forget. Ever. No matter how much I will want to. And Gods know I'm not showing you mine."

"You're going to be a doctor, right?"

I nodded. *Oh, no.*

"Then you are going to be doing things like this as a doctor, yes?"

*She had me there.* "Yes."

"Then, please, please, please, take a look. There is no one else I can ask."

I sucked in air. "I'm not a doctor yet, you know." *I'd rather have 14 daggers plunged into me.*

She shrugged. "True. But I can't go the Imurians doctors, can I? I'm *not* asking one of the guys to look! You are my only hope right now of knowing." Her fists clenched. *"I have to know."* She hissed the words through clenched teeth.

I blew out my breath. *Hells and damnation.* "I understand, Zoe. First tell me why you dislike me so much."

She tilted her head to one side and regarded me, then peered at her fingernails. "You remind me of my little sister, Princess," she spat out the name, "who can do no wrong." She held up her hand. "Yeah, it's wrong of me to make that comparison but I can't ever be right around her at home and that spilled over onto you. Also, in a lot of ways, I'm jealous of you for the attention you get for being so small and cute with your long, beautiful hair and those crushing blue eyes and all the things you're good at doing." Her voice faded out. "I'm so sorry, Jessi." Then she chortled, a startling sound. "We can be the Velvet Sisters and then I'll think of you as an adult, not as my pesky little sister."

"Or the Velve-twins." I blurted out and then laughed. After a startled pause, she joined in and we laughed until we were crying, another shock in this suddenly different universe. We laughed until we ran out of breath. Then, limp from the release of tension, pain, fear and anger from the long night, we looked at each other.

"You know, Jessi, I'll have to treat you the same in public because how can we explain a huge difference in our behavior, you know, just like that?" She snapped her fingers.

"I understand." I nodded as we linked pinkies in an unspoken promise. "Okay, Zoe, I'll do it. Just like a doctor would. But under no circumstances whatsoever am I touching you, you know, down there." I raised an eyebrow. "Just so you know." I had wanted to become friends with Zoe, true, but I never ever thought in a million galaxies it would be through something like this, something so intimate and private.

She nodded, relief on her face. "I have to know, Jessi."

I heaved a big sigh. "Okay. Let's get this over with. Show me your velvet."

A flashlight and a moment later, I knew and Zoe sucked in a breath. She could tell by the look on my face what I had seen, or to be more precise, what I hadn't seen. She was no longer a virgin.

## CHAPTER TWENTY-SIX

"So it's true, what I thought." She sniffed back tears, scrubbing a hand over her face, voice thick. "Is that coffee?"

Horse crap in a barrel. It was time to get ready for our classes that day and I'd almost rather break an arm than go. "Yeah, its coffee. I'm so sorry, Zoe"

She shook her head. "Not your fault. I'll deal with it somehow. I wonder if I had fun." She smiled a watery smile and wiped her eyes. "It is what it is. But I think I will stay with you from now on until we leave this ship. What were they trying to do? I don't remember everything that happened before they shot me."

"That doctor said something about impregnating you." I grabbed her hand and squeezed it. "I don't see how you could be since it would be inter-species and nothing like that happened to you tonight. I think we should report this to the authorities."

Her face went white again. "Oh, bloody gods, no! What would I tell them? 'I think I've been raped because I'm not a virgin now but I don't know who or when.'" She gave a brittle laugh. "Oh, yeah, that would be so darned believable. I'm sure the authorities would totally believe me, with no proof, no awareness and no memory of who or when." Her voice dripped sarcasm and bitterness as she clutched my hand tighter.

"You're right; gods almighty, I hate that you're right. We have no way to prove anything." I patted her hand. "However, on a better note, the doctor said something about how tonight would be 'the deciding factor in the experiment' and it wasn't completed, so I don't think fertilization could happen, Zoe. I think you're okay."

She squared her shoulders. "I would know, right? Wouldn't I? What would your mom say? She's a Reproduction Specialist." Then she looked at me with a puzzled look. "How do you know what the doctor said?"

Oops. "The Officer told me what was said. I'm just passing along the words."

"Oh. So, what would your mom say?"

"She'd say you would know, you would feel different." I peered at her. "Do you feel, I don't know, expectant?"

"No." She pressed her hands over her flat belly. "No, I feel the same as always, although my side hurts like unholy hell."

"It's good you feel the same as you normally do." I said in a brisk tone. I stood, still holding her hand. "We have to risk going to your room for your stuff because Lordy knows my robes won't fit you."

She made a face. "Yeah, I have to, don't I? I certainly can't wear your little girl gowns, that's for sure." She sniffed in a dismissive way. I guess a thank-you note from her would be too much to ask after all, velv-Twins or not. "Okay, Princess, help me up."

"I'm not your Princess, Zoe; I'm your velve-Twin." I cocked my head at her, eyebrows raised.

She flashed me a startled look as she stood on wobbly legs and made a face at me. "Fair enough. You're kind of pale, you know."

"I'm pale? You should see yourself! You look like you were dipped in flour, you're so white!" And there it was again, I couldn't stop it—laughter, soul relieving gut hurting guffaws hitting me with the suddenness of a sledge hammer. I doubled over and Zoe started laughing, too, clutching her side as she sat, both of us gasping for air. I blurted out, "You should see how you looked before I gave you blood."

Dead silence. "You did what? How?"

I wiped my eyes. "You desperately needed blood, I was afraid to call the medics, so I figured it out and the nannies took care of the rest. I am a doctor's daughter, after all. So just think, Zoe, at least for a while, you'll carry around a little of me." I reached out and tapped her nose. "You little lucky ducky, I know how much it means to you."

"You gave me blood." She said in a faint tone. "How did you know we'd be compatible?"

"I'm O negative, universal donor."

"Oh. But how—?" She shook her head. "I can't think about that right now. I need to pee again before going into the corridor." She made her wobbly way to the refresher room.

A chime sounded at the door. I made a face; what now? I asked, "Who is it?" and Room said, "Si'neada." Well, boogers. Why was he here now? I opened my mouth to tell Room to send him away when I felt a tug on my robe near my feet and I jumped straight in the air from fear, eyes wide, heart pounding and hands shaking.

"Good morning to you, too." Deester said. "Let Si'neada in. We both know what happened."

I drew in a breath to steady my nerves as I placed a hand over my galloping heart. "You scared me to death, Deester! How about a little warning next time before you just pop into sight?"

He covered a grin with his hand, eyes sparkling with mirth.

My eyes cut to the bloody cloths in the sitting room. Oh, crap-ola. How was I going to hide all that?

He flashed sharp teeth at me as he looked at the cloths. "Just let him in. We will to help you dispose of, ah, the stuff."

Nothing I could do; he'd already seen the bloody rags so I sighed and signaled the room to open the door. Si'neada bustled in, exclaiming, "My little cosmic ray, are you all right?" He looked around. "Where is Zoe?"

I pointed at the bathroom.

"Is she all right? Was she hurt badly? There is a ship search for her! But all on the hush-hush, you to know. I hurried here to make sure you are all right; the others looking for Zoe do not mean to treat her kindly."

"I gathered that from the officer who brought her here. She has a shoot wound to her right side but it was far enough out it didn't hit any vital organs. She did lose quite a bit of blood, however, as you can see."

"Oh, my little rescuer! It is so fine you were ready to take her in your room! I must to see her for myself, you to know."

Zoe came out of the bathroom as if her name summoned her, her skin still pale but tinged with color while her eyes looked bruised and tired. She gave me a scathing look. "You promised!" Hurt underlined her words.

I held my hands up in supplication. "I didn't tell them; I swear. They just showed up and said they already knew everything."

"They?" She looked around and then down, doing a double-take. "Deester? What are you doing here?"

My turn to stare at her. "You know Deester?"

"Yes, yes," Si'neada said, "everyone knows everyone here. Zoe, what happened? This is so very distressing; are you all right? I heard you were shot!" He covered his mouth with both hands as Deester patted her leg.

"Well, I feel like a thousand boulders and one big knife just rammed me to the ground but I guess I have to thank Jessi here for my life. Some officer brought me here, I passed out and when I came to, I found myself in Jessi's room."

Si'neada said with a frown, "Zoe? Do you want me to escort you to Medical? You are so very pale and I think you need to receive blood or something. I must to see this wound to be sure it is not vital."

Zoe said, "Jessi gave me blood already; it's the reason I can stand and walk."

*Thanks for the bomb, Zoe.*

Heads swiveled to stare at me. "I am a doctor's daughter, people. I have O-neg blood so it was a reasonable thing to do."

Si'neada blinked rapidly as he tried to assimilate this information. "How? You have medical equipment?"

"The officer grabbed supplies from the lab on his way out with Zoe." I lied. "He thought they might come in handy."

Zoe interrupted. "Do you know who the officer was? I'd like to thank him."

Si'neada shook his head. "No, we do not know who it is. There is turmoil in the science area, like someone kicked a hive, and the whole ship is being searched for the mysterious officer and for you. No one seems to know him."

*Yeah, and they won't find him. I'll have to be someone else next time.*

Si'neada snapped his head toward me. Uh oh, apparently I'd sent that thought out. *:Next time, little one? Be someone else? What do you mean by that?:*

Oh. No. He'd Heard me. I hadn't meant to broadcast the thought but obviously my control wasn't perfect yet. Well, poop in a bucket. How did I explain this?

Zoe clutched Si'neada's arm. "You won't let them find me, will you? Please say you won't!"

Si'neada patted her hand. "No, my lovely friend, I will to be sure they cannot have you again. You will not be alone again until after you leave this ship. You will to be safe on Amorpha."

She thumped down in the chair. "Please make it true."

"But I do wonder who the mysterious officer is." Si'neada mused. "There are, of course, many on board I do not know—after all, our population is around 20,000 Imurians, but I would to think I would have come across him before somewhere."

Deester giggled. "I think the mysterious officer is really Jessalya."

Our attention riveted on him at the same instance. "What?" "What did you say?" Our voices overlapped. I think my heart actually stopped for a beat or two.

Deester drew himself upright as far as he could and pointed at me with a flourish. "She is a Shape Exchanger. I have seen it myself."

Zoe's mouth dropped open. I glared at Deester while Si'neada gasped, then laughed. "Of course she is the impossible. What was I thinking? I would to expect nothing less from our little Human." He laughed again, then said, "Good joke, Deester."

"I have seen her." Deester insisted. "I have vid of her exchanging one body for the other."

That little rat bastard. Could I get away with strangling him in front of everyone?

Si'neada looked back and forth between us, tapping a finger against his lips. "Vid? You are not making a joke?" Bewilderment laced his voice.

Deester said, looking smug, "I am not joking. I have vid proof." I tried to kick him but he danced out of my reach.

Zoe said in a faint voice, "Will I become one of those, too, whatever it is? She gave me her blood."

Our heads swiveled her way. I think we'd all forgotten she was there. "No?" I offered. I had no clue; it certainly hadn't been the intention and besides, I didn't know how or why I shape changed so had no idea if I could give the ability to anyone else.

Si'neada asked me, "When did this to start, this exchanging? If it is, of course, true."

I looked at Deester and scowled as ferociously as I could at him, willing him to retract his words. He gave me a thumbs-up gesture with a toothy grin.

I snarled, "Of course it isn't true! It's impossible and we all know it! Right, Deester?" I glowered at him. He smirked at me in return.

Zoe objected, "I want to see this vid first. I demand to know what might happen to me!" She glowered at me. "Did you think this through before contaminating me with your blood?" She tapped her foot, fists clenched. "I can't frackin' believe this! *What have you done to me*?"

I flinched back. "I don't—I can't shape shift, Zoe! That's impossible!" I held up a placating hand. "I gave you enough blood so you'd survive, that's all, I swear. I don't have any diseases, you know that."

"Then who's this mysterious officer no one can find on this ship? Tell me that, Jessi!"

"I don't know! He showed up at my door with you dripping blood everywhere so I let him bring you in! You looked horrible and he suggested I give you blood to help you recover faster. After all, nannies are their tech so they should know what they can do. He said you didn't have enough left to heal yourself properly so it was the only choice!"

Why was I defending myself? Like it or not, I saved her ass.

We stood there glaring at each other, fists clenched, until Deester stepped between us. "Humans!" He pointed at Zoe and then at me. "She saved your life which you do not to remember because you were not aware enough. Her blood helped your nannies remove the drugs you were given."

I said, "See? I told you I saved your miserable life!"

Zoe stood as tall as she could so she could look down on me. "All right. You saved my life. Thank you." She said the words as if each one burned a hole in her tongue.

Deester chirped in a way too happy voice, "I will to show you this quick vid. Yes, yes, Jessi, I to know you wanted this kept a dreadful mystery from all but it is important everyone here knows; this is important for your own safety which is why I speak the truth to them. Since you are the impossible, we do not to know how she will be affected by your blood. It is only fair she gains knowledge if her life is to change, also."

I huffed out a breath. Okay, that was reasonable but that didn't mean I had to like it. "Oh, all right. Let's see this supposed vid."

*Maybe he didn't really film it, maybe I can come up with some reasonable explanation. Or maybe I'm busted.*

Deester said, with a toothy smile, "I have sent it to your PD, Jessi and Si'neada. Zoe, I do not to believe you have yours with you."

Zoe shook her head. "I don't."

I picked mine up as Si'neada did and we each opened our viewing screens. The vid from Deester was ready so with dread clutching my throat, I touched the "Play" button, Zoe crowding close to look over my shoulder. In the opening scene, I saw myself sitting with my eyes closed and fists clenched, suddenly crumpling to the floor. Then we gasped as my body began to malform, joints slithering and muscles regrouping as my hair wrapped around me, melting into my skin to become Imurian hair. My stomach lurched in rebellion; I was glad I hadn't eaten anything yet. Zoe's hand covered her mouth. It's bad enough to feel the pain of transforming but it was so much worse to see it.

"Frackin' fairy farts in an air tight bag!" Zoe said in a faint voice. "That has to be CGI, right? Something the computer made up to look like you're actually changing?"

In that instance, I loved Zoe for suggesting the explanation. "Yes! That's what happened, it has to be because everyone knows shape changing is utterly impossible." I clutched at the words like a life line.

Si'neada said, while slowly shaking his head, "I would to like to agree but I cannot. This is real." He looked at me with a look in his eyes; I wasn't sure if it was pity or excitement or both. "This is real." He breathed the words into the air. "Oh, my little exchanger, you are the impossible."

## CHAPTER TWENTY-SEVEN

"No." I said. "You said it yourself, it's impossible. It's CGI, has to be."

He shook his head. "No, my little pack of needles, you *are* the impossible. This is not CGI. Do not argue, little one." He held up a hand to forestall me from talking. "It is impossible but yet, it is not. This type of vid cannot be faked." He shook himself. "I must to speak to my—the Queen about this."

I opened my mouth but Si'neada shook his head again. "No. You cannot deny this. We all have seen this now with our own eyes." He pointed a finger at me. "I to understand your need for secrecy but we did to need to know and we will to keep your secret to preserve your life." :*I must tell the queen, however. It is imperative.*:

I deflated. How had I gone from zero people knowing to three? "What would happen to me if anyone else finds out?"

He made a face. "It would not be good and you would be fought over. The scientists would take you for experiments and to see if they can replicate your abilities. Any military would want you for a weapon. Any government would want you for a spy. There are those who would kill you to prevent you from being used for anything or for being replicated. There are those who would want you for clandestine things, like training you to be an assassin." Si'neada said. "We will to keep you safe, my little surprise package. All here must be sworn to secrecy as your life and your freedom are at stake."

I felt faint and groped behind me for the sofa. I sat down, ignoring the bloody cloths, dropping my face into my hands. "I never wanted any of this; I didn't ask for any of this to happen. I thought it was just—oh, bloody hells, I gave Zoe my blood."

Zoe gasped. "You—me. I could be—no. Oh, hairy balls of fire." I raised my head to look at her as she clutched her hair with both hands. Deester hugged her leg to soothe her. Zoe looked at me. "This is a disaster. If I hadn't seen that vid, I wouldn't have believed anything like this could happen." She looked at Si'neada. "You're telling the truth? It's not CGI?"

He smiled a little. "I am telling the truth, all of the truth. I am as shocked as you."

"I know how you feel. Believe me." I sighed. "For what it's worth, it didn't start until this trip so I really think you won't become a shape changer. For whatever reason, something happened to me, maybe the same thing that killed my brother, and that might be why I'm this way." Then a thought struck me and I swallowed back bile. "Maybe it's going to kill me, too."

That brought a startled silence to the room; no one seemed to know how to answer that. One thing for sure, I'd already outlived my brother by a whole lot of years so that was some comfort.

"Does it hurt to change? It looks painful." She asked with a frown on her face. "I'd forgotten about your brother; I'm sorry, Jessi."

I nodded to acknowledge her words. "Oh, hells, yes. The worst pain you can imagine, like knives slicing and dicing me into other shapes. It's not something I want to ever do again but it was the only way into the Science Lab area. And you're damned lucky I did; otherwise, you'd be a lot worse off."

She shuddered as she clutched her side. "You're right." She huffed out a sigh. "Yeah, you're right and I appreciate your showing up in time."

I looked around the room. "We'd better get this cleaned up or there'll be more questions than we want to answer."

Si'neada said, "Yes, please to do that. I will to speak to the Queen about this matter. I will to come to get you later, Jessi. Zoe, you will be safe as long as you are not alone so you will stay always with another. Please do not return to your room without me or another Human. And you must not speak of this to anyone. Ever. Promise."

She nodded. "I promise. Besides, who would believe me?" She tilted her head to side in a quizzical way. "Who is the Queen?"

"She is one of the females aboard this ship. All our females are called Queens."

"Can I meet her?"

"I will to ask if she wants to be met. It is her decision, not mine."

I quipped, "So it just looks like the ship is run by males but really, it's the Queens who do the real work, right?"

Si'neada lifted one side of his upper lip and then sighed. "Yes, that is more or less true."

Zoe tilted her head to one side. "Okay. I'd like to meet her if possible. If Jessi gets to meet her, I should be able to meet her, too."

*Don't hold your breath, Zoe.*

Si'neada said, with an easy chuckle, "Oh, rivalry!" He clapped his hands once. "It is not a contest, my dear Zoe! If the Queen wants to meet you, I will to let you know, I promise." Then he looked at me. "My little delight, if you will to finish cleaning yourself up, we will to stop at Zoe's room to get her things and then on to breakfast. But we must now hurry to do this before the others arrive in the corridor."

I did a hurry-up job on cleaning myself up, got dressed in one of my robes and hurried back to the sitting area. "What about the mess in here?" I asked, as I gestured to the bloody clothes and stains on the couch.

Deester held up his two top hands, palms toward me. "Not to worry, I will to clean up the area so no one will ever know this happened in here. I will to burn the cloths."

"Then I'm as ready as I'm going to be." I announced.

We three left the room, leaving Deester behind to contend with the cleaning. Zoe opened her room and let Si'neada enter first to make sure it was safe to come in. Even with all her haste and her wounded side, she looked a whole bunch better than I did. My eyes were gritty from lack of sleep, I'd not taken time for make-up and even my hair felt sullen and grumpy. I had swiped the toothbrush over my teeth in my room but even so, they felt mossy to my tongue.

She flipped her perfectly brushed blonde hair over her shoulders, make-up applied to hide her pallor and she made a determined motion of her hand away from her sore side. We stepped into the hallway with Si'neada as the guys emerged from their rooms and we waved to them. Keaton raised his eyebrows. "Whoa, Jessi. Rough night? You look rode hard and put away wet."

*Gee, thanks.* I yawned, covering my mouth with my hand. *See? I'm trainable.* "Yeah, I had trouble sleeping and I missed the alarm so didn't have much time to get ready." I rubbed my gritty eyes with one hand.

"Sorry to hear that." He punched me playfully on the shoulder. "I'll help you stay awake in class."

"Thanks." I smothered another yawn. "And thanks for pointing out how bad I look."

Mitchler chuckled. "Yeah, he's so tactful. Truthfully, Jessi, you don't look that bad; just tired." He picked up a hank of my hair, not knowing how close he came to losing a fingertip or two. "Your hair seems curlier than usual this morning."

"How can you tell, Mitchler?" Zoe snapped and wincing as she clamped her right arm to her side. "Her hair is always a coiled mess." *Newsflash: Zoe's baaaack. Just like she warned me.*

Mitchler said in a mild tone, "I doubt she can help how curly her hair is. I'll bet it would be really long if you didn't have all those curls."

I smiled. "Yeah, it'd probably reach the floor. At least it's hard to tell if I forget to brush it."

"True enough."

As we walked, I felt a deep ache in my side from my wound and my thigh wanted to cramp but I made sure I walked in a normal manner, tough as that was. I realized if I were feeling sore, then Zoe had to be really hurting. Deester had brought skin glue to fix her wound but it still had to be very painful. I sympathized; I wanted to be asleep in my bed, too, but if she could suck it up and act normal, so could I.

Classes that day dragged for me and it was worse for Zoe. Her color was pasty by the time lunch rolled around and she visibly drooped by the time we got to the lunch table. Soli said with concern, "Zoe? Are you ill? You look like you don't feel well. Perhaps you should go see the medics?"

She raised a hand in a dismissive way. "No, I'm okay. I had a headache this morning when I awoke and it hasn't gone away. That's all. I'm going to take some pills for it right now. Happens now and then."

"Are you sure?" Soli said with a frown.

"Not my first headache, Soli, but I appreciate your concern. I'll be all right after I take these." She displayed two pills in her hand, commonly given for minor ailments. She threw them in her mouth and washed them down with water. "I think I'll only have soup for lunch, though."

"Good idea," he murmured.

Somehow we made it through the rest of the afternoon and dinner. As we were being escorted back to our quarters, I dropped behind the group and tugged Zoe to slow down. I whispered to Zoe, "Do you want to come to my room now?"

She shook her head. "Not yet. I'm going to Keaton's room for a while to study for a bit like we normally do so nothing seems out of place."

"Zoe, remember you need to stay with me tonight."

"Yeah, I know. I'll ping you when I'm ready for bed. Okay? We can stop by my room first to get my stuff so you can take it to your room for later."

"That's a plan." I agreed.

We caught up with the guys and Zoe said to Keaton, "I need to get something from my room so you guys go on and I'll be right there." The three guys went into Keaton's quarters while I waited for Zoe inside her room. She came out of her bedroom in a couple of minutes with a bundle of things, handing it to me.

She went to Keaton's room as I palmed open my own door. As I entered, I saw my quarters were pristine as if nothing had ever happened and I promised myself to thank Deester first chance I got. As I sat down on the chair, my PD pinged and Si'neada's message said to meet him in 15 minutes at the elevator.

After meeting, we stopped at the same door to the Queen's quarters as before, both of us checking the hallway, heads wagging back and forth like a dog's tail. Si'neada, dressed this evening in a soft gray outfit with fanciful embroidery around the collar and cuffs, touched the announcement pad and the door opened as if on command. "Enter, please, Si'neada, Jessalya." The Queen's voice invited us in.

She reclined on the couch as before and she gestured for us to sit. This time she was dressed in utilitarian clothes: a pair of what I'd term cargo pants, a buttoned top with multiple pockets, both in matching shades of brown and gold. The sleeves were long but not cuffed and fell gracefully around her wrists. She wore slit-toed dark brown boots. Her series of earrings were gold balls halfway up the outer edge of both ears. I instinctively raised a hand to my own ears. First of all, they were my ears, oh, thank goodness, and second of all, yes, I'd remembered to put in my main earrings today. I never removed the blue topaz stones, but I felt naked if I forgot the main pair.

I nodded to her, Si'neada still standing while I'd chosen the same seat as before, across from her. "Greetings, Queen. How are you today?" I bowed my head a little toward her, sitting up straight, hands flat on my knees.

"I am busy as always. How are your studies going?"

I shrugged. "Well enough, I suppose."

"What do you to think about the talent show? I understand you and Tatro are to dance a Late Childhood folk dance together, as if you are father and daughter, because you are small enough to be a child."

Oh. That's why he chose that dance, to demonstrate how a father teaches a child to dance. Those are the kind of things I have to put up with as a very short person. "Yes, that's right. And I volunteered to do a line dance routine for the show." A sudden idea struck me. "I don't suppose any of your kitlings would like to learn a routine with me? I mean, line dancing is a solo dance but at the same time, it's part of a larger group all doing the same dance—in lines." I raised my eyebrows with a small smile. "It would be fun and perhaps something they haven't learned before."

She smiled, one ear tilting back as she raised one eyebrow. "That would be fun but not allowed."

Si'neada interjected, giving me a significant look. "Enough chat, we do not to have much time. There is something we must discuss right now and it is very, very important, so important I am not sure what to do about it."

The queen's eyes widened a little bit, ears flattening a little in uncertainty. "What is this grave matter, then?"

I held up a hand and said, "Before Si'neada says anything, I'd like to know why you summoned me here again."

She looked at me. "Your journey is coming to an end and there are important things to discuss, you and I. But first, let me hear from Si'neada." She turned her gaze to him, making it obvious she wouldn't say anything else until she heard his news.

Si'neada took in a deep breath and then said, "She," and he pointed at me, "is an Exchanger."

She tilted her head to the side. "But we all knew that."

"No, not an Alien Exchanger, well, I mean of course she is that, too, but I mean she is a *body exchanger*." He paused for a second. "She can change her body into other forms." The words fell with a heavy thump between us as I jerked with shock and hoped the Queen hadn't noticed.

Her eyes widened even more, whiskers tight against her face in surprise, ears tilting forward with total attention, her gaze riveting onto my face. "That is impossible. We to know it is impossible."

He waved his hands, his ears abruptly upright in excitement, whiskers quivering, his tail wrapping around his thigh. "She changes completely into someone else!"

She looked from him to me and when he was done, she stood with a brusque motion. "I must to see this for myself. If this is true, then this changes everything!"

I felt like a bug under a microscope the way their two gazes riveted on me; feeling defensive, I raised a hand as if to fend them off. Now there were four people who knew my ultimate secret; might as well have broadcasted it over the ship's system the way this was going.

A new voice chimed in. "I have vid of her doing it." A small hand patted my knee and I jumped a foot into the air—again. "Sorry, Jessi." He grinned, showing all his teeth.

I glared daggers at Deester. "You *have* to stop doing that!" I sputtered as I swatted at him. He ducked easily with a chuckle.

"Right now, I must to see this myself." She folded her arms and widened her stance. "We have always believed that shape changers are impossible so I to need to see *for myself* if this is truly a possible thing to happen."

Deester said with a gesture of apology to me, "I report to Queen Ler'a'neada, you see, Jessi. Please to trust me when I say this is the only way we must go for the plans."

"What plans?" I grumbled, frowning.

Deester handed a PD to the Queen, who watched The Jessi Show with her mouth dropping slowly open, ears riveted forward in attention, whiskers quivering and eyes becoming so wide they looked freaky. I chewed my lip in nervous anticipation of what she would say or think.

She looked at me with sympathy in her eyes, letting me take a breath of relief as she handed the device back to Deester. "There is so much you need to know and we to have so little time before you leave this ship. We will to need your help on Amorpha for the next year you are there." She looked over at Deester again. "Deester, destroy that vid. It must not be found or seen by anyone else. Do it now, Deester." She looked back at me. "Can you change to look like me?"

"I—I don't know. I don't have much experience yet."

Grabbing my hand, she tugged me to the wall where she murmured, "Mirror" and the wall became one. Well, I'd be a peanut flavored jelly bean.

She said, "See if you can look like me."

I wrinkled my nose. "Okay, I'll try."

*Can we be her?*

Y℈S.

I lifted my chin, already dreading what came next. *Okay, then, any time.*

Agony swelled from my bones as I closed my eyes, clenching against the hurt, holding my breath. :*Breathe with the pain, stop fighting it.*: Si'neada mind whispered the instruction to me.

I blew out air with a whoosh trying to ride the waves of pain with my breathing. It helped a little, to concentrate on regulating the flow of air into and out of my lungs.

After a million minutes, Ler'a'neada startled me when she clapped her hands together. "This is momentous! But as painful to feel, I think, as it is to watch."

I nodded as I took in a full breath. She moved to stand beside me; outwardly, we were identical in every way. "DNA?" She asked.

I nodded again.

Ler'a'neada snapped her fingers. "I have decided. Si'neada, she must be taken to the repository now. She is our insurance for the future."

My head swiveled back and forth between them. "What do you mean, insurance? Where are you taking me? What repository? Of what?"

Si'neada heaved a big breath and made a face. "Yes, I to think the queen is completely correct." He looked at me. "What we are about to show you is beyond secret, you understand?"

"Yeah, yeah, I understand. Top secret and all that stuff, like my shape changing is definitely top secret and *no one else* is to know!" I clapped a hand over my mouth. "What about Zoe? She can't be left alone for a second so what if I don't get back in time to let her into my room?"

"Not to worry," Si'neada said. "Deester will be there to scout your room for safety and let her in to stay. He will explain to her why you are not there yet but it will not be the upcoming reason, just that you had to meet with the queen and were detained."

I nodded; that should work. Surely she could step across the corridor to my room without incidence. "You know what? I'll text her to tell her Deester will let her in and that I'm still in a meeting with the Queen. Also to tell her to ask Keaton watch her to my door."

"Ah, my little starshine, that is a good idea." Si'neada said.

"So what are you going to show me?" My curiosity brimmed over like a rain-filled lake. I bounced up and down a little in anticipation. "And, Deester, if you tell *one more person,* I'll pull out your claws one by one and then the whiskers from your snout."

He giggled. That little rat bastard. He said in a airy tone, "Easy wheezy, I will to do a good job, like always," giving me a saucy salute before he scampered out of sight. "To have fun!"

Ler'a'neada said, "We will discuss what it is after we arrive. We need to be very careful on our way as the location is as secret as we can make it on a spaceship. Si'neada, please input to the ship she is safely asleep in her room."

He nodded and scooted over to her desk to tap on the interface to access the computer system.

I complained, "I didn't know you could do that. That's a little scary."

She shrugged. "Most people cannot, there are safeguards, after all. But Si'neada is a genius in many ways and he can to do it."

He looked up and said, "It is all set. Let us to go."

Ler'a'neada suddenly wrapped her hand around my forearm. She looked at me intently, making me feel a bit uneasy. *:CAN YOU HEAR ME?:*

I swear I jumped six inches off the floor. She shouted so loud it was like having an air horn go off inside my head. "Yes! Oh, my shattered nerves, *don't* shout at me again like that!" As I clutched my ears, I realized I was hearing several other voices in my head, voices overlapping. :Ler'a'neada, are you okay?: :Why are you shouting?: :Is something wrong?:

:Yes, sorry, everyone, I was annoyed at my brother although he knows that I am always right. It will not to happen again.:

She then looked at me again and said in whisker twitch talk, <Can you understand this, also?>

I twitched back at her, <Yes, I can.>

Her eyes widened in astonishment even as she grinned. Then very softly, she whispered, "That makes things much easier." She threw a dark look at Si'neada. "Why did not you tell me she could mind whisper *and* whisker talk?"

Si'neada said, "I did not to know. She has not told me everything." He crossed his arms over his chest. <We converse this way now to stay silent.>

The Queen said, <How did you learn, Jessalya?>

I shrugged. <Not know. I not good yet, not enough.> I shrugged again, whispering, "Practice." <Not know all words with whiskers yet.>

Si'neada then made some gestures with his hands. I didn't know what he was saying, if anything, so I shrugged, holding my hands out, palms up, to show confusion. In a hushed tone, I said, "If that's yet another way of talking, I don't know this one, sorry."

"It is," he said. "I bet you can learn it very quickly, also."

"Perhaps."

## CHAPTER TWENTY-EIGHT

Ler'a'neada gestured for us to follow as she opened a panel on the wall behind the couch after moving aside a hanging fabric curtain. There was a narrow corridor present, inky dark with a metallic smell wafting out. Ler'a'neada and Si'neada stepped into the darkness but I hesitated for a second until Si'neada's hand shot out, grabbed my arm and yanked me in. The panel slid closed and I almost gasped, panic starting to erupt within me—**Not enough air**—my brain shouted but then I felt the softness of a light breeze brushing against my cheek. My fear diminished as Ler'a'neada turned on a tiny light source. I heard her mind whisper. *:There is fresh air circulating through the utility passages and plenty for us to breath. Not to worry.:*

I moved silently behind them on my bare feet, still in my Imurian form, following the tiny light. The space was just wide enough to allow us to walk in single file and after a small while, I felt the sides crowding in on both sides. The trapped feeling started rising again but Ler'a'neada shone her light down as Si'neada reached back to touch my arm in reassurance and I saw a short access ladder for the next level down. *:Silence now, it is imperative.:*

I wondered again where we were headed, as we repeated the ladders several more times. The corridor followed the curve of the ship and I lost my bearings after about the 4$^{th}$ or 5$^{th}$ ladder. Finally, Ler'a'neada stopped, put her finger to her lips as she pressed up against an area of the wall. She listened intently and then nodded, my ears swiveling forward to listen, also. Just as she reached out to touch the wall, probably to press hidden buttons, she stiffened and returned to her listening pose. Her ears flattened against her head and she shined the light at her face as she said in whisker twitch <I hear voices inside.>

We both nodded as she held up her finger in a "wait one" motion. I could hear the faint susurration of voices but I couldn't distinguish words.

After an eternity of me shifting from foot to foot, Ler'a'neada finally nodded her head. She pressed on the wall in certain spots and the section slid apart like a pocket door. The sudden light of the room dazzled my eyes for a few seconds before they adjusted.

We slithered into the room between a narrow gap in shelving that was snugged up against the wall on either side of the opening and I looked around, puzzled. This was a storage area, almost a warehouse from the size and I still had no idea why they'd brought me here. Ahead were shelves with boxes of all sizes, tightly stacked to the very high ceiling. I squinted at them; the closest one read "linens", the next one read "table ware" and so on. There was dust built up on the narrow front edge of the shelves; otherwise, the boxes were so close together a piece of thinplas would have a hard time fitting between.

Si'neada switched places with me as we followed Ler'a'neada sidling her quiet way down a narrow passageway between the shelves. Boxes were stacked in orderly rows and lights from far above on the ceiling did little to penetrate the gloom at the bottom where we walked. I heard a swishing sound behind me and I peeked over my shoulder. Si'neada was swiping out our footprints behind us. I had to swallow a sudden chuckle; he had a rag tied to his tail, which was swishing back and forth, back and forth.

Finally, after umpteen rows, Ler'a'neada turned left. *Ok,* I decided to myself, *tracking a path is a skill I definitely need to improve!*

Ler'a'neada's mind voice brushed against mine in the barest of whispers. *:We're here:*

*:Ok.:* I sent back, trying to make my mind voice soft. I guessed I'm not good at modulation yet because she winced and waved her hand in a "Quiet!" gesture. I grimaced to say 'sorry'. There's another area of practice I need.

She held up a finger to indicate waiting as she looked at Si'neada. His ears swiveled as his eyes scrunched together in concentration. Ah. Got it. He was listening on all the frequencies for minds.

He finally looked up and nodded, smiling. *:We are alone and can to speak softly but I to suggest mind whispering only when necessary as I continue to scan for others.:*

He looked at me. *:To send in a whisper, you must only think of a whisper and it will to go that way.:*

*:Okay, I'll do my best.:* I thought as I imagined the volume on very, very low. They both looked pleased as they smiled and Si'neada gave me the universal finger circle of approval.

I sighed very softly. This whole thing was tiring, confusing, and disorienting. I'd no idea where we were except somewhere in the bowels of the ship, no clue how to get back to the entrance panel or even where the door to this room was, and I *still* didn't know why I was there. I drew in a breath, smelling mustiness, dust, metal and old, stale air among other, less identifiable scents. I was still in Cat form so the punch of odors was enough to occupy my brain.

:*So? Why am I here?*:

Si'neada looked amused. :*Ahhhh, my little golden star. We are about to tell you.*:

I grimaced. : *Let's hear it, then.*:

A slithering sound above me made me jump and I squeaked out a sound. What in the three hells was that noise? Where had the queen gone? She'd been right next to me a second ago. I scanned the upper shelves and saw a box moving towards me from high up in the gloom.

"Where's Ler'a'neada and why is that box about to fall on us?" In my panic, I scuttled out of the projected path of a falling box, forgetting to mind whisper. Si'neada grabbed my arm to stop me and made soothing gestures with his other hand. He whispered, "It is okay, my little friend! It is only Ler'a'neada getting the container we want and it will not to fall, I promise!"

I remained poised to bolt, my heart thumping in a staccato beat, my breath short and fast. She was way up there, we were way down here, the box was half off the edge and how was it going to get to us without falling? Si'neada's grip on me felt like a steel band, preventing me from running although I pulled against his hand. The box scooted further into the air, but it wasn't tipping forward as I expected. My jaw dropped as the container appeared to be suspended in the air and then drifted downward like a feather, only in a straighter path. I drew in a sharp breath. "Anti-gravity! Right?"

Si'neada nodded, pointing. Ler'a'neada floated in the air on her way down, holding something in her hand. The square box was much, much larger than it appeared when I saw it so many shelves up, and as it settled onto the floor, I realized it was taller than me and wider than my arms could span. Ler'a'neada scooted gently to one side, settling onto the floor beside me. She grinned. "Never seen anti-gravity before?"

"No! I thought it was only used on big space ships to land on planets."

She nodded as she murmured, "That is true, but we have miniaturized it so that it can to be used for purposes like this. However, hand held units are very, *very* expensive and scarce because they to use one particle of Akrion. This one was built while the properties of Akrion were being studied; it's been missing since then." She bared a grin, showing sharp fangs, "We figured out size is irrelevant with Akrion. So yes, it is used to land space ships."

I stared at her, my mouth dropping open. I grabbed her arm. "Akrion? Tell me about Akrion."

She raised one brow at me and then looked pointedly at my hand on her arm. I flushed, dropping my hand to my side. "Please. I must know about the Akrion."

:Si'neada, are we secure from other minds?: He nodded.

"Akrion. You found the machine in the repair area, yes?"

I nodded.

"Yes. When I was near it, I felt it calling to me. Do you know why this would happen?"

She drew in a large breath, then expelled it. "I am not totally sure, but I think it has to do with the Akrion experiment on your mothers during their journey."

"The *what?*" I yelped.

She folded her arms, staring into the distance. "Many of us were against this, but most of us were very young at the time and our words had no weight." She shook her head as if dispelling unpleasant thoughts. "Akrion is very difficult to find and to tame for use in our ships. It is the main component for our FTL drives; it makes starships skip through time like a flat rock on still water while rearranging that time. I do not understand all the physics of it. Anyway, where ever we go in any galaxy, we are always looking for and collecting Akrion whenever we can. Some think Akrion particles are shed from a Universal God; it never dies and cannot be destroyed, but can be redeployed for other uses." She sighed.

"It is the main ingredient in how we have conquered space and are able to do our exploring and finding planets for the Rent-to-Own system as it allowed us to conquer faster-than-light travel. Then the scientists decided they wanted to know what would happen if a pregnant person was bombarded with a particle of Akrion and they chose—against many people's will—your pregnant Human mothers. To be fair, they also did experiments on other species, as well, including Imurians. I am sure this is why you are a shape exchanger." She laid a gentle hand on my arm.

White hot rage flashed through me as I lost control over my emotions and my body. I fought the changing pain but the loss of control was too much. I started crying as my body writhed its way back to my Human form. Finally, I gulped in a breath, not caring my clothes were puddled around me. "This was an approved experiment? On pregnant women?" I whispered, feeling the weight of each word tearing at me, tears streaming down my face, clogging up my nose and voice.

She nodded while Si'neada patted my back with sympathy in his eyes. "Yes. It was not a unanimous vote."

"No human knew and gave permission?"

"Correct."

"Was everyone in that room affected?"

"Probably not. They only used one particle so they blew it into the room through the vent, from that machine you were drawn to, deciding randomness would suffice. They did not have a way to know which person or baby would be affected so you have all been followed since your births. That is why you were all chosen for this journey so the scientists could continue to observe closely to see if there is an effect from the Akrion."

A sudden thought hit me. "Is this what happened to my brother?"

She shrugged. "Perhaps. His body did undergo transformations no one could explain at the time."

"If there was only one particle used, how could that be if you think I have it?"

She shook her head. "We have not puzzled that out yet."

I filed that away to think about later as it didn't yet make sense to me how it could have killed Devon but I was still alive, if I had the particle.

Si'neada said, "We do not to have time for all this!"

I raised a hand to forestall him. "What about Zoe? Why are the scientists interested in her?

"I do not yet to know that answer and what he is doing is not an approved experiment. What I know is Dr. Le'nar'te is interested in getting an alien pregnant interspecies, in this case, Zoe, to study the outcome. He did not get approval for this so he did this out of the chain of command. Because of you, we have found out about this and are taking steps to stop him from continuing on this path."

"Why is he still allowed on this ship?"

"Because he is brilliant in many areas and we cannot lose his acumen." She patted my arm. "Many of us do not like this, either, and are doing everything in our power to get his removal."

I placed my steepled hands over my nose and mouth. "While I'm grateful he didn't pick me for this experiment, does he or any of the scientists suspect anything about my abilities?"

"No. Or you would not be free right now. You would be caged in the lab, something we must prevent at all costs."

"Like those youngsters in the cages?"

She nodded. "Yes, like them."

"How can we free them?"

She made a dismissive gesture. "We cannot. They are well cared for but unless you really want to start an internal war, they must be left there for the scientists to study for now. It will keep the scientists diverted. Removing those younglings? Where would you put them? How would you raise them? They will not be harmed, I to assure you."

I stared at her, not sure I believed her but they had looked well-fed and comfortable, in spite of being in cages and I wasn't in a position to argue. What she said was true; there was no way to rescue them while we were traveling in outer space. *Perhaps when the ship returns in six months, I'll have figured something out.* I kept the thought as tightly as I could to my own brain.

I shook my head sharply, left, right, left, right. "Those sons of bastards." I said softly, anger lacing my words. "If I could only get them alone, one by one, I'd—I'd...." Words failed me.

"You would to end up in a cage, Jessalya, having unspeakable things done to you. You would be cloned, poked, prodded, perhaps impregnated, and that's only for starters. Do not *ever* be alone with a scientist. You have no idea what their capabilities are and they are many, I to assure you. I to believe the reason you are overlooked is because you are very small. When we to look at you, we perceive you as a kitling and therefore, to be protected. Your small size is your protection right now."

Shocking me, she stepped close and put her arms around me, pulling me in for a long hug. She kissed the top of my head, stepped back, still holding my shoulders and said in a soft voice, "You have friends in us, kitling, and we will to do all to protect you and your secret."

Si'neada nodded in agreement. "It is true, my little star. We will to protect you with all we have."

Ler'a'neada said, "Now, for the reason we have arrived in this place." She turned me around to face the box and touched a panel on the front side. It melted away and I stared into a misty interior, suddenly shivering in the cold air blasting out, diverted from thinking about the horrid experiment done to us Humans.

"This," Si'neada said in a very hushed voice, "is a DNA storage unit." He nodded a brisk up and down of his head. "It is *our* DNA storage unit." He gestured toward his sister with his head. "It is very secret."

## CHAPTER TWENTY-NINE

I looked at him blankly. Were they going to collect my DNA? Why bring me all the way down here for that? They could've gathered what they wanted from my fork at a meal. It was freaking cold standing in front of it and I wished I had more clothes on or fur on my body. I felt my hair wrap around me and, okay, this was new, heating up to warm me. There appeared to be no limit of what my hair, or my body, could do. I said, "I don't understand; if you wanted my DNA, you could've gathered it from a zillion different surfaces already."

They looked at each other. "Ah, well, we have tried to gather it but we have not been successful. It renders itself useless within a fraction of a second. It is the weirdest thing we have ever seen."

I backed up another step or two to get some distance between them and me. "Then you're going to throw me in there? Whole?"

Si'neada guffawed. "No! Of course not! That is not why we are here. You are not useful if you are a, what is it called? A frozen bar?"

"A popsicle, you mean?"

"Yes! That is what I to mean."

Still suspicious, I wrapped my arms around me and narrowed my eyes. "Then. Why. Am. I. Here?" My patience with all this crap was suddenly exhausted.

Ler'a'neada said in a very gentle whisper. "Because you are the first and only shape changer and now we finally to have a chance."

"A chance at what?"

There were a few beats of silence as they looked at each other. "A minute of history, first, so you can to understand."

I nodded and made a "give it to me" movement of my fingers.

"These worlds we sell on the Rent-to-Own program?"

"Yes?" I narrowed my eyes at them. "What about them?"

"The ones without sentient beings on them?"

"Yeeeessss?" I drew out the word in a suspicious voice.

"First, you must to realize that habitable worlds are not common. Usually, only one planet per system, and most often not even that. We can do many things but the one thing we cannot to do is to move a planet into a better position to the sun. So many things have to be right to support life, any life at all. That is why we had to become a space faring people because we have to range so far to find new systems that hold worlds we can to claim and to sell. You to understand so far?"

I nodded.

"So many generations ago. So many. We started out with noble intentions: find worlds without civilizations, preserve what is there while making it attractive for other species who need new worlds to settle and will be compatible to existing subspecies, sell the world on the rent-to-own program and we move on and find another. And so it went."

"Until….?" I prompted.

"Until we, as a race of people, decided it was easier to remove budding civilizations not yet at the point of technology or advanced defenses and claim the world for the program. The worlds are very hard to find, after all, and many light years apart. This is what we were born into, my brother and me, after many generations of this way of discovery and were raised with this concept." She stopped and took a quiet breath and looked at me in a pleading way. "This doctrine is none of our doing, please to understand that. As we became adults, we realized how awful this policy is but the wrong word to the wrong person and people disappeared, never to be seen again. That kept us very quiet, you to understand, yes?"

Imurians murdered each other? That was enough to make my head reel but the fact that we believed all these settled worlds had not had prior civilizations? That made my head spin. The confusing thing was: would Humans or other peoples actually stop buying the planets for themselves or would they shrug and say, "Oh, well, we didn't do it and here's a nice world, let's settle it."?

I didn't know the answer to that question. This was a lot to digest, that was for sure. "Ye gods and little fishes. I had no idea."

"Si'neada and I—and a few select others—joined with those who have been preserving DNA of destroyed species in case we ever did to find a world where we can repopulate them. The problem is, we do not to have enough worlds to offer nor can we to afford to terraform a world to accommodate these wasted species. We can clone them, of course, but there will not to be enough diversity for the species to thrive plus we have no way now to know how any of them would interact with each other. So should the world be a zoo? Who would be the caretakers? Do we need multiple worlds if the species cannot co-exist? But we cannot make money doing that, at least to start with. You see the challenge? There are so many questions and problems.

I gaped at them. "But of what use am I to you for that? I don't understand!" A small voice inside me said, *What if you are the only person in all the endless space who can bring back even one of these species? How can I refuse this?*

Si'neada's soft voice reached me. "We to understand how difficult this is to grasp; after all, we have thrown a lot of information at you and asking the biggest, um, favor in all of space. We also know how deadly dangerous this is for you and, quite frankly, for us, too." He patted me on the arm. "But no pressure, my precious spool of thread. We merely want you to take samples of each species as a safeguard and, also, if you can to become them, we can do studies and find the diversity necessary for perhaps returning a species to a new world to watch their development. There is, of course, no time left on this trip for you to manifest and we do not want you to do so yet. It must wait until after your year when we can have the time to study this together."

That startled a laugh out of me. "This is a *lot* to wrap my head around." I pursed my lips. "I have no idea what I want to do or even how to do it. I'm not sure I want to be The DNA Bank of Jessi." Even as I said that, I felt my hair quiver in eager anticipation of taking samples.

DO IT.

Ler'a'neada said softly, "This is our only chance at this. I would love to give you a lot of time to decide but we are limited by access to this room, to this container, and also by your trip ending. I do not want to pressure you unduly but we have to know."

"And if I say no?"

Her eyes pleaded with me. "I do not to think you will. Please to consider how dangerous this is for us to even show you and for you to have this knowledge."

"To be fair, you have very dangerous knowledge about me, too."

She nodded. "This is true."

Si'neada looked at me intently. "I do not think I have underestimated you, Jess."

I huffed out a sigh and made a sudden decision, but it felt right. "I'll do one for now. To see how it goes. After all, I don't know how many types of DNA I can assimilate, especially at one time." I hesitated. "How do we proceed?"

They looked at each other. "Eh, we are not exactly prepared for this moment. The usual way is to inject it into you but we have no supplies like that with us. This warehouse room does not carry medical supplies."

I rolled my eyes. "For piety's sake, okay, let's pick a tube, any tube. I have a way." *Well, about to give away my hairy secret.*

Ler'a'neada pulled on insulated gloves, then reached in for the nearest tube. "Starting with one is a good idea, I think." She studied the label. "This is from the world, well, you will not to know this world, but this species is oxygen breathing."

I blinked. It hadn't occurred to me there might be species that didn't breathe air. If I'd thought about it more, I'd have realized there must be aqueous civilizations, maybe even gas breathing ones, existing on hydrogen or nitrogen or whatever. Anything was possible, I guessed, in the vast endless expanse of space. What if I turned into one of those? I held up a hand. "Better make sure they're all oxygen-breathers. I don't want to turn into a fish out of water."

Si'neada winked at me. "I think, my little jewel, that would be wise."

Ler'a'neada manipulated the vial somehow and a hologram popped into the air. A 3D image appeared of a creature with four legs, nubby upper appendages with elongated pads instead of fingers, claws tipping each of the four per paw, two tails that were longer than the wispy-furred fudge-colored body, two large bright blue eyes centered front and forward with slit pupils, large round ears and sharp curved teeth in the open mouth. I couldn't estimate size due to there not being anything to scale it against.

"So tell me about them." I indicated the hologram.

"They were on the world now known as Xeritida, definitely pre-civilized. However, they were starting to use tools and had rudimentary starts at a written language. They had language and cooperative skills in hunting, as they are—were—a protein-based species. They could run fast, climb high and throw projectiles." She squinted at the fine writing at the bottom of the hologram. "They were rendered extinct about 200 of your years ago."

"200 years? And no one has been bothered by this mass murdering before now?"

She grimaced. "Of course we have. It is just that our ships are far apart and those of us who resist are scattered and have to be extremely cautious in who we to speak to about these things. We like to make sure our members of the resistance can all mind whisper on a certain frequency for privacy and secrecy but it does makes opposition very difficult. Not only do we have to find people with the right abilities, they have to desire being a part of us and then we have to make sure they are not going to betray us. Remember that brain delve you did on New Eden in preparation for this program? We ask new potential members to do that, also, to be sure of their true intent.

I felt sick. Of course, we all believe what we are raised to believe and I could see how many of the Imurians would accept this as normal business procedure. However, as an adult, we can make different choices in spite of doctrine, but so few decide to go a different way, choosing the easier way instead. Imurians were not different than Humans in that. Something about being civilized brings out competitiveness, a need for dominance and quests for power. Or for the Imurians: killing entire populations for profit.

How many vials could be stored in this kind of container? How many DNA containers were there? How many species had been murdered in the name of profit? In an endless space, the only boundaries are the ones we, as civilized societies, draw. The Imurians apparently stepped across that line a long time ago. I felt heart-sick over this but the truth was, there was nothing I could to change their behavior, at least not yet, other than be the DNA Bank of Jessi. Logically, though, there couldn't be that many stored types of DNA. There just weren't that many worlds out there, civilized or not.

I sucked in a big breath. "I don't know if I can manifest the DNA, I don't know their size, I don't know if I'll truly "be them" or just be the shape….I just *don't know.*"

Si'neada laid a gentle arm around my shoulders, and I realized I had hunched them up to my ears. I consciously allowed them to droop downward and leaned into the offered hug.

"Jess, we do not to know, either. This is a great unknown that we," he indicated the three of us, "will explore together. We do not to know these answers but together, we will to find out."

He paused and patted my shoulder. "Jessalya, what is your greatest fear about this?"

"Well, I'd say my biggest fear is being stuck in some other shape and not knowing how to get back to *ME*. My second biggest fear is that I will only be the shape but not BE the shape, if you know what I mean? I'm not sure how far this changing goes; like do all my insides change, too…and what about my brain? Do I lose myself in there in being a new shape and person? How will I communicate? If I DO get stuck in a shape, *how does that get fixed?*"

I drew in a breath. My shattered nerves, that's a whole lot of fear! Who knew? "What if we pick a vial that manifests as needing to be underwater and I'm in air and I can't breathe? How do we fix that? By the three gates of hell and the hairy chin of a space monster, how do we do this??"

Ler'a'neada grabbed my arms, leaning her head on my forehead and whispered, "Breathe, Jessi, just to breathe. We will to figure these things out together. But not here and not now. Now that we have the possibility, we still must to be cautious and to keep you from danger. Because if the others find out about this talent of yours, they will do anything to get their claws into you for experimentations or worse. We will to keep you safe, Si'neada, myself and B'le'ru." She brushed some of my hair back from my face as she looked intently into my eyes.

"The first time and indeed, many times over, Si'neada will to ride your mind as you change so we can to retrieve you if needed. Also to remember you have your own memory chip to use if absolutely needed. It will also to help us to determine how you to change and what happens…all with your permission, of course. Just to know you will not be alone."

She looked around. "This, however, is not the time or place. We need to get back to my place and we will do our first offering there. And we will be circumspect about vials we to choose; they must be oxygen breathers and compatible to your body mass, for instance." She laid a soft hand against my cheek. "Also, to remember you have been an Imurian and retained yourself in spite of the change. This truth should also happen with any other DNA."

Again I sucked in a breath and then blew it out again. "O-o-okay," I said in a shaky voice. "That's true enough. If there's any chance we can bring back murdered species for viability and a world of their own, I'll try one. But only one to start with so I can see how it goes." I unclenched my fists and relaxed my shoulders. "How many others are part of this plan?"

Si'neada said, "That is not important right now. It is more important to get you back to your room for some rest and to formulate plans. The less you know of the others at this time is better for your own safety." He made a placating gesture. "You will find out who else is on our side when it is appropriate."

I gestured to Ler'a'neada, who held out the vial. I stepped close to it while they both watched me with puzzled frowns. One strand of hair floated over the top of the open vial, dipping into it, then pulling out.

OK.

I gave them a thumbs up. "It's done."

Si'neada's head turned sharply to his right and he put his finger to his lips, asking for silence. He turned toward the aisle we'd come down as he barely whispered, "Quietly, please, as we to leave this space." He held up a hand while he "listened" for others, his forehead creased in concentration. He turned to face us. <It is a

good thing we are not staying to take more samples; there are several approaching this space.>

Ler'a'neada returned the container to the highest shelf, moving it in a fast motion upward, then we went back the way we came in. This time, I remembered to count the spaces between the shelving units—18—and when we reached the gap, I watched carefully to see where Ler'a'neada placed her fingers. She caught me eyeing her motions intently, and she smiled a wry smile. :*It is keyed to my DNA to keep out others so it will not to help you to know how to do this.*:

*Wanna bet?* I kept the thought to myself.

We made our way back to Ler'a'neada's quarters and entered her apartment through the panel. As soon as I saw the couch, exhaustion swept over me in a tidal wave of weakness. I barely made it before I sagged onto the cushions and then realized my bladder was very full and making demands. On top of that, my stomach started growling. I put my face in my hands, leaning forward, but that put pressure on my bladder so I leaned back and slumped into the cushions behind my back instead, rubbing my eyes. "I am *so* tired. I'm *beyond* tired…and I have to pee. And I'm hungry. And I don't think I can stand up right now." I dropped my hands and yawned. "I couldn't change into my pajamas right now much less become anything else."

Si'neada offered me a hand so I heaved myself to my feet. "Pressing things to take care of. Which way to the bathroom?"

"I will show you, my little sweetling." He used his arm to steady me as I wobbled down the indicated hallway. "When you are done, we will have food ready for you."

I nodded. "Ice cream would be wonderful."

He laughed. "After you eat real food, we will see about that."

## CHAPTER THIRTY

When I returned to the living area, the smell of food made my stomach point out loudly how empty it was. I wanted to run over and stuff food in my mouth as fast as I could so instead I walked; I do have some pride, after all.

Si'neada said, "Come on and to eat, my little sweet, while it is hot and fresh."

I piled food on a plate, spilling some on the table in my haste, filled my fork and shoved it in my mouth and loaded my fork to shove more food in as soon as my mouth emptied. After about five forkfuls this way, I glanced up to see them staring at me with wide eyes. "What?" I said. "I told you I was hungry! It takes a lot of energy to do all that changing." That's when I realized I was hunkered down around my food like a dog guarding a bone.

"Yes….it is just that we have never seen anyone this small eat that much so fast."

"Glad I could entertain you." I muttered as I picked up a glass of water, draining it and then sat back to finish eating in a more leisurely manner. "Okay, I feel better now although there's a good chance I might fall asleep on the way back to my room."

We arrived back to my room without incidence or meeting anyone, thank the stars. As the door shut, I noticed Zoe asleep on the couch but I was already at my bedroom shucking off my robe so I could fall in bed as soon as my teeth were clean. When I slid between the sheets, I was asleep before I could even pull up the covers.

When I woke again, I kept thinking about their DNA stash. The Imurians were so much more advanced in so many ways, they could surely clone the stockpile they had. They had to have studied these budding sentient populations extensively to determine whether or not they wanted to keep or destroy; I shuddered to think they would so callously commit genocide. Why did they need me? I shook my head. I didn't know. I muttered, "Wake up, Jessi, get some coffee, let's think about this later."

Something niggled at me that had to be done today. Frowning, I searched my memory for what it was and finally looked at my PD for the answer. The talent show! Oh, my scattered stars, that's tonight! Luckily, I had many line dances memorized so all I had to do was brush off the cobwebs. I had a practice session with Tr. Aelotro later that day for our dance together.

Now I was down to one night left and I hadn't had that shipboard romance or figured what actually happened to my brother. I had a piece of the puzzle, the Akrion, but if they only had one particle and it affected him, why am I the way I am? I just couldn't put this puzzle together.

Zoe was already gone, so I left my room to join the others in the corridor to go to breakfast, rubbing my temples, and heard my name. "Jessi! Hey, Jess, wait up!"

I looked up to see Keaton, walking rapidly to catch up with me. "Wow, you look like left-over scrambled eggs."

I widened my eyes at him, raising my eyebrows and grimaced. "Gee, thanks, Keaton. You say the sweetest things to a girl."

He looked abashed. "Uh, sorry, that's not what I meant, well, I mean, you look like you had a rough night." He offered a grin at me and winked. "I mean, gee, Jessi, you've never looked better. In your life. Of course!"

I chuckled; I couldn't help it. "Ok, I'll admit, I probably don't look the best I've ever been, but…" I gave a small shrug. Keaton gave me a one-armed hug as we continued walking down the hallway toward breakfast and I leaned into it for a bit. It might be the last Human hug I'd get for a year and I wanted to savor it. I really liked the feel of his arm around me and thought again of that now-lost-chance shipboard romance with regret. Stupid body and hair, anyway, taking all my time from when I could've maybe explored more of a relationship with him.

We reached the dining area and sat at our table. Zoe looked at me from her seat, narrowing her eyes just a bit. "You're a little rough around the edges this morning, Jessa Little." Then she winked at me, just the barest suggestion of one.

Soli barked, "Zoe! Leave her alone!" He turned to me, then and said, "Are you feeling okay? Because you do look a bit under the weather, I must say."

I smiled at him. "I'm fine, really, thank you, I really appreciate you worrying about me." I gave my own narrow-eyed glance at Zoe with the barest hint of a wink with it. "I think I look worse than I feel, actually." I punched in my order. "Oh, my gosh, you all do realize this is our last day on this ship?"

Mitchler said, "It's hard to believe the end is here, really here, now. It seemed so long ago we got on board, even if it wasn't all that long ago and now it's almost over." He held up a fork, pretending it was a microphone, and intoned, "And here we have the last bunch of extremely intelligent and most gorgeous students ever seen about to embark on the awesomest adventure of their lives! Will they handle it with aplomb? Will they run screaming for their lives? Will they survive this year on an alien world?" He paused. "Stay tuned, folks, for the next episode of 'Exchangers: Their Lives as Aliens.'"

We were laughing before he was done with his announcing and when he laid his fork down, we applauded. Our food arrived, putting an end to the nonsense and I realized with a pang I was really going to miss them, all of them, even Zoe. *I have to hope my blood doesn't change her in any way, even if it was the only way to save her life.* I looked at Zoe; her color was almost back to normal and she seemed to have more energy. She caught me looking at her, so she nodded very slightly with a small smile, tilting her head ever so little. I read that as meaning she was feeling much better. The gunshot wound in her side didn't seem to be paining her, at least right now.

When we arrived at our classroom, Tatro Aelotro stepped forward, saying, his fingers coming together in a steeple, "We have been pleased to be your guides along this journey to our world. You have a good knowledge of our language, our culture and our society and we," sweeping one hand out to indicate the other two Tatrans, "believe you all will do well. Some of you have a better grasp of our language," he looked at Zoe and me, "And others not as well," looking at Soli, "but all have enough skill to get by and of course, you will improve as your year goes by."

We chuckled.

He continued to speak. "Your assigned bodyguards will be there to greet you as you leave the ship." He nodded his head to his companions, and Tatra Hilodria moved forward, tapping on her device. "She has sent photos of your bodyguards and pertinent information to your devices. Please open them now so we can go through them together. Also, a dossier on your assigned family has also been highlighted for your review, as tomorrow you will meet them and their provided information is up to date as of today."

I tapped opened the information, seeing photos of 12 Amorphans. I stared at them in bewilderment. "Uh, Tatro?" I raised my hand. "Why are there 12?"

Zoe gave me a scathing look. "They have to take shifts, dummy. You won't have one bodyguard 24/7, you know."

"Oh." I said, feeling stupid. Of course there would have to be enough to take shifts; I'd just never thought about the logistics before. "They're going to be with us at night, too, when we're at home with our families?"

Tatro looked over and nodded. "They will not be inside the house but protecting from outside, not only you, the student, but also the families. There are those who are not fond of having aliens on our world at our schools."

Keaton asked, "How do we know the bodyguards themselves aren't one of those?"

"Good question, Keaton. They have been examined in every way possible and so we can say with confidence, not only did they volunteer for the job, they have trained extensively and have undergone a thorough brain delve so we are certain they are not in any way prejudiced against you or your host families."

"That's a relief," I remarked. "Hard to think of myself as an alien, however." I grinned.

Tatro said, "Yes, I understand but to us, you are the aliens, just as we are to you. And most people are interested in you as the unknown alien and are eager to find out more by knowing you but some are…let us say, more provincial and have no desire for anything new like aliens in our schools. We will keep you protected at all times, accordingly."

I wondered how I was going to tell my bodyguards apart; I was embarrassed to admit they looked very much alike to me. I supposed we Humans looked similar to all of them, too. *Hmm, we haven't tried the Amorphan form yet.*

My hair quivered in anticipation. TONIGHT?

*No!*

Tatro was speaking again, and my attention jerked back to his words. "We will each go over your bodyguards right now and we will start with Zoe, Keaton and Mitchler. Jessalya, you can practice your dance steps for tonight while we work with them and Soli, you can work on your talent also. You two are dismissed for an hour."

"I need to return to my room; I wanted to keep my dance a surprise for tonight and I can't do that here."

Tatro steepled his fingers again, looking at me. "Then, I will work with you now and then you may go to practice. Zoe, you may practice your steps instead."

"Sure," Zoe said. "I don't need privacy to go through my dance, like little Miss Smarty Pants here, just need my partner, Keaton. I guess she's afraid we'll steal her dance steps….as IF." She rolled her eyes.

Tatro nodded, narrowing his eyes a bit as he glanced between us. "Then, you and Keaton practice, and Soli instead will start with his bodyguards." He pointed to Mitchler. "You will be with Tatra Hilodria and Soli, of course, with the other Tatra and I will work with Jessalya."

Tatro and I went to a corner and he brought up photos of the guards. "This first one is named Androlean and he is the Boss Guard of your 12." Tatro's words became a cloud of sound to my ears; I mostly nodded and said, "Okay, uh-huh, I see" where appropriate. For all I knew, Tatro was putting up the same photo over and over because they all looked so much alike. I hoped when I met them, they would become distinguishable to me by personality. I guessed it was like getting to know identical twins; they were exactly alike until, well, they weren't.

"Any questions?" That startled me back into the current reality.

"Um." I hesitated. "Um, well, one question." I picked at a cuticle for a second. "How do I tell them apart?" My face turned red from embarrassment.

"I see." He tapped a finger on the desk. "It is a problem for us, also, telling you apart except that your hair is different from everyone else's and also your height is so short. It is easy to tell the difference between Human males and females because you have the feminine bumps up front and pushing out. That helps us distinguish. But as we have worked with you, we have come to know you as individuals. I think this will also happen for you when you know each one in person."

"That's what I thought but I hoped I could from the photos. I'm really very embarrassed but they all look so similar to me."

"This being an alien is confusing for us all, I think, until we get it all worked out."

He tapped his lip with a thoughtful look on his face. "One thing, Jessi, you will have to know. You are the size of a young Amorphan, not an adult, and because of that, you will often be treated like a child. Please do not take it personally."

I laughed, startling him, if I judged right by the straightening of his top hair and his widened eyes. "Already happens to me, Tatro. I'm still treated like a child on my own world, too. People see my size, assume I'm in my Middle Childhood years and treat me accordingly. It's an annoyance I've learned to live with."

He nodded, pursing his thin lips, then smiling. "I am relieved to know you are already aware of this *conundrum*." He used Standard for the term.

It was my turn to look startled. "How in the world do you know that word? It's not a commonly used one."

"I have done my studying of your language. Your language has many delicious words to use, I must say."

I grinned. "I agree; our language is so—so malleable and that makes it difficult to learn. We have so many words spelled the same and pronounced the same and yet the meaning changes on how it's used inside a sentence."

"Yes, I have often been confused by your language."

I realized the whole conversation had been in Amorphan, which now seemed as familiar to me as my own first language. "You know, I've even been dreaming in Amorphan! I just realized that."

He tilted his head while he smiled at me. "That, I believe, is a sign of truly knowing a language." He stood, placing a hand on my shoulder. "You are ready, Jessi, you are ready. Now you are dismissed to go to practice for tonight. Please return in one hour so we may practice our dance together." He took a step away and then look back. "And please review your photos of your guards for familiarity."

I nodded, stood and bowed to him. "I thank you for your service and teaching, Tatro, and I hold you in the highest respect. I look forward to our dance together and my year on your world."

## CHAPTER THIRTY-ONE

As I left the classroom, I realized I'd meant my statement to Tatro. I truly looked forward to living as an Amorphan; they were a gentle race, graceful, and intelligent. Maybe this year away from my parents would help my mother get over my long-dead brother. At least I now knew she and Devon had been part of an unsanctioned experiment with this particle thing of Akrion. I still didn't know if Devon had received it or not but the logical answer was yes, he did. But if he got it, what happened to me? I shook my head; I didn't know the answer to this shifting thing, wild and impossible as it seemed. Exchanging one body for another was the wildest adventure of all. Then I frowned. *I have one night left on the StarFinder and I still haven't gotten a total answer to my brother's death.* Time was running out. From resenting my mom asking me to find out to now, when I was fully invested in the answer, had been quite a journey.

I wondered, then, what being a body changer was good for other than being the perfect spy or the DNA Bank of Jessi. *Maybe I can change forms to understand the alien being I might be treating? Do I have a limit on how many types of DNA I can take in?* Was I like a fuel tank? Would I get filled to the brim and then what? Would some spill out while others went in? My actual dream was to be the first doctor to all the worlds, not just Humans so knowing the form intimately might be of use in that.

I had no way to know and there were no answers out there. As far as I knew, I'm the only shape shifter ever, so the answers would come as I discovered them. Then it struck me: what if I ever became pregnant? Would I pass on the changer genes? Would I even be able to become pregnant? *Was I still even Human??*

Suddenly depressed, I shoved my hands into my robe's pockets as I trudged down the hallway toward my room. I realized with a start, for the first time since entering the ship, I hadn't been assigned an escort to take me to my quarters. *That's weird.*

Then I started thinking about how we Human students would be separated tomorrow morning into five different cities on the same world with no contact with each other except for emergencies for six months. At six months, they would allow video contact with each other and receive our letters and packages from home for one time until our term came to an end. That's a long time to go with no human contact and I felt an edge of anxiety settle over me at the thought.

Absorbed in my thoughts, the slippery thought of maybe no longer being completely Human distracting me further as I tossed it around in my brain, I followed the curving hallway to my room. My hair suddenly tightened around me in a protective shell just as a hand clamped over my mouth and a voice hissed in my ear, "Silent, now. You and I are going to have a chat. I am not going to hurt you unless you try to hurt me first. Understood?"

My breathing stifled from his hand, my heart rate zoomed upward and I nodded, feeling weak in the knees. His whole body was pressed against me from behind, trapping most of my hair, his arm clamped around me in a vice-like grip. I didn't have a clue who this was—whispering voices aren't distinctive—other than to know he was male.

He clenched me tighter and whispered into my ear, "Say nothing, *nothing!* We are going to walk backwards to the door. Do not even to think of fighting me or I will shoot directly into your spine. Understand?"

I nodded once, I could feel the weapon pressing into my spine. He wrenched me backwards several steps, then he stopped to butt-open a door; he must've kept it unlatched somehow. He pulled me through into a hallway and I scanned the closing door but it had no markings. He turned me around, pushing me forward while keeping his big hand clamped over my upper body. I squirmed a bit; he was hurting my breasts. I felt the cold blunt end of his gun push harder against my back so I concentrated on viewing my surroundings and not tripping as he shoved me forward again. Even my hair or changer abilities couldn't stop me from getting paralyzed with a shot that close and direct. Cooperation was my only choice.

We went several feet down the hallway to another door, as anonymous as any door can be, and went through a few more doors just as unremarkable. The walls of the final corridor were painted beige, no decorations of any kind hung along its length and there were no directional colored stripes like my own corridor.

My self-defense training seemed to have disappeared with the gun pushing into my spine. Had we even practiced this scenario?

I couldn't remember right then; all I could think of was how to stay alive. He was bigger, stronger than me, as were most people. I could kick myself for leaving my own weapon in my room, against the advice of B'le'ru, but I'd been afraid of it being discovered or falling out somehow during dancing. And how would I have gotten to it, anyway? Oh—of course, my hair could've gotten it but could I really use it faster than my kidnapper could shoot? I didn't know and it didn't matter right then, anyway. I was outgunned, outmuscled, and outsmarted.

We reached another nondescript door without names or numbers and again he turned me around so he could butt-open the door. Once inside with the door closed, he let me go with a little shove, locking the door one handed while keeping the weapon pointed straight at me without wavering as I stumbled forward, off balance.

He said, gesturing with his free hand, "Sit. On that chair there." I groped behind me with a hand to find it; I didn't want to take my eyes off his face—the officer that had stopped B'le'ru that night in the corridor on our way to the shooting range—as I sat between the chair arms.

As I did so, he pushed a button on his shirt. Loops of cable snaked around my wrists and ankles and bound me to the chair. I made a fist to thicken my wrists as soon as I realized what was happening, hoping to prevent the cables from being so tight my hands would go numb.

"Why have you kidnapped me? You know I'll be missed; I have a three o'clock appointment with Tatro."

He shrugged. "To give me the answers I need and you will to be there to meet him. If not?" He made a dismissive motion with his head. "Well, it is hard to track a body once it leaves the ship."

My heart squeezed in fear but I was alive right now and that's what mattered. I didn't really believe he would kill me. I hoped. "I don't understand why I'm here. Why did you kidnap me?"

He glared at me, twisting his mouth. "I to ask the questions; your job right now is to give answers."

"Well, ask me something, then. What in the seven blazing layers of the sun have I done to get this kind of treatment?" I demanded in a shrill voice. To my dismay, I heard a slight quaver to my words. My heart chugged at top speed in my chest, and I felt my hands jerking in time to the beat. My breath came short and fast; I was angry and scared. I looked around the room. Nondescript gray walls; a light source from overhead, and other than the chair I was on, there was nothing else. It was a small, bare room. There wasn't even a vent cover.

My head jerked as he slapped me across my left cheek. I was so shocked, my mouth dropped open as I stared at him and my skin started to burn. "I told you: no questions, only answers."

I spluttered, "How dare you hit me?" I glared up at him with narrowed eyes and clenched teeth. He was dressed in a green utility coverall, with leather boots to his knees, various items stuffed into small pockets on his large wide belt, including the gun he'd put back in his holster. He had insignia sewn onto his shoulders, but I didn't know what they meant. Two breast pockets bulged with unknown items. His fur was a reddish brown with dark brown stripes and his tail constantly twitched around his legs. He wore a large device on his right wrist, indicating he might be left-handed. His eyes narrowed as he stared back at me, irises a dark golden color. I took all this in as he deliberately raised his left hand and hit me across the cheek for the second time.

He shook his head. "I do not want to hurt you, I really do not but I have already told you: No. Questions. However, I to need answers and I will to have them and I believe you to know them." He tapped his foot on the floor. "You and Si'neada are friends, yes or no."

"Yes." I was so angry with him right then I would've killed him if I had a way to do so. I flashed back to my test where I'd "killed" my classmates and teachers, remembering how I'd sobbed myself to sleep that night. Right now I would happily shoot him and not shed one tear.

"Have you met his sister?"

"No." I glared at him. "What sister?"

He slapped my other cheek, this time with a bit of claw out, scratching my skin. "No questions, remember?"

I nodded. I was becoming blindingly angry; I'd never been so furious in my entire life. My hair was gathering itself to lash out at him, I felt it quivering against me, trapped against my back in the chair. I blinked tears away; I wouldn't let him see me cry. I sent a thought out to my hair: *Stay calm for now; I need to find out why I'm here and what is going on. If we take him out too soon, I won't learn anything. I'm as angry as you are but we have to hold off. He hasn't really hurt me yet, and much as I hate him, they're only slaps.*

My hair relaxed by an nth of a degree; the immediate danger of us attacking was on hold for now. I really did want to know what was going on even as furious and humiliated as I was.

"Why have you been going with Si'neada at night?"

I couldn't claim him to be a lover; everyone knew Si'neada as a two-fur. I'd been sworn to secrecy about the weapons training and the DNA cache and, oh, everything. What would be believable?

"To be fitted for clothing. And for language training."

"Which language?"

"Yours."

He then switched to Imurian. "Do you understand this?"

"Yes, of course. Translator."

"Answer me in Imurian, please. Tell me the beginning of your day. In Imurian. And it had better be fluent."

I replied in his language. "I got out of bed, made coffee, added cream, took a shower, got dressed, joined my classmates for breakfast and classes."

He narrowed his eyes to slits as he stared at me, a snarl on his face.

"Why do you need special fittings?"

"Because I'm so small, he wanted to work with me individually to make sure the robes didn't look like a child's. I'm very sensitive about that."

He prowled around the room, always out of reach of me or my hair, then barked at me. "What else have you done together?"

I jumped in my chair, his voice so abrupt and harsh. "Uh, nothing."

He loomed over me, although still at a safe distance. "Tell me about the DNA cache."

"I don't know anything about it."

"Why is your scent in the room where it is contained?"

"My scent? I have no idea. Maybe someone thought I'm a good perfume."

He growled. "You might want to think again about being flippant."

I cringed as he raised his hand, prepared to duck. He seemed satisfied with my fear and lowered his hand part way as he smirked.

"Your scent has also been in the weapons range and upon the officer who trains. Have you a sexual relationship with him?"

"No!" I said with heat. At least I didn't have to lie about that.

"Are you sure? He is not one who worries about cross-species dalliances."

"Yes, I'm sure! I've never had sex with anyone, Human or not." Crap, that was no one's business except mine, although Zoe knew. He looked at me like he was examining an insect under a magnifying glass.

"Then he has trained you in weapon usage?"

"No. I don't know what you're talking about! I trained for years with my gun on New Eden but was forbidden to bring my weapon."

"Do you have a weapon on you now or in your room?"

"No!" I lied.

"Your room will be searched for such a thing. And I will search you now."

He drew his weapon, keeping it trained on my face, as he reached out with his right hand, his eyes on mine. He tried to slip his fingers into my neckline but it was snug; as I sat in the chair, it had tightened with all the material gathered under me, and his fingers wouldn't fit. He pressed the gun to my temple as he gathered the flowing material from the front of me and slowly lifted it. He licked his lips. I couldn't press my legs together because of the shackles around my ankles but I was thankful I was wearing

panties and a bra. *If he tries to rape me, we'll have to do something.*
WORKING TO FREE YOU.

Oh. Okay.

He pulled the material up to my neckline while still keeping the gun tight against my head. "Huh." He snorted. "You do not have too much in the female department, do you? And you are much rounder than the other female in your tummy area. Good padding for a romp."

"Stop staring at me! So I like to eat; get over it. And it's none of your business, anyway."

He chuckled. "You are a feisty one." He draped the excess material over my shoulder where he pinned it into place with his wrist but never wavering with the weapon. He placed his free hand inside my bra onto my breast, first the left one, then the right, as he squeezed them. "A nice handful, more than I was expecting." He sighed. "No weapon, however." He grinned. "But there is elsewhere to look."

I squirmed in the chair, trying to get away from his groping, but his hand dropped into my crotch area, palm and finger pads against me. To my horror, I felt a zing of desire zip through me even as I hated him for touching me. He cupped my most private area and squeezed. "No weapon." He sounded disappointed as he sighed. "As fun as this discovery of your body is, I have other more pressing concerns other than the one in my male sac." His expression hardened. "As if I would demean myself with a different species."

He made it sound like I was debris, useful for a while until discarded. Then, to my enormous relief, he dropped the material over the front of me; I guess being considered rubbish had its advantages. One strand of hair sawed on the cables holding my wrists, zinging back and forth like a hacksaw to free my hands. *How much further do you have to go?*

SHH. WORKING.

He squatted in front of me, placing the gun level with my belly button, and leaned in. "I know you have something to do with the DNA. I need to know why and how and I need to know with whom." He traced the scratch on my cheek with a soft finger. "I am trying to save the DNA caches. There are those who do not want them to exist because they are a bad example of our own history. I advocate for keeping worlds intact with existing species, not the destruction of species for profit. I have enemies among my own people and I need to know who to team with and you know who they are. You only need to name them and I will to let you go." He stared me in the eyes.

Caches? I thought there was only one. At least he wasn't accusing me of changing shapes. I wondered how he'd gotten his information although cameras were everywhere, as was the informal, yet more accurate, information highway of gossip, plus Deester, who seemed to be everywhere, well, everywhere except here right now. Maybe he had one of Deester's kind for an informant? I wondered if the apartment was bugged with cameras where I'd met with Si'neada's sister. That was a possibility.

"I can't help you. I don't know anything about any caches." I shook my head, trying to look helpless. "Si'neada and I have become friends so he offered to show me other parts of the ship. It's forbidden, I know, but I was so curious and persistent he finally said yes to showing me some other parts of the ship. He showed me the weapons range, because I'm certified at home so I wanted to see how yours is set up. I'm sure that's why my scent was there. He showed me one of the permanent living apartments and for all I know, that was his sister's place. So, yes, I broke rules but it was just a tour. I don't know anything else, I really don't."

I didn't know if I should believe the officer's story of wanting to save DNA or not; he was very compelling but maybe he was only saying that for me to give up information so he could harm them or destroy the DNA—or both.

He remained squatting in front of me. I admitted to myself he was quite handsome, with intense eyes, a striking pattern to his stripes, well groomed, and smelling of something spicy and enticing.

He stood abruptly, moving back from me and started pacing. "I want to believe you but I cannot afford to do so." He looked sidelong at me. "There is something about you, I cannot put a claw on it, but there is something about you that defies explanation." He pulled in a long breath. "And you smell so unique, not like the other Humans." He reached out as he neared and started smoothing my hair against my head. "Your hairies are so long and silky."

It was all I could do to restrain my hair from wrapping one small portion around his throat. *Not yet!* What if he was genuine and really wanted to be part of the DNA project of reseeding worlds? Of course, what if he wasn't? Either way, I needed to know. I tried to duck away from his questing hand but he didn't take the hint.

He squatted in front of me again and looked into my eyes, weapon back on my belly button. His scent was intoxicating as it wafted into my breathing space. He smelled so warm and inviting;

I'd never smelled anything like it before. His eyes were now so close I was about to go cross-eyed in order to return his gaze. All of sudden, with absolutely no warning, he placed his mouth over mine and kissed me. His hand clenched over my restrained forearms, gun tight against my stomach and my knees pushing into his chest as he kissed me. I tried to turn my head away from him but there was nowhere to go. His tongue probed against my lips as my heart rate and breathing started racing for a different reason than fear. I felt a snap of electricity against my cheek, bringing me back to my reality. I shook my head to stop it from repeating the action and that broke the contact with the Imurian.

I gasped in a breath. "Look, I don't even know your name and you're kissing me? Really?" I glared at him.

He looked a little dazed. He pushed himself back and away with an abrupt motion and shook his head as if to clear it. "I—I had not planned on doing that. Your scent…your hair…there is something very compelling about you." He actually looked a little embarrassed. And his male sac looked even fuller than it had before. A part of me was fascinated.

"You must be the only one so compelled, then, since no one else has tried to force themselves on me!"

He gave a quick little wag to his head, again as if to clear his mind. "If only you would help me, Madame Jessalya. I have gotten nowhere on my own."

"Hmph. Well, this is hardly the way to get my cooperation, you know, kidnapping me, restraining me and slapping me!" I shouted at him. "And that kiss? Really? Is that to lull me into thinking all of a sudden you're a nice guy and I'll spill all my secrets to you?"

He reached out and gripped my face between his strong fingers. It hurt and I couldn't dislodge him, he had me in that kind of grip. "I told you, no questions from you. I am frustrated, yes, angry, and stymied at every corner. That kiss was not a ploy; I felt compelled into it. And I do not regret it. But I will regret hitting you again which I *will* do if you do not start giving me answers instead of questions." His voice had dropped to a deadly hiss and I believed him as I stared at his angry face with his ears laid flat back against his head, eyes narrowed, and whiskers bristled out to the sides of his face, fur standing on end. I felt claw tips pressing on either side of my face where he gripped me.

At that exact second, I felt the restraints around my wrists give way. *Now!* I thought fiercely. *Now's the time!*

I reached up, grabbing his wrist from below to push his hand from my face as a hank of hair wrapped tightly around his throat. He gasped for air, stumbling backward, pulling me forward as he reached the length of my hair. My ankles being still attached to the chair, me and the chair tumbled forward, knocking him onto his back and me on top of him, the chair dragging at me. His hands grabbed at the hair around his throat, all of his claws out as he tried to cut himself loose. He sliced through some strands, the pain of it raging through my hair and into me as they fell to the floor, lifeless. Several strands of hair reached out and flicked his face with zaps of electricity and he snarled in a breathy way as he continued to saw at the hair, closing his eyes at the assault.

I grabbed his weapon as I scrambled off him, standing to point it at him. "Ok," I panted out, "stop struggling and I'll let you live."

*Let him breathe.* The strands loosened and withdrew as he drew in air, making him cough. He sank back on an elbow as the other hand rubbed at his throat. He looked daggers at me. "So, it is true. Your hair can to act independently. There has been speculation among the researchers about that. What else can you do?"

I shook my head. "Oh, no. You don't get to ask questions. I get to ask them now. Are you in cahoots with the researchers?"

He looked confused, wrinkling up his nose and furrowing his brows. "What is cahoots?"

I sighed. "It's a Human term. Are you working with the researchers, are you one of them?"

"No. I only know about their actions as a Ranking Officer. I am informed about their experiments and results but I do not sanction killing presentient civilizations for the money. The scientists, they only care about results, especially positive results. They become very frustrated with failed experiments."

I stared at him. "What are you talking about?" A thought hit me. "Are you talking about the classroom incidence? Or when my brother died?"

He grimaced, looking away, clearly not wanting to answer. "You know you cannot hurt me with that gun."

I said calmly, "Oh, but I can." I shot the wall next to him, making him jump into a crouch.

"You cannot do that! It is triggered only by my DNA!"

"Perhaps you forgot to turn on that feature?" I wrinkled my nose at him. I reached out in a swift motion, tapping his nose. "Boop. We all forget sometimes!" I frowned. "Your name and rank. Then we'll talk more about experiments."

## CHAPTER THIRTY-TWO

He gave me a surly look and lifted one side of his lip in a sneer. "Why should I to tell you?"

I raised an eyebrow and waggled the gun. "Uh oh, that sounded like a question to me. Remember the rules: the one with the gun gets to ask the questions." Thanks to Ble'ru', I could flip the gun into any mode I wanted without looking and I flipped to mild stun mode.

He narrowed his eyes as his tail twitched back and forth in irritation. Then he heaved a sigh. "Fine. Captain Sn'eri. I am fourth in line of command."

Holding the gun steady on Sn'eri, I held up my left first finger in an admonishing gesture. "Do not move from your current position or I *will* shoot your leg. I don't want you suddenly springing on me, do you hear me?"

His body tensed as he glanced at the weapon, then nodded. "Oh, I would never to do that."

"That sounded like sarcasm to me."

His lips quirked into a small smile. "Perhaps it was."

"Well, stop it. I don't like it." I said in a cross tone. A thought struck me. "Did that experiment have anything to do with Akrion?"

His mouth gaped open in astonishment and his eyes widened, ears going slightly flat. "How do you to know about that?"

"I know a few things, like it is a rare substance used in your FTL drives. What else is it used for?"

He glared at me, tail twitching in a furious manner. "Anti-gravity."

I waved the gun. "And….?"

He shook his head. "I do not to know all the uses."

"Where is it from?"

"The Universe. It is very, very rare."

"How was it discovered?

He shrugged. "Some planet had exploded, the scientists gathered debris to analyze and they discovered this molecular level debris resisted all manipulation and defied classification so the scientists had to find out what it could do. They did many experiments before finding FTL capabilities and anti-gravity. It never decays, never dies and never changes. It is extraordinarily rare so scientists are very jealous of the particles they have and will only ever commit one particle to an experiment." He paused to pull in air. "If the experiment fails, they retrieve the particle. Some say they come from the Great Universe Creator, like shed cells from a body. But the body of the Creator is so vast, endless like space, it only leaves a few particles here and there and all our ships are always on the hunt for more. After many, many years, we have created an easier way to gather them in but, like viable planets, which are also rare, they are very difficult to find."

"Anything else?" I prompted.

"Only that one Akrion particle calls to another and scientists are still working on ways to use that feature to allow for instant communication between our ships and planets."

"That would be useful." I thought this over. I remembered the pull I felt toward the stars when I looked out the viewing window, the strange tug I had felt toward the Akrion machine and to the wall vent.

"Have there been experiments on living beings?"

He lifted one shoulder and dropped it. "Of course. If it fails, the Akrion particle can always be taken back from the body."

"On Humans?"

He looked at me, twisting his mouth slightly.

"Answer me!"

He shook his head.

"You don't know or you won't tell me?

He shrugged.

I shot him in the leg and he crumpled to the floor as his leg gave out from the stun setting.

"Be glad I switched it to mild. Now, answer me."

He held up a hand in supplication. "All right, all right! Yes, on Humans."

"Pregnant women?"

He blew out a breath, watching my hand with the gun while he rubbed his thigh. "Yes."

"And my brother died as a result." The pieces clicked together in my mind. The Akrion cart was the right size to blow into a room through a vent, like into a classroom where the air quality suddenly became bad. These scientists had a lot to pay for and I'd be the one to see them do just that.

He nodded.

"They blew the particle into the classroom where my mother was teaching the other women, didn't they? And my brother was affected by it?"

"That is the theory, yes."

"Did they retrieve the particle?"

"No." He shook his head. "The scientists could not find it in his body or the room."

"Where did it go? Was there more than one particle in the machine thingy? Maybe it returned itself to it?"

"No. They thought of that but no. They could not to find it. They examined all the women and your brother when they treated them for the air problem; they checked for the particle everywhere but it was never found."

"Why did they do it? To pregnant women?" I clenched my left hand into a fist. "How *dare* they?"

"They are scientists." As if that was a valid explanation. "They thought the opportunity to see if any babies would be affected was too good to pass up. They did not to know your brother would be in the same room at the time, but, truly, they would not have cared. Even though Akrion itself does not change, they decided to find out if it would cause a living body to change if placed at or before birth."

Stunned, I could only stare at him. "Why Humans? Why not Imurians? Or Amorphans…or any of the other species?"

"They did. Amorphans were first since they can already shift body parts as needed. It did not to change any of them. A few Imurians volunteered and it was not successful. And so on. They had no opportunities to try the Akrion on pregnant females until a whole group emigrated at once. The scientists thought of using Humans, with your ability to have live births in spite of DNA changes or DNA defects, although that is centuries in your past now."

"And you still don't know where the particle is?"

"It has never been found. All of you Exchangers have been carefully checked and none of you to have it, either."

"Why did my brother die?"

He shook his head. "Speculation is the Akrion passed through him, causing changes incompatible with life but not right away, it took a few days. His body underwent spontaneous alterations but none of them made sense and ultimately he could not live through them."

He sighed. "Before it was known he was affected, your family went to the Viewing Deck a few hours later after the air experiment. The scientists believe the Akrion particle somehow returned itself to space and that is why they could not find it. Your brother reportedly was drawn to the window, pressing against it, clawing at it, almost as if he was called to go through the window to the outside. He could not, of course, and your parents tried to get him to leave the area. He resisted, crying and fighting with them until, suddenly, he relaxed and turned away from the window as your mother was holding him close to prevent him from harming himself."

*Do we have the Akrion particle?*

YES.

*So it passed from my brother into me while my mom held him so close?*

THINK SO.

I drew in a big breath. "So my brother was murdered by your scientists."

"Not intentionally and certainly not directly! There was no malice involved. They are always working to find out the best uses for all unknown substances. Your brother was an unfortunate side effect of the experiment. And for that, I to speak for the StarFinder staff and crew as we apologize for the mishap."

I felt like shooting him just for that pompous statement. My brother died because of their scientists and their fracking experiment! All my parents got was hush money, threats and the overwhelming grief and guilt of losing their first-born son. "My parents need to be told about this. They need to know it wasn't their fault."

"If you help me, I will help you with a message to your parents." He held up a hand, palm side up. I didn't like the glint in his eyes or the slight narrowing of his gaze. This dude was a conniver and I was disinclined to trust him.

"I have no reason to believe you. I'll figure out a way to get this information to my parents without you." I would ask Si'neada to convey the message but he didn't need to know that. I felt my hair tap me on my butt to get my attention.

*What!?*

DEESTER.

*Where?*

LIGHT OPENING.

It finally occurred to me I could have used my mind-whispering ability to communicate....maybe. :*Deester?*: I watched for a reaction from Sn'eri. He was calmly watching me, a puzzled look on his face.

"I'm thinking, okay? You just stay right there. This gun isn't going anywhere."

He rolled his eyes, tail twitching, as he rubbed the leg I'd shot. I moved a couple of steps back from him so if he did make a move, if his leg was already back to normal, I'd have some warning. I hoped.

No answer from Deester. I'd not been successful before with mind communication with him so why would that change now? I glanced up at the lighting area, saw him put his finger to his lips in a shushing manner, then he finger-walked in the air to show he was leaving. I could only hope he would bring help.

I was only looking up for a second or two but Sn'eri took the advantage of that slight distraction. He leapt but it was wobbly and off-center. I stumbled backward and tripped over the chair, going down in a heap. "Damn it all to the hells and beyond!" I snarled as I tried to right myself. I still gripped the gun so I swung it over and shot Sn'eri as he loomed over me. Looking surprised, he toppled onto me. "Way to go, Lilianthal. Shoulda thought that one through." I muttered. I shoved at his inert body; at least he was breathing. "That's the good thing about stun, you're still aware and you can breathe." I wheezed out the words; damn it, he was like a boulder on top of me. I heaved with all my might and he rolled off me onto the floor. I stood and dusted myself off.

"I *told* you I'd shoot you again if you moved!" I poked him with the tip of my shoe. "Aren't you going to apologize to me? I think I require an apology." I arched both eyebrows, pursing my lips.

He rolled his eyes upward, looking like he was fighting for patience and air. "I am sorry." He panted out the words as he looked at me, lifting his lips to show his fangs. "You shot me!" He said with an indignant tone. "I am definitely sorry you shot me."

I barked a laugh. "You call that an apology?"

He frowned. "Yes. At least while a gun is being held on me."

"Then it seems to me you could put some frosting on that apology and make it sound a little bit sincere."

I bent down sideways, righting the chair, turning it around so the back of it was toward him, and sat down, keeping the gun level on Sn'eri. I didn't want the restraints to somehow repair themselves and fasten around me again so I really hoped it wasn't a stupid thing to do but I needed to sit. My adrenaline wearing off, I felt shaky, tired and scared and I needed the back of the chair to support my gun arm.

He sneered at me. "I said I am sorry and that is as much as I will say. I do not to know what this frosting is but I am sincere." One side of his mouth curled up, showing at least one sharp tooth.

:Jessi? My little bunch of flowers, are you all right?:

:Yes! I'm okay. I'm in a little room somewhere with Sn'eri. I had to use the stun mode on him with his gun.:

A startled pause. :You shot him?:

:Well, yes. He leaped at me. Now he can't.:

:I will to be there very quickly. Deester is bringing me.:

I noticed Sn'eri's brow furrow as he looked at me intently. "Who are you talking to?" He demanded.

My cheeks heated up with embarrassment. I must've been moving my lips while mind whispering with Si'neada. I realized with a start Sn'eri couldn't hear us; perhaps he couldn't mind whisper or this wasn't his frequency.

"I was thinking, that's all." I bluffed. "Sometimes I move my lips when I'm thinking. Yes, it's embarrassing but that's me." I lifted one shoulder. I hoped my cheeks were no longer red.

"And you are thinking about….?"

I sighed. "What to do next," I admitted.

"You could give me back my weapon and we can go our different ways."

I narrowed my gaze. "Yeah, like that's going to happen. You didn't drag me in here just to let me go. I want to know more about these DNA caches; you had questions for me. I don't believe you are, um, altruistic about all this but I'll make you a deal. You tell me about the DNA stuff and why it's stored on this ship and I'll do my best to give you answers if you ask the right questions."

He looked at me with a slightly narrowed look, twisted his mouth to one side, then nodded. "Deal." He drew in a deep breath as he clumsily rolled over to his side. The stun mode was wearing off, it seemed.

"Deal. But I hold the gun. And stop sniffing at me."

He blew out a breath in resignation. "All right. I should never have used a weapon but you were always with others and I needed to talk to you privately, as an Officer of this ship, if nothing else."

"But why me? Why not Zoe or Keaton or one of the others?"

He raised one brow. "How do you know I have not talked to them?"

That stumped me. "I guess I don't." I gave him a glare. "Have you?

He half-grinned, an interesting look on a furry face with whiskers. "That is for me to know and not for you."

I sniffed. Time to move on. "Tell me about this DNA stuff. Why do you have it stored?"

He glanced off to one side, appearing to think over his answer. "Okay. I will to tell you but it is top secret, do you to agree?"

I nodded. "Sure, top secret." I mimed zipping my lips together and using a key to lock it but that only got me a very puzzled look by Sn'eri. I huffed out a breath with exasperation.

"A long time ago, many Imurians lost their way in the universe."

I interrupted. "You mean their navigation failed or what? Where did they end up and how'd you find them? What did they find?"

"No! I do not to mean it literally, it is an analogy. Please do not to interrupt my story." He scowled. "As I was saying before I was rudely interrupted, they became greedy. Habitable worlds are hard to come by, you know; the conditions have to be just right for oxygen breathers, just the right distance from the sun, and many other things. They became impatient and made the," he cleared his throat, "unwise decision to hurry things along." He held up a finger. "What I mean by that is instead of watching and waiting to see if groups of life became truly sentient, which can take millennia, they decided to intervene by wiping out presentient beings in order to gain the world. Many of our ancestors protested these decisions but were subdued into compliance or killed. A secret select few became guardians of DNA collected on species being wiped out, hoping someday they could be brought back to life on some other world." He tapped his claw-tipped fingers on his knee.

"The thing is, there is always a population problem needing to be solved by selling another planet to be populated, so DNA is stored in deep freeze in the hope it won't degenerate as it's waiting for what is right to be done. After all, we make a lot of money selling planets to over-populated worlds."

He drew in a big breath. "As you can see, this is a monumental secret and if gotten out, would damage our relations with all our business dealings with all the species we have sold worlds in the Rent-to-Own program. This is not discussed with people other than us Imurians for security reasons but I feel compelled to include you." He pointed at his gun in my hands. "That is a very compelling reason." He spread his hands apart in an apparent gesture of good will. "I tell you this since you are an honorable person and will keep your vow of secrecy. If you do not, then your death may have to be arranged. Or be turned over to the scientists, in which case I think you may to prefer death."

He sounded sincere and I was very tempted to believe him. I still wasn't going to trust him but I was inclined to believe his story. It matched fairly closely what Si'neada had already told me. Sn'eri being an Office of the ship made his help more valuable as he was in a better position to know what was happening.

"How does this involve me?" I asked, still profoundly upset and disturbed by their avarice and genocide tendencies but this wasn't the time to go into that. I couldn't think about Devon right now or I'd shoot Sn'eri again out of sheer anger. "Who has been threatening my parents all these years and paying them off? I want the threats to stop and stop now and the monitoring device removed from their bodies."

He laced his fingers together and placed them around one knee, bewilderment showing through one ear slightly forward, one slightly back, whiskers drooping, nose and brow wrinkling. "I really do not know. Threats? What kind of threats?"

"Threats to kill them and take me or just have me removed. Someone has paid my parents a lot of money for their silence since Devon died."

He shook his head. "I do not to know, truly, I do not. I will to check into this and do what I can to remove the threats. It must be the scientists who did not want the peculiarities of his death revealed."

I didn't like his answer but I believed he didn't know. He was cunning, yes, but his initial reaction to my question was genuine.

"Why me?"

"Si'neada's interest in you piqued my curiosity and I know it is not sexual for him so there must be more." He then pointed a finger at me. "How did you to get your hair to strangle me?"

"I don't know what you're talking about. My hair is very curly, as you can see, so you must've gotten tangled in it somehow." I projected innocence.

"That was no accident! You made your hair do that!"

"Hey, you fell backwards, my hair got tangled around your neck and tightened because I couldn't move fast enough to keep it slack. What can I say? That's what happened."

"How did you get out of those restraints?"

I shrugged. "I'm little and they were big, so I slipped out of them." I knew he wouldn't believe me since the restraints were clearly cut in half but I didn't care. I wasn't telling him about my hair or anything else.

: Si'neada, where are you?:

:I am almost there.:

"Now that you know these secrets, are you willing to help us, the Resistors?"

"Huh? Help you how?"

"Let us study you to see if there are effects from the Akrion experiment."

"There's nothing to study! I certainly do not give permission for that so don't even think about it!"

The doorknob turned on the door. Sn'eri glanced at the door, looking startled. The lock held.

I asked, "Who's that outside the door?"

He said, "I do not to know. This room does not exist on the current plan of the ship."

"Jessi? Are you in there?" Si'neada's muffled voice came through the door. "Let me in; I know you are in there."

I gestured with the gun. "Let him in, Sn'eri. That sounds like Si'neada. Somehow he's found us."

He crossed his arms across his chest. "No."

"I thought you wanted to be part of his group or whatever? Well, here's your chance to talk to him about it privately, away from other Imurians. Let him in. Or I'll shoot you again and you know I will."

He looked furious, ears canted back tight against his head, his upper lip lifting in a snarl as his tail whipped viciously back and forth at the tip. He pushed a button on his lapel and the door snicked open. Si'neada entered, closing the door quietly behind him.

"Well, well, well." He pursed his lips, tapping his mouth with one perfectly manicured claw. "This is an interesting thing to find, you two alone in a room. An unknown room that is not on the schematics of this ship. With an Officer of the Ship, no less." He looked pointedly at Sn'eri. "Explain, please." He made sure he wasn't standing between me and the gun being held on Sn'eri, moving back and to his left a bit. "And this had better be good enough for me to not report this to the Supreme Captain."

Sn'eri glanced between Si'neada and me. "You can mind whisper with her! That is the only explanation for how you found us here."

Si'neada said in a calm manner, "There are other ways, too; I was looking for *you*, as it happens, for other reasons. I heard voices in here, decided to investigate and found you both here. No mind whispering involved," he lied in a smooth voice. "Now explain."

"First I want her to put the gun down." He threw a scathing look my way but I merely smiled and shook my head. "I am interested in preserving DNA caches stored on this ship but have not known who to ally with regarding it. I have suspected you and your sister are involved but I have not had proof of that. You took a special interest in her from the beginning so I have been working to figure out why." He rubbed his nose with his hand. "I think I know now. How she can work my gun is a mystery I will solve and how she got out of restraints without the key."

Si'neada quirked an eyebrow. "Perhaps you forgot to DNA stamp the gun. And what restraints?"

Sn'eri pursed his lips. "Right. That is so like me to do that." He then scowled. "You know we are trained from early on to never leave that feature off. Ever."

Si'neada shrugged. "We all have that one time, Sn'eri; perhaps this was your time. Or when she overpowered you, perhaps something flipped the switch. There are many explanations."

"Her hairies overpowered me! How can hairies do that? No other Human's hairies to behave like that! That is *not* normal! For any being!" He rubbed his neck where my hair had tightened around him in a throttle hold. "I am going to be sore for days."

Si'neada grinned. "Get over it, Sn'eri. Sounds to me you deserved what you got. What were you thinking, bringing her to this hidden room and restraining her? Did you expect her to be trembling in fear and eager to answer questions?" He pointed at Sn'eri. "She is not that person." He tilted his head. "I have never thought it to be a very effective technique, myself."

I stifled a snort; of course that's what Sn'eri thought. They both heard me, and Sn'eri turned anger-filled eyes toward me, Si'neada's grin only widened. "Humans are not as passive or soft as you have perhaps been thinking, Sn'eri." Si'neada then heaved a dramatic sigh. "Well, what a conundrum." This must be the Word of the Day.

"If I had all day, I would stay here to be amused but as it turns out, I have other things I must to attend to. So, my little pin cushion, let me to have the gun and you can go. I believe you have a time schedule, also. I will to take care of Sn'eri."

I looked at him for a few seconds, working out what he meant by "taking care of", then shook it off as having watched too many murder mysteries. If Sn'eri were to 'disappear', it wouldn't actually hurt my feelings. I briefly wondered if he had a family, then I shrugged that off, too. Whatever happened, happened. He should be thinking of his family, not me.

I was about to hand the gun over to Si'neada when a sudden question came out of my mouth before I knew I was going to ask it. "What happens to the DNA? He knows about it," and I indicated Sn'eri with the gun, "so what happens from here?"

"Ah, yes, the DNA." Si'neada looked thoughtful. "Well, Sn'eri obviously knows about it so we will have to let him be part of our preservation group."

I nodded at Si'neada, giving him the finger circle of approval, then I glanced at his time piece. Really? I'd only been kidnapped for 40 minutes? It felt like 40 years. "I have to get going! My dance rehearsal is in 15 minutes! Si'neada, I'll meet up with you after the show tonight and finish that task we started then." I nodded in what I hoped was a meaningful way to Si'neada. Judging by the sudden gleam in his eyes, I took that for 'message received' and then I glanced at Sn'eri.

"Next time," I remarked, "Try being nice to me when asking questions; you'll get a lot more information than from attack and kidnap." I crossed the room and as I opened the door, I angled back, handed the gun butt first to Si'neada and said, "See ya later, terminator."

They both furrowed their brows in puzzlement and I grinned as I slipped through the door, but then I hesitated. "Um, guys? I don't know where to go from here. How do I find my corridor again?"

"Ah. Yes, that is a good question," Si'neada said. "Sn'eri, shall we be her guides?" He swung the weapon around his forefinger in a lazy motion as if it were nothing but a toy. I guess for him it would be as the gun was—supposedly—tuned only to Sn'eri's DNA.

I heard Sn'eri heave a sigh. "Of course." They both appeared in the doorway, Si'neada tucking the weapon into his own waistband. "After you, Sn'eri." He swept an arm out in a dramatic gesture and I noticed it was his non-gun using hand. Si'neada's eyes were sharp on Sn'eri's back as Sn'eri passed by me to take front position. Sn'eri said, "What happened to that delicious scent you had earlier? I only smell Human now."

I caught Si'neada looking at me askance. I raised my eyebrows and shrugged, gesturing my hands in a 'I dunno' way. I knew why it happened; after all, it drew him in close enough to free myself, but it was definitely a new "talent" previously unthought of. Was there no end to the surprises this body was capable of producing? It seemed the only way I was going to find out about them was to be in danger and I wasn't particularly fond of that idea.

Gripping the idea that maybe my entire body could change its DNA was a very slippery thing to think about. What happened to my own DNA? Or any others I'd gathered along the way? I cringed away from those thoughts, feeling panic crouched in the corner ready to pounce if I went too deeply into those ideas.

And now the scent thing. Was that a defense thing I could do now? I didn't know and quite frankly was a little scared to find out more. Did it really happen? I had inhaled his spicy, enticing scent…unless that was me exuding it. I shook my head at myself as I remembered his kiss. Why had I gotten sensations from his kiss in places I only wiped or washed? It should've been Keaton. I wished it had been Keaton.

I sighed and looked up from studying the floor and with a start, realized that Sn'eri was opening a door. I'd been so lost in my own thoughts again I hadn't noticed the route we'd taken. Annoyance at myself raised up and I grimaced, thinking it was a good thing I wasn't going to be an undercover agent. We stepped through into the Human corridor and I breathed a sigh of relief at knowing where I was. Home territory. I flipped up a hand to wave good-bye at the two males and I turned and almost ran down the hallway to get to the classroom so my teacher and I could practice our dance routine. I could hardly wait to get there so I could push all these questions and thoughts aside and concentrate on footwork and nothing else.

## CHAPTER THIRTY-THREE

The five of us gathered in the side room of the dining area with our Tatrans. I had two costume changes, one for my line dancing routine and one for my dance with Tatro. Soli was dressed in his gymnastics outfit, which made for very interesting bulgy parts, at least to my eyes, and again I felt a quirking of sensations in areas I normally didn't pay attention to. I felt a flash of regret about Soli being male oriented; I really liked him.

I checked out Zoe, who looked killer in her screaming red flirty dress for her ballroom routine and Keaton was mouth-watering handsome in his black dancing suit with a red tie against a snowy white shirt, both outfits swinging with charms from collars and cuffs. Mitchler was dressed for his teacher dancing routine with a flashy purple and blue Amorphan robe on, hair tousled in a becoming way. He was checking his appearance in the wall mirror. I would follow Mitchler with my personal routine, and then change into my robe while Zoe and Keaton were on stage after me. Si'neada had been very busy making all these outfits the past few days.

I was horridly nervous; my heart pounding and hands shaking. Line dancing isn't normally a one-person routine but no one else would take on three routines to help me out. I'd wanted to recruit back-up dancers from the Imurians but that hadn't been approved so I'd be out there all alone, pretending it was a one-person style of dancing.

I wore my ankle boots which I'd managed to squeeze into my luggage allowance. The leather was worked in a becoming pattern of leaves and flowers and the colors intertwined with blues, golds and soft reds in an appealing pattern. My boot-cut jeans allowed flashes of pattern with the various kicks and spins in this dance. My blouse, a blue and gold pattern swirled over the slinky material, was tucked in at the waistband with a sparkly belt threaded through the loops, charms hanging from the bottom edge all the way around. I wore my flashiest pairs of earrings and my make-up was as good as I could get it.

I wished my stomach would settle out of its current rampaging butterfly mode and I'd quit popping out sweat on my forehead. I felt slightly nauseous from anticipation and my hair, cascading down my back, tried to soothe me. I fretted about changing shapes at any given moment due to my nerves, which would, of course, be disastrous. At that thought, my hair tightened around me and practically gave me a shake.

*No WORRY.* Shape changing wasn't an option here and everything about me except me knew it.

I heard the swelling of conversations from the crowd outside the doors and we turned to stare at the door, including our teachers. Tatro said in a firm voice, "We are all nervous; it is not often we perform in front of those who are not our own species. Students, please remember you are prepared, you are practiced for this, and all will be well. Everyone, take a big breath," and he demonstrated by noisily inhaling, "and now let it out." He let out a comical snorting breath and we laughed, taking a lot of the edge off our nerves. I felt my shoulders relax.

Zoe looked at me and said, "Ah, Jess. Aren't you just the cutest little thing in your little girl jeans and shiny belt? Why, you're so yummy, you could be eaten up like a cookie!" Then she smiled broadly. "Or like Red Velvet....cake."

Surprised, I gave a gasping laugh. "I can't believe you just said that!"

"Anything for my Velve-twin."

I narrowed my eyes at her, wiping tears from my eyes. "I needed that." I held out my fist for her knuckle-bump.

We trooped out of the room to follow Tatro to the edge of the stage area where chairs were awaiting us. This way, we could see most of the show unless we had to scamper back to the room to change for the second routine. We had front row seats so the order in which we were led there didn't matter for once and I was glad to not be at the front of the line. Mitchler and Tatra were led up to the stage, which had risen out of the floor for the occasion, and they bowed to the audience while being introduced.

Si'neada, as host, was dressed in a glittery green jumpsuit with decorations and stones twinkling over the material. His nails were painted to match and his fur was fluffed and coiffed and sprayed into place, his lashes darkened with their equivalent of mascara. He flourished an arm at the two dancers, announcing, "Mitchler and Tatra Hilodria will dazzle this august audience with their rendition of the traditional Amorphan interpretation of the Harvest Dance!"

He clapped his hands together. "Now pay attention, people! This dance comes from the countryside of Amorpha, having been done for hundreds of years, to celebrate the yearly gathering of foods for the coming cycle of time. It has never been seen before any audience except the Amorphans so it is indeed a special treat for us tonight!" He clapped again, grinning to show all his teeth, and then swept out a hand to indicate the couple, who were now posed for the beginning of the dance. The Imurians, and I was surprised to note children among the adults, hooted and howled and clapped their hands together.

Mitchler and Tatra started the dance as the music played and as I watched it, I was busy going over my own steps in my head so, although my eyes were directed at the stage, I didn't really see anything. I was too busy thinking, *Weighted left, right kick, kick, step, left kick, then step, left kick…or is it right kick again? Oh, my shattered nerves, I'd better remember these steps when I get up there!*

I knew once the music started, my feet would remember the moves but I couldn't stop myself from thinking over the steps in the meantime. The song, "Clappity Clap Happy Clap" was catchy, repetitive and I hoped they'd like it. The dance, 128 steps—not counting syncopated steps—was fun to dance, lots of footwork and because it had so many steps, wouldn't have a lot of repetition throughout the song. "Remember to smile, Jess, remember to smile." I muttered to myself, which provoked an elbow into my shoulder from Soli beside me.

"You'll be fine, Jess." He whispered into my ear. "It's not like it's a national contest or anything so go up, have fun and imagine all the Imurians naked."

I snorted, a quick laughing one, surprising both of us. "Okay," I whispered back. "That's quite a visual. All that fur standing on end." He snickered, we smiled at each other and then we both turned our attention back to the stage. I relaxed back into my chair. Heck, what was the worst that could happen? I might miss a step or so, but like Soli said, "so what?". The audience wouldn't know the difference and there was really nothing riding on this other than pride. I heaved out a big breath, dropping my shoulders away from my ears and actually saw the last few sequences of Mitchler's dance on the stage. His movements were graceful and made good use of the stage as they swept around the perimeter, coming to a stop in the middle of the stage. As they posed in the final step, the audience erupted into cheering and cat-calling (I smirked to myself) and stamping of boots on the floor as they clapped. I poked Soli. "They're certainly enthusiastic." He nodded.

The couple stepped forward and bowed toward the gathered Imurians, Tatra smiling, Mitchler grinning, hand in hand. Si'neada let the noise go on for a while and then raised his hands in a stop motion. He nodded to them and pointed at the steps to encourage them to move off the stage.

I wiped my hands on my jeans to dry them off. My foot wiggled up and down in nervous anticipation until Soli gently placed his hand on my knee to still the slight tapping sound. I gulped and nodded to Soli in thanks.

Si'neada beckoned to me so I stood, making my shaky way over to the steps, my heart hammering in my chest. An Imurian was there to lend a steadying hand up the stairs. I sucked in a breath, squared my shoulders and climbed onto the stage. Si'neada smiled at me as he said, "And here is our very own Jessalya to perform a unique form of dance known as line dancing. She tells me it is normally done with many people on the floor in lines, hence the name, but tonight she will to perform solo to the dance song "Clappity Clap Happy Clap". The advantage of this type of dancing is it can be done without a partner and can also be done in unison with more people. We will all to enjoy this performance by Jessalya with the long, long hairies!"

He swept his hand out to indicate me and I smiled at the audience, although, with the floodlights at the edge of the stage, I actually couldn't see them. I bowed forward, straightened up, and put my weight on my left foot.

The song had a very short lead-in so I leaped into action making sure my boots were making the right amount of noise along with the beat of the music. I started sweating shortly into the routine under the hot lights but I didn't care; I was having fun! I loved dancing, my feet knew the steps and I went along for the ride. On the turns, my hair whipped around me in graceful motions and the audience, at some point, started clapping along in time to the music. I hit every step exactly right and when the ending note sounded, I stomped my heel down to indicate DONE. I raised my hands over my head and grinning from ear to ear, I bowed toward the audience, who were hooting, shouting, stomping their feet and clapping. I think they liked it.

Si'neada appeared at my side and wrapped arm around my shoulders. "Well done, Jess! I can see a new form of entertainment coming to our Starfinder crew and families!" :*If only there were a few more days, you could teach us. But alas, my little teapot, you must leave us soon.*:

:*I leave in the morning, yes. After the party for the other thing?*:
He nodded while smiling at the audience.

I put my arm around his waist and squeezed slightly. The noise wasn't abating and Si'neada finally had to holler to make

*Exchanger*

himself heard over the noise. "THAT'S ENOUGH! QUIET! QUIET, PLEASE!" The crowd finally settled back into their chairs. He said, "Well, I guess I do not have to ask for applause for this little one, do I? You took care of that already!"

A ripple of laughter went through the crowd. "We want another!" someone shouted from the dark. I was still trying to catch my breath. Si'neada shouted back, "She will to be back later for a partner routine! Right now, we need to send her off the stage," and I heard a few boos, "and bring up our next act, which I promise you will also to enjoy."

I made my way over to the stairs, the same Imurian waiting to help me down the short set of stairs, but this time he was smiling. In a soft tone, he said, "That looks like so much fun! I want to learn it; is it hard?"

I shook my head. "Not really, but you have to start with the simple dances and move up to the harder ones. I'll give Si'neada some information on how to learn from vids, if you want."

He nodded with enthusiasm and squeezed my hand as I reached the bottom step and then let go so I could sit. Soli offered me a high five, Keaton gave me a thumbs-up gesture, Mitchler echoing him. Zoe grinned at me, nodding, giving me a V for Victory—or perhaps, for VelveTwin. I whispered, "Thanks, everyone; that was fun. You all are awesome, too."

Si'neada announced Zoe and Keaton as they made their way onstage. I really wanted to see their routine before I changed clothes into my gown. I went over to the side of the stage toward our changing room to watch before slipping into the room for my robe.

There was no doubt Zoe and Keaton were very graceful together as they moved into each other's arms and waited for the music. As it began, a soft smile appeared on Zoe's face and she looked intently into Keaton's eyes, and he looked back. A stab of jealousy hit me and I stuffed it down as best I could. *It's part of the act, silly. I hope.* They dipped and twirled, adding in lifts and elegant moves in their waltz and the audience oohed and ahhed. Quite frankly, they should've because it was a gorgeous dance with the two of them together. I hurried to the room to change for my next routine with my teacher. That was going to be a comic routine, all right, short little me and tall willowy him. Ah, well, everyone needs a little humor in their life, right?

As expected, when Tatro and I went on stage for the routine, there were chuckles in the crowd but once we started dancing, the audience quieted and we swept through the motions of the Amorphan Celebration of Childhood dance moves. When giving our bows, the Imurians did their usual response and I was relieved to be able to leave the stage and know I was done. I enjoyed the rest of the show along with the audience, Soli putting on a heck of a floor gymnastic routine. How anyone can twist their body around in the air like that was beyond me.

After all the acts, Si'neada asked us to all come up on stage. "Here are our lovely dancers and performers from the evening. We have prizes for these Exchanger Students; we, the judges, could not to decide on only one as they are all equally talented. We gift each one of you with one month's supply of our coffee. Each of you had asked to purchase this fine commodity during this journey so it is deemed to be a prize indeed!"

We clapped and cheered along with the crowd at his announcement. We high-fived amongst ourselves, congratulating each other on jobs well done, hugging each other, wiping away a few stray tears.

When we were done, they lowered the stage into the floor and waiters started circulating with drinks and appetizers and it became a party. This was the only time on this journey we were allowed to mingle with the Imurians at will although I noticed the children had been ushered away immediately after the show.

The five of us gathered as a loose group and we all slapped hands and grinned and swapped compliments on our performances. Zoe said, "Jess, I have to say, I was impressed with both of your performances. Even my little sister, 'The Princess,'" and she made air quotes, "couldn't have done that better."

"Just remember, Zoe; I'm no Princess." She nodded, smiling.

I snatched a beverage from a tray as the server passed by and took a few gulps. I looked around for Si'neada; we had unfinished business as tonight would be my last opportunity to take on DNA from their storage.

The five of us laughed, dancing and drinking whatever beverage went by, having a glorious time. Before I knew it, they were blinking the lights to signal the evening was over and I wiped my sweaty forehead with one hand, panting for breath. I hadn't seen Si'neada since he was onstage so I didn't know what to do about the DNA samples.

I thought again of sending a mind whisper to Si'neada but then remembered him cautioning me not to use it very often and especially around a lot of people, as so many frequencies overlapped and it wasn't a talent to broadcast. I decided he would have to track me down; after all, I had been visible all evening, certainly not hard to find if he and his sister had been ready.

We chatted and laughed together like a clutch of chickens as we left the dining room with our escort, comparing our stage performances, having a great time together as a group. "Time to pack!" I chortled as I palmed open my door. I gasped as I took in the sight before me and my hand flew up to cover my mouth. What the hells had happened in here?

Our escort, De're'dita, stepped over and looked in. He slapped the security alarm on the door and put a hand on my arm, restraining me from entering my room. We both stared at the mess in my sitting room; pillows were slashed open, cushions askew. I shuddered to think of what my bedroom looked like. Guess Zoe wasn't staying in my room tonight. I glanced over my shoulder at my classmates to find them all frozen in place with their mouths hanging open.

Security arrived faster than I thought possible as the Officer strode up to my room, looked in, then looked at my classmates. "Are your rooms all right?" He demanded.

"Oh! We haven't looked yet." Zoe turned to her room, palmed it open to look inside. "Mine is all right." The guys checked their rooms; everything was fine except mine.

*Sn'eri, it had to be him. He told me he was going to have my room searched. Damned good thing I've got my gun on me.* Suddenly furious, I clenched my teeth. What did he hope to find? My memory chip? My parent's chip? Both were safe in my arm. My gun? In my bra. The secret to my hair? My hair didn't shed. I fumed, fists clenched, eyes narrowed to slits.

De're'dita turned to me. "Madame Jessalya, are you all right?"

"No!" I snapped. "Someone trashed my room and I'm really pissed off!"

"Do you have valuables?"

"Only if you count my clothes, my PD, and my coffee." I snarled. "You guys were very specific in your limitations." I clutched the container of coffee from the evening tighter to me.

He laid a hand on my shoulder. "Please, Madame. Please calm down. We will to find who did this and rectify it."

"You'd fracking better."

The security guard came out of my room. "There is no one in there, but it will take all night to go through everything for evidence. We will to move you to another room."

"I'll stay with Zoe in her room. I don't want to be alone."

"Yes, of course." De're'dita looked relieved at an easy solution.

"Do you think, uh, could Si'neada make something for me to wear for tomorrow? Just in case I don't have clothes tomorrow? All those beautiful robes he made for me!" Tears sprang to my eyes, to my embarrassment, and I brushed them away brusquely. I felt violated and vulnerable. Then I shook it off. If I felt violated, imagine what Zoe had to be struggling with.

As he turned to look at me, the expression on his face softened for an instance, as if he were looking at his own child. Being ultra-short and looking so young did come in handy now and again, I hated to admit. He nodded, a slow, considering motion. "Yes, that is a very good suggestion." He looked over to his left. "Ba'runka, communicate with Si'neada and tell him to come here with all haste." The uniformed male said, "Yes, sir!" and pivoted on a boot heel to comply.

"I was worried I wouldn't have appropriate clothing for our grand exodus tomorrow if for some reason I don't get my stuff in the morning so I asked if Si'neada could maybe whip up a gown in my size for tomorrow." I explained as I looked at Zoe. "You know I would look like I was dressing in my older sister's clothing if I had to wear a standard size."

"Well, that's true enough." Soli said, laying a hand on my arm in symptahty. "Good thinking, Jess." He patted me on the back.

Zoe said, "I have an extra nightgown you can wear tonight and I think we can get a toothbrush for you from the Imurians. Better for neither of us to be alone tonight."

"Oh, my little tray of delights! What happened? Are all of you all right? Why are you in the corridor?" Si'neada was at his most flamboyant, fluttering his hands about but his eyes were keen as they examined everything as he fast walked down the hall toward us.

De'red'ita said in a stiff tone, "Madame Jessalya's room was ransacked, unheard of on this ship! We cannot let her to sleep in her own quarters for safety reasons nor can she have her belongings until we have determined that all is clean and safe. Madame Jessalya would like for you to provide her with a gown for tomorrow's disembarking, in case her clothes are not available. She cannot borrow one from the Amorphans, that is obvious."

Si'neada clapped his hands together. "But of course! What is a little lost sleep among friends, correct? I do to need to retake measurements, however, as I am certain that her numbers have changed and all must be perfect for tomorrow!" He bowed to the Security Officer. "May I to take her with me to do so? I did not to think to bring my measuring tools with me, not knowing what was needed."

De'red'ita nodded. "Yes. I to think it is safe enough. However, for your safety, I will send Ba'runka with you as an escort."

"Yes, of course! That would be delightful to know we are totally safe indeed."

## CHAPTER THIRTY-FOUR

Surprisingly, all of my classmates wanted to hug me before I left with Si'neada, Zoe whispering, "I won't go to bed until you're back, Velve-twin."

"Thanks, Zoe."

I gave a little wave and walked off with Si'neada and Ba'runka. Si'neada put his arm around my shoulders and mind-whispered, :*Who do you to think did this?*:

:*Sn'eri did this, I'm sure of it. He's way too curious about my hair, I'm afraid.*:

It could have been Sn'eri; he would have the clearance for access to your room. Is your gun safe??:

:*Yes. It's with me.*: I paused to take a breath. :*Can it be proven it was him?*:

:*Probably, but he is 4$^{th}$ to the Command and it will be difficult to hold him accountable.*:

:*What did he hope to find? There's nothing in my room to give him information.*:

He wrinkled his nose. :*Perhaps a hair for analysis? Proof we were training you with a forbidden weapon, if he had found your gun?*:

:Perhaps. I don't think a strand of my hair will help him; when my hair leaves my head, it loses all its abilities.:

:Better hope so, my little dumpling.:

We arrived at Si'neada's workroom and he opened the door, nodding to Ba'runka. "All right, I can to take it from here. We will be secure behind the closed door."

The guard bowed and waited until Si'neada palmed the door closed. I assumed he then returned to his other duties and dismissed him from my mind. Si'neada said while holding up a finger to his lips in a shushing manner, "All right, my little measuring tape! Let me to get your numbers to make sure I have it right."

We started chatting about the performances earlier that night and after a while, Si'neada nodded and pointed at the door. "He is gone."

Startled, I glanced at the door and back to Si'neada. It hadn't occurred to me the guard might stay outside to listen. Yeah, some spy I would make....not. Si'neada smiled and said, "It is better to be overly suspicious than under."

I nodded with a wry grin on my face. "Yeah, you're right. I'm just not suspicious enough, it seems."

He beckoned to me and looked over into the corner of the room. We softly walked over and he removed a pile of fabric revealing the DNA container underneath. I raised my eyebrows and looked a question his direction,

"It was very difficult to get it here unnoticed; we had to go through the corridors and took much longer than expected, which is why I was gone from the party."

"Then Sn'eri did us a favor?"

"It appears to be so." He gestured to the container.

I stared at the box, inexplicably nervous, my hands sweating but my hair eager; it was straining to hold itself back from pouncing on the box. I wiped my palms on my jeans and said in a breathy voice, "Well, let's do this before I lose my nerve."

Si'neada tapped numbers onto the control panel. When the red light turned to green and the door hissed open, my heart rate jumped a thousand-fold, I swear. As the vapor cleared, I stepped closer to the box and peered in. Maybe 10 or 15 vials? I sucked in a deep breath, squared my shoulders and said, "Ok, I'm ready."

Si'neada took tongs and pulled a vial out of the cold interior. A strand of hair quested forward and dipped into the vial and then as quickly pulled back, shaking itself out. I laughed, a nervous sound. "Uh, too cold still. Apparently"

Si'neada grinned, "Yes, I to see that. Tell your hairies they have to give it a few minutes per vial to defrost enough to sample."

"I think they've figured it out."

As he held the vial, the 3D hologram activated and I studied the information provided: the name of the species, preferred diet, body type and variations, the type of rudimentary civilization it was developing and other facts. I memorized it as quickly as I could, wishing I had a photographic memory.

WE REMEMBER ALL. Smugness radiated from the reddish mass.

*Oh, of course you will.* I rolled my eyes. A strand poked my cheek, a quick needle-like prick, in retaliation.

My hair strand came forward again when it was time and with slow caution, dipped into the vial again. I could tell the instant it snagged the sample and felt the triumph. I knew it took time for my body to sort through the DNA and figure out how to integrate it into a usable form. I knew this much about the process and had explained to Si'neada that just getting the sample would not mean I could instantly become that species.

Si'neada put the vial back and this time, using two pairs of tongs, drew out two vials and held them in the air long enough for my hair to retrieve samples and for us to view the data. On the fifth vial, my hair came snapping out of the vial, shaking itself violently and then wiping against my jeans while a band of hair grabbed the vial and threw it on the floor.

"That sample has gone bad." I remarked.

Si'neada chortled and said, "You to think?" He held out the last vial. "Jess? How are you doing? Are you okay? Are you feeling yourself?" Si'neada's voice drifted over to me.

I shook my head, more to clear it than to negate his questions. "I—I feel—like—I overate at an all-you-can-eat restaurant. I have no idea how my body will sort all this out." Then I looked at him and grimaced. "You don't suppose I'll become all jumbled up into an unsolvable mess, do you? I won't have the ears of an Imurian, the feet of an Amorphan and the torso of…something…from in there?"

"Ahh, my little pincushion." He drew me into a hug. "I do not to think that will happen at all. I think your body has an inborn gift of sorting it all out and keeping track of who's who."

"My starry heavens, I hope you're right."

"Now the best thing for you, my delightful buffet, is to let you sleep. I to suspect a lot of the work will be done overnight, the sorting and cataloging and all that important stuff."

"Why wasn't your sister here?" I asked suddenly. "I'd think she would've wanted to witness this."

"Oh, she did, in the worst way. However, she was called to a Queen's Meeting and she could not ignore the summons. She charged me with this important task and told me to tell you to enjoy your year on Amorpha to the fullest. She said to remind you to not become any of these things without me there to help if needed. The important part is being the back-up depository. And of course, no one, besides you, me and her, to know about this in any way."

I nodded in agreement. "It certainly has to be secret." I paused and drew in a breath that I let out as a sigh. "Tell your sister I'm now part of all this, or more literally, all this is now a part of me and I will not jeopardize this in any way."

He hugged me again. "We to know you are full of integrity, Jessalya. We will to see you in six months and then one year and by then, we should have plans well in hand in how to use this knowledge and DNA base for the betterment of all races." He kept his hands on my shoulders and took a step back to regard me with a somber look on his face. "What any God has created should not be destroyed for profit and we pledge to make the universes a better and safer place for all sentient species."

"I believe you, Si'neada, or I wouldn't have agreed to doing this. I also believe in the sanctity of life and that's why I've pledged to help you, all of you, in this endeavor." To my utter astonishment, tears welled up in my eyes and I hastily dashed them away with a finger. My hair patted me on the back and then flowed forward and around me in a comforting gesture.

"Before we go, Si'neada," I held up a hand, "I must ask of you a favor."

"Yes, of course, my little piece of heaven, if it is in my power to do so."

"I have no way to get this information to my parents, you understand, so I must ask you to convey to them this information."

I drew in a large lungful of air. "What happened to Devon is not their fault in any way, his death was part of an unsanctioned experiment gone awry. In fact, his death is *my* fault but through no design, malice or action of my own." I wiped away a tear.

Si'neada looked at me with sympathetic eyes. "My little 'changer, I will to deliver this message. Is that all you wish to explain?" He placed a hand on my shoulder, a comforting gesture. "None of this is your fault and your parents do not blame you, this I to know."

I nodded while I considered this. It was my fault; somehow as a fetus I pulled the Akrion into myself. I didn't dare tell even Si'neada I had that unfound particle of Akrion within me where it couldn't be sensed or detected. It had gone completely dormant when it entered my fetal body from Devon's to avoid discovery and didn't spark into action until I entered my Transition years and could accept the startling changes, from my sentient hair to now being an Exchanger in all the meanings of the word. For his own protection and mine, this must be my exclusive secret.

"Tell them I love them with all that I am and someday I will explain the whole story when it is safe to do so but this must suffice for now. Devon's death had everything to do with the experiment and nothing to do with their own actions. It's important they know that."

He nodded, a determined motion. "I will to let them know when I can safely do so." He then smiled and clapped his hands. "I have presents for you!"

"Really?" I blinked.

"Yes!" He reached behind him and pulled out a bra. "Here!"

I accepted it. "Uh, gee, thanks. Didn't know I needed any more of these."

He chuckled. "My little star, it is a special undergarment. Look at it; I built in a pouch for your gun."

"Oh!" I exclaimed. "How clever of you, thank you!" It indeed did have a pouch to comfortably hold my weapon and I didn't have to worry now about it falling out.

"That is not all." He gathered up an armful of robes. "These all have a secret opening in the front only you can access—DNA and all that stuff—so you can reach your weapon if needed. No one will know there is an opening in the front; the material will only open to your touch."

Tears welled up in my eyes. "Thank you, Si'neada." I said in a soft tone. I cleared my throat. "Just…thank you. For everything and especially for this."

He pulled me into a hug. "Only the best for my exchanging friend. I will to make sure these are packed into your suitcases."

## CHAPTER THIRTY-FIVE

I barely remembered getting to Zoe's room and putting on her oversized nightgown. Once my head touched the pillow on the couch, I was out into a deep sleep and when I awoke to the room lights coming on, I swear I hadn't moved all night. Maybe I'd been afraid I'd roll off the couch onto the floor.

I blinked my eyes open, wondering why the room wasn't familiar and then memories from the night before flooded over me. That's right; my room was ransacked, I'm now in Zoe's room on the couch and I didn't know if I'd have any belongings packed to take with me this morning. Oh, yeah, great way to start a new year as an exchange student. Nothing I could do about any of that.

What I could do was get up, use the bathroom and make my bladder happy. I heard Zoe stirring in her sleeping room and my hair pushed on my back toward the cleanser. I took that to mean all was well in DNA World. I washed and felt much better for being clean. I'd asked Si'neada to work with Sn'eri to find out who had kept my parents under their thumbs all these years and to do what they could to stop it. My message was safe with him for delivery, nothing written that could be traced in any way, and, although he pressed me, I wouldn't give any other details. I had to protect them all.

My stomach rumbled in hunger and amused, I wondered whose stomach was rumbling, mine or some other species? I then laughed at myself. It didn't matter, the hunger was real enough. I stepped into my Amorphan gown Si'neada had provided me the night before and then left the bathroom to greet Zoe.

"Thanks, Zoe; I think I'm ready to take on the Amorphan world now."

"Did you find out anything about your room?"

"Not yet," I shook my head. "Someone was looking for something, for sure, but I don't know what they thought they could find in my room." Best to keep my suspicions about Sn'eri to myself.

"It's odd it was only your room."

"They probably just got to mine first. Maybe they were after my memory chip, you know, the one from the brain delve we had to go through? If so, they definitely weren't going to find it in my room."

"Yeah, mine is safe back on New Eden. Just in case I lost it or something, you know?"

"Yeah, mine, too." I lied. I had both memory chips, the one my mom gave me and mine, both hidden under my skin.

The guard bowed as we left her quarters, asking, "Was your sleep good, Madames?"

"Yes, it was, thank you for asking."

"If you will wait here, Madames, we will to take your group as a whole to the dining area."

Keaton stepped into the hallway, raising a hand in greeting. He grinned his boyish grin and I wished again I had gotten my first kiss from him on this trip. I pushed that out of my mind, no time for that now.

"Hey, Jess, you look much better this morning. Getting off this ship to join your family must be agreeing with you." His guard escorted him over to where we were standing; guards had been posted at all the doors. He and I gave each other palm slaps.

"I slept the sleep of a breastfed baby, I'm telling you."

"That good, eh?" He winked at me and I chuckled, blushing a little bit.

"Yeah, that good." Then I sobered. "Nothing like starting the biggest adventure of our life having my belongings flung all over and not even knowing if I'll have my own luggage when we leave."

He tipped his head a little to one side and then back to straight. "Well, that's what stores are for, I guess."

"Yeah," I sighed. "I just I hope they packed everything up nice and tidy. Can you imagine me dragging a suitcase down the ramp with a sleeve or two trailing in the dirt?"

He chuckled at the image as Soli and Mitchler walked up with their guards.

"Is this a convening of the greatest Human minds of all time?" Soli joked.

"Of course," Keaton said. He looked around at all the guards. "Our last time we must go as a group to breakfast."

Mitchler ran a hand over his hair, smoothing the waviness of it. "At least we all got our beauty sleep and we'll get breakfast before leaving the starship. It's been, ah, an adventure, everyone.

Looking forward to meeting up again in six months. Until then, happy studies and happy family living."

We nodded in unison. "An adventure it has been so far," Soli agreed. "And the biggest one starts in," he checked the time, "1.35 hours."

"Not that you're being precise or anything." I joked.

"Why are we all standing in the hallway like a parliament of owls? Let's go eat; I'm starved!" Zoe said.

Soli said, "I don't think owls stand around, for the record."

"It's all I could think of, okay?" She said.

Soli said, "How about a clowder of cats, a tangle of kittens, a leap of leopards, a troop of kangaroos, a waddle of penguins—"

Mitchler interrupted, "What the heck is a kangaroo and a penguin?"

Soli shrugged. "Who knows?"

"You're a fount of useless information, aren't you, Soli?" I laughed.

He smiled and shrugged. "Those have always intrigued me."

"The only thing intriguing me right now is food," I announced as my stomach grumbled. "And oh, look, there's the dining room!"

We sat at our table for the final time to order and while we waited for the delivery of our food, Officer De'red'ita came to stand at our table. "Good morning. We are pleased to tell you your luggage will go with you to Amorpha. We did not to find anything harmful in your room."

"Did you catch who did it or find out why?"

"No, I regret saying we did not." His gaze shifted for a fleeting second.

They know but won't do anything about it, since Sn'eri is so highly ranked. I mean, they don't flinch at killing entire species, why would they be bothered over one officer trashing a Human's room?

"But it is not a matter that can be hidden forever; it is only a matter of time."

"At least I'll have clean underwear now. Since I didn't have anything of value to steal, I guess I'm okay." I remarked and the others chuckled.

Then Security Officer De'red'ita stiffened to attention. "Please! To stand up! The Captain is honoring you with a visit!"

We rose to our feet as a contingent of officers approached. I noted Officer Sn'eri at the shoulder of an impressively big Imurian dressed in a white formal uniform. Sn'eri looked at me and as I caught his glance, I thought I saw hunger in his eyes and a smirk on his lips. *I'm not sending out that odor again, am I? Oh, by the broken gates of hell, I hope not. Judging by that look on his face, he knows I know he ransacked my room and he knows I can't do anything about it. Yet. He'd better watch out in the future.* My nostrils flared and I lifted one corner of my lip in a snarl. His self-satisfaction deepened and I wanted to slap the look off his face.

The Captain stepped forward then, bowed to us and we bowed in return. "I very much to regret the intrusion into your room last night, madame Jessalya. I am very happy you were not present and are unhurt. We cannot let our Exchangers be harmed, after all, before your grandest part of this trip is yet to begin. Please to accept the Starfinder's apologies and be assured we, the crew, will do all in our power to find and to punish the ones responsible."

His ears came to attention as he straightened, his tail perfectly still next to his leg, the officers behind him stiffening to attention. He raised a hand to his brow and they mimicked the movement. "We to salute all of you for embarking on this adventure and learning experience and we are happy to be part of this experience with you."

None of us were quite sure what to do, having not been coached on this type of protocol. Did we salute back? Did we bow? Did we say thank-you?

Zoe came to the rescue. "Captain, we appreciate your visit." She saluted. "We appreciate your efforts on our behalf, the safety that was given to us and we have enjoyed our time aboard this great ship. We will remember you and the crew with fondness."

We followed Zoe's lead by saluting, also. Zoe's dramatic flair seemed to be just what the Captain wanted; he dropped his hand, the others following suit. "To a magnificent year as Amorphans." He intoned and raised his hand to us in farewell. "Please to enjoy finishing your meal. It is one hour to disembarkation."

We reseated ourselves and I said, "Well done, Zoe. I wouldn't have ever come up with anything as good as what you said."

She flushed a light pink tone on her face. "You're welcome. Someone had to say something!"

"Well, once again, thank you." I picked up my eating utensil and put a bite of egg dish into my mouth.

We took our time over the meal. It was the last one aboard the Starfinder and we really had nothing else to do until it was time to transfer to the shuttle to go to the planet.

Mitchler looked around at us, then picking up a spoon, said in his best sports broadcasting voice, "The crowd is feasting on the remains of their breakfast and all is well on the field. Shortly, they will begin their descent into the history books of all times as the Exchangers from Earth! They will separate once their feet are on the ground again, each finding their own destiny in their own way." He gestured in large, expansive moves. "But in one short, oh, such a short year, they will return and regroup to exchange their adventures once again! Let's hear it for the EXCHANGERS OF EARTH!"

We yipped and yelled and hoorah'ed, bringing startled looks and a rushing of guards over to our table. We were laughing so hard we couldn't talk, and the guards relaxed as they watched us with puzzled eyes.

"Only Mitchler could turn this into a sporting event!" I gasped.

He bowed from his seated position. "Only the best for all of you." His glance lingered on me and he winked, startling me. He'd never shown any interest in me this trip, flirting with Zoe and giving her his attention. I winked back which broadened his smile.

Breakfast was over. As we stood, we waved to the rest of the dining room, who were watching us. It was time, almost time. This was an auspicious event and the Starfinder was apparently ready to make the most of it. Our escorts gathered us into a group to go to the shuttle. Our belongings were already aboard so all we had to do was show up.

I checked my device for the thousandth time to see the faces of my new "family" so I would recognize them; I'd be very embarrassed indeed if I couldn't pick them out.

The shuttle ride down was as uneventful as the original one. As we waited for the atmosphere to acclimate to the outdoors, I wondered, *Was everyone else as nervous as me?*

I looked around, seeing Keaton wiping his palms against his robe, Mitchler smoothing his hair again, Soli swallowing a few times. Yup. They were as anxious as I was about departing the ship, going from the known into the unknown. I drew in a large breath, held it for a second and let it out slowly. Guards surrounded us as we waited for the departure door to open and I felt a little bit lost, like a mouse in a forest of tall, tall trees. On impulse, I grabbed Zoe's hand and squeezed it. She looked at me with a scared look on her face and then squeezed my hand back. :*Oh, Gods. I'm so scared.*

Shocked, I sucked in a breath as I winced; her mind whisper was more of a shout. No time for finesse here. :*Zoe, I can hear your thoughts. No! Don't react! Just know if I can hear you, so can others. Imagine a steel wall surrounding the inside of your head. You need to have that wall up at all times, only opening a window if you want to try and mind-whisper with someone else like me. No time to explain more now. Zoe, this must've come from my blood.*:

Stunned silence. Her fingernails dug into my hand as she gripped my hand so hard the bones grated. :*Telepathy. Ye Gods.*: A tendril of hope. :*Maybe we can converse this way even separated. I may need the contact to deal with....you know.*:

:Yes, I know. We'll have to figure it out but know I am here for you, Zoe, now and forever, and I'll do my best to help you deal with what was done to you on this ship.:

:Thank you.:

She loosened her grip, wiped away a tear, and straightened her shoulders. Her thoughts became dim as she built her internal wall.

"Good job, Zoe." I whispered.

My ears popped as the ship adjusted to the outside pressure. The door slowly slid open but I couldn't see through the tall bodies in front of me. The guards were going first to make sure nothing happened to us when the doors opened. I guess I appreciated that.

As the door opening widened and sunshine and scented air poured in, the others automatically grouped themselves behind me. The "Right to See" Law apparently still held sway with my classmates. Either that or if there was an attack, I would go down first. I rolled my eyes at thinking that but couldn't help wondering just a little bit which it was. Come to think of it, Zoe was the first one to move behind me. Hmmm.

The guards waited until the farewell vanguard was lined up on the ramp leading down to the planet and then stepped forward. One shouted out, "THE EXCHANGERS OF NEW EDEN!" The waiting crowd erupted in cheers. The guard turned, holding a hand out to me and as I stepped forward, taking his hand, he announced, "MADAME JESSALYA LILIANTHAL OF NEW EDEN!"

I bowed to the crowd, who continued cheering, although I thought I heard some boos out there, too. He moved forward toward the ramp as a mind whisper drifted into my head.

:*I wonder which one it is. Is it her? She is so little but even little beings can bear young.*:

:*Si'neada took a personal interest in her which makes her very likely. If the experiment succeeds, we can breed her or the other one to anything and start our own zoo world of wonders and make even more money from admission prices.*:

I couldn't tell who was conversing. My step faltered as I heard their words and only the guard's hand kept me from falling flat on my face, which would not only be a huge embarrassment but a dead give-away to whoever was talking. Unfortunately, I couldn't tell one mind whisper from another yet and didn't even know if it was possible.

A different tone to the mind whisper. :*We have to wait until we return to the planet to put our plan into motion. In six months, we will have determined if she or the other is fertilized and then we can make plans for our breeding program.*:

:*That is true. If we have to, we will take both of them. But time for that later. We cannot take any more chance of anyone overhearing this.*:

:*True.*:

My mind spun, my grip on the guard's hand tightening. Breeding program? What were they talking about? Could Si'neada or his sister have talked—no, they wouldn't do that. I trusted Si'neada.

Well, you know what? I had six months ahead of me before worrying about all that. Zoe and I could—probably—talk by mind-whispers if we practiced except I didn't know how limiting distance was. Maybe with a good wind? Hopefully we could figure out how to communicate. For now, warning Zoe was all I could do. :*Zoe. Be very, very careful. There's still danger to both of us. Keep this window barely open so I can try to talk to you later; hopefully we won't be too far apart. Keep your bodyguards around at all times, especially at six months. Every night at 10 pm local time, we'll try to find each other this way.*: I hoped she was the only one who heard me; I glanced over at her and she gave a barely perceptible nod my way.

I straightened my shoulders, put my chin up high, and marched forward down the ramp. I'd also keep my personal bodyguards close and even closer at the six-month mark. In the meantime, I had a new world to explore, a new family to get to know and a university education to gain, not to mention new DNA swimming around inside of me. If anyone was pregnant, it was Zoe and I would find a way to help her figure out what to do about it if it was true.

It was a grand world from what I could see. My eyes drank in the view of the beautiful azure blue sky, fluffy white clouds drifted overhead and a warm, light breeze brought the scent of flowers to my nose. In the distance, fully leafed-out trees swayed in the breeze, flowers adorning them in different colors: blue, pink, white. Foliage extended from the edge of the landing site, my eyes greedy for the green of it after the drabness of the ship's interior. I blinked at the richness of the colors around me, the welcome songs of birds and I took in a full breath of natural air. I could hardly wait to get on the ground to start my new life.

And then I was there, my Amorphan family running toward me and yes! I recognized them! The fact they were holding a sign with my name on it helped a lot with that. Datro Lariendo was tall like all Amorphans, wearing an aqua robe with red accents, eyes sparkling in the natural sunshine, Matra Teatriana hurrying close to his side in a yellow robe with frills and sparkles washed over the material, both of them waving frantically as if afraid I wouldn't notice them. Daro Simatrao, my new little brother, was scampering after them with a huge grin splitting his face, holding my "Welcome, Jessalya!" sign high in the air.

I bowed to them, they bowed to me and then they swept me into their midst as they chattered and exclaimed, welcoming me, hugging me as I hugged them back. I grinned so hard, my cheeks hurt and problems were forgotten as I fielded questions from them and threw some remarks back at them—in Amorphan, which delighted them. My little Amorphan brother hopped up and down, patting me, crowding close to my side and exclaiming over my perfect Amorphan. I felt suddenly safe and surrounded by happiness, worries disappearing for the moment. I loved my new family already and looked forward to my upcoming year with them. Plenty of time to deal with banquets, classes and problems later.

## ACKNOWLEDGEMENTS

Many years ago, when I was about 10 years old, I thought I'd write a book. My opening line was, "I ran into my room, threw myself on the bed and cried because I was so happy." That was not only the opening line but also the closing line. I suddenly realized the enormity of writing an *entire book* all by myself and abandoned it with as much suddenness as I decided to write it.

I took several writing courses many years later, well after college, and in doing so, wrote a Young Adult novel as part of a course, which will never again see the light of day (and don't ask!). Again, I found out how much work goes into a novel.

Now skip ahead another 15 years or so and here is my completed novel, which, if you're reading this, you've gotten to the end and I'm gratified. It is a lot of work, takes a lot of rewriting and gumption to do this.

I am grateful to my husband of 40+ years for allowing me space to do the writing. He is truly baffled how people can enjoy science fiction/fantasy (but it's not real! He says with a bewildered look on his face. I reply, "But it could be!") but he bravely says he'll read my books, anyway.

He tries very hard to leave me alone when I'm writing, although sometimes I'm just sneaking peeks at Facebook and email. (Shhh, don't tell him!) I'm very grateful for my core of friends, who are very impressed I've written a book *and* publishing it; without their sense of wonder at such an accomplishment, I would honestly think it was something everyone could do. (Well, not really, but they do reinforce the accomplishment). Even my older sister is impressed, and that is something not easily done with her!

So thank you for believing in my ability to do this: Larry Brungardt, my wonderful husband, my core of bridge friends, Carol K, Cheryl P, Mary Q, and all the rest of you Wednesday players (you know who you are), our friends from Maine, but now here in Arizona, Marie and Eddie L, for their enthusiasm for all endeavors and my sister, Thea, husband Fred, and daughters, Susan and Christine, and Larry's cousin, Kathy S. If you looked for your name here and don't see it—I'll catch you in the next book.

I also thank you, The Reader, for you are the most important part of this: after all, if people don't read our efforts, authors have no good reason to write.

## ABOUT THE AUTHOR

K. E. Brungardt, D.O., is a bridge player, author and a Watercolor Artist by day, sleepy by night. Since retiring from Family Practice Medicine in a small town in Wyoming, she now has the time to pursue all her interests and more. She and her husband moved to Arizona in 2002 because her arthritis rather loudly pointed out how much better warm weather feels. She enjoys her hot tub every morning and loves reading science fiction/fantasy as her main genre, although she doesn't turn down a well-written memoir or murder mystery. She has written articles for local newspapers and is also an award-winning artist and author.

If you enjoyed *Exchanger*, please consider writing a review on Amazon.

To read more about K.E. Brungardt, please see the author's page at: *www.karensauthorsite.wordpress.com*

Made in the USA
Columbia, SC
03 September 2019